KT-226-599

ANNE MELVILLE

The Lorimer Legacy

GRAFTON BOOKS
A Division of the Collins Publishing Group

LONDON GLASGOW
TORONTO SYDNEY AUCKLAND

Grafton Books
A Division of the Collins Publishing Group
8 Grafton Street, London W1X 3LA

Published by Grafton Books 1986

First published in Great Britain by
William Heinemann Ltd 1979

ISBN 0-586-06607-1

Printed and bound in Great Britain by
Collins, Glasgow

Set in Times

Contents

THE LORIMER LINE

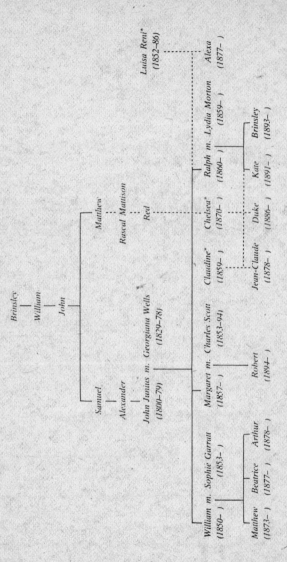

-------- = Illegitimate descent

* = Mistress

PART I

Alexa in England

1

A young woman whose greatest problem is that of filling her time ought to consider herself fortunate. Alexa Lorimer knew this well enough, but as she embarked yet again on an exercise which she had practised a dozen times that day already, she found it difficult to control her vexation. She had gone to the trouble of preparing a surprise to enliven the afternoon. But Margaret Scott, her guardian, hurrying off from Elm Lodge to inspect some village baby which had developed a rash, had not even noticed. Now the rest of the day stretched emptily ahead, offering no excitements. Alexa was bored.

Her hands slammed down on the keyboard of the grand piano and the discord of her ill-temper reverberated through the drawing room. She had been practising for over an hour, but to what purpose? What good did it do to improve her breath control, to extend the range of her voice, to increase its flexibility, to perfect the purity of its tone, when her guardian forbade the career on which her heart was set?

Indulging her discontent, Alexa jumped up from the piano stool and wandered round the room, fingering its ornaments, until the sight of her own reflection in the mirror above the fireplace reminded her of a second grievance. She was eighteen years old but still expected to wear boots and black woollen stockings beneath ankle-length dresses, which were suitable only for the school-room. Her hair fell to her waist because no one had recognized that it was time for her to put it up. What could she do to make someone realize that time was passing, that her life was slipping by?

For it was 1895 now – a year in which Alexa Lorimer found herself poised in the limbo between childhood and womanhood. Just as some children never quite grow up, so some adults seem never to have been children. At this turning point of age, Alexa achieved the feat of combining these characteristics. The childish style of dress was forced on her, but her immaturity displayed itself in more than appearance. As a small child she had felt a continuing need to give and to receive demonstrative affection, and she had not yet grown out of this longing. Every day she assured Margaret of her love and waited for a kiss or embrace in return. She craved for praise like a little girl and was hurt by criticism, even by silence. Her good looks, her needlework, her painting, her music – all were continually placed on show and must continually be applauded.

Yet there was a sense in which she had never had a childhood. Orphaned when she was nine years old, Alexa vividly remembered those earlier years with her dying mother: years of cold and hunger, of lies to landladies and stealthy removals from one shabby set of lodgings to another in the middle of the night. As for her father, if he had ever dandled her on his lap, she did not remember it. Indeed, even his name was unknown to her. She had been given the surname Lorimer because at the time of her adoption that had been her guardian's name. Margaret Scott had been born a Lorimer, a member of the great Bristol family of merchant princes. Her marriage to Charles Scott had taken place only some years after she had accepted the responsibility for Alexa's upbringing, rescuing from the workhouse a child without family or friends to care for her.

It was the nightmare of the years of poverty which made Alexa determined to become rich. Almost from babyhood she had known that she was beautiful. Her oval face, framed by the long blonde hair which glinted with red in the sunlight, would have inspired a Renaissance artist to paint her as a goddess. She was a natural actress too. Her expressive vivacity and the flash of her green eyes, though disturbing the classical beauty which her face displayed in repose, had the power to catch and hold attention. But Alexa's greatest asset was her singing voice; her goal, an operatic career. That was why she practised so conscientiously every day, and that was what she dreamed about every night. Yet how could the ambition be realized? In many pleading talks with her guardian she had been told time and time again that there was no form of theatrical entertainment in which a young woman could appear without irreparable damage to the most precious of her possessions: her reputation.

So deep were Alexa's love and admiration for Margaret that she tried to accept what she was told. But nothing could put an end to her obsession with a future in which she would be famous. Nothing could stop her fretting against the dullness of her life in the country, where the greatest excitement of a new day was that Margaret's little son, Robert, might cut a new tooth. The very thought of doing anything to offend or upset her guardian brought tears to her eyes, and yet her ambitions urged her to escape. If only she could see how to take the first step! When, oh when, was something going to happen?

As though to answer the question, Margaret Scott came into the drawing room at that moment, a small, neat woman whose bright auburn hair had only recently begun to lose a little of its youthful sheen. She had become a medical student at a time when great determination was needed to overcome the opposition of the medical profession, society in general and her own family in particular to the idea of a woman qualifying as a doctor, and the steadiness of character which had sustained her at that time still showed itself in the calm good sense with which she organized the household at Elm Lodge. Years of earning her own living before her marriage and since her widowhood had made her firm and efficient, but the businesslike side of her nature was never allowed to obscure the warmth of her love for her son and her ward. The smile on her face now was that of a woman with a treat to announce, and she did not look about her before speaking.

'I have just heard from Bristol. Matthew is coming to stay.'

Alexa's impulsive nature made her as easily excited as depressed. Gloom was banished in an instant as she clapped her hands with pleasure. 'But you invited Beatrice and Arthur as well, surely?' she exclaimed.

Margaret laughed as she sat down. 'Beatrice is out in society now. It seems from her mother's letter that her chances of finding a husband are not rated very high. Anyway, there is to be no question of taking time off from the search to bury herself in the country. And Arthur, it appears, has asked if he may leave school and join Matthew in their father's business. So both the boys now have little holiday time and must plan carefully how to spend it to advantage. I am quoting their mother's own words. Sophie has never troubled to waste time in being tactful.'

'But Matthew, you said – ?'

'Matthew would like to come by himself. His letter arrived by the same post as his mother's. He was not told of the invitation until after it had been refused on his behalf, and I detect a note of indignation in his hope that it is not too late for him to accept. Matthew and I have

10

always been particularly fond of each other. We needn't tell the others, but I shall be glad to have him here without them.'

Alexa made no comment, but her eyes sparkled. She too liked Matthew the best of all Margaret's nephews and nieces. He was someone to whom she would be able to talk about her ambitions, someone whose support might be enlisted.

Alexa had been adopted by Margaret nine years before. After barely supporting herself as a doctor, Margaret had returned with her ward to live in her childhood home, Brinsley House, which stood high above Bristol and the gorge of the Avon, a monument to the wealth of the Lorimer dynasty. Alexa knew that the move had been made so that she herself should enjoy comfort and young company. The house belonged to Margaret's elder brother, William Lorimer, whose ownership of the Lorimer shipping company had made him as prosperous as any other in the long line of slave-trading sea captains, merchants and bankers from whom he was descended. William had never made any pretence of liking Alexa. But he had always disapproved of his sister's determination to qualify for a profession and earn her own living. His position as head of the Lorimer family made it necessary in his eyes that as an unmarried female Margaret should become part of his household. By allowing her young ward to share the schoolroom of his own children, he had been able to force on his sister a situation more easily approved by Bristol society. So for several years – until Margaret married Dr Charles Scott and moved to Elm Lodge – Alexa had lived in the great mansion which the Lorimer family had built a century earlier, and had developed with the three children of the household a relationship almost as close as that of siblings.

Like true brothers and sisters, they had had their likes

and dislikes amongst each other. Beatrice, sharp-featured and sharp-mannered, had never accepted the intruder, although they were close in age. Alexa for her part tried to make friends, but was defeated by argument and sarcasm. Beatrice was clever, and took pleasure in leading Alexa's quick but less logical mind up knotted by-ways before laughing at her for a fool.

Arthur, the youngest of the three, was clever as well, with his father's quick wits and eye for a profit. He could see how to make money in any situation, and only Alexa's lack of pocket money when she was younger had prevented her either losing it to him or else, according to Arthur's mood, seeing it invested in some scheme which would double her fortune. They were friendly enough, but Arthur was too young for a real intimacy.

Alexa's relationship with Matthew, the eldest of the trio, was of a different kind. It was his overt admiration of her looks which was no doubt responsible for some of Beatrice's jealousy. Three years Alexa's senior, he had protected her when she arrived at Brinsley House, fending off Arthur's boisterousness and Beatrice's unkind criticisms. Both as a boy and as a young man he was reserved, even silent – kinder, though far less clever, than his quick-thinking brother and sister. Alexa recognized the affection which he never put into words, and was always happy in his company. The prospect now that she would be left to entertain him during his visit while Margaret worked gave her nothing but joy.

When Margaret turned to leave the drawing room, Alexa held her breath. Surely the surprise she had arranged would be noticed at last.

Yesterday the end wall of the room had been empty, but on it today hung a picture in a heavy black frame. It was the portrait of an old man. His thick hair and beard were completely white – although his bushy eyebrows, surprisingly, were as red as Margaret's hair. There was vigour in the firm features, and his eyes stared sternly out of the canvas, confident and commanding. Alexa found his expression tantalizing, for there was a hint of kindness mixed with the severity. She waited with interest to discover what Margaret would say – an interest which quickly turned to alarm. For when she caught sight of the picture, Margaret seemed to be not so much surprised as shocked. She stared at it for a long time before turning slowly back to face Alexa.

'How did this get here?'

'I found it in the boxroom with all those old pieces of furniture. I was helping Betty to look for a chair to put in Robert's bedroom, and there it was, propped against the wall and covered with dust. It seemed a pity to let such a handsome picture become dirty. I thought perhaps you had forgotten it was there, so I asked Parker to hang it this morning, as a surprise for you. Who is he?'

Margaret sat down. She was white-faced, and for a moment it appeared that she did not wish to reply. And yet the answer, when it came, was not one which should have caused any hesitation. 'That,' she said, 'is John Junius Lorimer. My father.'

'Then why didn't you hang the picture before? I should have thought – '

'Because it would have offended Charles to see the portrait here,' Margaret said.

It was Alexa's private opinion that husbands should not be allowed to have everything their own way, especially when they happened to be dead. But she realized how tactless it would be to say so. 'Tell me about him,' she begged instead. 'You never talk about your parents. What was your father like?'

'He was an autocrat,' said Margaret. 'Rich and respected. He was chairman of Lorimer's Bank until it

13

collapsed at the end of his life. He ruled it as though he were God, and his family was given much the same treatment. The portrait gives a good indication of that, I think. But he was generous as well. That may not be so easy to recognize from the painting.'

'Did you inherit anything from him?'

'My red hair,' said Margaret lightly. 'And I didn't think much of the inheritance when I was young, I can tell you.'

'But nothing else? If he was as important as that, surely he left you some kind of legacy. Some money, or some of his things?'

There was a sudden coolness, a barrier between them. If Alexa had not known that her guardian was always completely honest in everything she did and said, she would have suspected that Margaret was about to tell a lie. But that was only the most fleeting of impressions. The answer itself came with a definiteness which could only be sincere.

'No,' Margaret told her. 'I loved my father very much, and he loved me; but he left me no legacy at all.'

2

A question asked in innocence takes on an unintended significance in the mind of someone who is reluctant to answer it. Margaret found Alexa's interest in legacies disturbing, for her thoughts went at once to the black leather case which she had concealed in an unused attic. Had the child been ferreting about in the cupboards under the eaves as well as in the little boxroom? Was she hoping by her enquiry to elicit an official confirmation of something which she had already discovered for herself?

14

But Alexa's continuing questions suggested that she had accepted the answer at its face value. Margaret had been careful to tell no actual lie. It was perfectly true that she had inherited nothing from her father.

'Was it because he was angry about your wanting to be a doctor?' Alexa pressed. 'Did he divide everything between his sons? Or did he believe in leaving everything to the eldest?'

'I never dared so much as hint to my father that I wanted to take a medical training,' Margaret confessed. 'That came later, after he was dead. No; there was no quarrel. It was just that by the time he died he had nothing to leave. He lost all his fortune in the last months of his life, when the bank crashed. My brother Ralph is just as poor as I am. And if William is rich, it is because he had already taken over the family shipping line before the crash, and he has inherited the Lorimer talent for business. The most enduring legacy in any family is that of character.'

'How can you say that!' Alexa demanded. 'Your two brothers are quite different from each other. And you are different again.'

Margaret recognized that it must seem so to Alexa. For one thing, the physical differences were so pronounced, especially between her two brothers. William had always been small and sharp-featured, and he had inherited his mother's brown hair. Ralph, on the other hand, tall, broad-shouldered and blond, had been as handsome as a young god before he left England. If he was sallowed and desiccated now, that was the result of years of exposure to a tropical sun. It seemed worth while to explain, though, how in one way they were the same.

'William and Ralph are both very hard-working,' she told her ward. 'Able men, and ambitious too, in their different ways. William has put all his energies into running a business, and he has been wonderfully success-ful. Being well established before our father died, he was very quick at that time to seize every opportunity to increase his fortune. Ralph was only a schoolboy then, when Lorimer's Bank collapsed. He saw the crash as a judgement on the family for the years of slave-trading which brought us our wealth. That was why, as soon as he was old enough, he chose to go out to Jamaica as a missionary. But as far as I can tell from his letters and Lydia's, he seems to have taken charge of a congregation which was debilitated and unemployed and achieved a miracle by turning his parish into a thriving agricultural community. I hardly understand how he has done it, but clearly he must be as good a manager as William. What they each inherited was an insistence on being at the head of their own affairs, and a determination to succeed. My father had both these qualities to a very marked degree.'

'And you?' asked Alexa. 'What about you?'

'If I seem less successful, you must remember that I started from a lower level of expectation. I was brought up as a rich man's daughter, with everything provided for me. And might have expected to marry young and simply to move from one gentleman's care to another. To carry me through a medical training I needed the same will to succeed that I have just been describing in William and Ralph – and I had to face much more opposition than they did. I confess that I have been less ambitious since I qualified, but I still share my brothers' liking for indepen-dence. To manage my own household seems as much of a triumph to me as the running of a plantation is to Ralph, or of a shipping line to William. So you see, we all enjoy a fair inheritance.'

'I wish I could have shared it,' said Alexa. There was a touch of envy in her voice. For a moment Margaret hesitated, wondering whether to take this opportunity of telling Alexa something about her own parentage. But it was not a subject to be approached without preparation. The turn of the conversation had taken her by surprise and she had not had time to think what she might want to say and how it would be best to say it. She stood up and looked her father in the eye again.

'You were right, Alexa, to think that John Junius Lorimer should not be condemned to cobwebs for ever,' she said. 'I hope that as you practise you will find him an appreciative audience.'

Even as the door closed behind her, she heard the sound of the piano begin again. It seemed a good moment to dispel any remaining suspicions about Alexa's explorations. She hurried to the top of the house. The attics there were designed to accommodate a far larger domestic staff than Margaret could afford to maintain, and in one of the unused rooms was concealed the only treasure which Elm Lodge contained. It might have been wiser to entrust it to the strongroom of a bank, but Margaret had good reason to be suspicious of banks, and she had no fear of burglars. All the villagers knew that their doctor often had as much trouble as themselves in finding one penny to rub against another.

Her anxiety proved to be unfounded. The cupboard was securely locked, and when she unfastened it with the key she wore round her neck, the dust lay undisturbed on the old newspapers which she had piled high to conceal the box.

Margaret opened it and stared in silence at the black leather case whose contents had been the cause of so much trouble to the family, and to herself in particular. It was true enough, as the careful framing of her answer had suggested to Alexa, that her father had left no material inheritance to any of his three legitimate children. But it was not the whole truth. In the year before he died, John Junius Lorimer had contrived – by a ruse which fell only a hair's breadth short of being criminal – to salvage one treasure from the wreck of his fortune. And that treasure was in front of Margaret now.

Conscious of what it had done to her life, she could hardly bring herself to look at it. But how foolish it would be, she told herself, not to check its safety now that she had begun. Reluctantly she unlocked the case, raised the lid, and drew out one by one the three velvet-lined drawers.

For a long time she knelt in front of it without moving, mesmerized by the sparkle of the gems. The centrepiece was a necklace of rubies, with a pendant in the form of a rose; its petals were formed from more rubies, set in silver and framed with tiny diamonds. In the bottom drawer nestled a pair of delicate drop ear-rings which repeated the rose motif on a miniature scale. At the top, even more richly elaborate than the necklace, lay a tiara in which yet another ruby rose was surrounded by trembling leaves of silver and diamonds. These were the objects which alone could be said to constitute the Lorimer legacy; and they had not been bequeathed to Margaret.

Instead, John Junius Lorimer had left them to a baby whom during his lifetime he had not publicly acknowledged as his child. It was his mistress, Luisa Reni, who on her deathbed had handed them to Margaret and asked her to keep them until her little girl, Alexa, should come of age. That was the moment – nine years ago – when Margaret had first learned the name of Alexa's father.

Alexa herself did not yet know that she was a Lorimer by birth as well as by adoption. When Margaret accepted the responsibility for bringing up her orphaned half-sister,

18

she needed her brother's help. William offered them both a home at Brinsley House only on the understanding that Alexa should not be told the truth about her birth. He had laid down the condition for the sake of his father's reputation, and Margaret had accepted it for Alexa's. She had resolved to tell her ward the truth on the same day that the rubies were handed over – on her twenty-first birthday. Even then the taint of illegitimacy would be hard to accept.

Like the rubies, the portrait of John Junius belonged, unsuspected, to Alexa. Poor Luisa had almost as little money in her purse as Margaret on the terrible day in 1879 when the contents of Brinsley House were auctioned for the benefit of the bank's creditors, but she had spared what she could to make sure that Alexa would one day see what her father looked like. Fortunately, there was no one else in Bristol at that time who wished to be reminded of John Junius Lorimer, and the portrait had been knocked down to her for only a few shillings.

Thoughtfully Margaret packed up the case and locked it away in the cupboard. As she briskly snapped the lock on the door, she snapped shut her own memory at the same time. What had happened in the past was of little importance to her life today. All that mattered now was that the legacy which John Junius Lorimer had left behind him was safe, and no one but Margaret knew of its existence.

Even the most unsophisticated girl knows that the simplest way to secure a young man's company is to pretend an enthusiasm for his hobbies. Alexa had no talent for painting or carving, but she knew them to be Matthew's passions, so she took care to prepare her watercolour box before he arrived. Carrying a picnic hamper between them, they strolled each morning through the fields until Matthew found a flower or a view of the village church to inspire him. Margaret was fully occupied with an epidemic of measles which was spreading through the village, and asked few questions about how they spent their time.

On the last day of his visit Matthew's concentration appeared to be disturbed. He had been drawing a foal, making a series of quick sketches as it tossed its head or rolled on its back or trotted up to its mother to feed. Alexa heard the firm strokes of his charcoal faltering, although she pretended not to notice.

'Do you remember your mother?' he asked, so unexpectedly that Alexa blinked with surprise.

'Of course. I was nine when she died.'

'What was she like?'

'She was Italian. Dark-haired; not like me. Until she became ill, she was very beautiful. She had a lovely singing voice, and played the piano well. She was a teacher of music, you know; very patient. When I was small, she had to take me with her to the lessons, and I can remember all the things she used to say, over and over again. It's been a great help to me: I can give lessons to myself.'

'How was it that Aunt Margaret came to adopt you, then?'

'She came – as a doctor – to visit my mother, who was dying by then of consumption and starvation. But they had known each other earlier, as teacher and pupil. After my mother died, there was no one in the world on whom I had any claim. I was very fortunate to escape the workhouse. Why do you ask all this?'

Matthew was slow to answer. He had sounded awkward even when he asked the question, and now he was obviously embarrassed; but Alexa waited until he spoke.

'When you first came to live at Brinsley House, we were told that you had been adopted,' he said. 'But you look – I just wanted to be sure – I only wondered whether Aunt Margaret could possibly be your mother.'

His face was scarlet as he stared down at his sketching pad. Alexa gave an incredulous gasp.

'What an extraordinary idea! Why, she wasn't even married when I was born.'

'I know.' Matthew's voice was apologetic. 'I shouldn't have suggested it. You won't tell Aunt Margaret I asked, will you?'

'Certainly not. She would be very shocked. Why – ?'

But Alexa had no need to finish the question. Without asking, she understood why he had needed to know. For six years they had studied and played together as though they were brother and sister. Matthew had known that she was not really his sister. What he was checking was the possibility that she might be his cousin.

Alexa could move one further step into his mind. Only the previous evening, after dinner, Margaret had been talking about a death caused by the measles epidemic: that of a feeble-minded child. Alexa, who had often noticed the boy's shambling walk and idiotic grin, asked how such things were caused.

21

'There are a good many possible reasons,' Margaret had said. 'But the one that I blame, and the most easily prevented, is the habit of marrying within a very small community such as a village. The parents of this boy were first cousins. It means that the child had fewer grandparents than is usual. If there is any weak strain in the family already, the chance of inheriting it is greatly increased. Although it is not forbidden for cousins to marry, I would always advise against it, if I were asked. But then, young people nowadays never ask for advice until they have quite decided not to take it.'

Matthew and Alexa laughed together then, and Alexa had thought no more of it. If Matthew, taking the theoretical advice seriously, felt it necessary to check that it could have no practical application to himself, there could only be one explanation. For a second time she felt her breath snatched from her; this time by wonder. She looked across at Matthew, who sat with his head still bowed, and was almost overcome by a wish to run her fingers through his thick fair hair. He raised his head slowly to gaze at her. Alexa jumped to her feet and turned away – not because she wished to discourage him, but because she was overwhelmed by a kind of excitement she had never felt before, and needed time to steady her feelings.

'I would like to paint you,' said Matthew, with almost as much abruptness as he had used for his earlier question.

'Then why don't you?' Alexa pirouetted round him, her white skirts swirling and the green ribbons on her hat flying. An onlooker might have thought she was flirting, for her extravagant dips and dances contrasted strongly with Matthew's unmoving solemnity: but the gaiety which she acted was only the veneer on a sincere delight. She came to a halt in a Gainsborough pose, one arm lifted to

22

her filmy white hat. 'I shall be a better model than a painter. When will you start?'

'I'm not skilled enough to catch a likeness in water-colour,' Matthew said. 'I would need to use oil paints, and I didn't bring them with me. If Aunt Margaret agrees, will you come to stay at Brinsley House?'

'It would be necessary for your mother to invite me.'

'I shall ask her to do so as soon as I arrive home. If she writes tonight you will have the invitation almost before you have completed your packing. Will you come?'

'Can you doubt it?' Alexa gave another pirouette of pleasure. The mare and foal, disturbed by the movement, whinnied and cantered away to the far side of the field. Matthew seemed not to care that his subject had vanished. He too stood up and held out his hand towards Alexa.

His shyness might prevent him from speaking, but there was no need for words. As she allowed him to take her hand, Alexa knew that their old relationship had come to an end. At the beginning of his visit she had welcomed him as though he were a favourite brother: when he left that evening, she said goodbye to the young man she loved.

Always before she had confided in Margaret, but this was her secret, to be kept from all the world. She made the excuse to herself that there was nothing to tell. A touch of the hand – what significance had such a small gesture? Only when Matthew put his feelings into words could she be sure of his love, and admit her own.

The invitation arrived as speedily as she could have hoped. With her usual lack of grace Sophie made it clear from the wording that she was writing at Matthew's request rather than from her own choice, but this merely increased Alexa's pleasure. She held her breath as she waited for her guardian's decision.

23

'The invitation comes at a good time,' Margaret commented, passing it across. 'I'm too busy with the complications of the measles to be good company, and I shall be glad for you to be well away from the contagion. Would you like to go?'

'Yes, please.' Alexa ran from the breakfast table to her own room and began to lay out all her clothes. She was mending and packing them with the help of Betty, their housekeeper, when Margaret came into the room to say what travelling arrangements she suggested.

'Good heavens, child! You're not being invited to take up residence in Brinsley House for ever!'

'I need to take so much because none of my clothes are suitable at all for such a visit,' Alexa declared with a touch of sulkiness. Her excitement at the prospect of a return to Bristol had been dampened as she tried to imagine the various kinds of entertainment which might be offered her, and in each case realized that she had nothing suitable to wear. 'It's time that I ceased to dress like a schoolgirl. You don't seem to realize that I am eighteen now. You tell me that Beatrice is out: well, I am older than Beatrice.'

She was sorry for her snappiness as soon as she had spoken, for she could tell that she had hurt her guardian's feelings. It was a long time since Margaret had needed to dress fashionably, but her silence now suggested that she sympathized with Alexa's outburst.

'You are quite right,' she said quietly. 'I have been remiss, not noticing how time has passed. When you come back from Bristol, we must have a discussion about your future. And for now – well, Betty will show you how to put your hair up for the evening. And I will send some money with you to Sophie and ask her to help you choose a gown in which you may keep Beatrice company if she asks you to. In fact, you will need two: one for day and one for evening.'

Knowing how short money was in the household, Alexa was immediately remorseful and would have refused it. But Margaret insisted firmly that the new wardrobe was necessary, and Alexa's anxiety to show herself off as smart in front of Matthew overcame her scruples. She was happy again, and as affectionate as always, when a day later she kissed Margaret and little Robert goodbye. She could not have guessed then how much would happen before she saw them again.

4

Ambition feeds on discontent. In her quiet country home Alexa had often felt the desire to go out into the world and make a name for herself. With Margaret's hard-working example at hand, she was less easily persuaded than most girls of respectable family that a young woman should do no more than wait at home until someone came to offer her marriage. At the same time, she would have liked to make some financial contribution to the running of the household. So firmly had Margaret discouraged her wish to go on the stage that for a long time she had not dared to mention it. But if her future were to be discussed when she returned from Bristol, perhaps she could raise the question just once more. In her heart she suspected that it would be no use, but nevertheless she passed the time of the railway journey in planning what she would say.

Then, as the train steamed into Temple Meads, she saw Matthew waiting and realized that she wanted nothing more than to spend her life with him. Her day-dreams of applauding crowds, of flowers strewn at her feet, of jewels and admirers – all these disappeared in the few seconds which it took him to catch sight of her. He was so grave, so handsome, so kind; and he loved her, she was sure of that. He had not told her so yet, but surely before she left Bristol he would speak – and then she would never think again of theatres and applause.

Matthew also had ambitions, rooted as firmly as her own in dissatisfaction with the life which his parents had forced on him. He had never revealed them to her before, but they emerged gradually in the course of her sittings for the portrait.

He had made a studio for himself in the tower room. Alexa looked round curiously as on her first evening Matthew led the way into it, to show her where he had set up the easel and to choose her pose, ready for a start the next day. During all her years at Brinsley House the tower had been locked and unused. It was not safe for children, Sophie had said if ever she was asked about it.

'It was my grandfather's favourite room,' Matthew told Alexa as they stood together at one of the windows, looking down-river at the breathtaking view of the Clifton Gorge and the suspension bridge which seemed to float above it. 'In his day, most of the Lorimer Line ships were still under sail. He used to stand here and watch as they came up the river to the Bristol Docks.'

'Do you remember your Lorimer grandparents?' Alexa asked, recalling the portrait of John Junius which was now hanging in the drawing room of Elm Lodge, and her own fancies about him.

'My grandmother not at all. She was ill most of the time, and found small children too noisy. But I can just remember my grandfather: a very big man. I didn't like him kissing me, because the hair on his face tickled. But he was fond of me, I think. I can recall being jogged on his knee. And although I was only six when he died, I can remember having the odd feeling that other people were frightened of him, but that I wasn't.'

'I've heard that he was very autocratic,' said Alexa.

'Well, perhaps he had the right to be. He was very rich, and important at least in the society of his own city. As well as being chairman of a bank, Lorimer's Bank, he owned and managed the Lorimer Line for most of his life, as my father does now – in fact, he gave the company to my father as a twenty-first birthday present. I find it curious that nobody in Bristol ever speaks of him. Even my parents never talk about him. But sometimes I think, from the little I've heard, that Arthur and I have each inherited a separate part of his character. Arthur will be a successful man of business, just as my grandfather was. He will build up the Lorimer Line and expand it and find new companies to join to it, and make a great fortune for himself. It's curious how one can tell these things in advance. He's not yet seventeen, yet his ability is already clear.'

'But you are the elder son,' Alexa protested. 'You are the one who will inherit the Lorimer Line.'

'Not if my father has any sense,' laughed Matthew. 'Already he can see how much I hate the work. I lack the talent as well as the taste for it. My father moves me round his office and his ships, so that I spend a few months at each task. At the end I am expected to put all my experience together to provide a complete under-standing of the running of a shipping line. But I am inefficient in every matter of business which is set before me. Whenever I attempt to command a column of figures I find myself faced with a mutiny. Last week I accepted twice as much cargo for New York as the ship I was filling could carry.'

Alexa smiled sympathetically. 'What have you inherited

27

from your grandfather, then, if not his business ability?' she asked.

'I would like to be an artist,' said Matthew. 'But that's easier to say than to do. I know I have talent, but talent is not enough by itself. I should need to be trained, and at the end of the training I should find myself in the most precarious of professions – and perhaps still lacking in the ability or the luck to succeed in it. I feel that it's a crime to waste my one talent – yet it would be wicked to hurt my parents by disregarding their wishes.'

'I know exactly how you feel!' exclaimed Alexa. She had not intended to say anything to Matthew about her ambition to sing in public, but the similarity of their situations prompted her to be indiscreet.

'There is a difference between us, all the same,' he commented when he heard her wistful day-dreams. 'A young man trying to earn a living as a painter can suffer nothing worse than starvation. But a young woman who goes on the stage – '

It was out of respect for her innocence, Alexa supposed, that he did not finish the sentence. But she knew what he was thinking. The argument was one which she had heard too often from Margaret, and it still had the power to annoy her.

'That depends, surely, on the young woman,' she expostulated. 'There is nothing immoral in itself in appearing before an audience.'

'Perhaps not,' he said doubtfully. 'But you must admit that the temptations facing an actress or a singer are very great indeed. A young woman living quietly at home with her mother or guardian is automatically protected against unpleasant advances of any kind. But when the same young woman displays herself on the stage, she seems almost to be inviting such advances, and she must repel them for herself. It is not to be wondered at if she fails, because she is expected to fail.'

Just in time, Alexa remembered that this was a subject on which she no longer wanted to argue. She changed the subject back to an earlier part of their conversation. 'You were saying that you had inherited some of your grandfather's characteristics,' she reminded him. 'He was not an artist, was he?'

'No. Doubtless painting was thought as unsuitable a pastime for a gentleman in his time as it is now. But he was a patron of artists. And he bought carvings and Eastern paintings, the best he could find. He had a love of beautiful things. That is what I have inherited. I love beautiful things too.' He turned away from the window to look at her. 'And you are the most beautiful thing I have ever seen, Alexa.'

His kiss was gentle, but she could feel the violence of his heartbeat as he held her close. They did not speak again until it was time for them to go in for dinner.

The next two weeks passed in a haze of happiness for Alexa. She did her best to control her hopes. If Matthew was serious in wanting to become an artist, many years were likely to pass before he would be able to support a wife. And yet, although she was inexperienced in the ways of the world, she knew that by kissing her Matthew had declared his love and made a commitment – and she, accepting the kiss, had accepted that she too was committed. If they concealed the state of affairs from the household, it was in order that they might continue to enjoy the unusual freedom which was a consequence of their equally unusual closeness of upbringing. Matthew hurried home from the shipping office as early as he could each evening and worked on her portrait until the light faded. He kissed her only at the end of each sitting, as they prepared to return to the company of the family, but the anticipation of this moment excited Alexa all the time she was posing, and the memory of it carried her through the following day. She tried to hide her feelings, but Sophie must have sensed them, for on the second Saturday, when Matthew was free in the afternoon as well as the evening, the sitting was interrupted by the opening of the tower room door. Beatrice came in, bad-tempered, and sat down on a chair. They waited for her to speak.

'Oh, I bring no message for you,' she said. 'Mama has sent me to find Alexa and keep her company.'

'Then you need not trouble yourself, because I am already making sure that she is not lonely,' Matthew said.

Beatrice gave the sharp laugh that was characteristic of her. 'I think that is precisely what Mama had in mind,' she said. Her voice rose to a shriller pitch as she quoted. '"While Alexa is our guest, we must not allow her reputation to suffer from any failure on our part to chaperone her adequately." So I hope, dear brother, that you can catch a likeness quickly.'

She made herself comfortable with a book. Matthew worked in silence for a little, but his sister's presence made the atmosphere heavy, and Alexa was not surprised when he flung down his brushes and complained that the light was not good enough. Beatrice smirked with triumph as she followed them out.

Alexa did not allow herself to be despondent for long. On Monday Beatrice was due to attend an evening party, to which Sophie would take her. It had been made very clear that although Alexa was welcome to go with Sophie on her rounds of morning calls, the company of a young girl who was so very much more beautiful than poor Beatrice was not to be tolerated on any social occasion at which potential husbands might be present. It was possible that a maid might be sent along to the tower room to act as chaperone; but maids could be bribed.

On Monday, therefore, Alexa made her way there as usual. The time of Matthew's return from work came and passed, but his footsteps were not to be heard running eagerly up the steps. At first Alexa fretted; then she became annoyed; and, at last, anxious. She went back into the main house, arriving in the central hall just as Sophie and Beatrice were leaving for the party. Perhaps they had spitefully forced Matthew to accompany them. While pretending to wave them a cheerful goodbye, she managed to take a good look inside the carriage. He was not there.

Disconsolate, she wandered through the house, looking into each room in turn, but without success. The library door was open. Had she known that William Lorimer was inside she would not have disturbed him, but she had stepped through the doorway before she was able to see him standing beside the fireplace. He was reading a letter, and something in the intensity of his stillness told her at once that she would find the answer to her questions here.

5

Any efficient businessman is accustomed to calculate precisely the effects of his actions. If William Lorimer allowed himself to be observed by Alexa as he tore the letter he was holding into tiny pieces, across and across, it was because he saw the need to harness his anger to a positive policy.

That was not to say that there was anything feigned about his fury. But in fact an hour had passed since two letters from Matthew had been delivered by messenger. One was addressed to William himself; the other to

Alexa. From his own brief message William learned that his elder son proposed to travel to Paris and study painting with the intention of earning a living as an artist. As soon as he had taken that in, he had felt no hesitation at all in opening the letter addressed to Alexa.

Its tone was sentimental. Matthew stated brutally enough to her – as to his father – that the thought of a lifetime spent in the offices of the Lorimer Line appalled him. It might prove that his artistic talent would not be strong enough to support him, but if he were to abandon his ambitions without ever putting them to the test, he believed that he would be discontented for the rest of his life. He begged Alexa to forgive him for going. In particular, he beseeched her to understand his cowardice in not telling her of his decision in person: he had known in advance that if he were to see tears in her beautiful eyes he would never have the strength to leave.

But his desertion was not to make her think that he did not love her. On the contrary – what he had to say on the contrary had caused William's head to shake in amazement at the indiscretion of young men. If she could forgive the abruptness of his departure, Matthew begged Alexa to write to him, to consider herself as truly bound to him as he was to her. And in return he promised that at the end of three years, when she was twenty-one, if he had not succeeded in establishing himself securely enough to support a wife, he would return to Bristol and ask his father to take him back again into the family business in order that they might marry. In the meantime, he hoped that Alexa might use the interim to test her own ambitions as he proposed to test his. And she was never to forget that he adored her.

There were more endearments and protestations of a similarly romantic nature. But none of these were of any significance compared with the shock of learning that Matthew had fallen in love with Alexa.

William, so meticulous in his eye for business details, gave less attention to the relationships within his family. He had thought of Alexa as being a child, because it was as a child that she had shared his own children's schoolroom and she was still young when she left Brinsley House to live with Margaret at Elm Lodge. He knew that she and Matthew had always been friendly. Neither Matthew's visit to Elm Lodge this summer nor his return invitation to Alexa had seemed of any significance. How Margaret could have been so blind to what was happening was a question which he would have the right to ask. She knew, as William did, that any marriage between the two was out of the question – not because of any prejudice on his own part, but as a matter of law. But Matthew and Alexa were not aware that this was the case. Neither of them had ever been allowed to learn that Alexa was in fact Matthew's aunt.

So although William was angry with Matthew, and scornful of his foolishness in rejecting opportunities which most young men would have welcomed, there was no element of spite in his immediate decision that the two young people ought not to meet again. It was in their own best interests that this should be the case. But to explain the legal situation to each of them could only cause bitterness against the adults who had kept their true relationship secret for so long. It had been William who ordained that Alexa should not be publicly acknowledged as the daughter of John Junius Lorimer. Now he recognized that he must accept some responsibility for the consequences of that instruction.

With all this clear in his mind, the decision that Alexa should not be allowed to read the letter which Matthew had sent her followed almost inevitably. She would of course be hurt by the discovery that the man she loved had run away. To give Matthew back to her, in a sense, and then immediately explain why she could not be allowed to keep him, would be cruel. How very much kinder it would be to let a single outburst of tears and unhappiness bring the whole sad affair to an end.

It was part of the necessary charade that he should seem to be still in the first shock of learning what had happened when Alexa appeared in the doorway of the library. He looked up as though he had only just noticed her.

'It's too bad!' he exclaimed. 'Have young people no gratitude nowadays? No respect for their parents? No sense of duty?' He made an apologetic gesture with his hands. 'I'm sorry, Alexa. My anger isn't with you. It's Matthew who has behaved unpardonably.'

'What has he done?' Alexa's eyes widened in apprehension.

'He's gone, that's what he's done. Left home. To be an artist, he says. Of all the ridiculous ideas! As though he could hope to support himself in such a way! And to sneak away so secretly! You've seen a good deal of him in the past two weeks, Alexa. Did he mention any plan of the kind to you?'

If he had needed an answer, he could have found it in the pallor of Alexa's face.

'No, I can see he gave no more warning to you than to me. Come and sit down, my dear.' He helped her to the leather arm-chair beside the fireplace.

'He spoke of his wish to paint,' Alexa whispered. 'But only in general terms. There was no suggestion that he intended to take any action. And I thought – I thought – ' She was silenced by the need to control her tears.

'He talked to me in the same way,' William said, truthfully. 'Several times, in fact – on the last occasion

34

only a few days ago. I tried to point out how fortunate he was to look forward to a share in the family business and to have secure employment now. It's all very well starving in a garret by yourself, I told him. But one day you'll want to get married. Wives cost money. They like to buy clothes, to eat something more than air. You'll want your own home. You'll want to have children. You'll be glad then that you've got the Lorimer Line behind you. Of course, what he really wanted was for me to give him money: a private income. But a business like mine grows by using its resources to expand, not frittering them away on hangers-on. It wasn't the first time I'd said that sort of thing to him. But it was the first time that he gave the impression of seeing the sense of it. I thought he'd got over all these fanciful ideas. And now, suddenly – ' He gave a snort of indignation that was genuine enough.

'Where has he gone?' Alexa asked.

'How should I know?' It was the first direct lie William had told, but it did not disturb his conscience. Once he had decided what course of action would be for the best, it must be pursued single-mindedly. Because Matthew's letter had not only mentioned Paris but had given a poste restante address there to which he hoped Alexa would write, William did his best to turn her thoughts as far away from that city as possible. 'I wouldn't be surprised if he didn't make for New York. He knows I'd come and haul him back if he stayed in England. And I've no doubt he was able to fool one of my captains into thinking that he had authority to take a passage. Though what's New York likely to teach him? Tell me that.' He gave another angry sigh. 'I must calm myself down,' he said. 'Think about it later. Will you sing something for me, my dear? I remember from your earlier years what a sweet voice you have.'

He offered his arm, helping her from the chair and

leading her towards the piano in the large drawing room. The support was needed, for she seemed almost unable to move.

'Did Matthew send any message to me in his letter?' she asked.

'"Tell Alexa I'm sorry," he wrote. Sorry for what, he didn't say. Had you two had a quarrel? Is that why he's gone?'

'No,' said Alexa. She was still near to tears. 'We never quarrelled.'

'Then I suppose we must explain it by a warped feeling of ambition. I must confess, I thought the boy was too easy-going to act as decisively as this. In fact, though I think he's a fool to turn his back on a good position in society and the sort of prosperous future that most young men would give their eyes for, I suppose he's showing more initiative by leaving than ever he did while he muddled up my figures for me in the office. He'll be back in a year or two, I don't doubt, with his tail between his legs. I lost my temper because he ought to have asked my permission. But when I think of it, he did ask from time to time, and a dusty answer I always gave him.'

It was true, but it was not enough to excuse Matthew's unfilial behaviour. His need for distraction, as he again pressed an unwilling Alexa to sing, was a genuine one, and he forced himself to concentrate with greater attention than he was normally prepared to devote to any kind of musical entertainment.

She began unsteadily, suggesting that the struggle not to weep was robbing her of breath. But almost at once a curious change took place. It was as though, subjecting her emotions to the music, she was unable to give less than her best to any listener. A firmness crept first of all into her fingers, as she accompanied herself on the piano, and then into her voice. William was startled into an

36

unexpected admiration. He took a step back in order that he could watch her as he listened, and set his mind to consider the possibilities.

She had been beautiful as a child and she was beautiful now as a young woman. William wasted little of his time in observing the attractions of the opposite sex, but he could recognize beauty when he saw it. And her voice had a quality quite different from that of the young ladies whose after-dinner warblings he was from time to time forced to endure. It even seemed to him that Alexa was singing better than many of the professional performers who appeared in the city's subscription concerts.

The fact that he had never liked her made it easier for William to be dispassionate. Her very existence was a reminder of a side of his father's character that would have been better forgotten. But whatever his personal feelings might be, he had already accepted his duty to treat her as a member of the family, and now he discerned another responsibility. She was unhappy. She herself might believe that her unhappiness was caused only by Matthew's behaviour. William knew better. He was not a man to make sentimental gestures, but he had always recognized obligations.

'Thank you,' he said when she had finished. 'Alexa, my dear, I must congratulate you. Your voice has matured out of all recognition. You have a most remarkable gift.'

'I wish I might have the chance to use it,' said Alexa, miserably.

'What are your ambitions?'

'My true ambition would be to become a *prima donna assoluta*. But even the humblest role in the world of opera would satisfy me.'

'And what are you doing about it?'

'What *can* I do, Mr Lorimer? I have no money, no influential connections. My guardian doesn't approve of

37

my ambitions, so how can I expect her to help me? I can practise – I *do* practise: but although I improve my voice, no one will ever hear it.'

'Is this a true ambition, Alexa, or merely the sort of dream in which all young girls, I imagine, indulge from time to time? If I were to offer you help, would you accept it?'

'What kind of help do you mean, Mr Lorimer?'

'I have an acquaintance in London,' he said. 'He is a gentleman, not a musician, but is nevertheless very much involved in the musical life of the city. He sees himself as a patron. If he felt, as I do, that your voice would repay proper training, he might arrange this for you, and even undertake your support while the training lasted.'

'Why should he do such a thing for a stranger?' asked Alexa.

'He would do it only if he thought your reputation in the end would reflect credit on his judgement. And he would do it not exactly for a stranger, but for me. A good deal in the business world depends on goodwill. He owes me a favour, which he could repay in this way without much trouble to himself – and then he would be in a position to hope for another favour from me later on.'

'You're very kind to make such an offer, Mr Lorimer,' said Alexa, her eyes revealing a mixture of hope and apprehension. No doubt, after so many years of dreaming, it was difficult for her to grasp the possibility that her dreams might actually come true.

'I feel sorry for you,' said William. There had been no spite in his decision to keep Matthew's letter from Alexa, but perhaps at this moment he was influenced by memories of old disputes with Margaret, of his resentment at her repeated refusals to live as a woman without a husband should, quietly in her brother's household. He was careful, however, to appear loyal to her as he justified his offer.

'I yield to no one in my admiration of my sister,' he said. 'Not once but twice she has been the victim of misfortune through no fault of her own, and each time she has overcome her difficulties magnificently. Her first suitor deserted her as soon as he discovered that she was no longer in a position to bring him a fortune. And when at last she found another love and married, her husband was killed within a few months of their wedding day. Most other women who found themselves widowed so soon after marriage, and in the middle of a first pregnancy, would simply have gone into a decline; but not my sister. Her present life is satisfying for herself, for Robert, for her patients. But I'm not wrong, am I, in thinking that it offers little to you? Your guardian can perhaps not be expected to realize herself how narrowly she confines you. It's easier for an outsider like myself to see that the time has come when you should begin to live your own life.'

'But I ought not to make such a decision without consulting her,' said Alexa.

'Of course not. But on the other hand, to discuss what at this moment is only a vague proposal can be of little value either to her or to you. She cannot be expected to approve an arrangement of which no details are available; and you can hardly hope to convince her of its value until you too know what is offered.' He thought for a moment. 'My acquaintance, Mr Glanville, will need to meet you before he can be expected to offer his support. He will want to hear you sing. And if he approves, you will have to have a second audition in front of a teacher. The best kind of coaching would come from someone who accepts a pupil not so much for the fees as for the pleasure of developing a talent. But that could all be arranged within a short period. At the end of twenty-four hours in London you would either have met with a polite refusal – in which case my sister would not need to make any decision – or you would have a firm offer of training which you could discuss with her in detail. In that case you could travel straight from London to Elm Lodge if you wished.'

'Yes,' said Alexa. 'I ought to do that.'

'I could telephone to Mr Glanville from my office tomorrow,' he told her. 'There is a need for haste in the matter, because I know he is shortly to travel to Scotland for some shooting. Would you like me to undertake that?'

That she still hesitated was to her credit, he supposed; or perhaps it merely meant that she was young and unsure of herself. As a businessman he knew that arrangements such as the one he had offered ought to be clinched at once. But Alexa was accustomed to accepting Margaret's advice and probably now feared her disapproval. William allowed time for Alexa to consider that if she said No she would be rejecting the best hope of achieving her ambition that she was ever likely to enjoy, in a manner which must be final: while if she said Yes, she committed herself only to an audition. The possibility of a subsequent training was one which her guardian would still have time to forbid.

William knew what Alexa would decide. The dashing of her hopes of marriage must inevitably throw her back on her own talents and ambitions, for the unexpected disappearance of the young man she loved would make it intolerable for her to return to a quiet country life, with nothing to which she could look forward. If the girl had any courage or character at all – and, whether he admitted it openly or not, she *was* a Lorimer – she was bound to accept the challenge.

He waited, and saw the lost, unhappy look with which she had greeted the news of Matthew's flight gradually replaced by a determination which showed in her eyes and the firmness of her lips. She looked up at him trustingly.

'Thank you very much, Mr Lorimer,' she said.

6

An unsophisticated girl who has spent all her life in the same sheltered surroundings is apt to be either apprehensive or intolerant when she first ventures outside them. This was not, however, Alexa's situation. As a small child she had moved rapidly from one set of lodgings to another, each less comfortable than the one before, and had learned to adapt herself quickly to her surroundings. Then, when her fortunes were at their lowest, she had been rescued by Margaret and taken to Brinsley House. Here she was expected to behave in accordance with rules she had never learned and to fit into a domestic hierarchy which seemed at first to have no place for her. A dull child might have succumbed to bewilderment but, because Alexa was observant and imitative, she adapted herself as quickly as before. For this reason she felt no kind of social anxiety as she stood on the pavement of Park Lane and looked up at the imposing façade of Glanville House. There would be more servants here than at Brinsley House and because their employer was a nobleman, they would be haughtier – but she was not frightened of them.

William Lorimer had explained the position to her before she left Bristol. The head of the family, Lord Glanville, lived in his London home only when Parliament was sitting, spending the rest of the year either abroad or at Blaize, his country house. He was unlikely to be in residence when Alexa arrived. If by chance he *was* there, he would formally be her host. But the gentleman who had promised to receive Alexa was his younger brother, the Honourable Duncan Glanville.

She rang the bell and was reassured to find herself expected. As soon as she gave her name the butler summoned a footman to show her to a bedroom and carry up her luggage. Although her host did not put in an appearance to welcome her, the way in which her arrival was taken for granted was a relief. As the train chugged eastward that afternoon Alexa had felt a good many qualms of fear. She had no cause to distrust her guardian's brother: yet the kindness of his offer seemed so much out of character that she continually searched her mind to discover some way in which he might be deceiving her. But she could not think of any reason why he should be unkind, any more than she understood why he had chosen to help her.

She had concluded in the end that he was trying to make up for his elder son's behaviour. Alexa had found it difficult to hide the fact that she was in love with Matthew. Perhaps his father had noticed it and, angry on her account as well as his own, resolved to make what amends he could. At least it seemed that her worst fear had not been realized – that she would arrive in London without a penny in her pocket to find that no one was prepared to receive her.

When she was ready she went downstairs, as the butler had instructed her. She was wearing the new day dress that Sophie had bought her at Margaret's request, and her long hair was coiled on top of her head. She hoped that the dignity it gave her would conceal her nervousness. It came as a second reassurance to hear, as she walked slowly down the curved staircase into the hall, that someone was playing the piano extremely well. It might mean that the Honourable Duncan Glanville was an accomplished amateur musician, or else that he already had a protégé: in either case it confirmed the description of him as a patron of the arts.

It was easy to choose between her guesses. The fashionable clothes and arrogant expression of the pianist marked him out at once as a rich man. He glanced at Alexa as she appeared in the doorway of the drawing room, but did not interrupt his playing, merely nodding his head to indicate that she should take a chair.

As Alexa sat down, she saw that he already had an audience. A woman of about forty was lying on a chaise longue, her legs covered with a rug, although the afternoon was warm. She showed her weakness in the way she raised her fan as a gesture of applause as the piece came to an end.

The pianist stood up and bowed formally over Alexa's hand without troubling to introduce himself.

'Fanny,' he said to the woman on the chaise longue. 'May I present Miss Alexa Lorimer to you? Miss Lorimer, Lady Glanville.'

Lady Glanville smiled as she acknowledged the introduction. Her expression was kind, but Alexa could tell from her eyes that she was in pain.

Alexa turned back towards her host and found that he was looking her up and down in a way that no one had ever done before.

'Too thin!' he said, and she flushed with shame and embarrassment.

'Really, Duncan!' protested Lady Glanville. 'What a way to greet the child! She has a most elegant figure.'

'For a lady of fashion, perhaps. But if her ambitions lie in the world of opera, she will have to put on some fat.'

'You are too coarse!' This time Lady Glanville spoke

more sharply. Her brother-in-law bowed in acknowledgement of the rebuke but made no alteration in the haughty
tone of his voice.

'We will ask her to provide the finale to your little
concert, my dear Fanny,' he said. He turned back to
Alexa. 'I made it clear to Mr Lorimer that any help I was
prepared to give you was contingent on an audition. I can
hardly be expected to waste time and money on some
young lady who is only fit to squawk to her mother's
friends after dinner. Did he warn you of that?'

Alexa nodded her head: her throat was dry with
nervousness.

'When I put the condition to Mr Lorimer, he merely
laughed and commented that in such a case we might
consider it settled,' said Mr Glanville. 'I take it that he
admires your ability. Well, we will find out at once if he
is right. If I give you time to prepare yourself you will
become more nervous, not less. And you will find my
sister-in-law the perfect audience. She could not speak a
critical word to anyone to save her life. What will you
sing?'

'"Che faro senza Euridice",' answered Alexa. She had
sung it to William on the previous evening, with tears in
her voice for her own lost love. Now she would use it
again to mark her entry into a new life.

'Do you speak Italian?' It seemed that her choice, and
the accent in which she announced it, had made a good
impression.

'Yes, sir,' answered Alexa. 'My mother was Italian.'

This answer too earned a nod of approval, and her
confidence began to return. She had expected to
accompany herself, but Mr Glanville sat down again at
the piano and without needing a score began at once to
play the introduction to Orpheus's lament. Alexa sang as

44

well as she could, and was disappointed by the silence with which her performance was received.

'What makes you think you're a contralto, Miss Lorimer?' he demanded, turning on the piano stool to face her. His voice was so aggressive that Alexa's heart sank. She was not good enough, then. It did not occur to her that the question was anything but sarcastic. The natural range of her voice was a wide one, and she had taught herself contralto arias mainly because her mother had been a contralto and had left her a box of music, too shabby to pawn or sell. Because the register had given her no trouble, Alexa had always taken it for granted that she was a contralto as well.

Lady Glanville must have noticed the dismay on her face, for she gave a sweet smile. 'I thought the child sang beautifully, Duncan,' she said.

'Oh yes, yes. A pretty enough voice. But mezzo at the very lowest; and a full dramatic soprano if she holds her head up. Here, try again. We can take a few liberties with Gluck.' He turned back to the piano and played a series of chords to show that he was transposing the aria upwards. Then he nodded at her to sing it once more.

It was extraordinary what a difference the small change made. Instead of cradling her voice inside her chest, Alexa found that she had to stand up straighter, pull her shoulders back, project her voice outwards and upwards. She had no difficulty in reaching the higher notes, and now the sound was not merely adequate but glorious. Long before she came to the end she knew that she must have justified William's request on her behalf. As the last note died away she found herself gasping, with excitement rather than breathlessness. Her eyes were bright and expectant – but once again her patron was slow to comment. This time it was because his attention had been distracted.

45

Alexa turned to follow his gaze. A very tall man, his hair already streaked with silver, was standing in the doorway. Without being told, she felt sure that he must be Lord Glanville. He had the same immaculate appearance and aristocratic expression as the Honourable Duncan Glanville, but without the younger man's trace of cruelty. He too was staring at her, but in a quite different manner from his brother's earlier scrutiny. It was as though he could hardly believe what he had heard. As soon as he saw that he had been noticed, however, he nodded politely to Alexa but turned to speak to his wife.

'Fanny, my dear, are your boxes ready to be carried down?'

'All but the valise which is to travel in the carriage. I will see to that now.'

Lord Glanville bent over the chaise longue to help his wife to her feet. Alexa, seeing the difficulty with which Lady Glanville moved, hurried to assist on the other side but then hesitated, wondering whether she was being presumptuous. Lady Glanville gave the same sweet smile with which she had encouraged Alexa before, and accepted the support of her arm as well as Lord Glanville's. She walked with difficulty towards the foot of the stairs, where two servants were waiting with an invalid chair to carry her up.

'Thank you, my dear,' she said. 'If this is to be the first step in a great career, I feel privileged to have been present at it. I wish you every success.'

There was an immediate feeling of rapport – almost affection – between the two women. Alexa was warmed by it as she returned to the piano and her sympathy must have been obvious, for Mr Glanville showed no impatience at the interruption.

'My sister-in-law suffers from a muscular disease,' he said. 'She is in constant pain, which she can relieve only

46

in hot baths and poultices. My brother leaves with her tomorrow for Baden-Baden, so that she may take the cure again. Now then, let us continue. Mr Lorimer was not deceived. You have a good voice. I would like to explore its range.'

By now Alexa's confidence had returned. She had been so painstaking in her exercises over the years that she found no difficulty in singing the scale from each chord he played. When he stood up during the last of them and put his hand lightly round the front of her throat she was disconcerted – but continued to sing in order that he might feel the movement of her larynx, if that was what he wanted.

His next move was very much more disturbing. He asked her to sing a series of notes, starting softly and making a gradual crescendo, prolonging each note for as long as her breath allowed. As she did so he came to stand behind her, very much closer than Alexa liked, and put his arms round her waist, pressing the palms of both hands against her diaphragm.

She did her best to conceal her uneasiness. He was testing her breath control. It was a legitimate touch for a music teacher. She had seen her own mother do it to the little girls she taught, helping to show them how they should breathe. But her mother was not a man; and this man was not a music teacher.

He had the right to know whether she deserved his interest, she told herself. It need never happen again. And although he was not a teacher, he had conducted the audition in a reassuringly professional way. Alexa sustained each note as he had instructed, and tried not to notice that his thumbs were touching her breasts.

At last the ordeal was over. For a second time he looked her up and down. 'I think something could be made of you,' he said. 'I hope you're not stupid enough

47

to think that you can walk straight into an opera company. The training for a singer is long.'

'How long, sir?' asked Alexa.

'The best singers take six years.' He showed his amusement at the dismay on her face. 'And by then you think you will be old and ugly, with the best years of your life wasted! Well, if you work hard, three years may be enough. We will wait until the travellers have departed tomorrow morning, with all the fuss that will involve. Then I will arrange for a teacher and discuss a course of study for you. For tonight, I will have a meal sent up to your room.'

'You are so kind, Mr Glanville. I don't quite understand – I would like to say how grateful I am.'

From what she had been told, she half expected him to reply with some reference to his love of music, but instead he smiled in a manner which she found unpleasant.

'Good,' he said. 'I feed on gratitude. I shall expect to be succoured by regular offerings of it.' He dismissed her with a nod, leaving her to make her way back to her bedroom.

As he had promised, a tray was brought to the room. When she had eaten the lonely meal she went to bed, exhausted by a day of travel and anxiety. For a long time she lay with her eyes open in the darkness, trying to make sense of all that had happened and to see, if only a little way, into the future.

The past was something she must try to forget. Throughout the previous night she had lain awake, weeping, hurt and unhappy. That Matthew should have deserted her at all was almost impossible to believe; that he should have gone without a word of farewell had, in the end, caused her misery to be replaced by anger. She would take good care never again to give her love so easily. But no one should ever know how deeply she had

48

been hurt. She would show Matthew how little she cared for his desertion by becoming rich and famous. For a little while longer she would need to live as a dependant; but once her training was over she would make a great career for herself. How fortunate it was, she tried to persuade herself, that she had not after all been diverted from her ambitious plans into a life of domestic dullness.

As unexpected as Matthew's departure was his father's helpfulness. Almost against reasonable expectation William Lorimer had kept his promise. He had introduced her to someone who – in an equally unlikely manner – was apparently prepared to help her realize her ambitions. But how much could Mr Glanville be expected to do for a stranger? To provide her with board and lodging might cost him little. To arrange a musical training might gratify his pride. But did he realize, she wondered, that she had no resources of her own at all? She had brought with her – since she planned to return directly to Elm Lodge the next day – all the clothes which she had taken to Bristol, and the single valise contained all that she owned. Her two new dresses would be shabby long before the course of training was completed. Already she needed a new pair of shoes, since the money Margaret had sent to Sophie had not been enough to provide this. Would she be entitled to go to Mr Glanville for clothes and pin money? And if not, what was she to do? To ask Margaret for an allowance was out of the question. Every penny that came into Elm Lodge was needed to balance a tight budget.

This problem brought Alexa to another difficult question. Would she be able to persuade her guardian to give permission for the whole ambitious undertaking? Yes, it must be possible. Margaret herself had been ambitious as a young woman and had seized her chance to take a training and make a career for herself. She would feel at least a little sympathy for Alexa's hopes. Her doubts had always been about the threat which a theatrical life posed to the good reputation of any young woman. There could be no objection, surely, to this preliminary arrangement, made by her own brother with a family of such undoubted respectability as the Glanvilles. Alexa's anxiety on this score was not too great. The financial problems loomed larger in her mind than the social or moral ones – of which, indeed, she was hardly aware.

She was still lying awake, wondering how far Mr Glanville's generosity was likely to extend, and how far she could ever recompense him, when the question answered itself. She heard footsteps approaching along the corridor. They came to a halt, and the door of her bedroom opened.

7

When one unexpected event after another in the course of a single day has turned out to be for the best, even a disquieting occurrence may briefly seem capable of bearing a favourable interpretation. There was nothing stealthy about the opening of Alexa's bedroom door, and nothing furtive about the movements of her patron as he came into the room. Alexa was naturally alarmed; but for a second she managed to persuade herself that he had arrived only as a polite host to make sure that she was comfortable, perhaps not expecting her to have retired to bed so early. The reassurance vanished as he closed the door behind him and put the lamp he carried down on her bedside table. Earlier in the evening she had found his smile unpleasant. Now it terrified her. She pulled the sheet up to her chin.

'What are you doing here, sir?'

'Did you think the audition was over?' Mr Glanville enquired. Her eyes, wide with alarm, must have shown him the answer. 'I take it this was something that Mr Lorimer forgot to mention.'

The thought obviously increased his amusement. He sat down on the edge of the bed. Alexa scrambled out of it on the other side and waited, breathless with fear, to see how she could get past him to the only door of the room.

'Don't be stupid,' he said. 'A couple of hours ago you were willing enough to accept favours. Did you expect them all to come free? It's time you grew up. There's a price to be paid for everything, my dear. In this case, I flatter myself that you will find the price as acceptable as the career you are buying with it. I shall keep my side of the bargain. It is hardly too much to ask that it should provide me with as much satisfaction as you.'

'There is no bargain,' said Alexa. 'Yes, I have been stupid. I was told you were a gentleman. I thought – '

The smile faded from his face and anger made him ugly as he stood up and strode towards her. Alexa flung herself across the bed in an effort to reach the door. He caught her by one foot and she kicked him with the other, hard enough to send him staggering off balance backwards. Sobbing and slithering she flung the door open and rushed out into the corridor, charging head-first into Lord Glanville.

She clung to him in relief, still sobbing as she buried her head in his chest. But even now she could not feel safe. The two men were brothers. They might be in league – or at least not prepared to quarrel over a stranger. The silence seemed to last a long time; but Alexa dared not look up, in case she should see the same smile on Lord Glanville's face as on his younger brother's.

Certainly his voice, when at last he spoke, was light and apparently uncritical.

'My dear Duncan, you don't usually need to press your attentions on young women by force. One has been led to believe that as a rule they fling themselves at your feet.'

'This one's a fool. Says she didn't realize – '

'And perhaps she didn't.' There was a new edge of harshness to Lord Glanville's aristocratic drawl. He still spoke pleasantly enough, but definitely.

'Don't worry. I can persuade her.'

'No doubt you can, dear boy,' agreed Lord Glanville. 'But not tonight.'

'I could say that it's none of your damn business,' protested his brother.

'And I could say that while Miss Lorimer is a guest in this house I am responsible for her. Goodnight, Duncan.'

The answering goodnight was sulky, but not accompanied by any further protest. Alexa, who had held her breath during this exchange, began to cry again, gulping for air but still clinging tightly to her protector. He released her grip gently and led her back into her bedroom. As she sat down on the side of the bed, he leaned back against the door, looking down at her from his great height.

'One can only assume that there must have been some misunderstanding,' he said. 'You can go back to bed now. You will be safe enough tonight.'

'And tomorrow?' asked Alexa. She was still trembling with the panic she had felt as Lord Glanville's brother had grabbed at her.

'My brother has not favoured me with details of the arrangement under which you came here,' said Lord Glanville. 'If you wish to end it and return home, the servants will be instructed to see that you are safely set on your way. My wife and I will be leaving for the Continent early in the morning, so we cannot help you personally.' He took out his purse. 'You have come from Bristol, I understand. Have you enough money for the return journey?'

Alexa's tears began to flow again. In her frightened state, Lord Glanville appeared as the only protector she could trust, and the thought that he was about to leave increased her feeling of helplessness. 'I cannot go back to Bristol!' she exclaimed.

'Who sent you here?' asked Lord Glanville. 'My brother mentioned a Mr Lorimer.'

'Yes, he sent me. He was supposed to look after me, but he sent me here. And he knew, he must have known, what was going to happen. It's unthinkable that I should return there.' Even at the time Alexa – well aware that William Lorimer had never particularly liked her – had felt surprised that he should be so helpful. It was easy for her now to assume that everything which had happened was part of a deliberate plot.

Lord Glanville put his money back in his pocket and came right into the room to sit in an arm-chair. He stared at her with a serious expression on his face.

'I take it that Mr Lorimer is not your father, then,' he commented.

'No, my lord. My father died when I was a baby, and my mother a few years later. I was adopted into the Lorimer family. But Mr Lorimer is no relation of mine at all, and I never want to see him again.'

'Where else could you go, then, if you are unwilling to return to your guardian?'

Lord Glanville's natural enough mistake in assuming that William Lorimer was her guardian was hardly noticed by Alexa. There was an answer to his question, and she would have to give it – because of course she could go back to Margaret, who was expecting her return, although not at any precise moment.

And that, Alexa realized, would be the end of all her dreams. Only an hour earlier she had imagined herself persuading her guardian that an opera singer could live a life untouched by scandal, whether rumoured or real. She would have described herself as the protégée of a family which was above reproach. How could she honestly do that now? And if she told the truth, Margaret could hardly be expected not to point out that the incident confirmed all her previous warnings about the immorality of a stage career. There would never be another chance.

The disappointment of knowing her hopes to be dashed so soon after they had been raised caused Alexa to let out a groan of anguish.

'I want so much to be a singer!' she cried, with all the passion of her unhappiness. 'But I'm only eighteen, and I don't know what I should do. There's no one to help me. Except your brother; but I've been brought up to believe that what he expects of me is wrong.'

'You are quite right to think so, and your attitude does you credit. No, don't start crying again.'

He was too late. Alexa was no longer frightened, but she wept from self-pity – for the collapse of her hopes, the defeat of her ambitions, the loss of her lover, the dismal future which lay ahead. Lord Glanville stood up again.

'Wait a moment,' he said. 'Someone had better prepare you a hot drink. It will help you settle to sleep.'

He was gone longer than the giving of an order would have necessitated – so long, in fact, that Alexa began to feel she had been abandoned. Desperately she searched her mind for some alternative to the dullness of a country life, some plan which would meet Margaret's standards of respectability.

Her most immediate thought was the most impossible. Once before, when she was only nine years old, she had performed for a few months in music halls in order to earn money for her dying mother. Alexa had never forgotten those months, and her feeling of power and pride every time she had managed to reduce a noisy audience to silence, forcing them to listen to her singing and to love her. Even with no more experience than that, it was likely that her voice and appearance would gain her employment of the same kind again now. But not even Alexa could argue that a music hall was a respectable environment. And how hurt Margaret would be to learn that her ward preferred such a way of life to the one offered by herself and Robert. It was impossible. Of course it was impossible. But she must do *something*, she told herself. She must do something.

Lord Glanville returned at last, and sat down.

'Now then, Miss Lorimer,' he said. 'We must consider your future. It's difficult for me to know what help would be of most advantage to you. I may feel that my family has some responsibility for the difficulty of your situation – in point of fact, I do most strongly feel that – but without having very much opportunity to discharge that responsibility. You ought to be sent home, of course, but your reluctance to return to Mr Lorimer's house is understandable. I have been discussing your position with my wife.' He hesitated, as though an effort were needed for him to continue. 'We had a daughter who, if she had lived, would have been almost your age by now. Lady Glanville was greatly affected, I believe, by – well, the details are not important. She has suggested that what we could offer you, if you would like it, is a little time, so that you may consider what you want to do without the spur of insecurity. If you would care to travel with us to Germany tomorrow, Lady Glanville would appreciate your help as a companion while she is taking the waters. Her maid will be with her, of course, and there are attendants at the spa, so your duties would not be onerous. But to lie all day in a bath is tedious, and I shall have to return to England as soon as I have seen her comfortably settled. You could perhaps read to her, and accompany her on whatever walks she can manage. This would be for a few months only, but it would allow time for reflection. It's possible, too, that we could find a singing teacher for you in Baden-Baden.'

Alexa hardly needed to hesitate. She had already realized that a return to Elm Lodge now would mean the defeat of her hopes for ever. And the attraction between herself and Lady Glanville had been mutual as well as immediate. To act as a companion was the most proper of employments and the promise of singing lessons meant that her ambitions need not yet be completely buried.

There was one difficulty – that if she were to leave early the next morning she would have no chance to get in touch with Margaret first, and it would not be easy, either, to write during the course of the journey. But then, Margaret believed her ward to be safely at Brinsley House. There would be nothing in a few days' silence to worry her, and a letter which came in the end from a semi-permanent address and which described a working arrangement would be more reassuring than a tentative proposal. Alexa began to express her gratitude, but Lord Glanville's mind was running in the same direction as her own.

'Does your guardian have the telephone?' he enquired.

Alexa shook her head. She meant by that that Margaret could not be reached by telephone; but even if she had realized that Lord Glanville was referring to William Lorimer, it would have made no difference to her answer. There was no instrument at Brinsley House, but only at the offices of the Lorimer Line, which William would not reach until after the Glanvilles had begun their journey.

'Then you understand that I must write a letter,' Lord Glanville said. 'You are under age. I cannot simply take you out of the country without saying anything. However, since we must leave early, I see no reason why we should not take the answer for granted. If your guardian was willing to entrust you to my brother's care without a chaperone, there can be no possible objection to your travelling with my wife. But of course, if you are summoned back to England, you will have to come. Will you travel with us on those terms?'

'My lord!' Alexa sprang to her feet and held out both hands towards him in relief and thanks, forgetting that she was wearing only her nightdress. The events of the past few days had given her little reason to think that she was a good judge of character. She had believed that Matthew was in love with her, that William Lorimer had wanted to help her, that the Honourable Duncan Glanville was interested only in her voice; and in each of these beliefs it seemed that she had been mistaken. But this time, she felt sure, she was not wrong in believing that Lord Glanville was a kind and upright man.

Even with this confidence she was briefly disturbed as he took her outstretched hands and smiled at her. Her life at Elm Lodge had offered her no experience of men. Within the past few days she had seen Matthew Lorimer look at her with all the tenderness of young love – or so she had thought at the time. Within the past few hours she had seen lust in the eyes of Duncan Glanville. Lord Glanville's smile was different again. There was admiration in it, and sympathy, and something else which she could not quite identify.

But he was not a young man like the other two. He must be almost forty. Old enough to be her father, as he had indirectly pointed out himself: the explanation seemed sufficient at once. What his smile revealed was undoubtedly a kind of fatherly affection. She smiled whole-heartedly back at him.

'I shall be very happy to travel with you, my lord,' she said.

PART II

Alexa Abroad

1

Even a town wholly devoted to the cure of sickness is not a depressing place when most of its visitors suffer from nothing more than greed. Baden-Baden was one of the most fashionable resorts in Europe during its season. Beneath the glittering chandeliers of the Casino some of the wealthiest men in the world gambled away fortunes with gold and silver tokens; while in the arcade outside its doors their wives and mistresses chose beautiful jewellery, elaborate hats and the most exclusive styles of fans, shoes or gloves. The ladies who promenaded on the rich green lawns around the Trinkhalle, or along its colonnaded concourse, were often too plump to be elegant, but could certainly claim to be expensively dressed.

The glitter and animation of the spa brightened Alexa's eyes in excitement when she first arrived. Behind the town a romantic backcloth of dark, forested hills framed a ruined castle perched on a crag. The wild panorama and the swirling scandals of society both appealed to a side of her nature which had been for far too long smothered by the conventions imposed by the Lorimer family.

But her hopes of gaiety and entertainment did not survive for long. Baden-Baden was a resort for the wealthy and offered little to a dependant. Lord Glanville lost no time in settling his wife comfortably into the Haus des Kurgastes and discussing with the Kurhaus doctors what course of treatment could best alleviate the pain from which she suffered.

He had business to do in Vienna but would return, he promised, within a few days – to satisfy himself that all was well before he travelled back to England. Almost at once a daily routine was established which left Alexa little time for new experiences. Lady Glanville spent every morning in the thermal baths at the Friedrichsbad, taking comfort from their heat and aeration. Alexa was not expected to attend her there. It was in the afternoon and evening that her company was appreciated. At the invalid's slow pace they walked together along the Lichtentaler Allee and beside the shallow stream in which basked fish as fat and greedy as the old men who nursed their gout along its banks. There was a ceremony of drinking the waters at the Trinkhalle and hardly less of a ceremony in taking tea or hot chocolate with a small group of acquaintances. Lady Glanville did not play cards, and always retired early to bed. Such a routine demanded little of Alexa, but she could find no profitable way to spend her free time. She had hardly had time yet to be bored, but already she sighed with the anticipation of boredom.

Her ennui bred dissatisfaction, which increased as the season ended. The autumn sunshine lost its strength and the flowers which trailed from every balcony in the spa were chilled into bedragglement. Overnight the ornamental beds in the Casino garden were robbed of their brightness by the first touch of frost, and the neatly manicured trees of the Kurhaus park drooped sadly, their brown leaves falling with the soft rain. There was a feeling of life retreating in every sense – for with the approach of winter the wealthy men departed, leaving only the oldest and most infirm of their own sex and the most indolent or ailing of their wives.

There were never many young people in Baden-Baden: now suddenly it seemed that there were none at all. Except, of course, for the sturdy attendants who were employed to push wheelchairs – but although they could hardly fail to notice Alexa's youth and beauty, they had learned that it was more profitable to fawn on the elderly ladies who employed them. Alexa felt herself drooping like the flowers, overwhelmed by a feeling of time passing. To Lord Glanville in London she had cried out in anguish that she was only eighteen. Now the emphasis had changed. She was almost nineteen, and nothing was happening, nothing was going to happen: she was making no progress towards the goal on which she had set her heart.

The unhappiness of her thwarted ambition was increased by guilt. Every day which passed made her more ashamed of the fact that she had not yet written to Margaret. The realization that she had left a loving home to no advantage was part of the reason for her reluctance. It would be humiliating to admit that her unwise behaviour had brought her no nearer to fulfilling any of her ambitions. Margaret would summon her home and scold her for her impetuosity, and there would never be a second chance to escape. Even to explain how meaningless she found life at Elm Lodge would be hurtful. Alexa found one excuse after another to justify her silence: Margaret would believe her still to be at Brinsley House, and so would not be anxious yet; a letter would be more reassuring when there was something definite to say in it; it would reach England more swiftly and safely if she waited to put it into Lord Glanville's own hands. So every day she postponed what she knew to be her duty.

When she was in danger it was Lord Glanville who came to her rescue. Now, as her boredom increased, it was his wife who helped her. The musical life of the spa was vigorous, for many famous musicians had made their homes there. Even after the season had ended there were regular tea-time and evening concerts. In addition to this, the Haus des Kurgastes invited its residents to provide their own less formal entertainment as though they were in their own drawing rooms. Lady Glanville arranged that Alexa should be invited to sing after dinner one evening.

After the little concert was ended, Alexa returned to the side of her patroness and found her talking to a stout lady with a strong face and vigorous manner. Her name, Eva Becattini, was familiar – until her retirement she had been one of the best-known dramatic sopranos in Europe. Alexa hardly dared to breathe as she waited to hear whether she would be dismissed with a polite compliment or whether her singing had inspired anything more enthusiastic. But La Becattini – her fame was such that she was always spoken of in this way – appeared to be arguing too busily with Lady Glanville even to notice Alexa's arrival.

'My voice has gone, completely gone!' she was protesting.

'But not your experience. If you could only set her on the right road. She gives her time to me and I have no means of helping her. I can ask only as a favour. But you would find her responsive.'

La Becattini turned to stare at Alexa as though noticing her for the first time. 'What languages?' she asked.

'I speak Italian, diva,' said Alexa. 'I have learned French in the schoolroom, enough to study a role although not to converse fluently. And I am learning German here.'

'You are too slight for Wagner,' said La Becattini dismissively. 'His work demands a stronger constitution. But of course German would be necessary if you were to sing in Dresden or Vienna. Well, I could give you some exercises. Teach you a role, perhaps, if you are quick and promise not to bore me. There will be no society to amuse me here until July. You can call in the mornings if you wish. I am at home to my friends at noon. You should come at ten.'

She nodded brusquely at Lady Glanville, recognizing that no great thanks were due for an invitation designed so much more for Alexa's advantage than her own, and strode away. Alexa took the seat she had left and squeezed Lady Glanville's hands between her own. Her eyes were bright with happiness.

'Dear Lady Glanville, why should you do so much for me?' she asked.

Tired though she was, Lady Glanville laughed with an affectionate amusement.

'Boredom is a disease that the thermal waters cannot cure,' she said. 'You are bored because you dream of excitement without knowing how to attain it. La Becattini is bored because she remembers excitements she will never be able to repeat. And I am afraid that unless I can provide you with occupation you will return to England and leave me to be bored with my own company. But now, I hope, we shall all be happy. Will you help me to bed, Alexa? It's been a long day, and I am tired.'

Together, and very slowly, they went up the marble stairs to Lady Glanville's suite. Often at such times Alexa was overwhelmed with pity for a woman who was not yet forty years old but who would soon need to be pushed in a chair from one place to another. It had already become obvious that Baden-Baden could offer no treatment to cure Lady Glanville's condition, although the heat of mud or water made her limbs less painful while they were immersed.

Lord Glanville returned to Baden-Baden. The lack of

improvement in his wife's condition caused him to frown anxiously and ask quiet questions of the maid; but in Lady Glanville's presence he was as cheerful and as kind as ever. She had little news of her own to give him, but was enthusiastic about Alexa's progress, and the information appeared to give her husband pleasure.

'I'm glad that the hopes my brother raised are not after all to be disappointed,' he said, as they sat together in the Gasteshaus one evening after Lady Glanville had retired to bed. 'When you are rich and famous, I hope you will lend your name to my campaign.'

'I shall do anything I can to repay you and Lady Glanville, whether I become successful or not,' Alexa promised. 'But what *is* your campaign, my lord?'

'I believe that women should have the same right as men to vote in Parliamentary elections,' he told her. 'Do you agree with that?'

He was smiling as he asked the question, perhaps taking her answer for granted. But Alexa, applying the theory to herself, frowned doubtfully.

'I know nothing about politics: nothing at all,' she said. 'How could my vote be of value when it would be so uninformed? And most women, surely, are in the same position as myself.'

'Women have ceased to concern themselves with political affairs simply because they are not allowed to put any opinions to practical effect and are hardly encouraged to express them even in conversation. A woman can feel definite views on those spheres of life in which she is allowed responsibility. Once she is allowed to influence government in her choices, she will for the first time take pains to understand what the choices are.'

'It sounds to me, my lord, as though you are more concerned to change the nature of women than of Parliament.'

He gave a laugh more carefree than she had ever heard from him before.

'Perhaps you are right – and the subtlety with which you analyse my motives suggests that you are fit to have the vote without any change being necessary. I think it wrong that half our nation should be encouraged to be feather-headed by the lack of consideration given to their views. And this state of affairs seems to me particularly unfortunate when the care of our children is so largely entrusted to these same silly women. My opinion is that women are as capable of acting responsibly as men are. But they are unlikely to display their abilities while they are more apt to be criticized than praised for initiative. The meetings which are held in my London home are attended by women, and I can find no fault with either their reasoning power or their determination.'

Alexa puzzled over the problem. She still did not completely understand why Lord Glanville should have chosen the right to vote as the main point of his campaign.

'Will it not be difficult to change a state of affairs which has remained undisturbed for so long?' she asked tentatively.

'Very difficult indeed,' he agreed. 'But you are not quite right in suggesting that nothing has changed. For many years in our country the right to vote has depended on the possession of property. Property was owned mainly by men, and thereofre it was to men that the vote was given. But recently there has been a movement to extend voting rights, separating them from the ownership of property – but still confined only to men. And so, you see, the principle has changed. Where once the franchise excluded those who did not own property, now it excludes those who are not men. You understand the difference?'

Alexa understood, but was less sure that she thought it important. She was flattered, however, that a nobleman like Lord Glanville should try to convince her. He was not only an aristocrat, but almost old enough to be her father, yet he was willing to converse with her as though she were a friend instead of a mere dependant. As though he sensed her lack of interest, he changed the subject.

'I must return to England within a day or two,' he said. 'The Parliamentary session has already begun, and I should be in London. But Lady Glanville must remain here. The cold and damp of an English winter can do her no good. Are you happy to stay here with her?'

'Oh yes, my lord!' For a moment she was alarmed lest he intended to take her away from Baden-Baden and La Becattini; but it seemed that he was merely reassuring himself, for he nodded to accept her contentment.

'And you have been in communication with your connections in England since your arrival here?'

This time Alexa was more reluctant to answer. He interpreted her silence correctly.

'I know you felt that you had been ill-used,' he said. 'Nevertheless, it's necessary for me to consider my own part in the affair. You are not yet twenty-one. I ought to have your guardian's approval of your presence here. I wrote to Mr Lorimer, as you know, but he has not favoured me with the courtesy of an answer. It's hardly likely that he will accuse me of abducting you, but I think, all the same, that you should write a letter of reassurance. I could post it in England after my return. I have no wish to interfere in your affairs. But if you were suddenly to disappear from my care, I know what distress I should feel. I hardly like to be responsible for the same unhappiness in anyone else.'

He had looked at her with the same grave kindness at the time of their first meeting. Alexa remembered: she had not understood his expression then and she did not now. But she recognized the validity of what he said, and was ashamed that she had delayed. The next day she wrote to Margaret.

Long as the letter was, it did not contain the whole truth about her disappearance. She described where she was, and who had befriended her. She explained her ambitions and the progress she was making in her efforts to achieve them. With affection and sincerity she apologized for the distress which she knew she must have caused. But nowhere in the letter did she mention the name of William Lorimer.

It was a complicated mixture of feelings which held her back. There had quite certainly been a time, as she ran from the Honourable Duncan Glanville in her bedroom at Glanville House, when she had believed that William Lorimer had deliberately sent her to her ruin. Now that she was not only out of danger but was enjoying the very privileges which William had promised her, although from another source, she did not feel quite the same certainty. It was possible that his offer of help had been genuine, although misplaced. Because Alexa had never liked him she found it easiest to suspend judgement – she had no need to be grateful, and therefore had resolved never to see him again.

But such a course was not something to be inflicted on Margaret, who was his sister. Alexa realized that if she were to tell even part of the truth, she was liable to cause trouble. It would certainly upset Margaret if she were to believe that her brother had deliberately entrusted Alexa to a scoundrel – but she would be equally unhappy to learn that it was William who had advised Alexa to abandon the dullness of a country life and devote herself to a career of which Margaret was known to disapprove, without even pausing to discuss her plans. To precipitate a family quarrel would be unkind. A widow with a small son needed all the support that the other members of her family could give her. Treading a delicate path between tact and truth, Alexa left unsaid whatever could cause ill-feeling. When she handed her letter to Lord Glanville on the day of his return to England, her conscience was at peace for the first time in weeks.

2

The best antidote to the reproach of failure is hard work. On a wintry Sunday afternoon Margaret was sitting close to the fire, trying to keep her anxieties about Alexa under control by studying some figures which she had collected over the past two years. The subject was not a romantic one. She was considering how many schoolchildren in her area had been discovered to have hair infested with lice, how many days' schooling they had missed, and how soon and how often the infestation had recurred, in the hope that the pattern of the problem would suggest some means of eliminating it. When Betty announced a caller, Margaret was at first a little irritated by the interruption. Then she read the name on his card. It was Lord Glanville.

A few weeks earlier the name would have meant nothing to her. But when she had written to remind Alexa that she must not outstay her welcome at Brinsley House, William had been forced to reveal that her ward had left the country and – with a nearer approach to apology than was usual to him – had admitted his own part in Alexa's plan to escape from a country life which she found too dull. The meeting had ended in a quarrel. Seeking to excuse himself, William had hinted that the introduction he had given to Alexa, intended to keep her from home only for twenty-four hours, had been to a gentleman of the utmost respectability. If she had abandoned this arrangement in favour of an expedition to the Continent in the company of an aristocrat whose motives could only be guessed at, that was not William's responsibility. Margaret in return had suggested that he would never have allowed his own daughter to make even such a brief visit without a chaperone, and that she herself ought to have been informed immediately of Alexa's disappearance. They had parted in anger – but Margaret had at least been given the name of the nobleman and two addresses in England.

They had proved to be of little use. The housekeeper at Blaize, Lord Glanville's country house, and his secretary in the Park Lane town house, had given the same answers. Lord Glanville was visiting Germany and Austria and letters were not being forwarded: but he was not expected to be abroad for very long. All Margaret could do was to write again, asking that he should get in touch with her when he returned; and then wait. Now, it seemed, the waiting was over.

The papers slid unnoticed off her lap as she stood up, and her head swam with an inexplicable dizziness. Was it the heat of the fire, or had she so often feared disaster on Alexa's behalf that now she could only expect bad news?

'Is he alone?' she whispered, but knew the answer before she asked the question. If Alexa had accompanied him, she would already have burst into the room without any formality of announcement.

'Yes, ma'am.'

'Show him in, Betty.' She held out her hand as he came into the room. 'Lord Glanville.'

'It's very kind of you to receive me.' He hesitated for a moment, looking around as though he had expected to see someone else present. 'I had thought to find Dr Scott here.'

'I am Dr Scott.'

For a second longer he stared in surprise, and then burst into full-throated laughter which came unexpectedly from a man so intellectual in appearance. 'My dear Dr Scott!' He bent over her hand. 'I beg your forgiveness. In London I devote a large part of my time to considering how the cause of women's rights may best be advanced, and yet when I meet a woman who has achieved success by her own efforts, I fail to recognize her. I am deeply ashamed. Allow me to say at once how much I admire those women like yourself who have carved careers for themselves in spite of the disapproval of society.'

His laughter had given Margaret a moment to study his appearance. He was a tall, thin man – a year or two older than herself, she guessed. Perhaps it was only because she already knew his name that she found his long nose and face gave him an aristocratic expression; but without any other clues she felt immediately sure that he was intelligent, serious and kind. Her own quick summing-up amused her – and saddened her at the same time, for it was a reminder of how rarely nowadays she met new acquaintances with whom she could feel such an instant sympathy. But the conviction that she was right in her assessment had an immediate effect on her state of mind. This was a good man. Alexa, if she had been in his care, would have come to no harm.

The conclusion was irrational but overwhelming. All Margaret's unhappiness fell from her like a dirty shift. She was not now even in any hurry to hear his news, so sure was she that it would prove reassuring.

'I see that you're not wholly converted to your own cause, my lord,' she said, smiling. 'Obviously you don't think that men and women should be treated equally. You would never dare to unloose such a flood of flattery on a man. Well, that makes it easier for me to confess

70

that I have a thoroughly female curiosity. You have news for me, I trust.'

'I have a letter,' said Lord Glanville. 'I have just returned from Germany and was asked to carry the message to England and to post it here. But my curiosity is even greater than yours. I was anxious to meet the person to whom it was addressed – yourself.'

'Is it from Alexa? How is she?'

'In good health and good spirits,' said Lord Glanville. 'I can give you a full report of her, and you will not hear anything to dismay you. But I know nothing of her relationship with you, if there is one, or of her home circumstances.'

'She is my ward,' said Margaret.

'Not Mr Lorimer's?'

'No. Mine. Her father died when she was a baby, and her mother when she was nine. She lived with me from that time until she disappeared – disappeared without a word. I love her as my own daughter. I have been half out of my mind with worry. At first I didn't know at all where she was; and even when I discovered that she was travelling in your company there was no one to tell me under what arrangement she had left the country. And yet' – it was difficult to conceal a trace of resentment – 'you have known where she was all this time.'

'I have known where she was, certainly. She has been travelling as a member of my household and then living in Baden-Baden as a companion to my wife. What I have *not* known was that she had any connections in England other than Mr Lorimer, and he and Alexa showed no wish to correspond with each other. I had no reason to disbelieve my original impression that she was, apart from him, alone in the world. But as the time of my return to England approached, I realized that there was something else she wanted to tell me. She admitted at

71

last that there was someone whom she loved dearly and who must have been hurt by her departure.'

'But why did she not write earlier?' asked Margaret.

'I think she was ashamed, though she had done nothing she needed to regret except leaving you in suspense: she recognized that this at least she could put right. I promised to post her letter myself. But when I saw that it was addressed to someone whom I took to be male, bearing a name different from her own, I felt it my duty to make sure – to find out – '

At any other time Margaret would have been amused to see such a sophisticated man struggling to complete his sentence, but by now she had become impatient. 'May I read Alexa's letter?' she asked. 'Afterwards, perhaps you will help me to understand what has been happening.'

She tugged at the bell pull and asked Betty to bring in tea while Lord Glanville felt in his inside pocket for the letter. It was long and emotional. Before she had reached the end of the third page, tears were streaming down Margaret's face.

'Relief, not sadness, Lord Glanville,' she said as she came to the end, excusing her exhibition of weakness. 'You will forgive me if I leave you for a moment.'

The bowl of water which stood on the washstand in her room was chilled almost to freezing point by the wintry weather. She lifted handfuls of it to splash and cool her face. Then, calm and businesslike, a professional woman again, she went back to the drawing room.

Between sips of China tea, Lord Glanville filled in the lacunae left by Alexa's letter. Even his account, however, did not satisfactorily bridge the gap between Bristol and Baden-Baden.

'I can see that Alexa has been fortunate indeed to be taken into your household, Lord Glanville,' Margaret said in a puzzled voice. 'But how did you come to take the responsibility for a stranger in such a generous way?'

For the first time her visitor hesitated. Margaret could not judge whether the full explanation was one that he did not know or chose not to give.

'The circumstances of her arrival in London were unfortunate,' he said. 'I happened to be passing just at the moment when she had discovered, to her great distress, the difficulties which face a young girl who lacks the protection of her family. All I intended to do at first was to give her enough money for her fare back home. I can see now that I should have made very much stronger efforts to establish the details of her home life. But the circumstances were not appropriate for calm reflection. Alexa was in tears, refusing to admit that there was anywhere she could go, and I was on the point of leaving England with my wife.'

It still seemed to Margaret that the explanation was not complete, and Lord Glanville must have been sensitive to her doubts.

'Alexa could have returned to you at any time,' he said. 'You may blame me for not forcing the truth out of her. I can only say that I did not know it was there to be forced.'

'I don't blame you for anything at all. Quite the opposite! Alexa's letter makes it clear that you have been generous to her in a manner she does not deserve.'

'Do you want me to send her back?' asked Lord Glanville. 'As her guardian, you have the right to decide.'

'Do you wish to be free of her?' asked Margaret in return. 'As her guardian, I have the obligation to support her.'

'I hope you will let her stay,' Lord Glanville said. 'My wife has become devoted to her. Not many beautiful young women are prepared to be so patient with an invalid. And Alexa may have told you in her letter how we had the good fortune to discover that La Becattini had taken up residence in Baden-Baden after her retirement from the stage. The fact that someone of her reputation has agreed to accept Alexa as a pupil is almost in itself the first step towards an operatic career.' He paused, apparently sensitive to the significance of Margaret's slowness to comment. 'You may of course consider this an unsuitable ambition?'

She took a long time to consider, staring into the fire as though she could see the future there.

'When I was a young woman myself, Lord Glanville, my ambition was to be a doctor. My father's disapproval of such an idea was so certain that I never dared even to mention it to him. After his death, when I determined to begin the training, my brother denounced it as immoral. I was confident that he was wrong, and took my own way. I have never regretted it. No doubt Alexa feels the same kind of confidence that I am wrong about her. Doubtless I am being old-fashioned now, just as I thought my brother old-fashioned then. I cannot deny that I have a prejudice against the stage, even the operatic stage. But it's true that Alexa has a great talent, and I believe that any young woman in her circumstances ought to have the means of earning her own living. If this is the way she chooses to do it, I must give her my blessing. In any case, it's clear enough that if I were to call her back when she has already taken this first step which you describe, I could never expect her to forgive me. And what has life here to offer her? It was my fault in the first place that the only choice she saw was between dullness and flight. If you are prepared to continue as her patron, Lord Glanville, I shall be as grateful as she is; and happy to know that she is in such good hands.'

It still amazed her, as they smiled at each other, that

she should feel such an instant sympathy with a stranger from a different class of society and way of life. But their tête-à-tête was interrupted by the boisterous arrival of Robert. This was the hour which Margaret kept free for him however great her pressure of work might be.

Lord Glanville looked almost wistful as the sturdy little boy flung himself on his mother's knees and hugged her.

'I must sympathize with you for being a widow,' he said. 'But at least you will have the happiness of seeing your son grow up.'

'Have you no son of your own, Lord Glanville?'

He shook his head. 'We had one baby daughter soon after our marriage: but she, unfortunately, did not survive. Since then – my wife's illness first attacked her while she was still young, and increases in severity with every year that passes. I cannot hope for an heir. I find it ironical that I should have been so fortunate in my inheritance of wealth and title, but that I lack the power which most poorer men have, to dispose of my fortune as I would like. Still, I doubt whether my younger brother regrets my childless state as much as I do myself.' He stood up, towering over her. 'Alexa, then, will remain at Baden-Baden with my wife. If you have any further questions to ask of me, I shall be at Glanville House in Park Lane for as long as Parliament is sitting. And I hope very much, Dr Scott, that if you ever come to London you will call on me. A committee of ladies meets every month at my house to discuss how women may best be allowed some voice in the government of the country. The views of someone like yourself, someone who has entered a male sphere without losing any of her femininity, would be of great interest to us all.'

It was unlikely, Margaret thought as she said goodbye, that she would ever accept his invitation – unlikely even that she would ever see him again. The meeting, so unexpected in a life which offered few social pleasures, had warmed her day. But it was unimportant compared with the news he had brought. She played with Robert with the high-spirited youthfulness that she had known in her student days, chasing him with shrieks and screams of laughter through the dark rooms of the house until they were both over-excited. Later that evening she wrote a formal letter of thanks to Lord Glanville. Then, her lips open with happiness as her pen raced over the paper, she poured out her heart to Alexa.

3

When Royalty drops like a stone into the placid pool of a spa, the ripples touch even those who shelter in the backwaters. It was the habit of the Prince of Wales every year to travel straight from Cowes in search of a cure which would make his nickname, Tum-Tum, less appropriate. Alexa, like everyone else in Baden-Baden, knew when he arrived, but she had no expectations of meeting him. Age and his ever-increasing girth had made it impossible for the prince any longer to play the part of Don Juan, but his reputation was slow to fade. Although Lady Glanville would have the entrée if she cared to claim it, there was no possibility that she would introduce a beautiful young woman into the royal presence. In any case, she was by now too ill to take any part in social life herself.

Alexa did not care. She was not interested in elderly princes, and during the past few months her daily time-table had left her few free moments. La Becattini had pretended a reluctance to undertake her instruction, but the pretence had been dropped as soon as the first session of coaching began. She was a hard taskmistress. There was no means of telling whether Lady Glanville had been right in seeing her energy as a refuge from the boredom of retirement or whether Alexa could be justified in hoping that her own talents prompted the determination that they would be developed to perfection. Whatever the reason, the daily meetings grew longer and longer. The training of the voice was the most important part of each session: but in addition to this, operatic roles were discussed and prepared. Over a tray of hot chocolate and cream cakes the diva would reminisce abut her own past successes: then she sent her pupil off with ferocious reminders of the exercises to be practised before the next morning. There was no time for boredom now. By the end of each day, the concentration which the work demanded made Alexa almost as ready for an early night as Lady Glanville.

Nevertheless, curiosity made Alexa dawdle when one morning as she returned from her coaching session she saw the prince with his entourage, waddling through the park towards her. Deep in conversation, they all passed without seeming to notice her – except for one: a young man who sauntered at the end of the little procession with a bored look on his face.

He came to a full stop in front of Alexa and addressed her directly, in a voice as haughty as his expression. He spoke in German, but with an accent which Alexa recognized as English.

'Really, I'd begun to think that there was no one under the age of ninety in this home for cripples. Will you take a walk with me, Fräulein?'

'I don't believe we know each other,' Alexa replied in English, flushing slightly with the knowledge that she ought to have continued on her way without taking any notice of him.

'Easily remedied. Caversham, at your service.' He clicked his heels and bowed sharply from the waist in the manner of a German student.

The Duke of Caversham! To Alexa's still unsophisticated ears, the name rang with respectability. She told him her own, but continued to interrogate him as unobtrusively as she could. 'I suppose you are in attendance on His Royal Highness?'

'I've been summoned from Heidelberg by him out of curiosity. I succeeded to the title a few weeks ago, so His Royal Highness is aware that when he becomes king I shall already be a member of the House of Lords. He may be hoping to sound out my political views. He hardly needs to bother. Nothing would induce me to waste my time in such a dreary institution. Now that we are properly introduced, allow me to repeat my invitation.'

Alexa was well aware that a self-introduction was no introduction at all, but she had been starved of young company for so long that she could not bring herself to refuse the suggestion directly.

'I am expected at the Haus des Kurgastes,' she said, indicating the palatial building in which those who took their treatments most seriously rented suites. 'And I have too much to carry.' She was taking back a borrowed score of *The Marriage of Figaro* to study, as well as the manuscript books in which La Becattini scribbled exercises for her to practise.

'I'm prepared to wait for a moment or two.' The young duke sat down on one of the seats with which the gardens were well provided, and crossed both his legs and his arms. Without deciding what she would do, Alexa hurried on her way. To her surprise, she found that Lady Glanville had already returned from the Friedrichsbad and had retired to bed.

'I am beginning to find the waters here too strong for

me; too exhausting,' Lady Glanville murmured. 'I need to rest in bed for a few days. It's dull for you, Alexa. I'm sorry.'

Alexa was sympathetic, but too much engrossed in her own affairs to pay very much attention to the worried expression on the face of the maid who busied herself making the bed comfortable. Usually Lady Glanville liked to listen to Alexa's chatter about her lesson while she rested, but today she seemed too tired even for this. Alexa glanced out of the window and saw that the duke had not yet moved.

'I made the acquaintance of the Duke of Caversham this morning,' she said tentatively. 'He invited me to stroll with him in the gardens.'

'A very pleasant old gentleman,' Lady Glanville murmured. 'An acquaintance of my husband's. You need fresh air. But don't walk too far and tire yourself.'

Alexa hesitated for a second longer, wondering whether she ought to correct the misapprehension. But the invalid's eyes had closed in exhaustion. And there could be no harm in a simple walk. She picked up her parasol and hurried down the stairs, slowing to a languid stroll only when she was in sight of the duke.

It was impossible to maintain an attitude of indifference for long. Her companion was twenty-one and high-spirited, as delighted to be free of royal restraints as Alexa was to escape from chaperonage. For an hour they laughed and talked together.

'And you have never been to Heidelberg, although it is so near!' exclaimed the young duke in astonishment when he discovered how closely she had been confined to Baden-Baden since her arrival. 'You must come with me when I return, the day after tomorrow.'

'I can hardly – '

'You could bring a maid or whatever is necessary.' He

79

brushed her objections aside before she had time to make them. 'I will introduce you to my friends. The university term has ended, but the social life is so strong that many of the students, like myself, are unwilling to tear themselves away.'

It was impossible, of course: and yet, as the duke continued to talk, taking it for granted that she would accompany him, Alexa explored the possibilities in her mind. She had not missed a single lesson with La Becattini since her coaching began. To plead a sore throat just for one morning could do no harm. And Lady Glanville, in her present exhausted state, would be glad to be left undisturbed. No one need know.

It was the mention of the other students which clinched the matter. She missed the company of young men. The disappointment which she had suffered at Matthew's hands had made her resolve never again to bestow her affections too whole-heartedly, and the hard course of work imposed by La Becattini acted as an acceptable substitute for social life. But after concentrating for so many months on a goal which was still far ahead, the offer of a day's relaxation was too exciting to be ignored. A little flirtation, nothing serious, to be forgotten as quickly as it began, was just what she needed to raise her spirits. And although it might be dangerous to spend too long alone with a young English aristocrat, she would be safe in a group. Excitement animated her face as she told him that she would come.

She had expected that they would travel by the railway, so when the day arrived it came as a shock to find that they were to travel by four-in-hand. True, the duke drove the horses as though taking part in a Roman chariot race; but all the same, Heidelberg was further away by horse-power than it would have been by steam engine. Although Alexa laughed, holding on to her hat, as they sped through the wooded countryside, she was already calculating times to herself. Her conclusions were not reassuring – but it seemed that her companion was able to read her thoughts.

'The return journey will be speedier, of course, by railway,' he said. 'But these horses have to be returned to the livery stable.'

Alexa nodded to show that she understood the situation, and gave herself up to enjoyment of the drive. By the time the carriage rattled into the university city beneath the rosy ruins of the castle and clattered to a halt on the cobbled streets she was in her gaiest and most vivacious mood.

Caversham had been truthful when he promised her the company of his fellow students. The town swarmed with young men, walking stiffly in their high boots, and many of them bearing on their cheeks the fresh scars of duels. They wore the round caps which showed by their colours the corps to which each belonged, and it was those of the red band who quickly attached themselves to the duke and his pretty partner. Fêted, almost carried at times, Alexa was borne up and down the town, to stare at its monuments while the young men stared at her.

As evening approached the party swept into a beer cellar. It was already crowded with young men who sat in small groups near the walls, but a long table down the centre was empty. The arrogance with which Alexa's hosts claimed it made clear their right to have it reserved for them: no doubt it was with their initials, as well as those of their predecessors, that the wood was so deeply carved.

While they called for beer, Alexa looked curiously around her. It was difficult to see much in the smoky atmosphere, for there were no windows in the low-ceilinged room and the oil lamps which hung from the heavy beams were almost obscured by a dangling collection of boots, fencing foils, ladies' slippers and stolen street notices. The walls were covered with photographs of young men stiffly posed in groups, hung on panels as scarred with carved initials as the tables. It was clear enough that this was no place for a respectable young lady, but Alexa felt that she had no choice but to remain. The Duke of Caversham was her only protector here and she must stay in his company until the moment when she needed protection from him.

Although the beer was light, it came in huge, silver-lidded tankards. Alexa, unused to drinking, first of all fought against her increasing light-headedness and then succumbed to it. Someone was playing a piano loudly in a dark corner, and soon everyone was singing. Without knowing the words, Alexa was quick to pick up the tunes. One of the students, who had been scribbling something at the end of the long table, presented it to her with a click of his heels, and called out to the pianist. He had written a poem for her, Alexa saw. She flushed with pleasure as she read it – for by now her German was fluent – and realized that she was being invited to sing it.

It took her only a moment to learn the melody which the young poet had used for her verse; a lilting tune with an exuberant chorus. She sang her part and the students joined in with a roar which became more rumbustious at each repetition. In a steady beat they thumped their mugs and stamped their feet in accompaniment to Alexa's clear tones. Her excitement fed on the presence of so many admiring young men, the touch of apprehension about what was in store, and the exhilaration which always came when she projected her whole personality into her singing. She wished that the moment could last for ever. And then, abruptly, the bubble was pricked.

The door opened, and Lord Glanville stepped inside.

He stood still for a moment, his tall presence impressive even when, as now, his face was grey with tiredness. Alexa was the first to see him and the only one who could guess why he was there, but the recklessness induced by so much beer and the heady atmosphere of the beer cellar carried her on to the end of the song. Only then, as the students roared and banged approval, did she become quiet and ashamed.

As she stepped away from the long table, the Duke of Caversham looked round and sprang to his feet. He reached Lord Glanville before Alexa could, blocking her way to him. He was drunk enough to be belligerent, but the older man did not flinch.

'I have not had the pleasure of meeting you since your school-days, Your Grace,' Lord Glanville said. 'Allow me to take this opportunity of expressing my sincere regret at your father's death. And now, if you will excuse me, I have come to take Miss Lorimer back to Baden-Baden.'

'Miss Lorimer is here under my protection, my lord. You are not insinuating, I hope, that she has anything to fear in Heidelberg.'

Behind Alexa, the singing had begun again, but between the two men in the doorway there was a long silence which seemed charged with antagonism. Alexa, without understanding what was at stake in the confrontation, was frightened. They would surely not fight. There could be no doubt that they were both angry, both prepared to defend injured pride; and the scarred faces around them made the thought of a duel less impossible. But duels, although an accepted part of the Heidelberg way of life, were illegal for Englishmen, and aristocrats did not exchange blows. She told herself that she must be exaggerating their antagonism; yet still she was frightened.

The young duke, beer-blustering and with the need to maintain his reputation in front of his companions, might have pressed the challenge into an open quarrel. But the older man, tired with more than the rigours of travel, not only refused to be provoked but offered Caversham a means of saving face.

'Miss Lorimer is my wife's companion and her presence is required at once. My wife is gravely ill, and is to leave Germany without delay. I am sure Miss Lorimer is most grateful to you for entertaining her, but she will acknowledge that I have some claim on her services.'

Sulkily, the young man stepped aside and allowed Alexa to pass. She held out her hand to him, not wishing their acquaintance to end in anger.

'It has been a very pleasant visit, Your Grace. I hope very much that one day we may meet again.'

He bowed over her hand without speaking and watched her go. Lord Glanville offered his arm, and she took it. As the clear summer air refreshed her after the smoky noise of the beer cellar, she told herself that she must not be angry with her patron. He had presumed on his position; there could be no doubt of that. But although she was not quite sober yet, she was sensible enough to realize that – not for the first time – he had saved her from a situation which she could not have controlled. She was prepared to be grateful. What she was not prepared for was the realization that Lord Glanville himself was almost too angry to speak.

When she did understand it, she became indignant.

'I have not had a single free day since my first meeting with you, my lord,' she protested. 'I know how much I owe you, and I am truly appreciative. But it is surely not too much to ask that just for a few hours I should be allowed to enjoy myself as other young people do.'

Lord Glanville came to a standstill in the middle of the

cobbled street. 'You misunderstand my feelings,' he said. 'I am tired, yes, for I have travelled from England and then have been forced without resting to come in search of you. And I am angry with you, yes, because you have been blind to what has been happening. But most of all I am upset, because what has brought me to Germany is what you appear not to have noticed. Did you really not see that my wife is dying?'

Shocked out of her self-absorption, Alexa stared into her patron's eyes. Recognizing the truth as soon as he spoke it, she was appalled at her own indifference. She had liked Lady Glanville from the moment of their first meeting, and the older woman's kindness had deepened the relationship to one of affection. But to Alexa, young and healthy, the invalid's condition had seemed a sad one from the start. Lacking experience as well as sensitivity, she had failed to note the moment when a continuing deterioration carried the sufferer past any hope of cure.

'My lord!' she whispered: and the depth of her sympathy produced an unexpected effect, for at once she found herself enclosed in Lord Glanville's arms. With her head pressed hard against his chest she could hear him groaning aloud in despair, completely overcome by his emotions. They had stood like this once before, but then it was Alexa who was fearful and crying and in need of help. Now the positions were reversed, and the appeal for comfort was to Alexa herself. She gave it as well as she could, not caring what passers-by must think as he buried his face in her hair, his arms tightening convulsively around her waist. He was weeping, or else so near to it that his breath was forced out in sobbing gasps as he struggled to control his emotions. Alexa murmured in sympathy, hardly knowing what words she used, until his frenzy of grief had spent itself.

Gradually the bruising tightness of his grip relaxed. He

drew a very little away from her, although not far enough to let her look up into his face. There was a moment of quietness between them in which Alexa found herself suspecting feelings which in no circumstances could he ever have expressed. He loved his wife: she knew that well enough, but knew with equal certainty that it was a long time since Lady Glanville had last been able to live with him as a wife. What had never occurred to Alexa before was that he might love her as well. He could not confess it, and Alexa herself could not acknowledge it – nor, in fact, did she wish to do so. Lord Glanville was a kind man, a handsome man, an upright man; but in her eyes he was also an old man. She could take pleasure in his company: she certainly felt for him sympathy and gratitude and respect. But it had never occurred to her to love him, and it did not do so now.

The clarity of her perceptions had an unexpected side effect. The Duke of Caversham had flirted with her, had pressed her hand, would have kissed her before the evening was out if there had been no interruption, and she would not have cared. She would have fought off any attempt on his part to go further, as she had fought off Lord Glanville's brother; but that was a matter of reputation rather than of feelings. She did not love the Duke of Caversham any more than she loved Lord Glanville, but had she been asked an hour earlier she would have seen no obstacle to allowing some kind of relationship to develop. In this moment of emotional exposure, however, the memory of Matthew Lorimer, whom she had tried so hard to forget, flashed before her eyes. Almost as though he were standing in front of her she felt herself looking at his shy, serious eyes, his thick fair hair. She was still in love with him, after all. A flirtation could not have reminded her, but the intensity of Lord Glanville's suppressed feelings had the power to raise the ghost of her own.

The moment ended. Lord Glanville's arms fell to his sides and he gave a single deep sigh. The spring of emotion, briefly uncoiled between them, sprang back into a tangle of words that could not be expressed. Throughout the journey back to Baden-Baden, neither of them spoke at all.

4

To the unhappy, 'home' is always somewhere in the past: to the contented, it is in the present. Alexa, in the emotional sense, had never had a home at all, only a succession of addresses.

She was not conscious of the lack. Because she had never felt an attachment to any place, she hardly knew that such a feeling existed. The subject was far from her thoughts when, three weeks after her escapade in Heidelberg, she was shown to a room in an Italian villa. Lord Glanville had learned that on the tiny peninsula of Sirmione, projecting into Lake Garda, there was a thermal site which might prove more beneficial to his wife than Baden-Baden. The area was not developed as a spa, but a local doctor had agreed to take Lady Glanville into his own home and treat her daily with baths of hot mud. Like every other doctor, he held out no hope of offering more than temporary comfort, but even that was to be welcomed.

Alexa stood at the open window and looked out. The scents of cypress and rosemary were carried up by the warm air to caress her nostrils. There were cypresses everywhere, slim pillars of darkness, peacefully contrasting with the contorted shapes of ancient olive trees. At the foot of the garden lay the undisturbed surface of the lake, as placid as though it were coated with oil. While she watched without moving, its deep blue depths paled to a silvery turquoise: across it, a path of rosy orange led to the setting sun. She should have been tired after the slow journey, but instead she felt at rest, content.

A servant arrived with her luggage and asked in Italian where he should put it. Without turning round, Alexa answered in the same language. The words came to her lips without any pause for thought. By the time she left Germany she had been able to speak German, but as a foreign language. Ten years had passed since she had last conversed in Italian with her mother, but she recognized instinctively that it was her native tongue. She looked across the lake at the black silhouettes of the mountains on its further side and knew in the same way that this was her country. 'I have come home,' she thought to herself in wonder, and all at once the wanderings of her childhood and youth fell into place. They had brought her to Italy, because Italy was where she belonged.

It was like falling in love, but with a certainty and a happiness that love itself had not brought her. Margaret had written to her several times, asking when she would return – recognizing that she could not leave Lady Glanville while she was still of use, but begging her to remember that she would always be welcomed and loved at Elm Lodge. Until this moment Alexa had taken her eventual return as much for granted as her guardian did. Now – although with no good reason to support her certainty – she was suddenly sure that she did not wish to live in England again.

What happened at Sirmione was that Alexa grew up. The startling moment when she had found herself clasped in Lord Glanville's arms in the middle of Heidelberg had matured her emotionally. Never again would she be so completely the victim of her feelings as she had been during her brief relationship with Matthew. Now to that aspect of maturity she added a businesslike attitude to life – and, in particular, to the organization of her own career. Until this time she had relied on other people. In view of her sex and upbringing, this was hardly surprising, but it had put her at the mercy of events in a way which she did not intend to tolerate in the future. Her ambitions were clear, and equally clear was the fact that from now on she must achieve them by her own efforts. She recognized the good fortune that had come to her aid in the past year, but it was time to take control into her own hands.

Gratitude, however, had still a part to play. As long as Lady Glanville lived, Alexa was at her service. In the stifling atmosphere of the mud room she read aloud for hour after hour – for by now Lady Glanville's eyesight was affected as well as her muscles. Every evening she sang and played the piano, quietly and soothingly, without expecting any reaction from the invalid on the sofa. But as time passed and it became ever clearer that her services would not be needed for very much longer, she took one step to ensure that when Lord Glanville offered to take her back to England she would have the means to refuse.

The moment came when some shopping had to be done, requiring a greater variety of merchandise than the tiny walled village of Sirmione could provide. The maid had drawn up a list of necessities, but she spoke no Italian, so Alexa's offer to accompany her was welcomed. Lady Glanville herself insisted that Alexa should turn the chore of shopping into an interesting expedition – and Alexa had already made local enquiries which suggested the best place to choose from her own point of view.

So she and the maid did not go to Verona, in spite of the fact that this was the nearest and best-stocked city. Although it had already become Alexa's ambition to take part one day in the opera season which was mounted each year-in the Arena there, she recognized that she could not hope to make her start so near to the top of the ladder. Instead, they boarded the west-bound train and, passing through Brescia, came very soon to Bergamo. By the time the shops closed for the afternoon siesta they had obtained everything they needed in the modern town at the foot of the hill. The maid, isolated in a remote part of a foreign country for so long, was eager to spend an hour or two enjoying the animation of city life, even if she could not understand it, and Alexa willingly climbed with her into the old fortified town which was perched on a hilltop. Together they explored the narrow cobbled streets and dignified market squares which surrounded the great cathedral. Together they looked down from the walls at the green countryside around.

'I have one more errand to do,' Alexa said abruptly. All morning she had been wondering whether she had the courage. To express her intention, even though she gave no details of it, would commit her to the action. She appointed a time when they should meet again, ready for the return journey, and then walked alone down the hill.

By the time she arrived outside the Teatro Donizetti she was panting a little, more with apprehension than because of her speed of walking. To recover her breath, she paused in the shelter of a wide avenue of horse chestnuts and stared across at the theatre. Its stout wooden doors were closed, and the heavy blocks of grey and pink stone from which its façade was built suggested the massive strength of a fortress. She straightened her shoulders and summoned up all her courage. Even the strongest fortress could fall to someone who besieged it with sufficient determination.

She knew that by now rehearsals must be in progress for the winter season of opera. Finding a side door open, she was guided to what she sought by a confusion of noise. A piano was playing, someone was singing, someone else was shouting over the song with instructions about movement, a carpenter in the background was hammering, a shabby group of people – the chorus, perhaps – were chattering none too quietly in a corner. All these sounds, except for the hammering, came to a ragged halt as Alexa appeared at the back of the stage.

'What do you want?' The voice came from the darkness of the auditorium.

Alexa addressed herself to the man who was presumably the director of the opera. 'I want to join your company, maestro.'

There was a roar of laughter. The two singers already on the stage looked at her pityingly: the members of the chorus mocked her.

'Every street urchin in Bergamo would like to join our company,' the director called up as his amusement subsided. 'But I choose my own singers and they are chosen. Go back the way you came, if you please. You have no right to be here.'

Alexa did not bother to listen to what he had to say, knowing in advance that it could be nothing but a refusal. Instead, she began to sing almost as he began to speak. She had prepared herself for this moment, pondering for hours over the choice of an aria which needed no accompaniment, which showed her voice to its best advantage, and which contained no pause or quiet interlude which would allow of interruption. La Becattini had done her work well, developing a natural talent into a powerful instrument. As Alexa sang, the director's protests faded, allowing the unauthorized audition to continue. When she had finished, there was a moment's silence and only on the face of the woman who had been singing when Alexa arrived was there still any hostility to be seen. The director stood up and walked with great deliberation on to the stage. It took him some time. Alexa felt her legs trembling as she tried to maintain a look of confidence. He planted himself in front of her, his legs apart, and his voice was rough and disdainful.

'And I suppose you think, just because you are able to trill a little, that we shall fall on your neck at once and ask you to be our Marguerite, our Mimi, our Tosca.'

It had been difficult for Alexa not to hope exactly that in the day-dreams which at first had taken the place of plans. But she had her ambitions under tight control by now. She was asking for work, not indulging a fantasy, and she was determined to get it.

'Of course not, maestro. I hope that you might give me employment in the chorus. And that if you think me worthy, I might be allowed to understudy some of the smaller parts. I have studied under La Becattini and know how to prepare a role. But of course I realize that I lack experience. If you take me into your company, I will do whatever I am told.'

There was a second silence. This time it must surely be a hopeful sign. If he were going to send her away, would he not have done it at once?

'Your voice is too strong for the chorus,' he said. 'I'm sorry. You sing not too badly, but – '

A short, plump woman emerged from the shadows at the side of the stage to interrupt him, murmuring something that Alexa was not near enough to hear. For a third time the director looked her up and down.

'I am reminded of a baby expected in March,' he said. 'It may be that by December Signora Fiorentino will cease to carry conviction as a young unmarried maid. Well, you may attend rehearsals if you wish, and prepare to act as understudy for her roles when it becomes necessary. But it would be on the understanding that you are not employed until you are needed.'

Alexa accepted the arrangement with a promptness that gave him no time for second thoughts. It could not have fallen out better, for she would not have been free to join the company immediately even if her request had been successful. Now it seemed that she could not only stay on with Lady Glanville, but would have time to prepare the roles and might hope that they would not be too insignificant. It was not conceit but realism which assured Alexa that a single performance would be enough to secure her a place in the company. She knew her own ability.

The director asked her name. She had been known as Alexa Lorimer since Margaret adopted her, but now she replied without hesitation, 'Alexa Reni.' It would not have occurred to any of them that she was a foreigner, and by using her mother's name the illusion could be maintained. Her colouring might be unusual for an Italian, but not unheard-of – the blonde and chestnut-haired models of Botticelli and Titian had come from this northern part of the country.

That evening, back in Sirmione, Alexa told Lady Glanville that she had found herself a new teacher in Bergamo, and asked permission to return there once a week for a lesson. The lie did not disturb her conscience, for it was made with the kindest of motives – she could hardly announce that she was making plans to prepare for Lady Glanville's own death.

The deception did not have to continue for very long. Lord Glanville used Christmas as his ostensible reason for abandoning his affairs in England in order to be with his wife; but he arrived at the beginning of December and was vague about how long he would stay. A week was enough. As though she had only been waiting for the reunion, Lady Glanville died in his arms.

5

Deaths and homecomings so often follow each other that welcome and condolence become confused. Margaret already knew from Alexa's letters that Lady Glanville had not long to live. So when Robert called from his nursery window, one afternoon early in 1897, to say that he could see a carriage coming up the drive, she did her best to subdue her reactions. Neither sympathy nor etiquette, however, could prevent her from running to the door. Quite apart from the pleasure which she took in Lord Glanville's visits – for he had driven over from his country house, Blaize, several times since that first occasion on which he had acted as Alexa's postman – it was possible that today he might be bringing Alexa with him, her duties as a companion sadly brought to an end.

She was disappointed, but was given no time in which to be alarmed. Hardly had Lord Glanville stepped down from the carriage before he was reassuring her.

'Alexa is well, but she has remained in Italy,' he said as they shook hands. 'You shall have a full report. But first of all, I must have my Christmas present for Robert unloaded. It comes so late that he may think I have forgotten him.'

Margaret looked at the mourning ribbon round his arm. 'Lord Glanville, I am so sorry – '

Their hands were still touching in greeting as she spoke. He brought his other hand up to enclose hers as though

94

he were the one to comfort her, and not the other way round.

'Fanny's life in these past years was so full of pain that I can almost feel glad she is released from it,' he said. 'I spent long enough grieving when I first saw how tightly the disease was gripping her, and again when I learned that there was no cure. Now I must teach myself to be happy that it's over. But I am glad of your sympathy.'

Not for the first time, as he squeezed her hand slightly, Margaret was warmed by the surprising friendship which had grown between them. As an aristocrat he did not trouble himself with the sort of conventions by which life at Brinsley House had been ruled; and Margaret – a widow, a professional woman, and by now in her fortieth year – was equally free of any doubts about the propriety of holding long discussions with a gentleman in the privacy of her drawing room.

She recognized, too, that in a quite different way he enjoyed her son's company almost as much as her own. Robert was an active, mischievous little boy with carrot-orange hair and a wide, friendly grin. He was not yet old enough to understand that he lacked a father, but the need must have been there subconsciously, for he attached himself to his mother's tall visitor whenever he could escape from his nursemaid's clutches. On this occasion, however, he was easily persuaded to follow the coachman, who was carrying a huge rocking horse up to the nursery.

'You spoil him, Lord Glanville,' protested Margaret, as she watched her son delightedly practising his gallops even while he was still on the way upstairs.

'One of the pleasures of life which I have most missed in the past has been that of giving presents to children,' he said.

Margaret did not argue. She knew that the lack of an

heir, a son to whom he could leave all his property as well as his title, was a grief which had been made all the stronger because of the impossibility of ever discussing it with his wife. But he would not want to discuss it with anyone else, either.

'I returned to Sirmione as soon as the doctor wrote to tell me that Fanny had not much longer to live,' Lord Glanville said as soon as Robert's preoccupation with his new possession left the adults free to talk privately in the drawing room. 'In the days before her death, I couldn't bring myself even to think about the future, much less to discuss it with anyone. I simply took it for granted that when the time came, Alexa would return with me to England.'

'What alternative had she?' asked Margaret, as surprised now as he must have been then.

'She told me, to my astonishment, that she had the promise of a temporary engagement with an opera company in Bergamo. She thanked me very nicely for the help I had given her. Then – ' he laughed at the memory – 'she turned against me the arguments I had sometimes used in speaking to her of my work with the Women's Committee, reminding me how strongly I felt that many women were more capable of responsibility than either they or anyone else allowed. She hoped that I would be glad to hear her decision: that from now on she ought to stand on her own feet.'

He paused for a moment, as though remembering the scene, and began abruptly to pace up and down the room. 'I wish you could have seen her,' he said. 'Standing before me, with her arms clasped in front of her like a meek schoolgirl while she explained her plans; but all the time with her head held high and her eyes flashing with excitement and determination. In a curious way she reminded me of yourself at that moment.'

Margaret could guess why. John Junius Lorimer's two daughters had inherited his confident spirit in equal measure. But there was no need to provide any explanation. 'What did you say?' she asked instead.

'My first instinct was to refuse my permission. For a young English girl to live alone in a foreign country, with no security of income, unprotected, and surrounded by men whose nature it is to take advantage of young women – the whole proposal seemed ridiculous. But then I had to remind myself that I have no rights over her. I'm not her father. If I acted as though I were, Alexa would think of me as interfering and autocratic, but she would still be under no obligation to obey me. And I have to confess that the excitement in her eyes won me over. She was so happy and so hopeful, I couldn't bring myself to discourage her.'

'So you gave her your blessing?'

'I reminded her of her duty to you.' He laid a letter on the table beside Margaret. 'She has written, naturally. But she answered me at the time with such deep feeling that I can quote her almost word for word.' He turned back to face Margaret as he did so. 'She told me that you had been so good to her, and that she loved you so dearly, that she would not for the world do anything to hurt you. But she sincerely believed that you would understand her feelings because, when you were exactly her age now, you knew what it was to see a door opening ahead and to fear that you might be prevented from passing through it. And I remembered that at our first meeting you expressed very much the same sentiments yourself. So when Alexa told me that she had faith in your affection, it seemed likely to me that her faith was justified. I didn't attempt to argue any further.'

Margaret remembered the occasion to which he referred, but she could not help being troubled by Alexa's plans. 'You spoke of a temporary engagement, Lord Glanville,' she said. 'Does that mean that Alexa may return to England soon?'

'The winter season extends for only a few more months. However, it appears that in the Arena at Verona a summer season is staged. She hopes that if she can make a sufficient impression in Bergamo, she will be invited to Verona. It's difficult for me to guess whether her hopes will be justified. But her teacher in Baden-Baden told me privately that Alexa had all the potential of a great performer. Alexa herself seemed confident that she only needed one good opportunity to display her ability, and then it would be recognized at once. That was what made me feel it would be too harsh to deprive her of the chance. I took her to Bergamo myself and settled her into lodgings, so that it might be observed that she was not alone in the world. And I have banked for her there a sum which will pay for her journey home. Now she can leave at any time, even if her own resources are not sufficient.'

Margaret thanked him for his kindness and then considered the matter for a little while in silence. At last, smiling, she shrugged her shoulders in a gesture of helplessness.

'I have to let her go!' she exclaimed. 'I suppose I must have let her go already, when you first came to tell me where she was and I did not ask her to return. I told you then that I was not completely happy about her choice of career, but what can I offer her here instead? A country life so quiet that I could not even introduce her to a prospective husband, if marriage was what she had in mind. I had thought at one time that she might find employment as a music teacher – but I know well enough that even in that capacity she would be exposed to danger from the fathers and brothers of her pupils. The temptations of the theatre may not prove to be any greater, and of course its rewards will be considerable if she is successful. I have to hope that her upbringing will protect her. Since her ambitions are high, I'm happy that she has some hope of realizing them.'

'You should come to London,' said Lord Glanville. His pacing of the drawing room stopped as abruptly as it had begun and he sat down again to face her. 'If the country offers no company for Alexa, what society does it afford yourself?'

'I have never cared for society, as long as I can feel my work to be of value,' said Margaret, startled by the abrupt change of subject. 'And the country is the best place for a child.'

'Robert will be happy and healthy anywhere as long as he is in your care, and as he grows older he will benefit as much as you from the conversation of more intelligent companions than a village school can provide. As for the value of your work, I believe that you are wasting your training and energy. An elderly man, half retired at the end of his career, could be happy in this practice. But your abilities are far greater than you have any chance to demonstrate here. Not just as a doctor, but as an administrator. I have been making enquiries. I've learned, for example, that for six years before you married you had the sole medical responsibility for the children in the Ashley Down orphanage in Bristol – and that you organized a programme of child care and health inspection which prevented many common afflictions from ever showing themselves. The trustees of the orphanage speak of you still with great respect.'

'You have been making enquiries!' repeated Margaret incredulously. She had taken his first reference to London as nothing more than a surprising change of subject, but already she sensed that there was more behind it. Lord

Glanville's manner was normally grave, but now he leaned forward with an even more serious expression than usual.

'I have come to invite you to apply for an appointment,' he said. 'I am Governor of a hospital in Westminster. Of course I know very well that my only qualification for the post was my title, but I made it clear when I accepted the offer that I was not prepared to be a figurehead. If I was to take any interest at all, it must be an active interest. You already know how anxious I am to improve the educational possibilities open to women. Now I have the opportunity to combine these two activities. There is a vacancy for a staff doctor. At the same time – it is a teaching hospital – there is a possibility of admitting young women as students. The battle is not yet won, but I am hopeful. I would like to put your name forward to fill the medical vacancy, with the understanding that if you were successful you would also be responsible for supervising the studies of the female students.'

The suggestion came as such a shock to Margaret that she found herself unable to answer – even to express her astonishment.

'I have to make it clear that you would be used as a standard bearer, so to speak, in the heart of a battle,' Lord Glanville continued. 'There would be opposition to your application. It would not be on any personal grounds, but merely fuelled by the realization that your appointment would open a gate which has been locked for too long, and would in the end change the very nature of the hospital. I have to choose for my candidate a woman who is not only well qualified as a doctor, not only mature enough to provide a good example to young women and efficient enough to supervise them, but also stout-hearted enough to listen to criticism which may be hurtful even though it will not be personal.' He stopped, laughing at himself. 'Do I sound as though I'm making a speech in the House of Lords? I'm sorry. But finding that such a candidate exists is miracle enough. I wouldn't like the enterprise to founder through any lack of persuasion on my part. You could do it, Dr Scott. Will you try?'

'You are asking me to uproot myself, to change my whole way of life.'

'Yes,' he agreed. 'I wouldn't dare to do so if I didn't believe that it would be in your own interest, giving you a more satisfying occupation. And in the interests of the young women who would be accepted as students, and of the women's movement in general. But primarily I am speaking for myself, and I would accept the responsibility for the upheaval in your life. You would need to appear at an interview, but any canvassing of the appointments committee would be done by myself. It would naturally be unwise to sell this house or the practice too soon, but if the time came to do so my estate manager could handle the business for you, and I can offer you a house in London. City life is more expensive than country life, but at least you need have no burden of rent. And I should insist that the hospital offered a salary no lower than a man would accept.'

'I must consider this carefully, Lord Glanville. I imagine you don't expect an answer at this moment.'

He shook his head. 'It's enough to know that you don't reject it out of hand. Shall we go and see how the young horseman is getting on?'

Margaret found it less easy than her guest to dismiss his extraordinary proposal from her mind, but the subject was not raised again in conversation until he was on the point of departure.

'You will allow me, I trust, to call again and hear your decision,' he said. 'In all my high-falutin' speeches about the possible benefits to the women's movements, I forgot to declare my own interest. It would give me great personal pleasure to think that you were coming to live in London, so that we might meet more frequently.'

Was it Margaret's imagination, or was Lord Glanville for a second time that day squeezing her hand more affectionately than usual? The moment passed too quickly for her to decide, but it gave her a good deal to think about after he had gone. The friendship which had developed between them was one which gave her a great deal of pleasure. Was he now giving her notice that he hoped for something more? His wife's death was far too recent for him to express any such feeling openly; but it had been so long expected that he would not feel ashamed of dropping an indirect hint.

Margaret tried to criticize herself for the immodesty of her thoughts. An aristocrat, a rich man – how likely was it that he would have more than a casual interest in a country doctor, no longer young? Yet he was no ordinary aristocrat, and Margaret had often enough heard him declare how scornful he felt of the rich women in his own society whose days were devoted to nothing but clothes and the making or retailing of scandals. He was serious by nature, although when he laughed he could lighten the hearts of all who heard him, and Margaret knew that he was sincere in his respect for those women who, like herself, had struggled to improve their standard of education.

Respect was one thing: to wonder about anything more was to move into the realm of dreams. Like a good doctor, Margaret studied her symptoms and admitted to herself that there would be nothing to upset her in the thought of marriage to Lord Glanville. It was not by choice that she had enjoyed the company of a husband for such a very short part of her life. As a young girl she had fallen in love with David Gregson, her father's accountant at Lorimer's Bank, and could have asked nothing better than to spend the rest of her life with him. The quarrel with which their engagement was broken had been the fault of John Junius Lorimer, not of any lack of love on Margaret's own part.

A second chance of happiness had excited her when, during her years as a medical student, she first met Charles Scott. Once again obstacles sprang from the dark confusions of the Lorimer family history to separate Margaret for many years from the man she loved: but this time there had seemed to be a happy ending, when at last they were able to marry. Charles's death only a few months after the wedding was an accident which could not have been foreseen.

So Margaret had twice fallen in love, and twice had been robbed of her lover. But she had had time in each case to recover from her loss. It would be hypocritical to pretend to herself that she would never be capable of loving again.

Equally, she told herself severely, it would be foolish to assume on such slight evidence that she was loved. She was no longer young, and everyone knew that just as young men preferred to marry young women, so also did older men. Fortunately, the difficulties of Margaret's life had made her adept at disciplining her feelings and her hopes. When, after Robert was in bed, she settled down to consider seriously the proposition Lord Glanville had made, she forced herself to leave any thought of their future relationship out of her calculations, and to make the decision on professional grounds.

The answer came quickly, because all Lord Glanville had said was true. On one side of the balance was Robert's pleasure in country life. Everything else weighed down the other side. Margaret was well aware that the work she was doing, although useful enough, did not occupy her full energies. She had compensated for the fact that the practice brought in little income by developing country skills, but she had to recognize, if she were honest, that an ability to cure hams or make wines was not the most worthwhile use of a medical qualification. In London she could not only exercise her own abilities, but help other women to develop theirs. The combined task would provide great satisfaction.

There was another consideration as well. She had stayed on in Elm Lodge after Charles's death three years earlier because at first she was too upset to make plans and later too reluctant to add yet another move to the insecurities of Alexa's childhood. Later still, there had never been a point at which she asked herself if this was how she wanted to spend the rest of her life. Lord Glanville had set the question before her, and suggested an answer: it was an opportunity not likely to recur. Her fortieth birthday was approaching. If she stayed on at Elm Lodge now, nothing would happen except that she and Robert would grow older and older until Robert left home and she herself died there. It could hardly be called an exciting prospect.

Whereas, if she went to London . . . Was this, she wondered, how her father had felt when the chance of running some new business came his way; or how her remote ancestor Brinsley Lorimer reacted to the prospect of a new voyage? She could feel her eyes sparkling with excitement, although there was no one to see her; the blood tingling in her veins seemed to be racing faster than ever before. In much the same way, no doubt, Alexa was even at this moment sustained by the challenge of a new fight. It was the nature of the Lorimers to explore, to accept a challenge. Margaret was not so bound by her family tradition that she put this to herself in so many words. All she knew was that she could not turn her back on an exciting offer. She did not write to Lord Glanville, because to do so would be to deprive herself of the other visit he had promised. But her decision was taken that night.

6

Although an ordinary disappointment can best be borne if no one knows about it, one that goes deeper is only endurable when the secret can be shared. Margaret had been living in London for more than a year when Lord Glanville called on her one Sunday afternoon. He was a frequent visitor during the part of the year when Parliament was sitting, but he had left London two months earlier, as soon as the session ended, in order to travel abroad. Because she now often attended the meetings of the London Women's Suffrage Society which were held in his house, Margaret was familiar with his businesslike working manner as well as with the more relaxed mood which he displayed in her drawing room, but she had never before seen him agitated, as he was on this occasion. He tried to conceal the agitation under a description of his journey, but Margaret found no difficulty in recognizing the cause of disquiet when he reached it.

'While I was on the way to Rome, I decided to call on Alexa,' he said. His voice was casual, but Margaret's knowledge of geography was sufficient to tell her that Verona, where Alexa was spending a second summer, had hardly been on his direct route to the Italian capital.

'I wish you had warned me that you planned such a visit,' she said. 'Now that Alexa has passed her twenty-first birthday, there is a piece of property which should be in her possession – too valuable to be entrusted to any commercial mail or courier.'

'I'm sorry. When I left England I didn't know that I should see her, or naturally I would have mentioned it.'

'I hope you found her well.'

'I found her – ' He paused, as though he could not bring himself to put his impressions into words. 'I arrived in Verona late in the day, and discovered that Alexa was due to perform in the Arena the same evening, singing the part of the Princess Amneris in *Aida*. There was not time to call on her first, so instead I attended the performance. I cannot tell you – she is so beautiful! Both her face and her voice, and yet there is more even than that. Towards the end, as she listened to her lover being condemned to death, she seemed to control the whole Arena by the stillness of her body – thousands of people, a huge auditorium, the stars above making it seem as though she were singing to a universe rather than an earthly audience – everything was in her power. I knew already that her voice was strong and lovely. I hadn't realized until then the strength of personality which she can project. I wept for Amneris, and I was not the only one. The whole audience was moved. She stole the opera from Aida.'

'That may not have been quite what Verdi intended,' laughed Margaret, thinking that the discovery of Alexa's dramatic talents was what had unsettled her visitor. 'I can tell you that she had the same power when she was only nine years old. I was present once when she reduced a rowdy music hall audience almost to tears. You were able to see her later, I hope.'

'I waited after the performance,' said Lord Glanville. 'But of course she was not expecting me. She already had a companion for the rest of the evening.'

Margaret looked at him sharply, not needing to put the question into words.

'Ought I to tell you?' Lord Glanville asked himself. 'The news will disturb you, and yet you have the right to know.'

'Go on, if you please,' Margaret said quietly.

'I recognized the carriage which awaited her. Indeed, I recognized its owner. He is the son of an old friend of mine, now unfortunately deceased, the Duke of Caversham.'

The name was unfamiliar to Margaret and she was uncertain how to react. Alexa was bound to attract admirers. Margaret herself was not a snob, but she saw nothing wrong in the possibility of her ward becoming a duchess. Lord Glanville must have read her thoughts, for he lost no time in making his views clear.

'Once before I had to rescue Alexa from this same young man, while he was still a student,' he said. 'Now, his studies over, he is making the Grand Tour, and appears to find Alexa as great an attraction as the architectural sights of northern Italy. I can promise you that he will not marry her. It may take him a few years to run through that part of his inheritance which is not entailed, and no doubt during those years he will be generous to his companions. But before he is thirty he will have set his mother to scour America for an heiress with a fancy to be a duchess. He cannot afford to marry a girl without a fortune and he knows it as well as I do. The thought will never even have entered his head.' Lord Glanville stood up and walked across to the window, staring out of it with his back to Margaret. 'I'm sorry. I ought not to have told you. There is nothing you can do except worry, and it is too late for either prayers or actions to be of any use, I fear.'

'You spoke to her yourself?'

'I called on her the next morning. She expressed pleasure in seeing me, and I think it was genuine enough. But – well, I must try to see it through her eyes. She received me in a room full of the flowers and presents which her performances have attracted. In Italy, it seems, an opera singer is like a local queen. She had had a triumph, and she knew it. Doing what she always wanted to do, and doing it well, she was radiantly happy. It was to be expected, I suppose. She is twenty-one years old, and has a city at her feet and a duke to shower her with diamonds. What had I, or England, to offer her?'

Margaret did not move as he came back to the chair which he had left a moment earlier, sighing in unhappiness.

'I ought not to have pretended to you that I had no plans to visit Alexa when I left England,' he said. 'You are right that I should have warned you of my journey. If I did not, it was because I hoped to surprise you. It is eighteen months now since Fanny – since Alexa embarked on her own career. I had thought that I might find her lonely, perhaps disillusioned, ready to return to the love and security which you could offer her in London. And after a little while – ' He looked directly into Margaret's eyes. 'I had hoped that she might marry me. I can say that to you now, because I realize that it will never happen.'

A moment before, Margaret had felt as unhappy as he, on account of the news which he had brought. Now, suddenly, she was additionally numbed by a blow which hit straight at her own heart. But she was used to concealing her feelings, and forced herself to show only sympathy.

'I think you would have had a great deal to offer her, Lord Glanville,' she said quietly. 'But did Alexa ever know – ?'

He shook his head, impatient with himself. 'The last time I saw her was a week after my wife's funeral. What, with propriety, could I have said then? I recognized how excited she was at the opportunity before her. If I had forbidden her to attempt it, would she have loved me for that? I suppose I must have hoped in my heart that she would fail. My disappointment is well deserved. She tells me that she thinks of herself now as an Italian and expects to pursue her career in Italy. She sent you her love, as always, but said that she is unlikely to return to England until she is invited to do so by the Royal Opera House.'

It was clear that he had already said more than he intended, and Margaret saw that too great a show of sympathy would only increase his distress. She contented herself with returning the strong grip of his hands as he held both hers in farewell.

'I have done you no service in speaking my mind like this,' he admitted. 'You would have been happier to know less. But there is no one else in the world to whom I could express my feelings honestly. I know that I can trust you to respect my confidence.'

'Of course.' Margaret looked up at him and tried to smile. In a gesture which his great height made as awkward as it was unexpected, he stooped to kiss her on the forehead. Then, hastily, he took his leave.

After he had gone, Margaret stood for a long time without moving. If Lord Glanville had kissed her like that a year earlier – even so chastely, with such absence of passion – the gesture might have raised hopes which already were unwarrantably high. She looked back on her feelings then, remembering how she had dared to wonder whether his proposal to bring her to London meant that he hoped for an increase in the warmth of feeling between them until it grew into something more than friendship. All all the time he had been in love with

Alexa. How clear his intentions seemed to her now! He had needed to establish Margaret in London so that Alexa could be enticed back to live with her guardian once her bid for fame had failed.

No criticism could possibly be made of Lord Glanville's behaviour. He had acted throughout with the strictest honour and generosity, giving everything he had promised. Without immodesty Margaret could recognize that he respected her and had during the past two years developed a warm affection for her, as she had for him. But that was all, and nothing he had said or done had suggested anything more. He had even dropped hints which Margaret should have been able to interpret. His longing for an heir, a son of his own, had been made obvious enough: she should have been able to deduce that when the time came he would look for a wife who was young. Any false expectations which she might have entertained were entirely of her own making.

Twenty years earlier, Margaret might have wept for her disappointment. Now she was strong enough to deny to herself that any disappointment existed, and to make herself believe it. She had come to a mistaken conclusion a year ago, but it was of no importance. What mattered was that she had had other valid reasons then for leaving the country and coming to London, and they were still valid now. Instead of crying, Margaret held her head high and laughed. It was just as well, she teased herself, that she was happy in her work.

Later, unable to prevent herself from going over the conversation again in her head, she realized that there was one other conclusion to be drawn from it. If Alexa did not propose to return to England for some time, she must be told about the rubies which were her birthright. Margaret wasted no time in writing.

'This is a letter which ought to have reached you on your twenty-first birthday,' she began. 'But I hoped at that time that it would not be too long before you returned to England, so that I could speak rather than write, and also could put into your hands something which I consider too valuable to post across Europe. Today, though, Lord Glanville has told me of your decision to stay in Italy, and I must not allow you any longer to remain in ignorance of what is already rightly yours: a legacy from your father.

'You may have guessed already that your mother was not married when you were born. I cannot know how much she talked to you about your father, but I doubt whether you can remember him, for he died while you were still very young. One day I would like to tell you about him, but not in a letter. Before he died, he gave your mother a box of precious stones – rubies – to keep for you; and she in turn handed them to me when she knew that she too was dying. They are yours now, and they represent a legacy of love. But they are also of great value. You must tell me what you would like me to do with them – but consider when you do so that they will need to be kept in a secure place.

'I shall await your answer – but most of all, of course, I hope that you will come in person to collect your legacy, so that I may see you again after this separation which already seems so long.'

Alexa's answer, when it arrived a few weeks later, was as long and affectionate as always; but it brushed aside the subject of the legacy as though this was of little account.

'You are right to suggest that the frequent moves which my career makes necessary pose difficulties in regard to valuable objects,' she agreed. 'All I can do is to make sure that my jewel case is always within sight of myself or my maid. So if the gift from my father has been safe with you all these years, I suggest that you should leave it where it is. I am not short of jewels, and I take greater pleasure in wearing a present in the company of the generous friend who gave it to me than I would do in flaunting the cold legacy of a man I never knew.'

She could not have known how much Margaret would be hurt by such a casual dismissal both of a father who had loved his last baby so deeply and of the fortune in precious stones which had been the cause of so many separate unhappinesses in order that it should one day adorn Alexa's hair and neck.

It was tempting to write back with a fuller explanation of John Junius Lorimer's circumstances at the time of Alexa's birth. But even after so many years had passed, the shock and shame of the collapse both of Lorimer's Bank and of its chairman had left a different kind of legacy imprinted on Margaret's own mind.

The wish that Alexa should feel proud of her father and be assured of his love conflicted with Margaret's memories of the way in which her own love for John Junius Lorimer had been betrayed. Even if she had ever completely understood the situation which had led to her father's death, it was too complicated to be explained on paper. Margaret promised herself now that she would tell the whole truth when it could be done face to face. There was no reason to believe that the delay would be of any importance.

PART III

Margaret in Jamaica

1

It is women's work to preserve family ties – at least in the eyes of men, who expect communications to be maintained, but scorn to make the effort themselves. A woman who pursued a full-time career at the end of the century, however, had little time for the trivia on which such relationships depend. Margaret had never had much in common with her brother William, and their already strained relationship had been further weakened by her decision to remain independent of him after Charles's death. Since her move to London at Lord Glanville's instigation, she had ceased to visit Brinsley House even for holidays. She saw Beatrice from time to time, for her niece – still unmarried at twenty-seven – was by now the secretary of a Bristol group campaigning for women's suffrage, and represented the city on a national committee which met at Lord Glanville's house. But although Margaret corresponded with the Bristol branch of the family, remembering birthdays and exchanging news and good wishes, she had not actually spoken to William since the stormy conversation in which he had admitted his part in helping Alexa to escape from Margaret's care. It came as a surprise, therefore, when she arrived home from the hospital one evening early in 1905 to find him waiting to see her.

William wasted little time in polite exchanges about health or children, but came straight to the point.

'I've just returned from Jamaica,' he said.

The statement came as a second surprise to Margaret, for it was not often that he tested his own ships. 'Was the voyage for pleasure or business?' she asked, realizing even as she spoke how foolish the question was. William was not a man to do anything for pleasure alone.

'Trading conditions are changing,' he told her. 'For a long time the sugar industry has been showing low profits. I've had letters from planters in Jamaica, declaring their intention of changing their crop from sugar cane to bananas; and Ralph, who started in the banana trade in quite a small way, has been extremely successful.'

'Ralph!' exclaimed Margaret, astonished. It was as a Baptist missionary that their younger brother had gone out to Jamaica in 1882. Such was his devotion to his congregation that he refused to take all the home furloughs to which he was entitled, so that Margaret had not seen him for some years. But he had married her best friend, Lydia, and the two women corresponded regularly. Nothing in Lydia's letters had suggested that Ralph had abandoned his vocation.

'I mean, in the plantation which he manages on behalf of his congregation,' William explained, impatient of the interruption. 'Well, in their letters, the planters enquire about markets, but most of all they need to know that ships could be waiting when the crop is ready. Sugar and rum can wait for their passage, but bananas begin to ripen as soon as they are cut. I thought it wise to go myself to see how the ships should be equipped and whether the expense will be worth while.'

'And what did you decide?'

'To enter the trade,' he said. 'I was able to evolve a satisfactory plan to make sure that the fruit would arrive on the quay only as the ship enters the port. But that's of no interest to you. My news is that I advised Ralph of my arrival and he came to Kingston to meet me. We were

114

able to spend a pleasant evening together. I am charged with a message to you. He and Lydia hope most particularly that you will pay them a visit. Ralph was anxious for my opinion as to whether this would be possible. But I had no idea, of course, how much you are tied by your professional responsibilities.'

Margaret did not make any immediate comment. Because the supervision of students comprised a large part of her hospital work, the contract of her appointment had been drawn up in academic rather than purely medical terms. Like a university teacher she was allowed, if she wished, to take a sabbatical year at any time after completing her first six years in the post. The prospect had been a tempting one when she first qualified for it a year earlier, for she would have welcomed the chance to travel, collecting information and statistics on the subject in which she now specialized, infant mortality. But she had postponed her decision because she wished neither to interrupt Robert's schooling nor to abandon him to the care of servants. To spend part of the year in Jamaica would be of only limited value to her proposed research, but it would not be impossible. She had always had a particular fondness for her younger brother, and her girlhood friendship with Lydia had been strengthened by all the strains and pleasures of the life they had shared as medical students; so she had a double reason for considering the request.

'Has he any special reason for the invitation?' she asked.

'He has sent a letter.' William handed it over. Margaret frowned over Ralph's tight handwriting as she read its first paragraphs slowly.

'My dearest sister,
    'William will have told you of my hope that you will visit us.

115

There have been many times during these past years when I have wished for your company, but I have known that I had no right to distract you from duties as important to you as mine to me. My request now is not so much to offer you a holiday as to appeal for your help. Lydia finds herself again with child. I will not disguise from you the fact that the discovery of her condition was not altogether welcome. The loss of two of our little ones in the fever epidemic three years ago inspired us both to feel that we should praise God for the health of our surviving children, and not risk the lives of any other infants in a climate such as this.

'But God's will must be done, and we prepare to rejoice in the gift. Lydia is of course anxious because during the period of her confinement our community – which by now is a large one – will be without medical attention. It was she who first voiced the thought of the good turn you could do us by coming here. Although I adopt that thought as my excuse for writing to you, in order that Lydia shall not guess the cause of my own anxiety, I am, to tell the truth, a little troubled in my mind. At Lydia's age childbirth may not be easy. I cannot too strongly express the relief I should feel if I could know that you would be here as our guest when the time comes. I owe to you my good fortune in marrying the best wife any man could have. Will you help me to keep what you helped me to find?'

The letter continued for several pages, but as soon as Margaret had satisfied herself that the news they contained had no further bearing on the subject she left the rest to be read later.

'Do you think I should go?' she asked William.

'It's not for me to say whether you're able to do so. But I can confirm that Ralph is worried about Lydia's condition. As a doctor you will know best whether his fears are justified.'

'Lydia is younger than I am,' Margaret said. 'But even so – ' She calculated in her head that her friend must be almost forty-six. 'Yes,' she said. 'There is a risk. Two risks, in fact, to the mother and also to the child. But – ' She thought anxiously for a little while. 'Two of her own

116

children have died. Can they really expect me to endanger the life of my only son?'

'I can offer two answers to that,' said William. 'The first is that Ralph assures me that the threat to health is now much less. There is very little malaria. Nor has there been any epidemic of yellow fever since the children died. The climate is certainly a difficult one for babies and small children. But Ralph considers that a healthy boy of Robert's age should suffer no discomfort. The sea voyage, in addition, will be good for you both.'

'And your second answer?' prompted Margaret, since he seemed to have forgotten.

'That you can if you wish leave Robert in England. He's old enough now to go away to school – and since he has no father, I think it would be to his advantage to do so. A good many schools offer special arrangements for boys whose fathers have died. I could settle this for you, and shoulder what costs may still be necessary. And in the holiday while you are away he would be welcome to make my home his own.'

'Why should you do so much for him?' Margaret asked the question to keep the conversation alive while she continued to think about her decision.

'Because I'm a rich man. Because I sympathize with the misfortunes you've suffered. And because at one time – indeed, on two occasions – I would have expected to maintain you in my household for the rest of your life. You saved me that expense. I regard myself as still in your debt.'

'Shall we have dinner?' said Margaret. 'And of course you will spend the night here. I'll tell you tomorrow what I've decided.'

By the morning she was clear in her duty. She ought not to have forgotten, even for an hour, how Lydia had come to her help in the weeks which followed Charles's death, when in the misery of bereavement she had put the life of her unborn child at risk. Even if friendship were not a strong enough reason for the voyage to Jamaica, there was a debt of gratitude to be repaid, and it was a fortunate chance that she was entitled to leave her hospital duties, with the right of return.

She had already decided, however, not to take Robert with her. Perhaps her concern for his health was a fussy one, but she knew that she would not enjoy her stay if she was worrying about the risks. The offer of a home for his holiday from school she would accept, regarding it more as a gift to Ralph and Lydia than to herself. Her reluctance to owe William anything perhaps still stemmed from the memory of a cold interview many years before, when she had needed to ask a favour of him in order to embark on the medical studies of which he so deeply disapproved. She was sure, she told him now, that if a reduced fee could be arranged for Robert she would be able to pay it herself.

'You will at least accept your passage from me, I hope,' he said. 'I plan to include accommodation for ten passengers on each of the banana boats. The crossing will be fast and I expect it to be very popular when it becomes known; but for the first few voyages there will be berths to spare, so the offer costs me nothing.'

Margaret could not help smiling when she realized that William understood her feelings. She had quarrelled with him often enough – but perhaps, she told herself, he had always acted for the best as he saw it. She watched without protest as he called Robert to his side, questioned him gravely about his school work, and dismissed him with the usual tip of a rich uncle, a whole sovereign. There had once been a time when she might have seen such a gesture as patronizing, but she realized now that such a reaction would have been touchy. The observation gratified her. It was because she earned a good salary on her own merits and was able to live in comfort, not needing to be helped or pitied by her brother, that they could be friends again – not as brother and younger sister, not as rich man and dependant, but as equals.

2

Babies fortunately allow plenty of time to prepare for their arrival. Several weeks were needed before arrangements were complete both for Robert's schooling and for Margaret's own replacement at the hospital. It was on a day late in March that she stood on the deck of a Lorimer Line banana boat at the end of its voyage to Jamaica. For a moment, as the vessel turned past the Palisadoes, the reef which stretched its long arm to shelter Kingston Harbour, she stared down into the sea. Somewhere below were the remains of Port Royal, the home of Sir Henry Morgan's privateers and once known as the richest and wickedest city in the world before it was engulfed by a tidal wave. But there was nothing to be seen now except the suddenly calm water. Raising her eyes to the island ahead, she was surprised by its mountainous outline. Kingston itself lay in a flat crescent at sea level, but the hills pressed round the port in a tight semicircle, cutting off the breeze so that the atmosphere suddenly became oppressive.

As the ship drew near to land she saw Ralph waiting to greet her on the quay, wearing a wide straw hat and a black suit made of a thin cloth. He had always been tall, but since their last meeting he had become too thin, and at the same time had begun to stoop, so that his coat hung shabbily from his shoulders. His face looked anxious. Perhaps that was because he had not yet caught sight of his sister. As soon as he did, he took off his hat and waved it in welcome.

The gesture revealed that his hair, once the colour of bright straw, had been bleached by the sun until it seemed from this distance to be already white; and he had been so long away from English fashions that it straggled over his neck instead of being cut close to the head. Looking at this tired, rather drab figure, it was difficult to remember the bright vitality of the young man in a white blazer who twenty-seven years ago had been Captain of Cricket at Clifton College.

As she stepped ashore, rocking slightly on her feet after the voyage, it occurred to Margaret that Ralph was the only person who made her feel conscious of her age. William had in a curious way always been middle-aged. The passing of years had carried him by now into his fifties, where he had properly belonged ever since his youth, so that his appearance and personality had come into accord, giving him an air of authority where once he had seemed only crafty. But Ralph, so handsome and athletic as a boy, had always been someone whom Margaret regarded as young. Seeing his lined face now in the bright tropical light, she was reminded that he was not young any longer. And whatever his age, Margaret herself was older.

But Ralph's energy had not diminished. As soon as he had greeted her, with even more than his usual affection, he issued a series of orders which caused her baggage to be brought off the ship and carried away towards the railway station. Margaret would have preferred to keep it in sight, but the quay was piled high with boxes of bananas and almost before the ship was finally tied up the work of loading had begun, making it difficult for the passengers to move easily away. The loaders sang as they worked, tossing the boxes from hand to hand as though they weighed nothing. Margaret had seen plenty of coloured men in the Bristol docks, but nothing had prepared her for the blackness of these Jamaicans with their close-cropped curly hair and the powerful muscles of their legs and shoulders, which their shabby clothes hardly covered at all. She marvelled at the steadiness with which they worked. Although it was still early in the day, she herself felt overpowered by the heat and humidity.

'Is it always as hot as this?' she asked Ralph.

'This is the cool season.' The answer was not reassuring. 'It will end soon, I'm afraid. That's yet another cause for my concern about Lydia. One would not by choice bring a baby into the world at the hottest and wettest time. My first wish, before I wrote to you, was that Lydia should return to England for a few months. But she wasn't willing to be away from me and our people for so long. You'll at least find Hope Valley less oppressive than Kingston. We have a little height, and very often it catches a breeze. I'm afraid the approach to it may prove fatiguing, when you've travelled so far already. But there's no help for it. And the train will leave almost at once.'

He was right to anticipate her fatigue, but the warmth of her reception made up for it. Laughing women and children greeted her with cheerful shouts when they reached the village, and Lydia was waiting outside her home in welcome. It was such a pleasure for Margaret to see her friend again that their kissing and chattering continued for some time, while Ralph smiled indulgently and the two children, Kate and Brinsley, hovered shyly in the background.

Lydia was as merry as ever, although no prettier. Even in England, neatly dressed in the smocked blouses and skirts of their student days or in the grander gowns of her social life, she had never been handsome. But now in addition she had become too thin, and the faded cotton dress she wore would have been dowdy even if it were not stretched so tightly by the state of her pregnancy. None of this, however, made the slightest difference to her good humour.

That day and the next there was a good deal for Margaret to inspect. Ralph showed his sister with particular pride the fine stone chapel, built on a platform of rock which stood up within the valley. It had been constructed since his arrival and under his guidance, he told her, to replace the mean wooden structure which he had found there. The stone had been cut from their own ground to a plan which terraced the steeper parts of the village and provided a sewage channel for the whole.

Lydia was equally anxious to show off her dispensary. Margaret sat there quietly for an hour to see how the morning surgery went. She realized that she would need to learn about some of the local herbs which Lydia used to treat rashes or stomach upsets, but there would be plenty of time for that.

It was Lydia, too, who in the cool of late afternoon proposed a walk round Pastor's Vineyard.

'Do you grow grapes here?' asked Margaret in surprise.

'Not a single bunch,' laughed Lydia. 'But the land is managed by the pastor, and the pastor every Sunday reminds his people that they must go forth and labour in the vineyard. The name has come naturally. Most of the congregation, I imagine, would not recognize a real vineyard if they saw one.'

It was a longer tour than Margaret had expected, even though they did no more than look across the extensive fields from the path which ran through their centre. There were pastures in which white cattle grazed, and groves of orange and grapefruit trees. Banana plants stretched in long lines, their heads drooping with the weight of the crop and their huge leaves tattered by wind and rain to resemble the fronds of palms. A smaller area had been dug for the cultivation of squash and callaloo and other vegetables equally unfamiliar to Margaret.

Lydia was still laughing as she explained. 'Your brother has become a farmer, although he doesn't realize it,' she said. 'He believes in all sincerity that I am the one who cares for the bodies of his people, while he looks after their souls. But he can't help organizing them to their own advantage. All this land was once part of an estate – the Bristow plantation – which had been wholly abandoned after the emancipation of the slaves. It was a form of neglect which can be seen all over the island. The plantations became unprofitable as soon as the slaves had to be paid for the first time; the owners went back to England, and the overseers they left behind had no incentive to manage the land well. The old plantation house here is still called Bristow Great House, but it's completely derelict. When Ralph first saw the plantation, it had reverted to jungle – but as you see, it's as well ordered now as it can ever have been.'

The name of Bristow Great House was a familiar one to Margaret. She knew that it had been built by a member of the Lorimer family many years earlier; he had called it after the ancient name of his home city, Bristol. It was curious, she thought, that Ralph had never mentioned it in his letters, and more curious still that it should have come under his control at all. He was, after all, only a younger son – and his decision to become a missionary had been taken after his father's death. Margaret would have liked to interrupt her friend with questions, but Lydia was still describing the situation with affectionate enthusiasm.

'Tidiness and planning for the future don't come naturally to most of our congregation,' she said. 'They've learned that in such a lush land they need only push a stick into the ground and it will root and grow. But you can imagine that such a carefree attitude doesn't suit Ralph's temperament. He believes in efficient management. The food is distributed amongst his people, and the profit spent to their benefit, but he is the one who decides what shall be grown and who sells the surplus. Sometimes I tease him that he's as hard a task-master as any of the old-time plantation-owners. They lashed their slaves with whips, while he goads them on with the hope of heaven and the fear of hell. He should have been a businessman, like his father and brother. He pretends not to be, but at heart he's a true Lorimer.'

'I hope this doesn't disturb you, Lydia.' Margaret knew that she herself was largely responsible for her friend's marriage. Years ago, when she had invited Lydia to stay with her at a time of crisis in Ralph's life, she had been well aware of the likely consequence of the invitation. Everything had turned out then as expected – but Lydia must have believed herself to be marrying a missionary, not a farmer or a businessman.

'To tell you the truth, Margaret, I'm not as concerned as Ralph about either heaven or hell. I don't tell him so, and every Sunday I go twice to chapel and teach in Sunday School as well, but I can't bring myself to share his faith as devoutly as I ought. There are parts of the Bible that I know cannot be literally true, but Ralph insists that everything written in it must be taken as fact. I don't even think that the people understand half that he tells them. But they shout out phrases from the Bible and it seems to make them happy and altogether I'm sure it does more good than harm. Because of the food from the farm they're as healthy, I dare say, as any other group of people in Jamaica. And with the money from the cash crops, Ralph has built a school and employs a teacher. He's promised me a hospital as the next project. The community is entirely self-supporting. What he's doing must surely be good when the results are so beneficial. You mustn't tell him that I sometimes laugh a little, because I admire him all the time.'

'And love him too, I hope.'

'That goes without saying.' Lydia took her friend's hand and they turned back towards the valley. From the moment when Margaret had first read the letter in which Ralph asked her to come, she had felt an indefinable uneasiness. But now she saw that Ralph and Lydia had created a way of life for themselves which brought them personal happiness as well as satisfaction in the work which they did for others. There was no cause for anxiety.

3

The secret lives of children are foreign territory to their parents, but an outsider often finds it easier to cross the frontier. In the first excitement of her arrival Margaret had had eyes only for her brother and her friend, but on Saturday she set herself to make friends with her niece and nephew.

Kate and Brinsley had spent only two brief furloughs in England since they were born but, although their aunt was almost a stranger, a sympathy sprang up between them immediately. At their last meeting, Kate had been a sturdy, tomboyish little girl, and the intervening years had made no change in her independence of spirit nor in the unladylike definiteness of her firm movements and long strides. Her tawny hair was tied with bedraggled ribbons into two thick bunches, but only to keep it out of her eyes – every detail of her appearance proclaimed the fact that she did not care what impression she made on anyone who saw her. The whole family, as a matter of fact, was shabbily dressed. Margaret was freer of vanity herself than most women, but even she thought it a shame that a young girl should be allowed to grow up without at least a standard of neatness to observe; and resolved to spend some time during her visit with a needle and thread, mending old clothes and perhaps even making new ones. It was too soon in the visit now, however, to criticize. Instead, joining the two children on the verandah, she asked the fourteen-year-old girl what she was studying so intently in her notebooks.

'Some of the Valley people don't come to Mother for help when they're ill,' Kate told her. 'They have their own medicines and poultices to clean a wound or draw off a fever. They don't like to tell Mother their recipes, but they tell me. And sometimes they let me watch when they change the poultices, so that I can see whether the mixture works or not. I've been making some notes, to see which recipes appear to be the most successful.'

'Does your mother mind having such competition on her doorstep?' asked Margaret.

'I asked her once,' Kate said. 'And she just laughed. She told me that some people who fall ill get better even if a doctor never comes near them. And some will die, however good the doctor, because they are too old or too weak or because the illness is without a remedy. There will be a good many, of course, who are truly cured by the care or the medicine which a doctor gives them. But there are always a few, she says, who recover – if they *do* recover – mainly because of their own certainty that they will. So the remedy prescribed by a qualified doctor might not do them any good if they had no faith in it. But if

126

they believe that a potion smuggled in by Old Emmy on the night of the new moon has a special power to cure them, then they'll be cured.'

'You're learning the secrets of our profession very young,' said Margaret, laughing in her turn. 'And do your studies confirm what your mother told you?'

'I think some of the old formulas work in an ordinary way,' Kate told her earnestly. 'I mean, if Old Emmy binds strips of papaya fruit over an infected wound, you can see that the infection is being drawn out. She's using the same sort of medicine that Mother does, although she may have different ingredients. But then there was a woman who went nearly mad after she had a baby. She kept banging her head against walls and trees, and gabbling in a way that didn't make sense. That time Old Emmy smeared a green ointment on the soles of the woman's feet. It smelt foul, but I can't think of anything in it that could really have done any good. But the woman fell asleep within an hour, and when she woke up she was well again. So yes, I do think that Mother's right about the importance of faith. It's the other medicines that I'm trying to study carefully, so that I can find out which of the ingredients is the one that works.'

'I can see you're going to be a pharmacist when you grow up,' said Margaret, and was taken aback by the indignation in the girl's eyes.

'But I'm going to be a doctor, of course!'

'Yes, of course.' Margaret's voice was apologetic, but her smile was full of sympathy. The certainty with which Kate expressed her ambition reminded her of her own frustrations at the same age, and the excitement with which she had seen one barrier after another fall before her determination to succeed. 'And you, Brinsley?' she asked, turning to her nephew.

'I'm to be sent to school in England next year,' said

127

Brinsley, an energetic twelve-year-old whose eyes sparkled with liveliness. Margaret had already noticed that he had inherited not only his father's yellow hair but also the careless gaiety which had characterized Ralph in the schoolboy days before guilt drove him to religion. It was obvious that Ralph adored his only surviving son – but at the same time seemed to feel a continual need to curb the boy's high spirits. Margaret herself found Brinsley's light-heartedness delightful, but perhaps her brother saw in it only a reminder of his own sinful youth, from which he had been at such pains to escape. At any rate, he had already told his sister that it was time for Brinsley to be subjected to greater discipline than was possible in a community which had spoiled him from birth.

'Are you looking forward to that?' she asked.

'I wouldn't look forward to it at all if it were to offer nothing but the diet of Latin irregular verbs which my father suggests,' said Brinsley, making a face at the grammar which lay unopened beside him. 'But Mother has told me something about his own schooldays – how when she first knew him his enthusiasm was only for cricket. That's a more interesting prospect.'

'You don't play cricket here, I imagine.' The houses of the Hope Valley community were built on the two steep slopes of a gorge formed by the stream which divided them; and in addition to that, the land descended sharply from the mountains to the flat coastal plains which formed the plantations; there was no room for a cricket pitch there. As for the estate which Ralph had taken over, Margaret's tour of inspection suggested that every possible inch of land had been brought under cultivation, with nothing wasted on frivolities.

'Don't I just, though?' said Brinsley. He looked at his aunt with mischief in his eyes. 'Would you like to see,

Aunt Margaret? But if you come, you mustn't tell anyone.'

'I'd love to see.' Margaret was amused as well as curious. She fetched her hat and they set out together, leaving Kate to study her notes. Brinsley led the way at first along the same path which Lydia had taken towards Pastor's Vineyard; but after a little while, looking anxiously at his aunt's clothes as though to gauge whether she would be willing to risk spoiling them, he came to a halt beside a row of palm trees. These – in marked contrast to the rest of the tidy estate – were almost strangled by a variety of vines and creepers which had wound their way up towards the sky and then dangled down to root in the ground again. The curtain of vegetation appeared to be impenetrable, but Brinsley took hold of a huge golden-veined leaf and tugged at it, raising a flap of greenery which had been cut to provide a doorway.

'This way,' he said, and Margaret bent low to go through. As she straightened herself on the further side of the tangled screen, she looked round in surprise. She was standing in a garden. It was unkempt and overgrown, but there could be no possible doubt that these grounds had been laid out for pleasure rather than for profit. The steep fall of the land had been tamed into terraces, hedged with poinsettia and hibiscus: the stone steps which joined them were flanked with ornamental urns, cracked now but still imposing. Specimen trees, bright with blossom, were scattered over what had undoubtedly once been a lawn, although now the broad-leaved crab grass which had carpeted it was almost invisible beneath a smothering of weeds.

As well as a garden, there was a building. 'That's Bristow Great House,' said Brinsley, noticing that his aunt was staring at it.

Margaret could not help laughing at the grandiloquence

of the name – and not just because it was a roofless ruin now. Surely, she thought, it could never have been particularly imposing. There were only two storeys, raised from the ground to allow a dark storehouse underneath, and only three rooms on each floor. Brinsley was able to provide an explanation.

'It wasn't called a Great House because it was specially great,' he said. 'The main house of every plantation was called that. They were never built high, because of the danger from hurricanes. And they never had many rooms, because the people who lived there spent almost all their time outside.'

Margaret could see that the verandahs which encircled the building on both levels must once have been cool and attractive places, although by now the wood had rotted and the whole area was fouled by bird droppings. She was curious enough to walk towards the stone steps.

'There were other buildings separate from the house,' Brinsley told her. 'The slave quarters on one side and the kitchen quarters on the other. My best friend lives there, in the old kitchen. And there was a bakehouse and a laundry, although they've fallen down now.'

By this time Margaret had gone up the steps and picked her way carefully across the crumbling floor of the verandah. Inside the house and so protected from the weather, the rooms on the lower storey were in good condition. What must have been the drawing room was of a noble size. It was possible, with a little imagination, to furnish it with polished wood and gleaming silver and people it with the rich plantation owners of a century earlier, gossiping and flirting with all the formal style of a closed society.

A slave based society, Margaret reminded herself, refusing to admit sentimentality. She moved into a smaller room, and stopped in surprise. Brinsley, she realized, was watching her reaction with a pride which made clear what had happened.

The room – once perhaps a study – had been cleaned and furnished. The furnishings were shabby and unsafe – a rug that had probably been thrown out by Lydia as being too disgracefully threadbare, and tables which had almost certainly been made by Brinsley himself with an inexpert touch. But the floor and the fluted panelling of the walls had been polished until they shone with a red richness.

'It's the thing about mahogany,' said Brinsley behind her. 'You can let it get damp and dirty for years and years, but then all you have to do is to rub hard and it looks like this. This is our room, Kate's and mine. We don't tell anyone about it.'

He was giving her a warning, but Margaret had no intention of betraying secrets. She examined more closely the designs carved into the doorposts. There was no doubt at all, now that she could see them clearly, that the pattern was the same as that used in the building of Brinsley House in Bristol. Margaret had recognized the name of Bristow as soon as Lydia first mentioned it, and this small detail of construction confirmed her belief that she was standing in the house which Samuel Lorimer's younger brother, Matthew, had built at the end of the eighteenth century.

'Did your parents ever consider coming to live here?' she asked.

Brinsley shook his head. 'It wouldn't have done,' he said. 'I mean, I never asked them, but I could see why they wouldn't want to. No one's lived here since Massa Matty died, because the plantation was run by overseers after that. Massa Matty seems to have been quite decent, from the stories the old ladies tell about him; but all the same, he was a slave-owner. It wouldn't be right for a pastor to live like a slave-owner. That's really why Kate and I don't talk about this room when we're at home, in case Father feels he has to stop us coming. I think he tries to pretend that the house isn't really here at all. That's why he's let a strip of jungle grow up all round it, when everywhere else it's been cut down.'

There was still a good deal that Margaret did not understand about the situation. Had John Junius Lorimer managed to conceal this part of his possessions in the same way that he had concealed the rubies, and with the same intention – to provide a legacy for one of his children who was still a minor at the time of his ruin? Well, it was a question which should be put to Ralph, not to Brinsley, who from the tone of his remarks appeared to have no suspicion that any member of the Lorimer family had ever owned property so near to Hope Valley. She returned instead to the subject which had originally brought them on this tour of inspection.

'Where do you play your cricket?' she asked.

Brinsley led the way outside again, and round to the side of the house. A young man who had been sitting in the shade of an ackee tree rose to his feet as they approached. Older than Brinsley, and more powerfully built, his face displayed the same kind of alert intelligence as did the white boy's. He was very much lighter in skin than most of the inhabitants of Hope Valley, but his smile was just as broad and cheerful as theirs when Brinsley introduced them.

'Aunt Margaret, this is my friend Duke Mattison. Father taught him to play cricket at the same time as me, and he's a rattling good bowler. He can spin the ball and make it break any way he chooses. Show her, Duke.'

They had constructed a practice net, levelling the ground and weaving palm leaves together into screens which would prevent the ball from travelling too far when it was hit. She watched the demonstration for a few moments, smiling at the energy with which the two boys defied the oppressive atmosphere. All their concentration was on the practice, so that they hardly noticed when she said goodbye, assuring them that she could find her own way back. And Margaret herself was thoughtful as she passed through the frontier strip of jungle and into the cultivated part of the old plantation. How had it happened, she wondered, that the Bristow estate had once more come under the control of a Lorimer?

4

Direct questions provoke direct answers, but not necessarily truthful ones.

'Tell me how the Bristow plantation came into your hands,' Margaret asked her brother when they were next alone together. 'I have been very puzzled, trying to think what could have happened, for I can't remember Papa ever mentioning it at all.'

'He can hardly have been aware that he had any claim on it,' said Ralph. 'Certainly in those last troubled months, when he had so many other worries, he would not have given it a thought. I've seen some of the old papers relating to the finances of the plantation. The overseer wrote several times to our grandfather, Alexander, who inherited it from his uncle Matthew, to point out that the land was no longer profitable – that instead of money being sent back to England, it was necessary for the owner to supply more capital in order that new crops might be planted and more efficient methods of working developed. It appears that Alexander never answered the letters. With the bank and the shipping line

133

to occupy his time, I can see that he would have little interest in a property so far away which threatened only to drain his resources.'

'If Papa knew so little about it, how did it descend to you? Does William know? And the Receiver who had to satisfy the creditors after the collapse of the bank – was he aware that Papa had this asset?'

'You are describing a plantation which has been well cultivated for twenty years when you talk about an asset, Margaret. When I first came out here and saw it, I can assure you it was only a liability. It could not have been sold because no one would have bought it. It was a wilderness, requiring an investment of much time and labour before any reward could be expected. If our community has succeeded in turning it into a profitable venture, it's because they gave their labour free in the beginning, expecting no payment until harvest time.'

'But even so – '

Ralph interrupted her with a laugh. 'It's all a coincidence, Margaret. I'm sorry if it makes the story seem untidy, but it's only the position of the Bristow estate which has led by accident to this new connection with the Lorimers. It could just as easily have been the property of some other family which lay abandoned here, and I should still have applied for it because it lay beside our own boundary. So much good land was neglected, and for so many years, that in the end the government took powers to reallocate it. So this plantation was taken away from the Lorimers because they had ceased to fulfil the obligations of owners. It's by chance, not by inheritance, that it has fallen into the hands of another Lorimer. You can imagine that I have no wish to be associated with the reputation of a slave-owner, so I'm sure I may count on your discretion in that respect. I've never described the past history of the plantation even to Lydia or the children – and it seems that our great-great-uncle has been remembered here solely as Massa Matty, so that my name is not a problem.'

'Does Bristow then belong to you personally, or to the Hope Valley community as a whole?'

Until that moment Margaret had had no reason to doubt anything Ralph had told her, surprising though she might find it. Was it her imagination now that made her suspect a reluctance on her brother's part to answer this last question?

'The deeds legally are in my name. That is a formality, an administrative convenience. It's easier for the authorities to deal with one owner, just as it's easier for one owner to manage an estate with the greatest efficiency. But all the profits of our crops – '

He was repeating now what Lydia had already told her, and Margaret allowed her attention to wander. She was remembering a conversation a good many years ago, when Alexa had asked what legacies John Junius Lorimer had left to his children. Margaret's answer then had been an honest one; it was true that her father had no power to bequeath anything to anyone in his will, for at the moment of his death all his known possessions had been sequestered. And yet now, twenty-six years later, William owned a shipping line, Ralph controlled a large plantation, and waiting in England for Alexa to collect was a fortune in rubies. The children of the rich, it seemed, were not always as effectively ruined by disaster as the children of the poor. Only Margaret herself lacked any visible sign that she had been brought up as the daughter of a wealthy man, and she wasted no time on pitying herself for that. The capital from which she drew her livelihood was her professional qualification, and she felt all the more pride in it for having achieved her success without help.

135

That evening, just before sunset, it began to rain with a noise and unexpectedness which drew Margaret on to the verandah to watch. Even the worst thunderstorm she could remember in England had never been as forceful as this – the water seemed to be not so much falling to the ground as propelled to it under pressure. As densely as fog it obliterated the hills; as viciously as a bad-tempered child it bent the leaves of trees and climbing vines downwards and battered their blossoms to the ground. It drummed on the roof of the verandah and poured off it in a cascade to flood the ground below. It turned the main track along the valley into a river and surged down it like a tidal wave. Margaret found the sight frightening until she realized that the people of Hope Valley had had years enough to learn what precautions to take. This was why the church stood on its raised platform. This was why every house, from the meanest to the most substantial, was lifted from the ground on piles of bricks or rocks. This was why each one had a steeply pitched roof of corrugated iron to divert any cloudburst to the ground.

The sound of the beating rain softened for a moment as though the downpour had exhausted its energy. But then for a second time it hurled itself downwards, this time splashing into the verandah so that Margaret was forced to step backwards. Marvelling that Ralph and Lydia should not find such violence extraordinary, she went back into the house and, long after the rain had stopped, lay awake listening to the dripping of water off leaves and roofs. Yet next morning she awoke to sunshine again. The ground was steaming and the humidity so high that each breath seemed an effort; but the new day's blossoms were as bright as though there had been no massacre in the darkness and the trees and shrubs were bright with health. The valley had used the rain and already had forgotten it. A new day had begun.

Sun after storm; it was a contrast typical of the island. Margaret felt something of the same guilt which had prompted Ralph to devote his life to these people whose ancestors had been chained by early Lorimers and their captains into the reeking holds of the Middle Passage. To find the people of the valley still sullen and resentful in their dealings with white men would not have surprised but rather satisfied her, giving her the excuse to feel vicariously apologetic. But men and women alike were friendly, always smiling. Ralph criticized them for laziness, but to Margaret it was a miracle that they should be happy against the heritage of their history. She was as little able as Lydia to share Ralph's dogmatic beliefs, but if the Christian faith were responsible for this sunny contentment of spirit, the pastor had reason to be satisfied with his work.

On her first Sunday in the village Margaret put on her best clothes for church and found that everyone else had done the same. The number of men in the congregation was not great, but every woman in the valley must have been there, each wearing a severe straw hat and a cotton jacket and skirt laundered to crisp cleanliness. The children, too, had been scrubbed until they shone. Small boys who tumbled about all week almost naked were transformed by shirts and shorts into little black angels, whilst their sisters wore frilly white dresses and sashes, with ribbons in their frizzy hair. The hymn tunes were new to Margaret, although the words were in many cases familiar, but they were sung so beautifully that she was content to listen and to marvel at the sweet sadness of the harmonies.

To hear Ralph preach was another surprise. In England she had known him best in his moments of doubt and unhappiness. But the confidence which he felt in his life here tumbled out in words which were shouted rather than spoken. Margaret remembered that Lydia had recognized in her husband the man who might have been a businessman like his father, but she herself was suddenly reminded of the way in which John Junius, at the time of family prayers, had been accustomed to give God his orders for the day. Ralph – though ostensibly acting as a channel in the other direction, transmitting the word of the Lord to his hearers – was his father's son in this way as well.

Margaret allowed the words of the sermon to resound against her eardrums without greatly exercising her mind. There were too many quotations from the Bible for her liking, used as though they were bound to have significance merely because they had authority. If she tried to think about their meaning, it often had little relationship to the argument, so after a while she ceased to trouble herself with the effort.

Instead, she let her memory slip back over the years since her father had died. If he could see his children now, she wondered, what would he think of them all? William had behaved as a Lorimer elder son should do, but John Junius would have been startled to find Ralph administering an agricultural community on a tropical island. He would have been even more astonished to learn that Margaret was accustomed at any one time to take responsibility for the health and even lives of thirty mothers and babies, while also supervising the studies of an increasing number of female medical students – a species which hardly existed during his lifetime.

As for his other daughter – well, it might not have surprised him to know that she had grown to be one of the most beautiful women in Europe, but could he have anticipated that she would be a prima donna while still in her twenties? The thought of Alexa distracted Margaret's thoughts still further. She smiled to herself as she studied her own present surroundings and contrasted them with the dazzle of operatic life. Last night Alexa would have been singing in some opera house, greeted almost certainly with bravos and flowers, and carried off for a rich dinner in glittering surroundings by one of her admirers. To judge by the subject of the sermon, Ralph would not have approved. Margaret did not precisely approve herself, but she had learned to accept the news which Alexa regularly sent her and tried not to distress herself with moral judgements when they could be of no effect. She did her best to remember, as the congregation rose with relief and energy to sing a hymn, exactly where in Europe Alexa was at this moment, but failed to find the answer.

5

Spring comes to Paris in the style of the Impressionists. Sitting on the bank of the Seine, Matthew Lorimer did his best to capture in paint the energy of trees whose new leaves swelled inside their buds and broke through, stretching their fingers almost fast enough to be seen.

Artists commonly disparage that part of their achievement which causes them the least effort, although others may think it their best work. Matthew could have been the most fashionable portrait painter in Paris if he had set his mind to it. He had a genius for catching a likeness and a facility for adding an extra touch of beauty with such subtlety that everyone who saw the sitter after studying her portrait found her even lovelier than before.

This ability, because it came so easily, seemed to him to be of little value. Three or four times a year he would accept a commission to paint a rich man's wife or mistress

– but only in order to buy the paints and canvases which he needed for his real work, and to keep himself alive while he did it. In the nine and a half years since he left his comfortable home in Bristol he had become thin and shabby, but remained young. At the age of twenty-two he had been a shy and serious young man; now, although he had entered his thirties, he was as light-hearted as a schoolboy. Paris was a city bubbling with artistic excitement, the Mecca for young artists from all over the world. They were all as poor as he, and their poverty united them in high-spirited companionship. The excitement came from their experiments in style. Although Matthew had learned his craft from the example of the Impressionists, by now he was moving in a different direction, exploring subjects far removed from faces and flowers. But just as an occasional portrait served to pay the bills, so the dazzle of sunshine on water and the freshness of spring blossom brought a holiday temptation, with all the pleasures of truancy from more serious purpose.

As he strode home at the end of the day, Matthew sang aloud. Passers-by turned to look at him and smiled, sharing his good humour. Approaching the Opera he sang even more loudly, as though auditioning to be employed there. Suddenly he broke off in mid-phrase. A row of posters advertised the evening's performance. He had never heard of the opera: *Salome*. Even the composer's name was unfamiliar – who was Richard Strauss? But one name was familiar enough: Alexa Reni.

That she should use the surname Reni instead of Lorimer did not confuse him. He knew that opera singers frequently tried to appear Italian even when they were not. In this case, he remembered Alexa telling him that her mother was Italian – and the Christian name by itself was sufficiently distinctive. For a long time he stood and stared at the poster. When he resumed his walk back to Montmartre it was in a slower and more thoughtful mood.

Matthew had long ago severed all links with his parents. For some months after he left England they had professed themselves ready to forgive him; but once they understood that he never intended to return, their anger had become hysterical. William had taken a spiteful pleasure in letting him know that he could no longer expect to inherit any part of the fortune built up by the Lorimer Line. It was possible that both his parents still expected him to be starved out of his chosen career, but that was a pleasure he did not intend to allow them.

With his aunt, however, he had kept in touch by letter. Since babyhood he had felt a special affection for her. From Margaret he had learned of Alexa's disappearance from England and, later, of her training and first steps towards an operatic career. More recently she had ceased to mention Alexa's name in her letters, perhaps assuming that Matthew had no special interest in someone he had not seen for so many years.

Matthew's feelings about Alexa were in fact very complicated. Foremost amongst them was the memory of guilt. Alexa had loved him and he had deserted her. At the time he had hoped she might understand how important it was that he should enjoy at least a taste of freedom before submitting to the bondage of his father's business for the rest of his life. But her refusal to answer his letter even with a reproach had made it clear how much his selfishness had hurt her. He had not deserved forgiveness, and he had not received it.

All this had happened a long time ago, but there was an important sense in which his love for Alexa had never changed. If he had stayed in Bristol, he might one day have grown to blame her for all the chances he had sacrificed: by leaving, he had been able to preserve unchanged for almost ten years his picture of a beautiful and innocent young girl. For a moment now he was tempted not to challenge his memories to the test of time, not to expose himself to coldness or angry recrimination. But in practice it was impossible to know that Alexa was in Paris and not to see her.

He watched the opera that evening from the gods, so far above the expensive seats in which more fashionable opera-goers displayed themselves that he could hardly distinguish Alexa's features. In spite of that, her acting at once enthralled and horrified him. He went to the opera as often as he could afford and was accustomed to listen to the warblings of heroines who were either noble or unfortunate: this heroine, if the word could be applied to her, was lustful and vengeful. He took it for granted that young girls in the last stages of consumption should be portrayed by stout middle-aged matrons; but the glimpses of Alexa's slim body as she cast away each of the seven veils in turn while she danced made it seem natural that the officers of Herod's court should desire her. On this same stage he had seen Melba, whose reputation for acting was almost as high as for singing – but even Melba rarely did more than raise one majestic arm as a sign of emotion, or both arms at once to indicate uncontrollable passion. Alexa, by contrast, *was* Salome.

When the performance was over and the stage was littered with the flowers thrown by the audience, he jostled his way down to street level and went round to the stage door. He was known there, for he had several times been invited to attend rehearsals, making sketches which could be used to embellish the printed programmes: the guardian of the door turned a blind eye as he went inside.

The gentlemen who had been more generous with their bribes than himself were already crowded round the door of Alexa's dressing room, anxious to heap her with compliments or more flowers. None of them, Matthew noticed, was admitted; although he could guess from their expressions that they were rewarded with smiles. For his own part, he waited in a dark corner of the corridor until they had all at last departed.

The dresser opened the door to his knock. He handed her a sheet of paper. On it – before leaving for the opera – he had painted a picture of a rose and signed it with his name.

The door closed. It was opened again by Alexa herself. 'Matthew! Matthew!' she said – and then, it seemed, could say nothing more. Matthew for his part swallowed hard and clenched his fists, reminding himself that he had no right to embrace her.

'A painted rose was all I could afford,' he said, trying to keep his voice light.

'It's very beautiful. And it won't fade. Come in, Matthew.'

He followed her into the untidy room. Her dresser moved about, putting flowers into water. Then she picked up an armful of clothes and disappeared, leaving Matthew alone with Alexa. The charged silence between them lengthened unbearably, until Alexa at last broke it with a laugh.

'So often I've wondered whether we should ever meet again. And now that we do, I can think of nothing to say.'

Matthew found his tongue at last. To him, after all, the meeting had not come as a surprise. He congratulated her on her performance and on the success she had won in her career. 'We have both achieved our ambitions,' he said.

'You earn your living as an artist, then?' After her first

143

emotional reaction to the shock of seeing him, she had steadied her voice into one of polite coolness.

'Yes. And I never hoped or expected to be a famous one.'

'You found New York uncongenial, I suppose. Paris certainly has the reputation of being the most stimulating city for a painter.'

'New York?' he queried, not understanding what she meant.

'When you left Bristol, it was to go to New York, was it not?'

'I never had any thought of doing so. What gave you that idea?'

'Your father seemed quite convinced that America was your destination. I suppose, though, that it may have been only a guess on his part. Perhaps he had no more true information about your plans than I did.'

'But you knew that I was coming to Paris,' protested Matthew. 'I told you that most plainly.'

'You told me nothing,' said Alexa. 'You left, that was all. No warning, no explanation, no regret, no Matthew.' She moved around the cramped room as she talked, her hands moving carelessly as though to show that the matter was of little importance to her. Matthew caught her by the wrist and forced her to turn towards him.

'I gave you my address,' he said. 'I asked you to write to me.'

'And where did you hide this important message?' she asked.

'It was a long letter. I sent it to my father and asked him to put it personally into your hands.'

As though she had picked up a costume and found it to be for the wrong operatic role, Alexa discarded her pretence of indifference.

'I never received any letter. I asked your father if you

had left anything for me and was told that you had not. What did it say, Matthew? If you remember.'

'I remember every word.' But bewilderment and anger and an almost uncontrollable need to kiss her jumbled his thoughts into incoherence. 'I told you that I loved you. I was not leaving you for ever. It would only have been for a little while, if you had told me that you could understand. If I've stayed here, it's because there seemed no reason to return. I wanted you to write. For weeks after I came here I waited for your letter. I hoped that perhaps you would feel some sympathy for me, because you had your own ambitions and knew how it felt to see no way of fulfilling them. I even hoped that you would use the time – as you have done – to work towards your goal, so that you would never reproach me for depriving you of the chance. But all the time, what I wanted was to marry you in the end. If you had called me back, I would have come. If you had expressed yourself as hurt or uncomprehending, I would have tried to explain, to console you. But when there was no answer at all, I had to believe at last that you found it impossible to forgive me. And I knew all the time that I'd behaved badly. I deserved to be punished for it.'

'Oh!' Alexa's breath was forced out of her in a long sigh. She stood up again and began to pace up and down in an intensity of anger which for the moment seemed to transform her back into the part of Salome. At last she sighed again, calming herself.

'I've hated your father for many years,' she said, 'because when he sent me to London he put me in bad hands. But even while I blamed him for that, I never thought that the whole arrangement might be based on a deception. He found it easy to persuade me because I was so unhappy; and I was unhappy because you had gone without a word. And yet all the time, you say . . .'

She shook her head as though still almost unable to believe it.

'Why should he behave in such a way towards you?' asked Matthew wonderingly.

'I suppose I was not good enough for his elder son. He must have seen how fond we were of each other – and he knew already, what I only found out for myself later, that my parents were not married. I'm illegitimate.'

'What does that matter?'

'Obviously it mattered to him. He assumed, I suppose, that my moral standards would be no higher than my mother's – and he did his best to make his assumptions come true as quickly as possible. If things had turned out as he expected, I should have been too much ashamed, and you would have been too shocked, for us to return easily to our old relationship.' Alexa hesitated for a moment, and there was regret in her eyes as she looked steadily at him. 'I was fortunate at that time, and was helped to escape from the situation your father had arranged for me. But since then – ' She raised her head and listened to the sound of brisk footsteps approaching outside. 'We are going to be interrupted, and this is a conversation which ought to be completed. The conventions of opera have their uses at times. Hide behind the screen, Matthew, and keep still. It will be easier for me to tell a white lie if you are not here to arouse suspicion.'

She flung herself on to a couch as he did what he was told. From his hiding place he heard the knock on the door, the dresser's announcement.

'Le duc de Caversham, Madame.'

'Alexa! Another triumph! A small present to celebrate.'

'Jack, you're too generous. How beautiful! Did you enjoy the evening?'

'It's the least enjoyable opera I've ever seen in my life, which makes your own performance all the more amazing.

146

You've certainly proved the point that it's possible for Salome to do the dance herself, instead of using a substitute – but only when the dancer is Alexa Reni. Can you imagine any of those stout females at Dresden casting off a single veil?'

'They may turn out to be wise after all,' murmured Alexa. 'The dance is too tiring for a singer. I'm completely exhausted, Jack.'

'But you're going to dine with me.'

'I couldn't eat anything. Tomorrow we'll have lunch and ride together. But tonight I must rest.'

The young duke did not give up so easily, but Alexa was adamant, her voice seeming to fade away with weariness. Matthew listened with amusement until at last the door closed behind the petulant suitor.

'Are you really exhausted?' he asked, emerging cautiously from behind the screen.

'Not in the least.' Alexa bounded to her feet. Matthew found her sudden changes of mood startling. First indifferent, then angry, she had now suddenly become young and carefree, exciting him by the gaiety which sparkled in her eyes. 'And I'm ravenously hungry. I never eat before a performance. What did you plan to have for supper, Matthew?'

'A long loaf of bread and a bottle of wine. With a little goat's cheese for a treat.'

'Then I hope you have enough for two. Wait for me outside. I shall be dressed in fifteen minutes.'

She was better than her word and took his hand like a little girl as she came running out. His own excitement grew as he led her up the steep and narrow streets of Montmartre.

'You mustn't expect too much,' he warned her as they reached the foot of his staircase. 'A garret to you may be

147

merely part of the set of *La Bohème*, but to me it's home.'

'I begin to understand why Mimi collapsed,' Alexa laughed as she followed him up one flight after another. 'Why do artists always live in attics?'

'Because cellars rarely have skylights. Here we are.'

Even as he flung open the door he realized what a contrast his room must provide to the hotels in which she presumably spent most of her time, but he was not ashamed of it. He could joke about poverty because at least for the past five years he had known that he could earn money whenever he needed it, although he chose not to do so very often.

The studio was tidy. Alexa could not be expected to guess the significance of that. It was the first time for nine years that he had not returned at night to a chaotic mess of canvases leaning against every piece of furniture, brushes in jars, discarded rags on the floor and an unmade bed in the gallery. Part of Matthew's revolt against the well-ordered home of his childhood and the neat columns of figures he had been expected to produce in his father's office was a refusal nowadays to notice his surroundings at all. But in the three hours before returning to the opera house he had swept the floor and stacked the canvases neatly and found a clean pair of sheets to put on the bed. His description of the frugal meal which awaited him had been a true one, because in order to take the sting out of his likely disappointment it had been necessary to tell himself over and over again that of course Alexa would not come, and therefore to cater for himself only in his usual style. But in tidying the studio he had revealed his true hopes.

As he had intended, she went straight across to the canvas which stood unfinished on the easel and stared at it in perplexity. He stood beside her to explain.

'All these cubes and triangles are merely on the surface, to break up the image,' he said. 'When you look hard beneath them, you will see the true subject of the picture.'

'A piano,' she said, pleased with herself for the identification. 'But why must it be covered with these shapes?'

'To prevent you from noticing that you are looking at a whole piano and not merely one view of it. When you think of the instrument you almost certainly visualize the keyboard as it looks to the player, but at the same time you're aware of the shape of the raised lid as it is seen by the listener, from the side. I can combine both these views in a single painting by the use of these angles.'

'Do people buy pictures like this?'

'Not yet. One day they will. Don't you find sometimes in the musical sphere that a composer moves faster than the ears of his listeners? But they catch up with him in the end. It's the same with the eyes of people who look at pictures.'

For a moment longer she studied it, and then turned to smile at him with mischief in her eyes.

'And where are the others, the pictures you have hidden?'

'What do you mean?'

'This room is far too spick and span. You've been tidying your paintings away. Why am I not allowed to see them?' She turned the lamp higher, revealing the canvases which he had stacked against the wall in the low dark corner where the roof sloped to within a few feet of the floor. Her laughter bubbled in gaiety as she turned each one round in turn. 'How odd it is that paintings of naked women should be fit only for the eyes of gentlemen, while ladies who can study the same shape every day of their lives in the glass if they wish are expected to turn away blushing.' She turned the sixth canvas in the stack and her laughter came to a sudden stop.

149

Matthew took it from her and set it up on the easel. It was a painting in his earlier Impressionist style, bright and sunlit. A young girl was standing in a meadow of ankle-high grass. She wore a white frock: a wide-brimmed hat with green ribbons tied under her chin lay flat across her back, leaving her long hair, reddish gold, to fly loose about her shoulders. Her arm was raised and her skirt was swinging. Her eyes smiled from the canvas, and the woman she had become stared gravely back. Matthew looked at them both.

Alexa broke the silence with a little sigh. 'I'm glad you remembered me, Matthew,' she said. 'Although I was hurt when you left, I tried to persuade myself that it was the best thing for you, and so I was not angry for very long. And I hoped you would remember me.'

'Did *you* remember?' asked Matthew quietly.

'Oh yes. But all the same – ' she swung round to face him – 'I made myself learn a lesson from our parting.'

'What did you learn?'

'That men are not to be trusted. That nothing is permanent, no one is to be relied upon – except your aunt, who is the most loyal, loving creature in the world, even when she ought to be angry. It seemed to me that I must grasp at whatever came near me and make use of it while I could.'

'What are you trying to tell me?' asked Matthew.

She had been joyous and carefree when she first came into the studio with him. Now her blue-green eyes were serious as they looked into his.

'I'm trying to tell you that I am no longer the girl in that picture,' she said. She stretched out an arm so that he could see the emerald bracelet on her slim wrist. 'I'm telling you that young men like the Duke of Caversham do not give such presents only because they love music.'

'Nor does the model who poses for me always go home

150

when it grows too dark for me to go on painting,' said Matthew. 'But I can say goodbye to her tomorrow.'

'And as soon as Caversham has spent all his money he will have to marry, in order that he may start on his wife's. He has probably begun to wonder already how he may free himself from me. Shall we try again, Matthew, away from your father's reach?'

Half an hour earlier he had hoped to persuade her to spend the night with him. Half an hour earlier she would, he suspected, have agreed. But the happiness which warmed his whole body with a deep sense of peace had a curious effect. Alexa had been right to warn him that they could never return to the innocence of their first love. But they could make a fresh start of a different kind. Marriage played no very great part in the bohemian society of Paris, and he suspected that Alexa's friends might be equally casual in their attitudes. It was curious that, after so long away from Bristol, he should suddenly feel himself ruled by the conventions of Lorimer respectability. One did not sleep with the woman one proposed to marry until after the marriage. 'How long are you staying in Paris?' he asked.

'I leave tomorrow. *Salome* is not going into the repertory here. Tonight's performance was only an experiment. I shall be in Naples for the summer. And then to London in September. The management of the Royal Opera House is proposing to experiment with a winter season, and they need some popular singers. Once before I was invited to sing at Covent Garden, but only in small parts. I preferred to wait until the invitation allowed me to select my own roles, and now that time has come. I must warn you, Matthew, that I don't intend to stop singing. I have the taste for earning large fees.'

'That may be just as well,' laughed Matthew. 'Very well, then, I shall come to London too. I shall paint your

151

portrait and put it on exhibition and within weeks every beautiful woman in the country will be queuing at my studio. I shall see you in England, then, Alexa. Dearest Alexa.'

'Do you intend to tell your father that we have met again?' asked Alexa, after he had kissed her.

'My ties with Brinsley House are already broken,' he told her. 'Until today, the coldness has been on my parents' side. Now it's my turn to be angry. But to raise the matter with my father might tempt him to interfere again. So I shall find lodgings in London and make no contact with my family. Will you be staying with Aunt Margaret?'

'She's in Jamaica now, visiting your uncle Ralph,' Alexa said. 'But she will surely have expected to end her stay before September. And she has so often begged me to come to London that in any case I know she would hurry back to welcome me as soon as she learns my plans.'

'Then we can be married from her house.'

Alexa gave an amused sigh. 'All over Europe men fall on their knees and beseech me to marry them. And the man whose proposal I might consider seriously doesn't even trouble to ask the question.'

'Will you marry me, Alexa?' he asked.

'Of course I will, Matthew,' she said.

6

A resident in a foreign country soon ceases to realize how strange the environment must seem to a newcomer. Ralph, forgetting for a little while his anxiety on Lydia's behalf in the pleasure which his sister's company brought him, and observing how easily Margaret fitted into the life both of the family and of the community, needed to be reminded that many things commonplace to him must come as a surprise to her.

One such reminder came on her first Sunday in Hope Valley. Although darkness had fallen, they were all sitting on the verandah enjoying the coolness of the evening. Ralph himself was reading aloud to the children; whilst Lydia and Margaret, although listening, busied themselves at the same time with the sewing of baby clothes. So familiar was the sound of the drums to him that he would not have noticed when it began if he had not seen his sister look up suddenly from her work and stare into the darkness, listening to something in the distance.

Fearing she might be nervous, he interrupted his reading to explain.

'What you can hear is the last of the Sunday services,' he explained. 'One of the brothers leads it. When the weather is good, it's held out of doors.'

'May we attend it?' she asked him.

'It would be thought an intrusion on my part. And you would find the path too dark at this time.'

He was reluctant to give a more honest explanation, and on this occasion Margaret accepted what he said without further comment. He could tell that she was curious, however, and on each subsequent Sunday as the noise began he was conscious of her distraction. So he was not too greatly surprised when on one such evening, a month after her arrival, she went inside to say goodnight to Kate and Brinsley and did not return to the verandah afterwards. He waited only a few moments before going inside to call. As soon as he was sure that she had gone, he lit a hurricane lamp and hurried after her.

As he had expected, he found her standing in the darkness at the point high in the valley where a waterfall crashed down over the rocks to be abruptly absorbed in the calm of a large pool. He had taken her early in her visit to see the Baptist Hole, but then it had been in daylight, providing a picturesque view of water splashing and sparkling in the sun. That was how he had first seen it himself. His predecessor as pastor to the community had tried to warn him that a natural feature which seemed to lend itself to the baptismal service might earlier have had a part to play in some more primitive ceremonies. He had been too slow to understand the warning, and what Margaret saw now was the result of his insensitivity.

The whole adult congregation – including the men who rarely came to the chapel – had assembled round the pool. But instead of sitting in neat rows in pews, they were throwing themselves about, shaking their heads and shoulders in a wild dance. Their leader, standing on the flat rock which Ralph himself used as a pulpit whenever he had anything especially important to tell his congregation, shouted out phrases which were meaningless in themselves, and the dancers repeated them in a sound something between a scream and a groan. As they writhed and stamped, so their torches flickered, casting eerie shadows amongst the trees which clothed the gorge so densely: the accompaniment came only from the shaking of gourds and the rhythmic and steadily more frenzied beating of drums. Ralph had left his lamp behind on the path before coming near and it was not surprising, in view of the atmosphere, that when he put out a hand to attract Margaret's attention, she gasped in alarm.

As soon as she had seen who it was, Ralph drew her quietly away. Neither of them spoke until they were back on the verandah of the pastor's house.

'It comes straight from the jungle,' said Margaret at last.

'It comes straight from their hearts,' Ralph countered.

His sister nodded. 'The same thing, perhaps,' she said.

'I ought to have brought it to an end when I first came here. No doubt you think it weak of me to have given in.' He had struggled long with his conscience before deciding that the best solution was to insist that a ceremony which clearly would survive whether he countenanced it or not should be brought, if only by name, into the Christian observance.

'I respect all the more the success you have had here,' she said quietly. 'To overcome even partially an old culture of such strength seems to me a most impressvie achievement.'

Ralph was pleased by her approval. He was not as unaware as his wife believed of the disproportionate amount of time and energy which he devoted to the running of the Bristow estate. He had never confessed to Lydia that the plantation had once belonged to his great-great-uncle Matthew, and even more carefully had he concealed from the whole world the lie which had resulted in it becoming his personal property; but perhaps the pricking in his conscience increased his determination that the congregation should profit from its fertility. His nature was that of a man who needed to see results, to reap the harvest of his sowing. It was difficult always to feel confident that his Sunday sermons fell on receptive ground, and without the successful organization of the farm lands he would often have been depressed. From his observation of Margaret's reluctance to discuss her own religious beliefs with him, he deduced that she was not in sympathy with his opinions – but this very fact made her praise more welcome.

By now the time of Lydia's confinement was approaching. As she grew heavier, so did the atmosphere. The torrential outbursts of rain continued for longer and were then replaced by a sun which burned with a fierce, debilitating heat out of a cloudless sky. Ralph could see that even Margaret, who prided herself on her good health, was having to struggle against lethargy and tiredness, and Lydia's exhaustion was more conspicuous still. The smallest exertion out of the shade was enough to make the sweat run off her forehead to cloud her eyes, while the humidity made her gasp for breath. She could only take a few steps at a time before needing to stop for a moment and rest.

Remembering the lively way in which she had continued to work throughout all her previous pregnancies, Ralph could not help but worry. But he said nothing, because Margaret without fuss or complaint was already taking over all Lydia's activities. She was running the morning surgery by now, and visiting the sick in their homes. Kate and Brinsley were old enough to look after themselves – and Kate, in fact, chose to accompany her aunt to the surgery, producing from memory the past history of the patients who came there. Margaret even spontaneously continued the campaign towards community hygiene which had been one of Lydia's chief enthusiasms ever since they arrived. Ralph watched with affectionate amusement as his sister followed the course of sewage channels to trace a blockage, chased cattle away from the drinking stretch of the stream, lectured the mothers of children who squatted in the middle of paths, and paid surprise visits to the Bristow slaughterhouse to see that her instructions on keeping flies away from the meat were being observed. Whoever had trained the two women in the principles of public health had achieved a lasting success.

At times he worried, seeing that Margaret was almost as worn out as his wife at the end of each enervating day. But his first anxiety was for Lydia, and he knew that his sister shared it. That was why she had come, and she was not a woman to do things by halves. So he said nothing, even when – two weeks before the baby was due – she insisted that Lydia from now on must remain at home all day, and for most of the time in bed. His wife accepted the edict with a lack of protest which worried Ralph as much as anything else. Although it brought his anxieties to a head, it was a relief when in the early hours of one morning he felt Lydia's hand on his shoulder, waking him to say that her labour had begun.

They had agreed in advance that when the time came Ralph should take the children down to the coast, to leave them with another minister who was a friend. Kate and Brinsley were both excited by the prospect of swimming in the sea, and Brinsley confessed to hopes that he might also be taken on a crocodile hunt in the mangrove swamps, so both children said goodbye to their mother cheerfully.

Margaret had ordered Ralph to spend the night with his friend, since otherwise the double journey would have occupied fourteen hours. She made no secret of the fact that she would rather have him out of the house when the baby arrived. But when he returned to Hope Valley the next day there had been no change in the situation. One of the two village girls who had been chosen by Margaret to take turns in helping was sitting by Lydia's bedside, keeping her forehead cool, and a small boy on the verandah was tugging on a rope whenever he remembered it. This operated a makeshift *punkah* to fan the air into movement during those times of the day when the breeze dropped altogether. But there was not yet any sign of the baby.

Ralph spent ten minutes with Lydia, holding her hand and talking of the children and their journey. Then he took Margaret outside, where they could not be heard.

'Why is it taking so long?' he demanded. 'Even her

first labour lasted only eighteen hours, and the others were all so quick that we scarcely had time to send for help.'

'The baby is not very active; and Lydia herself was tired even before her labour began,' Margaret said. 'I prefer not to interfere with a natural birth if it can be helped, but the time has certainly come now when I must do so. I suggest you go away, Ralph. Make your usual visits. I'll send a messenger as soon as there is anything to say.'

Reluctantly he accepted his sister's instructions. All the doors and jalousies were open to catch whatever breeze might come, and if he stayed in the house he would not be able to escape from the sound of Lydia's breathing, half panting and half moan.

No message came, but after an hour he could stay away no longer. He returned to the house to find Margaret just coming out of Lydia's room with a baby in her arms.

'A little boy, just this moment born,' she said. 'Ralph, will you bring the cradle out of Lydia's room? She's very tired. As soon as you have had a word with her, she must be allowed to sleep without disturbance.'

He moved the cradle as she asked, and then sat by his wife's side for a few moments. But Lydia could hardly keep her eyes open. She was extremely pale and her energy as well as her blood seemed to have drained away completely. She managed a wan smile, but could not speak. Ralph's heart chilled as he held her limp hand in his own. If she should die, he thought to himself, and his spirit groaned with a fear which he must not express. No new baby would ever be able to console him for the loss of his wife. But it would not, surely it would not come to that. Lydia was exhausted, that was all, and it was natural enough. He told himself to be sensible, but in his imagination he saw her slipping away from him, and his true feelings burst out in an agony of guilt. 'I'm sorry, my dearest,' he cried, knowing that she would understand what he meant. 'Oh Lydia, Lydia, I'm so sorry.'

She was too tired to reassure him, too tired even to squeeze his hand. He realized very soon that his presence was no kindness to her, and went quietly from the room.

He found Margaret looking down at the cradle with an expression that he did not understand. There were times in the past when he had seen her unhappy, but never before had he caught such a look of startled uncertainty on her face, as though she were unsure of some decision she had made, and might even have been on the point of changing it. But his own anxiety left no room for him to consider his sister's.

'Margaret, is Lydia in any danger?'

Her quickness to recognize his fear suggested to him that perhaps she shared it, but she moved at once to embrace and reassure him.

'No, I'm sure she isn't. She's not a young woman any longer, of course. You mustn't expect her to recover as quickly from this birth as from the others. We shall both need to look after her for quite a long time.'

'Of course.' He was so anxious to believe her that his relief did not admit of any doubts and now at last he felt able to look for the first time at the child.

All his other children, after their first birth cries, had lain placidly in their cradles, as though feeling even in their first moments the security of the family into which they were born. This one was different. His face was screwed up in an expression of pain or fury, and what little hair he had was so fair as to appear white. He looked like an angry old man, and his father could feel no warmth towards him. Ralph stood in silence, trying to force the correct emotions into his heart. Then, slowly and compassionately, Margaret drew away the blanket which covered the little boy's body.

At first it seemed to Ralph that the baby was lying in an awkward position. Only when he looked more carefully was he able to see the deformity of the hip and the unnatural angle at which a stunted left leg grew from it. His earlier terror repeated itself. If Lydia should die for *this*, he thought. He said nothing as Margaret replaced the covering.

'Does Lydia know?' he asked.

'Not yet. She was too tired to ask, and I thought it best not to break the news until she was stronger.'

Ralph nodded his agreement to that, and summoned all his emotional strength to accept what he had seen.

'It's God's will,' he said. 'We will call the boy Grant. Because God has granted him the gift of life, and one day we shall learn why. Even his misfortune must have some purpose. And none of us was sent into the world to be happy all the time.'

'It seems to me that some from the beginning have less chance of happiness than others.' Margaret was still looking at the baby as she spoke, but now she raised her eyes to her brother. 'You're fortunate in your faith, Ralph. Those of us who don't entirely share it have no such certainty that everything is for the best. We feel ourselves to be faced with choices. And we can't always be sure that we have made the right decision. If your son had not lived, would that also have been God's will?'

'Of course. Everything.' Understanding suddenly what she meant, he stared at her with a horror undiminished by any of the doubts which he himself had felt a few moments earlier. 'The soul of a new-born child is perfect, however imperfect the body may be. You could not have killed a living creature, Margaret.'

'No,' she agreed. 'There was a moment in which I

thought the baby might never draw his first breath, and I wasted that moment in asking myself whether I should take any steps to help him. But, for all his deformity, his constitution is strong. He struggled with his own body and pulled himself into life. And then, as you say, I could not have killed him. Because it is my instinct and my profession to preserve life, because I would never have been able to face you and Lydia either with a lie or with the truth, and because I should never have been able to live with my own conscience. At the moment when you came in I was asking myself whether, when he grows to be a man, he will ever be able to forgive me. I'm grateful that you are able to bring me reassurance. The choice was never my own. The will of God had already determined what should happen.'

As a preacher Ralph knew that he ought to argue with his sister and banish the bitterness from her voice. But as a father and a husband he was too anxious and unhappy. Ignoring the cries of the baby in the cradle, he opened his arms to embrace Margaret, and they clung together for consolation.

7

When a great fear proves to be groundless, lesser worries expand to take its place. Lydia did not die, and Ralph ought to have been happy. But even after Margaret assured him that the moment of danger had passed, he fretted at the slowness of his wife's recovery, wondering whether she would ever regain her normal energy and resentful of the demands of the new baby who sapped whatever strength she had with his constant demands to be put to the breast and disturbance of her sleep with his cries. There was little he could do about it, for Lydia refused to surrender her responsibilities to any of those members of the community who would willingly have helped her. Ralph could feel grateful only that Margaret agreed to stay longer than had at first been arranged, continuing to care for the health of the village while Lydia devoted herself to Grant.

But as the weeks passed, he realized that his sister was beginning to feel her absence from Robert. Ashamed that he had extended his demands on her time by so long, he sent to Kingston to discover the dates on which William's banana boats would be leaving the harbour.

The answer had not yet arrived in Hope Valley when Margaret, joining Ralph in a stroll through the orange groves of Pastor's Vineyard, suggested quietly to him that Lydia ought not to risk another pregnancy.

'Do you think we intended this one!' he exclaimed. He was silent for a moment. But his feeling of guilt was so strong that he could not resist the opportunity to abase himself.

'After the deaths of the younger children, of course we were both very unhappy. It affected us in different ways. I wanted to be reassured by love. But Lydia's reaction to the tragedy was different. She was upset by the wastefulness of bringing children into the world if they were to be stolen from her, and was determined to have no more. And it was worse than that – as though she hardly dared to allow herself to love anyone for a little while, lest he too should be suddenly snatched away from her. She withdrew from me in a way – although not, I think, because she loved me any less.'

'I can understand that,' said Margaret.

'It was a worrying time. I longed to comfort her, but she couldn't accept comfort. For eighteen months, or even longer, the situation between us was a difficult one.

And then, about a year ago, the school was opened in Hope Valley. The first teacher who came was a woman. A very beautiful woman – well, you've seen her. She's still here. Chelsea Mattison.'

Margaret nodded. In a community where many of the women grew fat when their youth was over, she must have noticed the teacher's slim grace as well as her intelligent eyes.

'I'd known her when she was a girl. In fact, she was the one – ' Ralph paused. Many years had passed since Chelsea, then only sixteen, had offered herself to him at a time when illness had left him too weak to resist. He had discussed his problems with Margaret at the time, but could not remember how far he had gone into details. He decided not to be specific now. Chelsea had been discreet about the consequence of that night, moving away from the valley for the birth of her baby and returning only when the boy was old enough to live with his grandfather. Even Duke himself did not know who his father was. 'She was a clever girl. I provided the means for her to be educated. That made it difficult for me to refuse her the position when she wished to return. She was grateful, and like so many of the women here, she had few inhibitions about the way in which she could demonstrate her gratitude. The temptation put in my way was very great.'

'You resisted, though?'

'Yes,' said Ralph. 'But at a price. I needed Lydia's support. She gave me everything I asked for, but I asked too much. Or gave too much. Because of course I hoped that she too could be helped to forget her loss.' Ralph remembered that time in silence for a moment. Sometimes during these past weeks he had wondered whether it would have done less harm if he had followed the instincts which had so much shamed him at the time, and

163

had looked for comfort in Chelsea's bed instead of his wife's. But of course his conscience would not have allowed him to take that path. 'Lydia's age and the state of her health deceived us both into thinking that the danger of another pregnancy was past.'

'What about her health now?' asked Margaret. 'And the children! Are you satisfied that it's safe to stay here?'

Ralph shook his head helplessly. 'How can we know what is safe?' he asked. 'This is our home. We've made our lives here, and there's nothing waiting for us anywhere else. Lydia, like yourself, needs to feel that her time is usefully employed, and her work here is of inestimable value. As for the danger of fever – ' It was difficult for Ralph to speak without emotion about the killing disease which had struck so cruelly into his family. But he forced himself to tell her the facts as scientifically as he could.

'You in England probably learned before us of Major Ross's discovery that malaria is carried by mosquitoes,' he said. 'It came to Lydia's attention through a medical journal only about three years ago. I had suffered several times from malaria, and she determined that there should be no more attacks in Hope Valley.' He was able to smile as he remembered the efficiency and energy with which she had conducted her campaign. 'She set all the children to work, making them report every place in which mosquitoes could breed. Some places we covered and some we drained. She showed the children pictures and specimens of the mosquito and its larvae, so that they could recognize their enemy, and as she set about the work of eradicating it from the valley she discovered that there were two distinct varieties breeding here. We cleared both of them out together, of course, and encouraged other villages nearer to the big swamps to do the same. Since that time we have had no case in our community of either malaria or yellow fever, and Lydia has become convinced that if one type of mosquito spread the malaria, the other may well in the past have been responsible for the epidemics of fever. She is still vigilant, but we have lost our old fears of another attack. In other respects, the climate is a healthy one.'

'I find it very hot,' said Margaret.

'But we now find England too cold.' He looked up as Lydia, walking slowly, came along the path to join them. 'I've been telling Margaret of your campaign against stagnant water.'

'So you've persuaded her, I hope, to visit us again in a more leisurely way – to enjoy a holiday instead of allowing herself to be overworked. Will you promise to come back, Margaret? Now that Robert has gone away to school, and with Alexa so independent, you will have much greater freedom. It's because of Alexa that I came out to find you. A letter has just arrived from her.'

'You'll want to read it now,' said Ralph. He could see the eagerness in his sister's eyes, but his true reason for suggesting that they should all sit down for a few moments was to allow his wife to rest. He chatted with Lydia as Margaret tore the letter open and began to read it.

Everywhere in the orange grove there was noise. Birds shrieked and chattered, cicadas and tree frogs shrilled out their incessant high-pitched notes, water tumbled along the irrigation channels and, from a neighbouring field in which yams were growing, a group of workers sang as they hoed. But around the three Europeans there was a sudden electric silence, charged by the intensity of Margaret's reaction to what she was reading.

'There's no bad news, I hope?' Ralph asked.

Margaret put the letter into her pocket. When she looked up to answer, her eyes were both anxious and angry.

'There's news to disturb me,' she said. 'If you feel well enough now, Lydia, I would like to go home. I have written often enough to Alexa in these past years, hoping that she would return to England. Now it appears that she plans to do so, and I must be there when she arrives.'

'Of course,' agreed Lydia. 'But I would have expected you to look forward to that only with happiness.'

'Although she doesn't go into detail, I suspect that she is looking forward to more than merely a season at Covent Garden. It seems that she has met Matthew in Paris. And he also is proposing to return to London.'

'I remember that they were great friends as children in the schoolroom,' commented Ralph. So much of his life had been spent abroad that he could not pretend to know either of the young people well. He had the feeling now that he was being in some way obtuse, for it was certainly not apparent to him why it should so clearly be costing his sister an effort to control her feelings.

'If I read between the lines, I have to wonder whether they are planning to be more than friends. Alexa has been able to explain to me now what neither she nor I were ever properly able to understand before – why William, who disliked her, should have taken active steps to start her on a career. He realized, it seems, as I did not, that during her stay at Bristol ten years ago Alexa and Matthew fell in love with each other. Everything he did was designed to make sure that they should not meet again. Alexa writes in great resentment about his behaviour to her. But I have other grounds for anger. William never told me what the situation was.'

'Would that have made so much difference?'

'I haven't been open with Alexa,' Margaret said. 'She doesn't know who her father was. I intended to tell her the truth on her twenty-first birthday.'

'I see. And you didn't do so?'

'She was abroad by then, and to make a bald announcement by letter – ' Margaret checked her excuses and shook her head. 'No,' she said. 'I didn't do so. I'm very much to blame. But if William had given me even the slightest hint – '

It had taken even Ralph several minutes to understand what it was that was causing Margaret so much anguish. Lydia, whose weakness made her less quick-witted than usual and who was in any case less familiar with the history of the Lorimer family, made no pretence of being anything but puzzled.

'Why do you feel guilty about it? What is the problem?' she asked.

'If Matthew and Alexa have met again, isn't it all too likely that they may have fallen in love again? And as far as they themselves know, there need be no impediment to their happiness. What I shall have to tell Alexa now, and what I ought to have told her long ago, is that she is Matthew's aunt. They will never be able to marry.'

8

To travel from one country to another may be tiring, but when the same journey crosses the frontier of a new sort of life, it increases in excitement at every moment. By the time Alexa arrived in London she had forgotten the tedium of the hours which had passed since she left Naples and her eyes shone with the delight of seeing Margaret again after such a long separation.

Before they could do more than embrace and stammer their first greetings, the luggage must be carried in. Alexa had brought back to England everything she owned. She was not accustomed to travel with all her possessions at once and was amused by Betty's wide-eyed astonishment as valises, hat-boxes, jewel cases and portmanteaux were carried upstairs.

Her maid could look after the unpacking. Alexa herself followed Margaret straight into the drawing room, and for an hour or more kisses and compliments were interspersed with jumbled items of news drawn from the past ten years.

Gradually Alexa felt herself becoming calmer. She was able to accept a drink of tea, to sit and smile.

'What are your plans?' Margaret asked her. 'Is this only a brief visit, or do you intend to return permanently to England?'

It was too soon for Alexa to answer that question fully, but in one respect she could be specific. 'I have agreed to sing at Covent Garden during the first half of the season,' she said. 'After Christmas, nothing is decided. I was invited to return to Naples, but I've turned that down. And only the day before I left there I received an invitation to sing with Caruso in San Francisco next spring. I shall reject that offer as well. How can anyone seriously expect me to travel halfway across the world, away from all my friends, beyond the bounds of civilization?'

'A city which has an opera house can't be wholly uncivilized,' laughed Margaret. 'But for my own sake I'm glad that you don't propose to go so far away. Speaking of your friends, Alexa, I told Lord Glanville that you planned to return. He has arranged a ball for you at Blaize. I am to tell you that he is sure you will be the star of the winter season; he intends to presume on his acquaintance by being the first to present you to society.'

'He's very kind, considering how long it is since we last saw each other, and under what unfavourable circumstances.'

168

'What were they?'

'He called on me one evening after a performance – an evening on which I was previously engaged to dine with another gentleman. I owe Lord Glanville so much that I ought to have freed myself for his company. But I was taken by surprise, and the two men had quarrelled once before – well, I mismanaged the occasion. It's generous of him to forgive me. You've continued your own acquaintance with him, then, since he found your hospital post for you?'

'We see a good deal of each other when he is in England,' Margaret said. 'We are friends, in fact.' The tone of her voice as she spoke of him intrigued Alexa, and she would have pressed for further details, but Margaret was still speaking. 'And have you maintained your relationship with the Duke of Caversham?'

Alexa was tempted to be annoyed. She could never have expected Margaret to approve, but she had hoped that the news would not have reached her. Certainly she herself had never mentioned the duke's name in any of her letters. 'You know about that, then?' she said.

'It's no great secret, is it?'

'Are you shocked?'

'I was when I first heard. Shocked but perhaps not surprised.'

'I remember, you always regarded the theatre as a cradle of sin. Well, all that is over now. I gave Caversham his *congé* in the spring, and he announced his engagement while you were in Jamaica. His debts were pressing, because the estate is entailed and he had mortgaged its revenues for many years ahead. His mother succeeded in finding an heiress from Boston whose parents were prepared to pay handsomely for the pleasure of seeing their daughter a duchess. She's said to be a young lady with a mind of her own, and scornful of some of our European customs. It's thought that – at least for a little while – she may expect fidelity in exchange for her fortune. She's welcome to him as far as I'm concerned. I can promise you, my heart is far from being broken.'

Had she chosen to do so, she could have taken the opportunity then to tell Margaret her news. But the happiness she felt in her love for Matthew made her hug the secret to herself a little longer. He would come soon to see her, she was sure, and they would make their announcement together.

The maid who had come with her from Italy appeared in the doorway and began to murmur questions in her own language.

'Will you excuse me for a few moments?' Alexa asked. 'There are one or two decisions to be made. Which jewels should go to the bank: that sort of thing. And I ought to change my dress. The journey has left me dirty.'

'Of course,' said Margaret. 'You must be very tired. But Alexa, when you are refreshed, and before you go out or make any arrangements, will you allow me time for a serious discussion?'

'That sounds most forbidding.'

'I don't intend it to. But you already know that I have something which should have been handed to you on your twenty-first birthday. And there is an explanation which must go with it.'

'I shall be back very soon.' Alexa embraced her guardian again and ran lightly up the stairs. She threw off her travelling clothes and wrapped herself in a light robe of smocked silk as she supervised the stowing-away of her possessions. At one moment, while she was speaking to the maid, she heard the ring of the front door bell, but took no notice. Margaret's callers were no concern of hers. It must have been twenty minutes later that she glanced out of the window and was startled by the sight of a young man in the street below, walking away from the house with a reluctant lack of speed.

Surely that was Matthew! Barefoot as she was, Alexa flew downstairs and arrived panting in the drawing room.

'Has Matthew been here?' she demanded.

Margaret was standing beside a small table, looking down at a box which lay open on its surface. Her expression was unhappy, and Alexa was forced to repeat the question before it was answered.

'He has called, yes. And he will call again tomorrow.'

'Why should he need to wait?' Alexa moved towards the door again, but Margaret put a hand on her arm.

'Alexa! You can't go outside like that. Nor could you receive a gentleman in such a state. I guarantee that Matthew will return tomorrow. He told me that you had agreed to let him paint your portrait. His call was to arrange a time for the sittings. But one day's delay will do no harm. And you have promised me time for a conversation before you embark on your social life in London.'

Alexa's mouth pouted in petulance. She was quite accustomed to receiving gentlemen in the dressing rooms of opera houses in a much less modest attire than her present robe. But it would never do to quarrel with Margaret on the very first day of her stay. She sighed a little, and then smiled. 'Then let us have this conversation now and get it out of the way.'

'First of all I have some jewellery to hand over to you,' Margaret said. 'When you see its richness, you will understand why I was so unwilling to send it out to you in Italy. And you seemed to feel little impatience to receive it, even after I told you it was here.'

'You told me the jewels were a gift from my father, and I have no interest in my father,' said Alexa. She spoke indifferently, but that did not prevent her from moving to stand beside Margaret.

A small leather case stood open on the table, with its velvet-lined drawers pulled out in front of it. Alexa caught her breath as she looked down at the necklace of rubies, set in silver and diamonds, with matching ear-rings and a hairpiece in which diamond-veined leaves trembled round a rose petalled in more rubies.

'It's true,' she said slowly, 'that I had never imagined they would be so beautiful.' She unbuttoned the top of her silk robe and held the necklace against her skin, moving across to a glass in which she could study herself. 'The stones suit my colouring as though they had been chosen for me.'

'And so they were,' Margaret told her. 'Tell me, Alexa, why have you felt such a coldness towards your father, when you cannot really remember him?'

'That is the reason,' Alexa answered. 'He is a stranger to me. How should I feel warmth towards a man I've never met? What do I know of him? Only that he allowed my dear mother to starve. And if he could afford a gift like this, it would hardly seem that he could plead poverty on his own part as an excuse.'

'He died,' said Margaret. 'He couldn't help that.'

'It's usual for some provision to be made in such circumstances.' The coldness of Alexa's voice reflected her feelings.

'This was the provision he made,' said Margaret. 'If your mother refused to turn jewels into food after he was dead, that was not his fault either.'

Alexa shrugged her shoulders. 'I'm not concerned to attack him,' she said. 'What I told you before was true. I have no interest in him. If he were still alive, I would give him back his jewels. Since you say he is dead, I might as well accept them, because they are certainly

172

very pretty. But if you are proposing now to tell me who he was, you needn't trouble yourself. My dear mother and my dear guardian have been all the family I need.'

'It's necessary for me to tell you,' said Margaret. 'And then you will tell me that I should have done it long ago. I'm afraid you will be very angry with me.'

'How could I be angry with you when you have accepted all my own follies without a word of reproach?' Alexa kissed Margaret affectionately and then sat down with a patient expression on her face to hear whatever she had to be told.

'Your mother was my music teacher when I was a girl,' Margaret began. 'She was very beautiful. You may not remember that, because the time of her poverty began almost as soon as you were out of babyhood. Her colouring was dark, not like yours at all, but she had the same grace and slender elegance as you. At that time, the time of my music lessons, my mother was still alive, but was an invalid – or at least, she called herself one. She had retreated from my father. He was an old man by then, but still vigorous. And he was lonely.'

Alexa's quick mind understood at once what Margaret was about to tell her, but the conclusion was too extraordinary for her to accept at once. 'Your father?' she whispered incredulously.

'My father, John Junius Lorimer. Your mother was proud. When she discovered she was pregnant, she made no claim on him. She went away, in fact, to London. But later he discovered where she was, and saw you for the first time. His daughter. You must never feel cold to him again, Alexa, for in the time that was left to him, he adored you. He gave your mother an establishment of her own and for a little while she lived in comfort and gave comfort to him. But – well, you've heard often enough from me the story of how Lorimer's Bank collapsed. My father was ruined both in reputation and in estate. Everything he owned was owed to the bank's creditors. He was able to conceal the rubies from them only by a subterfuge which came near to being criminal. There was no way at all in which he could have given you or your mother more, and I know this caused him great unhappiness. He spoke of you in the very moment of his death. Your father loved you very much, Alexa – more, I believe, than he loved any of his other children.'

Alexa was too stunned to speak. Everything that had happened to her in her life, it seemed, must be reappraised in a new light, and she hardly knew where to start. 'So you are my sister,' she whispered at last.

'Your half-sister, yes. And William and Ralph are your half-brothers.' With an unexpected firmness Margaret looked straight into Alexa's eyes. 'And Matthew,' she said, 'is your nephew.'

'No!' There had been a moment, or perhaps only a second, in which Alexa had been poised on the brink of happiness at the thought that she was linked by blood to the woman for whom she had always felt a deep affection. Now, abruptly, delight turned to disaster. 'It's not possible!' she cried. 'He is older than I – he cannot surely – ' But even as she fought against the discovery she knew that it must be true. Groaning, she buried her head in her hands and felt Margaret sitting beside her. A comforting arm gripped her shoulders, but she could not accept comfort. For a long time neither of them spoke.

'This is why William behaved as he did all those years ago,' said Margaret at last.

Alexa dried her eyes and tried to steady her emotions by breathing deeply. 'Neither Matthew nor I could understand what led him to be so unkind,' she said. 'Why could he not simply have told us the truth?'

'He has always refused to recognize the relationship with you publicly, and presumably he felt satisfied that as a result of his deceptions you and Matthew would never meet again.'

'And you?' Alexa tried to conceal the bitterness she felt, but Margaret's unhappy expression made it clear that no accusation was needed to make her feel guilty.

'When your mother died, you were still a child,' she said. 'I wasn't married then – in fact, I had no expectation that I would ever marry. Although I had qualified as a doctor, I was experiencing difficulty in finding employment. If I was to bring you up, I needed William's help. His generosity was conditional on my promise of silence. At that time, I must confess, it didn't seem important. Later on I most certainly ought to have told you. I had intended it all to come together – the jewels and the truth – on your twenty-first birthday, but by then you had left England. To send the jewels seemed unsafe and to make a written announcement of your parentage was somehow too formal. I wanted to break down your coldness to the memory of your father by convincing you of the warmth of his love. And of course I didn't expect you to stay away so long. I'm afraid I allowed the matter to drift. I warned you that you would be angry with me. Neither you nor William had ever mentioned your attachment to Matthew. Until your letter arrived in Jamaica, I had no idea how important it was that you should have known years ago – and no suspicion that it was important still. I've been very much at fault. I'm sorry, Alexa.'

'You've guessed, then, that Matthew and I planned to marry?'

'Yes. Although only today did I feel sure of it.'

'And does all this matter?' Alexa asked. 'We are of the same generation. To say that we are aunt and nephew is only a form of words.'

'It's a legal impediment,' Margaret pointed out. 'No one who knew the truth could perform a marriage service. And anyone who told the truth could prevent the marriage.'

'I remember when I was eighteen,' Alexa began; for a moment she paused to savour the bitterness of the memory. 'Matthew asked me whether there was any chance that I might be *your* daughter. You had given us a lecture the previous day – I wonder whether you remember? – on the dangers of in-breeding, of marrying a first cousin. And yet if we were first cousins there would be no legal bar to our marriage. Why should this be any different?'

Margaret's gesture was compassionate. 'I can only say that it is. And if you consider the matter, the child of an aunt and nephew would be genetically more at risk than that of cousins. It would be a risk which you ought not to take even if the law were to permit it.'

'Does Matthew know?' Alexa demanded.

'Not yet. I wanted you to hear it first. He will have to be told, of course.'

Alexa received this in silence and could see that her lack of agreement was causing her guardian – who must now be thought of as a sister – anxiety.

'Alexa, there is no choice! It would be easiest, I imagine, if I were to tell him, so that you need not meet again. I understand what an unhappy situation it is for you both.'

'But he is going to paint my portrait,' Alexa pointed out.

'It would surely be wise to abandon that project. The strain – '

Alexa interrupted with a sudden determination in her voice. 'Matthew has left his life in Paris, and all his friends, for my sake,' she said. 'It was agreed between us

176

that he should paint me at a time while I am of some interest in London, so that all the most beautiful women in society will see the picture and hurry to commission their own portraits from him. If I have to deprive him of his hopes of marriage, he must at least have the chance to make his fortune. Will you leave it to me, Margaret, to tell him?'

It was Margaret's turn to be silent, and Alexa could guess why. Nor were the older woman's doubts unjustified, for already Alexa's mind was searching for some solution to the problem.

'I reminded you earlier of the risk to any children who might be born to you and Matthew,' Margaret said at last. Alexa could tell from the way she spoke that the subject was distasteful to her. 'You must realize as well that standards in England are different from those which you may have encountered on the Continent. If you lived with Matthew as anything but a wife, you would not be received in Society here. Nor would many rich gentlemen allow their wives to visit Matthew's studio, however great his skill as portrait painter.'

'I'm not tied to England. I can make a living anywhere. I don't care about Society. I don't care about marriage ceremonies.'

'All this has come as a great shock to you, Alexa, and it's natural that you should be upset,' said Margaret quietly. 'I've told you already how much I blame myself for what happened. Please don't add too much to the weight of guilt on my shoulders. And remember that if you were to deprive yourself of a proper family life in the way you're suggesting, you would be robbing Matthew of the same thing.'

'Yes, I'll remember,' said Alexa. 'But we've both suffered, Matthew and I, from his father's refusal to let us discuss the true situation frankly between us. Now that we're adults, we have the right to settle our own affairs. When Matthew calls tomorrow, I will see him. And as soon as the time is right, I'll tell him the truth. And now, if you will excuse me, Margaret, I think I'd like to retire at once. I've been travelling so long that I'm very tired.'

Alexa was exaggerating. Physically she was almost inexhaustible and could have travelled on for another week had it been necessary. But it was true that the day had drained her in a way she could not have anticipated. The joy of her reunion with Margaret had been over-shadowed by the news she had learned, and her emotions were strained to breaking point. She kissed her sister and prepared to leave the room.

'You're forgetting your legacy,' said Margaret.

Alexa turned back to the table and stared down at the jewels as they lay on their beds of black velvet. She did not move to touch them.

'The Lorimer legacy!' she exclaimed, unable any longer to restrain the bitterness she felt. 'It seems to me that the true legacy I have inherited consists of lies and deceptions and miseries. I wish I had not been born a Lorimer. I wish that I had no right to these. They bring me nothing but unhappiness.'

'You are not the first to suffer on their account,' said Margaret, her voice dropping almost to a whisper. Alexa glanced at her in surprise, but was given no explanation. 'But no one else has any claim on them. You had better take them. If you choose to sell them or give them away, that is your own affair. They are yours. And try to believe that your true legacy is one of love, a father's love for his daughter. The lies have come later. You must not put any of that blame on him.'

For a moment longer Alexa looked down at the jewellery. Then, nodding to herself, as though to acknowledge that Margaret had spoken the truth, she carried the case upstairs.

<h1 style="text-align:center">9</h1>

A house which descends through a single family acquires a special atmosphere of security. Often during the past ten years Margaret had spent weekends in Lord Glanville's country house, Blaize, and she found that in a curious way it reminded her of Brinsley House. Anyone else might only have been conscious of the superficial differences. Blaize was older and very much larger than Margaret's childhood home, designed on a spacious scale which would have been impossible on the limited site above the Avon Gorge; it was surrounded not just by gardens, but by a large park, with farmland extensive enough to be divided amongst a dozen tenants. Although, like Brinsley House, it enjoyed a river view, the gentle wooded slope towards the Thames had nothing in common with the sheer cliffs above the Avon. The true resemblance between the two houses was one of history.

Blaize was the seat of a rich family whose place in the social order had been undisturbed through many generations and seemed settled enough to endure for ever. Lord Glanville did not live ostentatiously, but his wealth was considerable and he took it for granted, expecting to leave to his heirs the same estate that he had inherited from his ancestors.

In just such a way had John Junius Lorimer believed that his style of life was secure. There was a difference of scale, naturally, between both the fortunes and the expenses of the two men, and John Junius had always expected to work for his living, an attitude not shared by any of the Glanvilles. But Margaret had been brought up in a prosperous household which took for granted the leisured comfort of the family and the unobtrusive efficiency of the servants. During all her visits to Blaize she felt at home in a way which might not have been expected of a woman who depended on her own professional work for her income.

Most of her previous visits had been quiet ones, but this was different. The ball which Lord Glanville was giving for Alexa – for which even his house in Park Lane had proved too small – had been organized on a grand scale.

Margaret had brought Betty with her. It was a very long time indeed since Betty had acted as a lady's maid. Nowadays she was a housekeeper, in sole charge of running Margaret's home while her mistress worked at the hospital. The reversion to her old role might have seemed a come-down, but the hierarchical society of the servants' hall at Blaize ensured that for the duration of her stay she would enjoy a luxurious holiday with few duties to interrupt her. She insisted, of course, on justifying her presence by preparing her mistress for the ball.

'It's a good many years since you last dressed my hair so elaborately, Betty,' laughed Margaret. 'Dancing and doctoring don't seem to go together.'

'More's the pity,' Betty said, biting her lip in concentration as she pinned a spray of feathers into the swept-up coiffure she had created. Even with Queen Alexandra's example to point to she had not been able to persuade her mistress that a fringe of curls over the forehead would be becoming. 'There. You're done. I remember that last time. It was when the Prince of Wales came to Bristol.'

'Yes.' Margaret stared at herself in the glass, remembering a time when her forehead had been smooth, her hair bright and springy – oh, how she had hated the unruly redness of her hair! – and her eyes had sparkled with happiness, untroubled by any premonition of what was to come. When Alexa swept into the room to be admired before the first of the guests from outside arrived, it was difficult for Margaret to smile with the gaiety required of her.

'How lovely you look!' she exclaimed. 'And you've decided not to reject the rubies after all.'

'It seemed an occasion on which to be respectable,' laughed Alexa. 'My other jewels have come from sources which I might not wish to confess. But a legacy from a father cannot be criticized. Why does the sight of them make you want to cry?'

Margaret was disconcerted to find that her reaction was so noticeable. She had no intention of ever revealing to anyone the fact that it was the existence of the rubies, suddenly discovered by Charles in the first year of their marriage, which had caused her husband to ride furiously away from the house to his death. But these jewels had been responsible for so much unhappiness over the years that it was not difficult to think of another explanation of her mood.

'I remember the first time my mother wore them,' she said, and had intended to go on when Alexa interrupted.

'*Your* mother? Surely you mean *my* mother.'

Margaret shook her head. 'Our father had the setting made ostensibly for his wife. Only after she had worn them once did he give them to Luisa to keep for you.'

'And what was the occasion you remembered?' Alexa asked.

'My mother wore the jewels to a ball in 1878,' said Margaret. 'The Prince of Wales had come to visit Bristol. It was the grandest event the city had known for years. But I didn't care a fig for the Prince of Wales. The important thing, as far as I was concerned, was that my engagement was announced on that evening.'

'To Dr Scott?'

'No. This was long before I met Charles. I was engaged to a young man called David Gregson.'

'What happened?'

'He was the manager of Lorimer's Bank and was involved in the criminal proceedings which followed its crash. He left the country to avoid imprisonment, and asked me to go with him. But we quarrelled over the extent to which my father was involved in the irregularities of the bank's affairs. David was right and I was wrong; but by the time I discovered that, it was too late. He'd gone.'

'Where?' asked Alexa.

'I never knew. There were ships sailing out of Bristol at that time to almost every corner of the world. He could have taken passage on any of them. I had no way of guessing which he chose. All I know is that he left England and I haven't heard from him since. None of that has anything to do with the ball. It's just that on that evening, dancing with the man I loved, I was happier than I'd ever been in my life before. Everything seemed too wonderful to last.' Margaret forced herself to laugh and spoke more briskly, pushing away sentimental memories. 'And it *didn't* last. The troubles of the Lorimers began almost before the bandsmen had finished packing away their instruments. That was the last evening of my life on which I could look ahead and see nothing but joy.'

'Perhaps tonight will bring you an equal experience of hope.'

'I doubt it,' said Margaret. 'Only the young can persuade themselves that perfect happiness will last for ever. And this is *your* night, not mine.'

'You are not to speak as though your life were over,'

Alexa commanded her. 'And if we don't stop talking about the ball of 1878 and make haste to appear at the ball of 1905, it will take place without us.'

'I'll leave you to make your entrance alone,' said Margaret, accepting the change of mood and smiling at her beautiful sister.

'Tonight, as I warned you earlier, I intend to prove that even an opera singer can be respectable. I have no intention of appearing without my chaperone.'

She drew Margaret to her feet and kissed her affectionately. The band was already playing as they walked together down the wide staircase.

For all Alexa's protestations, she spent little time at Margaret's side. Not only was she more beautiful than the fashionable society guests whom Lord Glanville had invited; she was also vivacious in a way which made them seem vapid by comparison. The sparkle of her personality dominated the ballroom as strongly as at other times it could hold spellbound a theatre audience. She refused to make a programme, so that after every dance she was surrounded by would-be partners pressing their claims. She danced energetically, although always with grace, and her laughter rippled round the room. Only for a few moments after the supper dance had ended did she seem to withdraw herself in some way from the gaiety which surrounded her; but Margaret, noticing this as she returned from her own supper, saw also the manner in which Alexa straightened her shoulders and held her head even higher than before, putting on the cloak of vivacity again as though it were an operatic role.

'Will you sit this dance out with me?' asked Lord Glanville, appearing at Margaret's side.

'I would very much prefer to dance it with you,' answered Margaret, preferring honesty to conventional politeness. She was not altogether reconciled to the fact that the expected place for a widow of forty-eight was a small gold chair at the edge of the ballroom, and for some time her toes had been tapping to the beat of the music. Lord Glanville smiled as he offered his arm and led her on to the floor. But it was clear that his real wish was to talk to her. The dance, a polka, was too energetic to allow for conversation. As soon as it was over he repeated his previous invitation.

They stood together on the stone terrace immediately outside the ballroom. The moon was bright, and caught the sheen of silks and satins as some of the younger dancers left the floor to stroll in couples between the clipped yew hedges of the formal garden below.

'Alexa added the names of some of her own friends to the guest list tonight,' said Lord Glanville. 'Do you know who the young man was with the thick fair hair? I think he may have left by now.'

Margaret's heart warmed with compassion for her host. She had been quick to notice that Matthew had been present earlier in the evening. Although only she could have been aware of the true situation, everyone in the ballroom must have noticed that at the start of the ball Alexa had danced more often with him than with any other partner, and had chosen to give him those dances, such as the waltz, in which he could hold her in his arms. But although Lord Glanville had reason for jealousy as far as Alexa's emotions were concerned, the fact that Alexa loved Matthew but had discovered that she could not marry him might in fact prove to be to the older man's advantage.

'That was my nephew, Matthew Lorimer,' Margaret answered. 'You may remember my introducing you to his sister, Beatrice, at one of your women's suffrage meetings. She is the representative of the Bristol group.

Alexa was educated in Matthew's schoolroom. They are childhood friends – like brother and sister.'

'One could wish that one's own sisters had ever been so affectionate!' His attempt to speak lightly was not very successful. Margaret could see his knuckles whiten with tension as he gripped the edge of the stone balustrade. 'She is so beautiful!' he exclaimed, as though unable any longer to control his feelings. 'She smiles at me and my heart breaks with happiness, and then I see that she has the same smile for every other man who dances with her. I recognize that she will never care for me. With any other woman I would have accepted the fact years ago and looked somewhere else for happiness. But Alexa is so lovely that if I cannot have her, no one else will do. One can call oneself a fool without being able to put foolishness aside.'

'There is still time – ' began Margaret, but Lord Glanville shook his head.

'There is plenty of time for her, but not for me,' he said. 'She's twenty years younger than I am. For long enough already she has thought of me as an old man, and soon it will be true.' He shook the subject away with a sigh and accompanied Margaret back to the warmth of the ballroom. They stood together for a moment and watched Alexa as she whirled round the floor. Her cheeks, usually pale, were flushed, and there seemed to be an element almost of desperation in the gaiety with which she tossed her head to the beat of the music. Matthew was no longer to be seen.

Twice in her own life Margaret's heart had ached when she found herself parted from a man she loved by circumstances she had no power to alter. As her eyes now followed Alexa round the ballroom her heart ached again, this time in sympathy for another young couple who were separated by the very same family heritage which had caused so much unhappiness in the past. Alexa was an actress, who perhaps found it easier to perform the part of a beauty without a care in the world in front of an audience. But it had been cruel of her, Margaret thought to herself, to force Matthew as well to come to terms with the facts of so unexpected a situation in a public setting. Margaret took it for granted, as she recognized the tension in her sister's slim body, that Alexa had at last told Matthew the truth and sent him away.

10

Sympathy with the mood of another person makes it easy to anticipate what she will do. Much later on the night of the ball – in fact, only a little while before dawn – Margaret ignored her weariness and went in search of her half-sister. All the other guests had by now left the house or, if they were members of the house party, retired to bed, but Margaret was sure that Alexa would still be awake and could guess where to find her.

She was in the music room, playing the piano with no light but that of the moon. In spite of the darkness she was aware of Margaret's entry. Her hands dropped on to her lap and she swivelled to face the door.

'You've had a triumph, Alexa.'

Alexa's laugh was soft, almost bitter. 'I've had four proposals of marriage this evening,' she said, 'although each time I tried to prevent the words being spoken, so that I need not be cruel enough to refuse them. Was it you who said I would never find a husband in London?'

'I'm glad to hear that I was wrong. Were you not prepared to accept any?'

The moonlight caught the blonde glint in Alexa's hair

as she shook her head. 'I'm not the plain daughter of a poor man, who must marry at all costs the first suitor to approach her,' she said. 'A woman who commands fees as high as mine can afford to be sentimental and wait for a true love to come along.'

'Very often love grows after marriage,' suggested Margaret.

'And very often it does not. If my only ambition were to be a countess or a baroness I might take the risk; but I care nothing for that.'

'Was Piers one of your admirers?' asked Margaret.

'Yes, Lord Glanville did me that honour.'

'And could you not feel – ?'

'No,' said Alexa. 'I could not. I was able to assure him of my great affection for him, as well as my undying gratitude. But in the time of my trouble he was like a father to me, and I can't think of him in any other way. He should marry someone like yourself – someone who loves him and is of his own generation, able to give him companionship.'

'Alexa! You surely didn't say anything like that!'

'Why should I not? I could hardly help noticing your feelings as soon as I returned, but men are very often blind until someone shows them where to look.'

'How could you! Oh, Alexa, you had no right to talk of me in such a way.' Margaret's cheeks flamed as she remembered the conversation on the terrace. 'You've humiliated him by forcing him almost to apologize to me for being unable to love me, and you've humiliated me by forcing me to listen. How shall I ever be able to face him again?'

'I think you make too much of it,' said Alexa, but there was a doubt in her voice. 'I'm sorry, Margaret, if I have been unkind. I was thinking only of myself and Lord Glanville when I spoke like that. He has been so kind to me that I could hardly bear to hurt him, and I thought it might help if – oh yes, you are right. I ought not to have spoken in such a way.'

For a moment neither of them broke the silence. But Margaret had sought out Alexa for a special reason, and did not intend to leave without the reassurance she hoped for. 'I saw that Matthew was here earlier in the evening – and noticed that he left before the end of the ball.'

'Yes,' agreed Alexa, her voice giving nothing away.

'May I suppose that you have told him of your relationship?'

'Yes, you may suppose it,' said Alexa. 'I have told him that he is my nephew. And I told him at the same time that I loved him, and that I cared nothing for marriage lines, and that I could not be frightened by talk of incest.'

'Alexa!'

'Well, it's so ridiculous!' exclaimed Alexa. 'A matter of convention only. There have been societies in which kings habitually married their sisters and were praised for doing so. Why should my whole life be ruined by some arbitrary rule? I told Matthew that I wanted nothing more than to live with him in some place where no questions would be asked, or where the answers would not be important. The talents we each exercise are not dependent on social approval.'

Margaret was shocked by what she heard, but did not express her horror. There had been no explanation yet of Matthew's departure or Alexa's own tense expression. 'What did Matthew say?' she asked.

'He withdrew for a little while. To think about it, he said – but also, I suppose, to watch me. And the result of his consideration was that he thought I ought to marry. He even went so far as to choose my husband. Like you – I suspect – he saw me as a peeress. He was not prepared, apparently, to feel responsible for my social ostracism.

He will not allow me to be anything to him but a wife; and since that is not possible, he has said goodbye to me. He claimed that it was because he loves me. But what sort of love is that, to run away at the first difficulty?'

'His behaviour is wise,' said Margaret. 'And kind, in the long run.'

'What have love and wisdom to do with each other?' Alexa's voice revealed that she was on the brink of tears.

'I understand how unhappy you are,' began Margaret, but she was interrupted before she could apologize once again for her own part in the affair.

'I am unhappy, yes, but most of all I am angry,' declared Alexa passionately. 'Why should I have to accept Matthew's judgement like this? He says he loves me – but he decides that he will go without consulting me, without listening to my wishes. What right have men to take it so much for granted that women will always accept their decisions? With any other man I at least have the choice to say yes, I will marry him or no, I will not: for that one moment of his life I have power over him, even if never again. But with Matthew I have been deprived of even that one moment. Even though he may plead that it's only for my sake that he deserts me, I'm entitled to be angry.' She paused for a moment to calm herself down and then spoke more quietly, although with an equal firmness. 'Well, that's that. Finished. Just as you thought it ought to be. I've come to a decision in the past hour, Margaret. I propose to accept the invitation to sing in San Francisco. And there are other opera houses in the New World which are anxious to attract the best singers from Europe and whose reputations are already not to be despised. It will be possible, I think, to arrange a tour. I might even decide to settle down in America. In fact, if I'm made welcome, I think it's very likely.'

Margaret's reaction to the plan were mixed. She sympathized with the feeling that a complete change of scene might prove stimulating to someone whose emotions had been under such strain. In unfamiliar surroundings Alexa might more easily forget Matthew.

'You may be right,' she agreed. 'Although I had hoped that after such a long separation we might enjoy a longer time together.'

'My wish is the same,' said Alexa. 'That's why I'm asking you now to come with me.'

For a second time since her arrival in the music room Margaret was almost too much taken aback to speak.

'But Alexa, my sabbatical year is almost at an end. I shall have to return to work at the hospital.'

'There must be opportunities for a trained doctor in America,' said Alexa, sweeping the objection aside. 'You might well meet with less prejudice in San Francisco than in London. And your experience is such that you could do nothing but good by working there. There are hundreds of people, thousands, pouring across the Atlantic every week, and most of them are poor and ignorant. The need for skills like yours must be immense.'

'But I have Robert to care for. Already this year he has been left for far too long while I visited Ralph and Lydia. And on that occasion he had William to look after him during the school holiday. I have no intention of ever allowing William to do me any favour again.'

'On the day of my return to London you spoke of the possibilities which a new life in America might hold for me,' Alexa reminded her. 'Wouldn't they be even greater for Robert? It's the land of opportunity. A boy of his age could grow up as an American, with a whole continent open to his ambition. Margaret, let us all three go. I will sing for a season. That much can be settled at once, and it will provide enough money for us to look around and decide where we might make a home, and what work we might do.'

'Why are you so anxious suddenly for this?' asked Margaret.

Alexa shrugged her pale shoulders. 'You've given the answer yourself,' she said. 'I'm in the mood to start a new life. To return to my wanderings in Europe after saying goodbye to them would seem a defeat; and since I had hoped to make a home in England as Matthew's wife, it would be painful for me to live here in any other style. The solution seems to lie in some new place which will hold no memories, and it's fortunate, I suppose, that I already have exactly the invitation I need. Matthew has set me free in order that I may marry, and perhaps I shall do so, although not at once. And if that is to happen, I must be respectable from the moment I arrive in San Francisco – chaperoned and decorous. What do you say? Will you come with me?'

'Alexa, you are too impetuous. I cannot possibly make a decision of this sort at a second's notice, without time to reflect.'

'Then I'll leave you to think about it. But I hope very much that you will come. I've been foolish in the past and run away from you, but you have never left me or ceased to love me. There is no one else to whom I can look for support.'

She stood up to face Margaret in entreaty. The whiteness of her low-cut dress and the paleness of her skin and hair gave her an ethereal look in the cold light of the moon. Only the rubies were dark, like drops of blood falling from her neck. Troubled, Margaret kissed her goodnight. As she left the music room, the piano resumed its plaintive lament.

By now it was almost morning and Margaret's body longed for rest. But her mind was teeming with questions and she knew that she would not be able to sleep until she had resolved them. Instead of returning to the bedroom allotted her, she climbed the stairs to the Long Gallery which ran the full length of the Tudor core of Blaize. She paced up and down beneath the line of Glanville portraits as she attempted to sort out her thoughts.

Her first reaction to Alexa's suggestion was to dismiss it as impossible. She was forty-eight years old. That was hardly the time to begin a new life. Yet Alexa, whether she intended it or not, had spoiled the friendship with Lord Glanville which provided the chief warmth of her life in London. And with Ralph in Jamaica, Margaret had no family ties to keep her in England. She had never been close to William, and now to past resentments was added the belief that none of Alexa's present difficulties would have arisen had he been frank both with Alexa herself and with Margaret. Alexa's account of the letter which had never been delivered had brought to the surface of her memory other half-forgotten lies. She had learned, long after the event, how William had engineered David Gregson's flight after the collapse of the bank, and she had often wondered whether she had been misled in any other way, never revealed, in order that her relationship with David might be ended. William was, to put it bluntly, a deceitful man, and her anger with him made it easy for her to break all her ties with Brinsley House.

It was true, in addition, that Robert was of an age to find adventure in a new country, and might well discover opportunities open to him there as he grew up. There was nothing in his case or her own which would decide the question either way.

Alexa's situation was a different matter. No one could force her to marry Lord Glanville, however much he wanted it and however advantageous such a marriage might seem. It was not her own fault that her hopes of happiness with Matthew had been doomed to disappointment – in fact, Margaret herself was mainly to blame, for the situation could not have arisen had she spoken out sooner. It was a responsibility which must be taken into account in considering Alexa's appeal. The angry disappointment caused by her enforced parting from Matthew might well have directed her into a way of life even wilder than had been offered her by the Duke of Caversham. If instead she was prepared to continue her career and at the same time to consider settling down in a respectable society, the choice was to her credit and deserved support. She had made the decision on impulse, no doubt, but there was good sense in what she said.

One question Margaret still had to put to herself. Accepting the fact that it would be desirable to make the journey, had she the courage? She abandoned her pacing of the gallery and threw open one of the windows, staring out at the quiet woodlands as she considered this most important point of all. Once before, as a young girl, she had been prepared to begin a new life with the man she loved – in any part of the world to which he wished to take her. But that was a long time ago, and she had put all such plans behind her when she knew that there would be no loving arm to support her in a strange country.

As vividly as though it were yesterday she remembered the names and the dates which William had written down so that she might question the captains of his ships when they returned from their long voyages. The *Rosa* from Australia; the *Diana* from Jamaica; the *Flora* from San Francisco; the *Stella* from New York. She had crumpled the paper up and thrown it away on the day she was accepted as a medical student, and had done her best never again to think of David Gregson or any of the cities in which he might now be living.

It was a coincidence that one of those cities should now be offered to her for a second time – but a coincidence which strengthened her growing resolve. When she was young she had faced disaster with determination. She was not yet too old to accept change with an equal courage.

Through the open window she could hear Alexa singing at the piano in the music room, the pure voice of her girlhood matured by her training and experience. The whole world deserved to hear such a voice. Was it possible for a woman to appear on the stage and yet to live a respectable life? It was difficult for Margaret to free herself from the prejudices of her upbringing, but the challenge stiffened her determination. If it could be done, she would help Alexa to do it. Together they would make a new life in the New World.

PART IV

San Francisco

1

Men and women, like other animals, instinctively establish themselves in a strange territory by covering the
ground and delineating boundaries on foot. On the day
after her arrival in San Francisco with Robert and Alexa,
Margaret went for a walk. She felt confused and unwell –
but there were no symptoms which would enable her, as
a doctor, to diagnose her own case. No doubt the main
cause of the turmoil in her mind was the strain of turning
her back on all her well-loved friends and the familiar
scenes of her past life. The future, uncharted, invited
apprehension as well as excitement by its unpredictability.
The only certainty was that the long journey by sea
and railroad had left her under-exercised. She needed
movement and fresh air. It would be a relief to experience
the ordinary tiredness caused by physical exertion instead
of the exhaustion brought on by the discomforts of travel.

From the moment, twenty-four hours earlier, when the
ferry left the railroad terminal at Oakland to carry them
across the Bay, everything about their reception had
come as a complete surprise to Margaret. How could she
have anticipated that Alexa would be welcomed by
crowds and cheered all the way to a hotel room filled
with flowers from admirers who could only distantly know
of her reputation? Nor had Margaret expected the brisk
helpfulness of strangers who had borne Robert off to
school on his very first morning in the city and had
arranged for Alexa to visit the Opera House on that

same morning. To Margaret herself, they had revealed that a furnished apartment – and the servants to run it – awaited her inspection in the afternoon. In London, the reputation of the New World had been one of self-help, in which newcomers were expected to fend for themselves. It was ungrateful, Margaret knew, to wish that they could all have been allowed just one day in which to rest before being rushed off their feet by friendliness.

In the meantime, left alone for an hour or so, she used the mechanical movements of walking to calm her disordered system. Her years as a medical student had accustomed her to explore new areas on foot, and there would be time enough after she began to make acquaintances in San Francisco to discover whether the conventions of the city approved such freedom. She was equally accustomed to steep slopes – and indeed, as she climbed the switchback hills she found herself irresistibly reminded of Bristol. True, most of the roads in San Francisco climbed straight up the hills, while the narrower lanes which tackled the gradient from the Avon waterfront to the Clifton heights curved in a manner more considerate to the horses which plodded up them. But there was the same feeling of exhilaration as the brow of a hill was approached, the same freshening of the wind, the same smell of the sea. The skies, too, were grey here today just as they so often were in Bristol, filled with clouds which did not bank oppressively but scudded across the sky like the sailing ships which Margaret remembered from her youth. They promised rain, but were in too much of a hurry to deliver it. An illogical association of ideas had caused Margaret, before she arrived, to connect California with gold and gold with brilliant sunshine. She had expected brightness of San Francisco and did not find it, but the misty dullness which greeted her instead did not come as a disappointment. Rather, it seemed almost a welcome, an invitation to feel at home.

There were other resemblances between San Francisco and her childhood home, sometimes requiring a subtle eye for their recognition. The houses she passed, built of shingled wood, were less substantial than the solid stone crescents and squares of Georgian Bristol, and more colourful in their various choices of paint. Nevertheless, they had the same smell of money about them. As she climbed Lombard Street Margaret – a stranger to the city – had no means of knowing whether Russian Hill was an area more or less wealthy than the average; but the atmosphere was one which she found instantly familiar. The merchants who had lived in the terraced tiers of the Bristol hills had for the most part been in the third generation of wealth, pausing for a few years before – like one of Margaret's own ancestors – they took the final step in the hierarchy of trade and built themselves mansions on the Clifton heights. The residents of this part of San Francisco, she felt instinctively, were poised in exactly the same way – rich already, but not yet quite prepared to take the final step into ostentation. She wondered where that final step, when it came, would take them.

There would be plenty of time to find out. Meanwhile, she took a few steps more herself and was brought to a halt in delight. In front of her now the ground fell away, and if she allowed her gaze to drop to the nearest part of the coastline, where scores of ships were busily loading and unloading, she could have pressed even further the parallel with Bristol and its prosperous trade. But instead she stared at a view far more beautiful than anything her home port had ever been able to offer, of a wide vista of wooded heights rising on the far side of the bay.

As though in welcome, the wind gave a last strong

scurry that tugged her hair untidily from its imprisonment under her hat and at the same time parted the clouds above to reveal a canyon of clear sky. The water of the bay responded, changing before her eyes from grey-green to sparkling blue. Margaret breathed deeply in the crisp, fresh air, taking the city to her heart. The atmosphere was at the same time reassuringly familiar and excitingly new. She could be happy here.

Half reluctantly, she turned to go back. Alexa would be returning to the hotel soon, and then they must go together to inspect the apartment. As she began the steep descent, she noticed someone coming up the hill towards her. He was dressed as smartly as any English gentleman – although his high hat and frock coat were of a style which had gone out of fashion in London a good many years ago: a fit resident, she thought idly to herself, for this district which she had identified as a prosperous one. As they approached and passed each other, he raised his hat.

'Morning, ma'am.'

He continued on his way with a briskness which made it clear that he did not expect any acknowledgement, but the effect upon Margaret was one which he could not possibly have imagined. Taken aback, she stood still. Did he know her? Did she know him? She turned back to look at him, but he was continuing on his way without any pause. It must simply have been a courtesy. Margaret was well aware that she would need to accept new social conventions in a foreign country. Until she learned what they were, she must try not to be surprised. And yet this small matter disturbed her, nagging at her mind as she walked on. Was the gentleman perhaps one of the many who had welcomed them on the previous day? She had been too tired at the time to be properly conscious of names or faces. He might have seen non-recognition in her eyes even as he spoke, and hurried on to avoid embarrassment to either of them.

But there was another possibility. Abruptly, Margaret changed direction, turning towards the harbour. It was time to bring out of the back of her mind the thought which she had pushed aside throughout the long journey.

It was possible that, just over twenty-seven years ago, David Gregson had landed at the very harbour which she was now approaching. And if he had done so, if he had stayed in San Francisco and made his fortune, he might at this moment be living in one of the shingled houses on Russian Hill. He could even have been the gentleman who raised his hat to a woman whose red hair was blowing untidily in the wind, because he recognized her as the woman he had once wanted to marry.

He could have been – but in fact he was not. The man had been a stranger, and in any case too young to be David Gregson, who would be fifty-six by now. On that point at least Margaret could be definite with herself. The only importance of the stranger was the reminder he had brought that at any moment she might come face to face with her one-time suitor.

It was time to put the probabilities to herself methodically, and to accept them. There was only one chance in four that David had come to San Francisco at all. Even if he did come, there was no reason why he should stay. As a man without fortune, he might have looked for land in some less developed part of the continent. Or he might have been tempted by the prospect of gold to travel north to Alaska. He might even be dead.

Suppose all these guesses were wrong. Suppose he were alive and living in San Francisco, what could it mean to her? He had had plenty of time to make a life without her. Long ago he would have acquired a wife, children, a career of some sort. If he were to meet

Margaret in the street by chance, the first likelihood was that he would not even recognize her. And if he did, he would not raise his hat to her, with all the risks that such a greeting would entail. He would cut her dead, and would be quite right to do so. Margaret herself would have no right to complain. David had parted from her in well-justified anger. She had no claim on his loyalty – and had not even been faithful to his memory herself. Her husband, Charles, had monopolized her love not only for the brief period of their marriage, but through all the unhappy years when it seemed that the feud between their two families would separate them for ever.

Margaret was a sensible woman. She knew well enough how foolish it was, and how illogical, to allow her thoughts to ramble in this way. Only the tiredness caused by the rough sea voyage and the long railroad journey, combined with the strain of starting a new life in a strange place, could explain why she found herself staring at every man she saw with both apprehension and hope. With a last clutch at rational behaviour she asked a passer-by to direct her by the quickest route back to the hotel, and a cable car took her almost to the door. Her head was swimming, and she found it impossible to tell whether it was her mind or her body which was on the point of collapse. Her final resolve, as she lay down on the bed for a short rest before Alexa's return, was that she would not allow herself to think of David Gregson again.

Amateur nurses regard sleep as the best cure for almost any illness. Alexa could not imagine what had caused the nervous and physical collapse which had overwhelmed her sister on the day after their arrival in San Francisco, but she was reassured rather than frightened by the prolonged drowsiness which followed it. Margaret was still asleep now, in a darkened bedroom; and Robert had gone off to play with his new schoolfriend, Brad. Alone in the drawing room of an apartment on Van Ness Avenue, Alexa was singing a duet with Enrico Caruso.

Caruso – in the flesh – had sung with Alexa before, on the stage of the Opera House at Naples. It was almost certainly his approval and recommendation which were responsible for her invitation to San Francisco. But it happened that they had never performed *Carmen* together, so she had accepted with amusement and pleasure the loan of what she called a gramophone but its owner described as an Edison-box. Caruso himself would not be coming west from New York until April, but the revolving cylinder of wax from which his voice emerged with surprising richness gave her the opportunity to practise harmonizing her voice with his.

She was startled by Margaret's sudden entry into the room – and it was easy to see that Margaret herself was flustered; for although she had dressed, her appearance lacked its usual neatness. Alexa smiled mischievously as she watched Margaret trace the tenor voice to its source.

'Did you fancy that I was entertaining a gentleman here in your absence?' she teased.

'Indeed I did, and I was very much upset to believe

that I was neglecting my duties as chaperone so early in our stay.' Margaret made her way to a sofa and sat down as the song came to an end. 'I find myself in every way confused. This is not our hotel room, is it?'

'No,' agreed Alexa, and could not resist continuing to tease for a moment. 'I hope you feel rested after your nap.'

'I can't remember ever having a sounder night's sleep,' said Margaret.

Alexa laughed, and went across the room to kiss her sister. 'You have slept almost without a break for six days,' she said. 'You allowed us to move you here from the hotel in a kind of dream, and once a day you have been sufficiently awake to take a little food, but you have always gone straight back to sleep again.' The horror on Margaret's face increased her amusement. Alexa knew well enough that laziness on such a scale must seem unforgivable to someone as briskly hard-working as Dr Margaret Scott. 'Had you been your own doctor, a rest of this kind is just what you would have prescribed for yourself,' she said. 'If you hadn't collapsed like that, you might have become really ill.'

'I'm never ill,' protested Margaret. It was true that Alexa could remember only one occasion, in the twenty years since she had been adopted, when her guardian had allowed an over-wrought mind to sap her body of its natural strength, and that was when Charles Scott had died only a month or two before Robert was born.

'You have not been ill now.' Alexa did her best to be reassuring. 'You were very tired, that was all – and it was hardly surprising. I blame myself greatly for inflicting such a journey on you. When you had all the strain of packing up your possessions and leaving your friends and reconciling yourself to a new life amongst strangers, it's no wonder that you should be affected by the weeks of

202

such discomfort. Besides, you had hardly had time to recover from your earlier voyage to Jamaica and back.'

'But six days! And one of your reasons for asking me to come was in order that your entry to San Francisco society should be conventionally chaperoned!'

'It has all fallen out magnificently,' Alexa assured her. 'I have refused all formal invitations until you should be ready to accompany me, and the result has been to make us the most sought-after guests in the city. Strait-laced mammas who were alarmed at the prospect of a gold-digging English singer getting her claws into their darling sons are now even more perturbed by the prospect of some other hostess being preferred to themselves. We shall have to consider seriously who is to be allowed the honour of entertaining us first. Our future social status may depend on it.'

'You sound happy, Alexa. I'm glad to hear it.'

Alexa's true feelings were more complicated than she intended to reveal, even to Margaret. She had determined to show herself to the whole world as light-hearted, and was glad that the person who knew her best was willing to accept what she said at face value.

'I seem to have been surrounded by kindness and admiration ever since we arrived,' she said. 'In Italy, it's normal for a prima donna to be fêted, so I'm accustomed to being spoiled, but I confess that I hadn't expected it to happen here, where I am not well known. I'm sure you must have had secret doubts about the wisdom of our journey, and so sometimes did I. It's delightful to be surprised in such a way. In fact, I find this in every respect an unexpected city. Do you know that there are no fewer than seven theatres? And that two of them are offering opera seasons? Anyone who disapproves of my Carmen at the Morisco Opera House will only need to move to the Tivoli to hear Tetrazzini's Gilda instead. It's a good thing to have a rival. Competition creates an atmosphere of excitement.'

'As long as you emerge as the champion,' Margaret suggested.

'She sings nicely enough, but she is too fat!' Alexa dismissed Tetrazzini with a flick of her own slim wrist. 'Well, I must wait until I have made my début before I can be quite sure. But I think I shall want to stay. And – ' Alexa allowed her voice to change, making her next remark so deliberately casual that it must appear tentative. 'I think I may decide to marry.'

Margaret made no attempt to hide her incredulity. 'You can't have met someone in so short a time!' she exclaimed.

'That was only a statement of intent. It doesn't mean that I'm interested in any particular man.' She allowed herself to be serious. 'I've loved Matthew for twenty years, Margaret – ever since you first took me to Brinsley House as a child. I know that I must make myself forget him. But it's so difficult, when he himself has done nothing to hurt me. I tell myself that there's nothing to be done, that we must never meet again. Ever since the night of Lord Glanville's ball, I've been trying to put Matthew out of my mind; and I can't do it. Well, perhaps a husband would be able to help me.'

'I remember your saying, on the night of the ball,' Margaret began slowly; but Alexa interrupted her.

'I said and did a good many foolish things that evening,' she admitted. 'But I remember one thing *you* said. That sometimes love comes after marriage.'

'It's unfortunate for Lord Glanville that it's taken you so long to accept that.'

Alexa sighed with the impossibility of explaining her true feelings for Lord Glanville – especially to Margaret, who almost certainly loved him herself. His kindness to the young singer he had befriended had been so great that Alexa had always had a particular affection for him. She did indeed love him in a way, but it was not a passionate way. Perhaps because she had never known a father of her own, she could not prevent herself from thinking of him almost in that relationship. What love she did feel was sincere enough to hold her back from anything which might in the end disappoint and hurt him. With a stranger it would not be too unkind to experiment. She could set herself the task of falling in love with someone. If she succeeded, she could marry him with a good conscience: if she failed, it should be possible to disentangle herself before too much harm was done. But with Lord Glanville, who knew her so well, no such experiment would be possible. A single kiss would have been enough to raise his hopes and open the door to disappointment. All this, however, was too difficult to put into words.

'To marry Lord Glanville without loving him would have been to take a risk – and he would have been the one to suffer most if the marriage failed.'

'I think you may have misjudged him, Alexa. He is stronger than you seem to believe. And he should have been allowed to estimate his own risks. Well, it's too late now to regret that. But didn't you refuse an earl that night as well?'

'I told you then that a title means nothing to me,' said Alexa. 'It would have imprisoned me, in fact. How could a countess be allowed to earn her living? I don't intend to let any husband prevent me from singing. I think it may prove easier to make that point in America than in Europe. And there are other kinds of aristocracy. Seven days in San Francisco have been enough to teach me that.'

'What do you mean?'

'I mean that the heights of the city are made of money. The men who live here build their homes of wood, not stone, because they know that one day another earthquake will bring the buildings down on their heads. But the foundations of the houses are of silver and gold and the iron tracks of railway lines. San Franciso is full of millionaires, Margaret. There are respectable ones and crooked ones, each with his own place in a hierarchy which it will take us a little time to understand. I shall rely on you to stop me making any mistakes. But as soon as we have made our map of society, I shall marry a millionaire. Or, at least – ' she checked herself. 'That's not quite right. The men who have made fortunes themselves tend to be rather rough. But their sons – that's something else again! Educated, cultured, with enormous expectations of wealth but a certain lack of imagination when it comes to spending their riches. They need expensive wives to show off their fortunes. I shall find the most suitable of the eldest sons and encourage him to fall in love with me. He will allow me to continue singing professionally until he comes into his inheritance; and then he will build me my own opera house, and we will make it the most famous musical centre in the world.'

'I don't like to hear you being cynical,' Margaret said quietly.

'That's not fair!' Alexa protested. 'I'm only saying out loud and in advance what a good many other young women think secretly. Don't marry for money, but marry where money is. Not everyone is fortunate enough to have the choice. Am I expected to throw away all my natural advantages? I can promise that whoever marries me will get a good enough bargain. I have never been a cheat. And I could say that *you* were the cynical one, when you advised me to marry first and hope that love came afterwards.'

'I was thinking only of Lord Glanville.'

'That demonstrates the danger, then, of generalizing from a particular case. So you must not frown too heavily if I decide instead to take a general truth and particularize from it. The general truth being that – other things being equal – a rich man makes a better husband for an extravagant woman than a poor one. Matthew had hardly a penny to his name, so you can't accuse me of *always* being greedy. As I grow older, I become more realistic, that's all.' She leaned over the back of the sofa and hugged Margaret apologetically. 'And I should have realized long ago that the only reason you allow me to rant on like this is because you are weak with starvation after all this time in bed. We have a Chinese cook who is longing to tempt your appetite with something more exciting than broths. I will set him to work at once.' She moved towards the bell, but burst out laughing before she reached it. 'Do come, Margaret. Look out of the window.'

Walking with an unsteadiness which made her weakness clear, Margaret came to stand beside her. Together they looked down at the wide avenue below. Two thirteen-year-old urchins were walking across it, dodging the busy flow of horses and bicycles and an occasional automobile. They were of the same height and covered from head to foot with the same coating of sandy mud. Only a glimpse of bright red hair through the covering of dirt suggested that one of them might be Robert.

Alexa could tell that Margaret was startled by the sight. The tone of her exclamation combined delight at seeing her son with shock at his appearance.

'Robert's instincts seem to be more democratic than yours,' she commented. 'While you look for your friends in the homes of millionaires, he finds his in the gutter.'

There was nothing critical about her voice, nothing to

suggest that she disapproved. She laughed in fact, as she saw her son's new friend wave goodbye and set off down the avenue at a run, turning a cartwheel as he went out of sheer high spirits. Nevertheless, Alexa supposed that she ought to explain. She missed her opportunity, however, for Margaret was already hurrying out of the room to greet Robert.

It didn't matter. Margaret would be as polite to a guttersnipe as to a prince, if he was a friend of her son. Alexa changed her mind about providing more information. It would be amusing to delay any introduction for a little while. She would have a word with Robert, asking him not to spoil the joke. Then they could both look forward to teasing Margaret when the truth finally emerged.

3

The social structure of a cosmopolitan city offers to a newcomer the same excitement that an explorer finds in the landmass of an unmapped continent. Alexa wasted little time before plunging Margaret into a preliminary expedition.

'Who is Miss Halloran?' Margaret asked, looking at the first name on the list which was set before her.

'Brad's aunt.'

'But who is Brad?'

'Bradley Davidson is the guttersnipe,' said Alexa, laughing. 'Robert's new school friend, with whom he went tunnelling yesterday. No doubt his aunt wishes to establish Robert's respectability by scrutinizing his family. She called last week, while I was at rehearsal and you were asleep. I gather that Brad's mother is dead, and his father travels a good deal on business. So Miss Halloran has to a large extent taken her sister's place in running the household.'

Deliberately Alexa made no attempt to explain why their first formal call should be in Robert's interest rather than in that of her own début into the highest level of San Francisco society. For the same reason, she gave Margaret no advance information about the area of the city they were about to visit. This enabled her to watch with amusement the astonishment on her sister's face as they paused before entering Miss Halloran's home.

Like almost every other house in the city, it was made of wood – but wood which had been carved into so many twists and scrolls and knobs and cross-hatchings that it had taken on the appearance of a gingerbread house. The ornateness of the architectural design rivalled the decoration: there were turrets and pediments, bow windows and a pillared colonnade. The building, itself four times as large as any normal family house, was surrounded by a garden which was huge by the standards of the densely-packed city, landscaped to take full advantage of the steep fall of the hill.

Alexa allowed Margaret a moment in which to adjust her picture of a filthy thirteen-year-old to this surprising setting. 'This is to San Francisco what Clifton is to Bristol, I suppose,' she said. 'It's nicknamed Nob Hill, after the railroad nabobs who developed it. If you find Miss Halloran's residence ostentatious, I can only suggest that you take a look at the Hopkins's house.'

'Is that all the information you're going to give me?' Margaret asked her. 'I'd like to know more about Miss Halloran than only the name of her young nephew. Was her father one of the railroad builders you mentioned?'

'Only in the sense that with his pick and shovel he actually helped to carve out a section of the track. He was an Irish labourer. He arrived in America with a wife and two small children, who lived in a tent beside each new section of the railroad. He hadn't a penny in his pocket more than his week's wages, and he couldn't even read or write.'

'Then how . . .?'

'He happened to be working within striking distance of Nevada when the Comstock lode was discovered,' said Alexa. 'I suppose he ran there a little faster than anyone else, and dug a great deal harder. He did only moderately well there, I'm told – he wasn't one of the original bonanza millionaires. But it set him up in San Francisco comfortably enough. And by the time the next big strike was made, in Alaska, he'd married one of his daughters to a man who could do considerably more than sign his own name. They went into partnership and really made a killing. Hence this fine example of domestic architecture. I've been warned that we shall find Miss Halloran excessively stiff and formal, and with a strong prejudice against the English which she may or may not express in our presence. She wouldn't thank us for mentioning her own father's origins, but she will be snobbishly curious about ours.'

'How did you discover all this?' asked Margaret.

'Oh, I made a few enquiries. Shall we go in?'

Alexa was not quite as confident as she tried to pretend about how she should behave. Her social life had for a good many years now been conducted on a very much less formal basis. But she was interested to discover that her sister knew exactly what was expected. Although Margaret had certainly never had time in her busy professional life for the making and returning of calls with which more leisured women of her age filled their days, she had already noticed that the fashions in dress here were a good many years behind those of London. It was reasonable to guess that perhaps social conventions also bore some relation to the rules of etiquette which had ruled Bristol society thirty years earlier.

Her own role, she realized as they sat stiffly in a huge gold and white drawing room, should be that of the shy young ingénue. It was not a time to parade her fame and independence. Alexa was as well able to act the part of a demure eighteen-year-old as that of a princess or a gypsy, and she did so now – speaking when she was spoken to, and listening with amusement to Miss Halloran's unsubtle attempts to research into Robert's pedigree.

The door opened, and Alexa's smile changed from amusement to pleasure as two young men came in to be presented. She wondered whether Margaret would recognize that she had caught a glimpse of one of them before. On this occasion Brad was clean. His face shone with scrubbing, his hair was sleeked down with water, and he was formally dressed in a suit whose style – of woollen stockings and knee-length knickerbockers – was odd to Alexa's eyes, but typical of the well-dressed young citizen of San Francisco.

Alexa, however, had no great interest in Brad. She was waiting to see how Margaret would like his brother.

'My elder nephew, Frank Davidson,' announced Miss Halloran. 'Though what he's doing in the house at this hour of the day I can't imagine. Frank, this is Dr Scott. And Miss Reni.'

Frank's face was boyish and handsome. Frank's hair was dark and curly. Frank's brown eyes sparkled with mischief and conspiracy as he bowed his acknowledgement of the introductions.

'I've been making some adjustments to the Panhard,' he said in answer to his aunt's criticism. 'And I have polished every piston and fender until the whole machine is glowing with elbow grease and pride. All I need now is

211

a passenger worthy of its excellence. I came here to offer you an automobile drive through the Golden Gate Park, Aunt Halloran. A pleasure for you, I hope, but a test drive for myself. I'm almost ready to build a complete engine which will be more reliable than anything at present on the market. So you see, I'm hard at work even while I seem to be lazing in your drawing room.'

'You know how I hate the noisy brutes,' said Miss Halloran.

'They are the transportation system of the future,' Frank assured her. 'And I intend to entrust my own future to them. You should be pleased that instead of being content to share my father's fortune, I propose to earn my own. Well, if I cannot persuade you, perhaps I could induce Dr Scott instead to accompany me. And Miss Reni, of course.'

'Oh yes, do let us go!' exclaimed Alexa, introducing a note of excitement into the debutante voice she was practising, for all the world as though she had never seen a horseless carriage before. To her delight, Margaret was willing to pick up the cue.

'As long as you don't expect me to be the eventual customer, Mr Davidson, that would be a treat for both Alexa and myself.'

Frank gave Margaret his most charming smile. 'I salute your enterprise in being a lady doctor, Dr Scott,' he said. 'But even you, I imagine, hardly expect that ladies will ever wish to drive their own autos. Even if they had the taste for covering their hands in dirt and grease, they would not have the strength to start the engine. So you will be safe from my sales talk.'

Alexa made no secret of her satisfaction as she followed Frank and Margaret outside and tied her hat on securely: she had taken the precaution of including a suitable scarf in her outfit. The visit had been a necessary formality.

Now that she and Frank had been officially introduced, she could rely on Frank to make sure that there would be other invitations.

Margaret, as it quickly transpired when at last they returned to their apartment after the drive, had not been deceived.

'I'm well aware that my role as your chaperone is as much of a pretence as any of your characters on the stage,' she said. 'But you would not accept a part without first being shown the libretto and the score. It was hardly fair of you to talk so much about Brad's aunt when it was Frank's aunt in fact whom you wished me to meet. Does the family hold any further surprises?'

'Brad and Frank have a sister, Cassie,' said Alexa. 'She is nineteen. About a year ago she married a young man who is trying to develop a vineyard in the Napa Valley. And there is their father, of course. I haven't met either Cassie or Mr Davidson.'

'And how did you come to make Frank's acquaintance?' Margaret asked her.

'I went to meet Robert after his first day at school here,' Alexa told her. 'You were asleep, if you remember. Robert and Brad arrived at the gate together, and Frank had come to meet Brad. He had one of his autos with him then, and was proposing to take his brother for a ride. He offered a ride to Robert and myself as well. But naturally I realized that I ought to refuse.'

'Naturally!' agreed Margaret. 'And naturally you were careful not to make your refusal too blunt. Alexa, you are behaving disgracefully.'

The two women burst out laughing together.

'But as a matter of fact,' Alexa protested, 'Nob Hill is the best starting point for our conquest of San Francisco. We need the approval of someone like Miss Halloran. And although Brad and Frank have provided a short cut, we should have been able to pay that call quite soon in any case, I think. Miss Halloran and her brother-in-law are patrons of the opera. They have their own box. When I make my début here, Miss Halloran will be as pleased to claim my acquaintance as I am to know her.'

'I suspect from some of her comments that I shall sink rapidly in her estimation once I become a working doctor,' Margaret said.

'You need be in no hurry, surely, for that time to come?' Alexa made her voice as persuasive as she could. 'You deserve a little leisure after all your years of hard work, and my fees are quite generous enough to support us all.'

'I've lost the taste for idleness, if I ever had it,' Margaret confessed. 'Certainly I'll keep my part of our bargain for as long as you need me, but I would be glad to know when you expect to set me free.'

Alexa recognized that Margaret had the right to a serious answer. 'For my first performances here I shall be singing with the resident company,' she said. 'But in the middle of April the Metropolitan Company of New York will be arriving, and Caruso and I will be singing with the company as guest artists in three of their productions. The first one in which I am to appear, *Carmen*, will open on 17 April. By the end of April I shall have had the opportunity to impress – or not – two of the most important managers on the North American continent. I hope very much that as a result I may be offered a contract with one of them. But it could as easily be in New York as in San Francisco. So if you would be willing to wait until then before making any firm arrangement of your own . . .'

'Until the end of April. All right, then. Robert will be surprised to find himself for three months at the mercy of a mother who has nothing to do but fuss over him. But that may be something he has missed. I hope you will win whichever offer you want, Alexa.'

Alexa smiled her thanks. She had no doubts about her own abilities in the operatic field; and the admiration she had seen in Frank Davidson's eyes suggested that within the next few months she could expect to receive more offers than merely those which came from managers. She would have a choice of rich prizes, and she intended to turn whatever she chose into a triumph.

4

It is a curious inversion of values which causes an operatic performance to be more highly regarded as a social than as a musical occasion according to the degree of wealth and sophistication in its audience. The opening night of *Carmen*, on 17 April 1906, was to be a gala event in San Francisco, and in turn was only the prelude to one of the main events of the social season, the Opera Ball. Margaret did not expect the occasion to offer any great excitement to herself, but she took for granted her duty to accompany Alexa.

Unlike the society guests who planned to attend, Alexa would only be able to dress for the ball after the performance was over. When Margaret went into her room in the late afternoon, she found it littered with clothes, as Alexa prepared to make her choice and send the garments over to the Opera House in the care of her dresser.

'What are you going to wear?' Margaret asked.

'As you may see, I am having some difficulty over the choice. But I've decided that what I wore to Lord Glanville's ball, at the end of my life in Europe, can fittingly mark my acceptance of a new world.' Alexa held

215

up the white satin dress. Margaret remembered how lovely she had looked in the ballroom at Blaize, and nodded approvingly. Then she caught sight of the black leather case which lay open on a table.

'Not the rubies, Alexa!'

'Why not?'

'I thought you didn't like them.' Margaret was reluctant to give the real reason for her objection.

'It's true that I had no interest in them before I saw them,' Alexa agreed. 'And I was ungracious, I remember, when at last you handed them to me. But in a curious way – how can I explain? They are very beautiful, I recognized that at once. And they are beautiful in a way that is exactly right for me. You said that my father had chosen them especially to suit me – well, as I wear them, I'm conscious of how well he succeeded, and it's given me a warmer feeling towards him. I've never truly felt myself to be part of a family, but these jewels are my link with the Lorimers – and especially with you.'

'Nevertheless, wear something else tonight. You have other jewels of equal value.'

'Certainly I have,' Alexa acknowledged. 'But it was these I wore for that evening at Blaize.'

'And did the evening bring you happiness?' Margaret did not wait for an answer. A fear which could not be rationally explained made the words trip over her tongue as she tried to persuade Alexa to close the box. 'Every time I have seen these stones, some disaster has followed. My mother wore them to a ball, and caught a chill there from which she died. Your mother showed them to me before she asked me to keep the box for you, and before morning she too was dead. And then my husband – ' Margaret's voice choked to a standstill. 'You know that I am not superstitious in the ordinary way, Alexa. But these jewels have brought real, not imaginary ill-fortune every time they have appeared.'

'Then we must be already doomed, for here they are displayed before us.' Alexa's smile made it clear that she did not accept Margaret's apprehension, but she closed the box nevertheless. 'Well, I certainly don't wish the evening to be spoiled by your premonition of some new disaster. I have some opals which are equally suited to this gown.' She looked at Margaret with eyes which sparkled with even more than their usual brightness. 'I have my own premonition about this evening,' she said. 'But all *my* expectations are happy ones. I think it possible that in the excitement of the occasion I may receive a proposal of marriage. I think it also possible that I may accept. Would you be prepared to welcome Frank Davidson as your half-brother-in-law?'

'I like Frank very much indeed,' said Margaret, and her approval was sincere. In Alexa's company she had seen a good deal of him in the past few weeks. She liked his humour and the merriment with which his eyes continually flashed. But beneath his light-hearted good looks she was conscious that he had all the firm character of a young man who knew himself to be technically skilled and justifiably ambitious. Alexa had enjoyed so many years of independence that it would need a strong man to control her. There was only one respect in which Frank Davidson might seem less than an ideal husband. 'He is a good deal younger than you, of course,' she pointed out.

'Eight years is nothing!' scoffed Alexa. 'Although as a matter of fact he believes that I am twenty-four, not twenty-nine.'

Margaret frowned in disapproval, and Alexa hurried to explain.

'I ought to be ashamed to admit to a lie, I suppose, but

it wasn't originally meant to deceive Frank. There comes a moment in every singer's life when she's tempted to add a few years to her career by subtracting them from her age. The temptation usually seems to arise as a fortieth birthday approaches – but by then, of course, it's difficult to carry off the deception because too many people know the truth. All that happened was that I looked ahead and realized that the beginning of a new career in a new continent would be a good time to make a small adjustment. I mentioned my new age in a newspaper interview even before I had met Frank, and afterwards I could hardly allow two versions to circulate publicly. I can rely on your discretion, I hope.'

'I think it unwise for any marriage to be founded on a deception,' said Margaret.

'Good gracious, this isn't a foundation stone. A small embellishment to the decoration, that's all. It's not as though he's choosing a bride by proxy. He will have what he sees. And of course I shall tell him the truth as soon as we are married.'

'It should be before you are married,' said Margaret, conscious that she must seem to be behaving priggishly, but sure that she was right.

'Very well, then; before. It's a matter of no importance. But of course I wouldn't want him to learn the truth from anyone but myself.'

Margaret accepted the command, although with reluctance. She hoped that Frank would never refer in her presence to Alexa's age. If the matter were not raised – and why should it be? – she could pretend to know nothing about it. She changed the subject to that of the evening's arrangements.

Although she lacked Alexa's incentive for taking pains with her appearance, Margaret dressed for the evening as well as a wardrobe designed for a less glamorous life allowed. Not for the first time she bemoaned her lack of inches. Her waist was as slim as Alexa's, and she held her shoulders as straight; but without the slender height which gave the younger woman the air of a princess, she could never attain true elegance in her own eyes. She did her best, however, and when she arrived at the Grand Opera House that evening she could hope that Alexa would not feel ashamed of her companion at the ball.

A seat was waiting for Margaret at the front of the manager's own box, but she was in no hurry to take it. There was a little while to go before the overture began, and the audience was still buzzing with excited gossip. Even without the additional spice of Caruso's appearance tonight, the theatre on its own was able to impose an atmosphere of grandeur. Above Margaret's head a series of galleries and balconies ascended so high into the roof that those who had paid their twenty-five cents for a seat in the 'seventh heaven' could hope to see little but the top of the singers' heads. But the more fashionable members of the audience, who patronized the boxes and the orchestra pit, were received in greater style. There was a huge lobby, with a wide promenade above it, lit – like the auditorium itself – by chandeliers whose crystals reflected the lights on to mirrored walls and received them twinkling back again.

For a few moments Margaret became part of the restless flow in which the richest citizens of San Francisco displayed themselves to their fellows. Then she allowed herself to be shown into her box. Here, too, she enjoyed looking round for a while, watching the bows and smiles as members of the audience searched for acquaintances and acknowledged them. She stood in the dim light at the back of the box, where she could observe without herself being clearly seen.

Two boxes along, Frank Davidson was helping his aunt

into a seat. As befitted a patron of the opera, she had one of the best places in the house. Margaret watched the young man's solicitude approvingly, wondering with some amusement whether Frank himself knew as certainly as Alexa did that he was likely to end the evening as an engaged man. Then her heart stopped beating. There was someone else in the Davidson box.

She had tried to prepare herself for this moment. She had told herself that there was virtually no possibility that she would ever see David Gregson again. She had done her best to persuade herself that after so many years they might not even recognize each other if they were to meet. Above all, she had reminded herself many times that there could never be anything between them again. They were strangers now.

All these deceptions were swept away in the single flash of recognitiin. Margaret would have been hard put to it to explain how she could feel so sure of the identification. Twenty-seven years ago she had slammed the door on a young man who was shabby and under-nourished, shivering with cold and shaking with anger. What she saw now was a man of fifty-six whose hair – although it curled up from his forehead as exuberantly as before – was completely white. His evening clothes were perfectly cut and the stones which sparkled on the front and cuffs of his shirt were undoubtedly diamonds. He had put on enough weight to emphasize his appearance of prosperity, and the easy way in which he took his seat beside Miss Halloran and began to look around the audience revealed his social confidence.

Giddy with the shock, Margaret sat down at the back of the box. Was David then Frank's father? Although their appearance in the same box was not sufficient to prove it, the probability went that way. William had warned Margaret once that a man escaping from a criminal charge would almost certainly change his name. For David to become Mr Davidson would be a short step, but sufficient to evade any official enquiry which might be made. It would explain, too, the immediate liking which Margaret had felt for both the Davidson boys. Certainly she had never recognized them as David's sons: the possibility had not even occurred to her. But in the moment when she saw them standing side by side in the great gold and white room on Nob Hill she had found them instantly attractive, almost as though she knew them already.

The orchestra began to play, but Margaret did not hear it. The curtain rose, and the huge stage was illuminated with gaslight as the light faded in the giant chandelier which hung over the auditorium: Margaret did not notice. She paid no attention when the girls from the cigarette factory poured on to the stage – not even when Alexa, almost unrecognizable in her dark wig, began to sing. Within seconds the customary miracle had occurred, as though Alexa had gathered the whole audience into the palm of her hand, allowing no one even to breathe until she should turn away with a flick of her castanets. Margaret had succumbed to this strange power at every other performance she had attended, but tonight her own circle of enchantment protected her. Pressed back into the shadow of the box, she thought what she should do.

The decision was not a difficult one to reach. Whether or not David was Frank's father, it was almost certain that he would be escorting Miss Halloran to the ball later in the evening. So Margaret herself must stay away. She longed to meet David again, but she could not face a public encounter. It could be alarming, she told herself, for a respectable citizen to find himself suddenly confronted by someone who would be able to reveal that he had come to America as a fugitive from justice. Even as she formulated this excuse, she knew how weak it was. A man who had built up a successful new life from nothing was not likely to be troubled about the remote past. The truth was that she dared not risk seeing in his eyes at an unexpected meeting either the polite stare of non-recognition or the flash of remembered anger.

She wanted them to be friends again. If she were to be honest, the confusion of her feelings told her that she wanted him to be more than a friend – but to start with it would be enough if David would smile at her, either forgetting or forgiving their old quarrel. And to expect this in the middle of a social gathering, without warning, and without any opportunity on her part to apologize, would not be realistic. Margaret made up her mind. She would write him a letter, warning him that they were likely to meet, telling him something about her life since their last meeting, and admitting the mistake she had made at that time. She would write the letter at once, this evening, and send it round as soon as she had checked with Alexa the next morning that it should indeed be addressed to Mr Davidson.

On the stage, Alexa had begun to sing the Seguidilla, while Caruso, as Don José, attempted in vain to resist her enticements. The three tiers of her flounced skirts swung to the swaying of her hips. The movement, lithe and sensual, would have been grossly improper in private life. On stage it was in character, but the effect on the audience was almost as intense as the acted reaction of Don José. Recognizing that the first act would soon be ending, Margaret scribbled a quick note to Alexa to be delivered after the performance was over. She made her apologies to the manager, and returned to the apartment.

The letter took her a long time to write. A good many drafts were crumpled and discarded before she could feel

222

satisfied. By that time, the hour was so late that the opera must be over. The ball would be in full swing – although Alexa, needing time to change from a dark-skinned gypsy to a pale princess, would probably be one of the last to arrive. Too late, as she undressed and went to bed, Margaret realized that she had deserted her duty. Thinking only of her own affairs, she had quite forgotten that this was just the kind of occasion on which Alexa should have been chaperoned. It was true that Alexa was perfectly capable of looking after herself, as she had been doing in Europe for several years. But it was also true that one reason why Margaret had made the journey was to provide respectability of the kind expected in good society, if not in theatrical circles. Her failure tonight horrified her. But the mischief was done now. It could only be hoped that Miss Halloran had taken the young singer under her protection for the evening.

Margaret tried to sleep, but anxiety kept her awake. As the hours passed, she asked herself whether Alexa should be home by now. How long could a ball of this kind be expected to extend? Who would escort her home, and could the carriage be relied upon to come by the shortest route? Every time she heard the hooves of a tired horse clattering on the cobblestones of the avenue she strained her ears for the sound of a door opening, but was always disappointed. She was still awake, and increasingly worried, at thirteen minutes past five in the morning.

5

Theoretical instructions for action in case of emergency are reassuring and easy to follow – until the emergency actually occurs. Robert had been given detailed advice by his friend Brad Davidson on what to do if there should be an earthquake. It was not, he was warned, a remote possibility, for small tremors were felt in the city quite frequently. The first step, if he was indoors at the time, was to dash for the shelter of a doorframe and stand underneath it, so that when the roof came down he would have some protection against being crushed. The next necessity was to get out into the open as soon as possible. It had all seemed perfectly clear at the time; but at a quarter past five on the morning of 18 April it was distinctly less easy to behave in the prescribed manner.

The suddenness of the shock, waking him from sleep, paralysed Robert. While everything around him trembled, he felt himself unable to move. He clutched the sides of his shaking bed, as though by holding tightly he could keep it still. There was noise all around him – the sudden loud noises of smashing windows and falling chimneys, with a deeper undercurrent as though the earth were grinding its teeth. Even the air seemed heavy with vibration, pressing down on top of him as he lay with his eyes wide open, waiting for the ceiling to fall.

There was a brief pause in the shaking, followed by an odd flying feeling, as though a giant hand had lifted the whole apartment block off the ground before allowing it to drop again. His room, which had been indirectly illuminated at nights by the light of a street lamp outside, was abruptly darkened. The floor lurched sideways and tipped him out of bed. He half rolled, half scrambled towards the door. The room was swaying slightly, so that for a moment he had the feeling that he might tip the whole building over, like a see-saw, if he took one step too many past whatever centre of gravity it still possessed. He stood very still in the darkness, waiting to see what was going to happen. The moment of fear was over, but it still seemed necessary to be cautious.

The quaking of the earth had already come to an end. Gradually the building also ceased to quiver. Robert heard his mother calling him. He crossed to her bedroom door and tried without success to open it.

'Mother, are you hurt?' he shouted.

'No; but the door's jammed. Are you all right, Robert?'

'Yes,' said Robert. 'Stand away!' He turned his shoulder towards the door and charged at it. The hinges splintered away from the frame and he and the door tumbled together on the bedroom floor. His mother helped him to pick himself up and gave him a quick hug before patting him up and down as though to assure herself that he was unhurt.

Now that he had taken some action, Robert felt more in control of the situation.

'We must get out into the street straightaway,' he said. 'I'll go and make sure that Alexa's all right.'

'Wait a minute.' His mother was looking out of the window. 'It's foggy outside,' she said. 'Wet fog, and it looks cold. The tremor seems to be over for the moment. We will go out, certainly, but only when we've put on our warmest clothes. Get dressed as fast as you can.'

On the way back to his room, Robert knocked on Alexa's door, but there was no answer. He looked inside. By now his eyes had adapted themselves to the dim light. He could see that a wooden beam had fallen across the foot of her bed, but there was nothing to suggest that she had been lying in it at the time.

'Alexa's not here,' he called.

'I know. Hurry up.'

He struggled into his clothes and was then sent back, grumbling, to brush his hair. His mother, meanwhile, had dressed herself and was packing some of Alexa's clothes into a bag. 'A ball dress is hardly the ideal wear for a day on the streets,' she explained. 'Right. Down we go.'

There were elevators in the Marie Antoinette building, but they were jammed in the distorted shaft. Robert took the bag from his mother and they joined the other residents of the apartments who were already jostling their way down the stairs.

Outside, on the wide avenue, groups of people were standing in a dazed silence, as though even the sound of speech might be enough to start the ground cracking again. Robert felt as uncertain as everyone else about what should be done next. But his mother, after a moment of the same hesitation, spoke decisively.

'Stay here, Robert. Don't get lost.'

'Where are you going?'

'To see if anyone needs medical help. I won't go far away.'

'Can't I come too?'

His mother looked doubtful. 'I'd prefer you to stay here in case Alexa comes to look for us. But if you'd rather not be left alone – '

Indignantly Robert repudiated any suggestion that he was frightened of being on his own. He was genuinely anxious to make himself useful – but from his mother's worried expression he realized that he could help best by staying. After she had left he looked round for somewhere to sit down. The buildings along the avenue were dangerously out of true, so that there was no temptation to linger on the sidewalk beneath them. But the avenue was unusually wide. Cautiously he skirted the humps and deep cracks which had appeared in its surface and found a fallen chimney stack to act as a seat. There was no traffic about, so that even in the foggy darkness his position seemed safe enough. The frightening experience which had turned into an exciting adventure changed quality yet again and become merely dull.

After an hour his vigil was interrupted by flurries of activity. Several of the families who had come out on to the streets decided that it might be safe to return indoors and prepare breakfast. In the block next to Robert's the chimneys, although not fallen, had cracked, and the lighting of the first stove was enough to set the building on fire. All the men in the street, including Robert, rushed to beat out the flames, and no great damage was done. But the incident revealed that, like the chimney flues, the water pipes were also cracked. When, an hour later, a second foolish cook lit her stove and accidentally ignited a broken gas main, it was clear to everyone on the avenue that amateur fire-fighting efforts would be useless. The electrical fire alarm system had ceased to operate, so runners were sent to the nearest fire station, and Robert found a second way of making himself useful. With another boy he agreed to run along the avenue for a few blocks shouting instructions that no fires should be lit inside or near any building.

Glancing up a side street as he was on his way back again, he saw a crowd jostling around a baker's shop. The front of the shop had collapsed, spilling the contents out into the road. Robert hesitated, his mouth watering. He had been brought up never to steal. But he was very hungry, and he could not exactly see where his next meal was likely to come from if he did not find it for himself. His problem was solved when he saw a long loaf of bread just about to be trodden underfoot by a group of people who were pressing towards the inside of the store. In a quick movement which he had learned on the rugby field he scooped it up. That was salvage, not theft, he told himself as he broke off a chunk and began to gnaw it.

His mother arrived back soon after he had returned to his place. Her face was pale and her clothes were splashed with blood. She shook her head at his offer of bread.

'I'm not hungry, thank you.'

'Are a lot of people hurt?' Robert asked.

'There have been some very unpleasant accidents,' she said, and he could tell from her expression that she did not want to go into details. 'In this area, though, there are a good many large houses with only a few people living in them, so the actual number of casualties isn't too large. It's different, I hear, in the Mission Street area: whole tenements crowded with people have collapsed. And there's a bad fire in Chinatown. Robert, if we can make our way to the Davidsons' house, would you be willing to stay with Brad while I see whether any kind of emergency medical service is going to be organized? I imagine every doctor in the city will be needed.'

Before Robert had time to answer, Brad himself arrived, swerving on a bicycle between the groups of people in the avenue.

'Alexa sent me,' he panted. 'She's at the St Francis Hotel with my folks. Half the city's there. They're serving out meals as though it was a soup kitchen. She told me to show you the way.'

Robert and his mother hurried to the hotel. The fog lifted as they went, and the sky lightened. Throughout the city, the first atmosphere of shock seemed to have been replaced by one of picnic. Already families were building stoves on the streets out of fallen chimneys or cobblestones. Robert began to feel excited again – but it seemed that his mother had thought of something to slow her footsteps.

'Brad,' she asked. 'Was it your father who was at the opera with Frank and your aunt last night?'

'That's right,' agreed Brad. 'He came back from the mine late yesterday, and Aunt Halloran had him into his stiff shirt before he had time to know what hit him.'

'He'll be at the hotel now, will he?'

'Don't rightly reckon so. He made sure we were all safe and comfortable there, and then he went off to see what needed to be done. Sounds as though this 'quake was worse than usual. There'll be an emergency committee, he said, to get things organized. Here we are.'

Alexa came running out to greet them as they arrived. Robert noticed that she and Margaret did not embrace at once, as usually happened when they had been separated for a little while. Instead, they looked at each other with the same expression on each face. It was an expression which Robert found interesting, because he recognized it as one by which he was occasionally trapped himself – the look of a person who has done something of which he ought to be ashamed but who is hoping that nobody else knows about it.

Alexa was still wearing her ball gown, although now it was crumpled and dirty. Her bare shoulders were covered with a gentleman's jacket; but even so, she was shivering, and looked relieved when Robert held out the bag of clothing which he had carried from the apartment.

'Were you still at the ball when it happened?' he asked.

Alexa hesitated for a moment before she shook her head.

'No. Frank and I had gone back to the Davidson's house to have a celebration drink.'

229

'What were you celebrating?'

Frank came out just as Robert asked the question, and stood with his arm round Alexa's shoulders. Unlike her, he had been able to change his clothes and was wearing a practical motoring outfit.

'Has Alexa not announced the news yet?' he asked. 'We didn't get around even to opening the bottle, as things turned out, but that doesn't alter the fact that the most beautiful woman in the world has agreed to become Mrs Davidson.'

Robert heard the news with interest, although not with any surprise. He was pleased at the thought that he would have some sort of relationship now with Brad – although he could not work out what it would be. He was grateful, though, that he was not expected to take any part in all the hugging and kissing that went on now, and wondered how Frank managed to put up with it so cheerfully.

It came to an end at last. While Alexa disappeared to change her clothes, and Frank went to find out what was happening in the city, Robert sat down to a proper meal with his mother. But he could tell that she was restless.

'You want to get away, don't you?' he asked.

'Yes. I can't just sit here when so many people may be hurt. But I don't like to leave you.'

For a second time Robert pointed out that he was hardly a child any more.

'It's not that,' she said. 'It's going to be difficult to keep in touch: that's what I mean. We're used to living in a society where everyone has an address and a routine – a bed to sleep in and some hope of meals appearing at regular times. Well, that was yesterday's way of life; not today's. The only safe way is for us all to keep together all the time. But I should find Alexa a hindrance. She's never been able to stand the sight of blood.'

'I'll look after Alexa,' Robert assured his mother. 'And

we could fix to meet at the hotel here between six and eight this evening. If either of us finds somewhere better to go, we leave a message here for the other instead. We might be able to go back to Nob Hill. Brad said that although his main house has shifted, they've got a little summer house in the garden which may be all right for camping out.'

He could tell that she was still unhappy about leaving him, so he gave her a brisk goodbye kiss and bustled her out of the hotel. By now he had discovered that there would be no bill for whatever he ordered, so it seemed a good idea to eat as much as he could before the food gave out. He was still sitting at the table when Alexa returned, wearing more suitable clothes than before.

'My jewel box is still in the apartment,' she said as soon as she rejoined him. 'Margaret must have forgotten. I feel anxious about it – with every building in the city abandoned, it will be tempting for looters to see what they can find after nightfall.'

'Would you like me to fetch it for you?' Robert asked. He could tell what she wanted to say, but she hesitated for a moment.

'Is the building safe?' she asked.

'It seemed all right when we left. On the tilt, but not sliding any further. There were lots of people going in and out of their apartments to fetch their things.'

'I wouldn't want to put you at any risk,' Alexa said, still doubtful. 'If there's another 'quake – '

'If there's another 'quake, then nothing will be safe and I'm just as likely to get a brick on my head here as I would be in the apartment. But until that happens, it's the sensible thing to collect as much of our stuff as I can. Everybody else is doing it. I could fetch some more clothes for all of us. And some blankets, in case we have to sleep out tonight. Where shall I find the jewel box?'

'Underneath my bed,' she said. 'It's a black leather case.'

On his way out of the hotel, Robert met Frank hurrying back with a grim expression on his face.

'Where are you going?' Frank asked him.

'To get some more things from the apartment. I'll be back as soon as I can.'

'You may not find us still here.' Frank looked worried, as though wondering whether he ought to prevent Robert from going. 'The whole of the Chinatown area is on fire, and it's out of control. There's no water to fight it. Some bright engineer apparently laid the city's water main right across the fault.'

'What's the fault?' asked Robert, bewildered.

'The San Andreas Fault is a weak part of the earth's crust that's been responsible for most of San Francisco's tremors. Everyone knows about it. How anyone could be such a fool – anyway, the fault shifted and the pipes parted and the result is that there's no water, except for the cistern on Nob Hill, and that won't last long. The fire could spread to the whole downtown area of the city. Van Ness is safe enough, so I suppose there's no harm in your going there. But if the wind blows this way, we shall have to leave the hotel. In that case, I shall take Alexa and Aunt Halloran out to the Presidio hills. You know where I mean?'

Robert nodded. It was in the open north-west corner of the peninsula that he and Brad spent their free time constructing a network of tunnels; and with other boys from the school they often fought mock battles in the old fort which guarded the Golden Gate.

'The military authorities are opening the whole area as a refuge. Ask in the streets before you start back whether the hotel is still safe. If it's been evacuated, look for us on Buena Vista.'

'Right,' said Robert. The tension in Frank's voice had affected him, and he began to run as fast as he could. But the way was impeded by a slow procession of people leaving their homes. They were not hurrying, but instead moved with a shocked sadness, their backs bent with the weight of their burdens as they tried to save as many of their household goods as they could. Some were dragging sledges or even upturned tables loaded with possessions. Others, more fortunate, owned or had appropriated delivery vans and were able to move furniture as well as clothes. From time to time they stopped and looked back. Robert looked too, and saw that the whole of the eastern sky was blanketed with smoke. He started to run again.

The Marie Antoinette block of apartments was still standing, and looked no more dangerous than when he had left it. Relieved, Robert ran to the entrance. A soldier who had been lounging by the broken doors straightened himself and put out an arm.

'No one admitted to this building.'

'I live here,' said Robert. He assumed that the man was acting as a guard against looters, and was glad of it. 'If the janitor's still here, he'll tell you. I've just come back to collect some clothes.'

'No one admitted for any purpose whatsoever. Safety reasons. I've got my orders, son. Don't hang around.'

Puzzled and annoyed, Robert retreated. There must be a back entrance to the block, though he had never had cause to use it. When he found it, this too was guarded, and his attempts to pass were equally unsuccessful.

Back in the main avenue, he looked around. Somewhere there must be an officer in charge of the soldiers. But he, when discovered, proved even less sympathetic than his men. He was clearing everyone out of the avenue as Robert approached him. The families who had been sitting in clusters on the ground were grumbling but obedient. Robert's request was turned down out of hand, and his attempt at an explanation brought only an explosion of fury.

'For Christ's sake! We've got a whole city burning and you're worried about a spare pair of socks. Get out of here, and don't let me see you again.'

Robert's freckled face pouted with resentment as he walked slowly away. Even if it were true that much of the city was burning, there was no sign of fire here. And he would only have needed a few moments. He would have great difficulty in persuading Alexa that there had been no way to get past the guards. She had had a night without sleep, and Robert knew that she must have hated having to appear in public looking as dirty as when he had first seen her that day. Now she would be preparing to spend a second uncomfortable night, this time perhaps in the open. Robert recognized that anyone's temper might become strained under such circumstances. He was likely to be given the rough edge of her tongue if he reported failure.

The thought persuaded him to wait around. The guard would change at some point, and the new men might prove more sympathetic. Or perhaps it would be possible to sneak past them after dark, when there would be neither gas nor electricity to light the streets.

He waited, out of sight, but without success. The evening guard was reinforced by a foot patrol which kept the whole avenue under surveillance. Just as he was screwing up his courage to make a dash through the entrance hall in the hope that he could hide immediately in an abandoned room, he heard the officer in charge of the new patrol shouting out his orders for the night.

'Looters should be challenged first where practicable, but you have authority to shoot on sight.'

Robert was a level-headed boy, well able to judge when

the odds had changed from adventure to recklessness. He was not a looter but it seemed that he might not be allowed time to convince anyone of that if he were seen. Even to slip quietly away was risky enough. As soon as he was safely out of the guarded area he walked despondently, trailing his feet through the debris which littered the road. In the adventure stories he had read, the heroes never gave up like this. They dodged through a hail of bullets, always in the end managing to rescue whatever needed to be rescued. But then the bullets were guaranteed never to hit them. This real-life adventure offered much less certainty that there would be a happy ending for everyone. The blood on his mother's skirt had been a sufficient indication of that.

The way back to the hotel proved to be barred. The troops who stopped him on this occasion were more sympathetic than the guards, but equally definite. The fire, they told him, was spreading so rapidly that there was little hope of saving any of the downtown area. Only approved firefighters were allowed within the triangle edged by Hyde Street and Mission Street.

Alarmed to find that the rendezvous with his mother had become impossible to keep, Robert remembered Frank's instructions and turned towards the Presidio. By now he was very tired, and the walk was a long one. As darkness fell, it was difficult to pick his way safely along the unlit streets, but at last he arrived in the hilly open area.

The whole of San Francisco seemed to be there already. Tents had been pitched in long lines, and soldiers were still hard at work erecting more. Families not yet fortunate enough to be offered shelter squatted in circles round their piles of possessions. A few cooking fires were burning, but it was impossible to recognize anyone without going right up to a group and staring. Without warning, Robert found himself gripped by panic. He had promised to look after Alexa, and now he did not even know where she was. She and his mother must both be somewhere in the crowd, but how could he ever hope to find them amongst three hundred thousand people?

Robert had been frightened for the brief period of the earthquake itself, but that fear had quite quickly given way to a feeling of excitement, and a determination to make himself as useful as a grown man. The new fear which swept over him now was worse than anything he had felt as he waited for his bedroom ceiling to crash down on his head. He was tired and hungry; he had failed in his errand and lost touch with his family. He was in a foreign continent, in a strange city – a city which was collapsing before his eyes – and he didn't know what to do. For more than an hour he ran between the lines of the tents, calling his mother's name and Alexa's. Tears began to run silently down his cheeks and he was too tired even to be ashamed. At last, stumbling over a guy rope, he allowed himself to lie where he had fallen, sprawled in misery on the ground. Within five minutes he was asleep.

6

Terror disappears when danger ends: shame lasts longer. At the moment when the earthquake struck the Davidson mansion on Nob Hill, Alexa was in bed with Frank. She had not until that moment felt guilty – for they were, after all, engaged to be married now. As they clung together in that terrifying moment when some demon seemed to be shaking the house from side to side in an attempt to eject its occupants, it was difficult to feel

236

anything more specific than physical fear. Only afterwards, as they held their breaths, wondering whether there would be another shock, did it occur to her how unfortunate the timing had been. Even the most liberal-minded aunt – and Miss Halloran was far from being that – could not be expected to condone such immoral behaviour if it was unmistakably brought to her notice.

Alexa's anxiety on this count was quick to control any temptation to panic. As soon as the first violent tremor had subsided to a residual quivering, as though the air were trembling like a jelly, she hurried into her ball dress again – while Frank, equally conscious of the need to preserve his fiancée's reputation, acted as her dresser.

'I brought you home for a celebration drink,' he instructed her as he fastened the tiny satin buttons with surprising dexterity. 'Servants all asleep. You were sitting in the drawing room when the 'quake struck. I was fetching the champagne. If you're seen on the stairs now, then you're looking for me.'

He opened the bedroom door and glanced quickly up and down the gallery. Alexa waited for his signal that there was no one about. Then she slipped out of the room while he in turn set about dressing himself. There was no need to be quiet, for the air was full of noise. From outside the house a ragged jangling of church bells provided a discordant background to the crashing of falling walls and the hiss and crackle of electric cables. Inside, Mr Davidson's collection of clocks, suddenly set askew, protested with a whirr of broken springs or the untimely striking of some hour which had not yet arrived, and somewhere in the background the water from a broken pipe could be heard cascading down a wall in a noisy waterfall.

The curved central staircase of the house had collapsed, but it was possible to climb down the wreckage. Alexa heard her gown rip as a splintered banister tore at its skirt, but she did not allow this to delay her. She looked quickly round the drawing room as she entered, choosing the situation which would best explain her tousled hair. Even if she had had the ability to dress it again herself into the elaborate style which had caused gasps of admiration to greet her appearance at the ball, there would have been no time. When Frank's father hurried into the room a few moments later, he found her apparently in the process of extricating herself from beneath a fallen lacquer screen.

It was the beginning of a day in which nothing could be taken for granted. The morning developed the atmosphere almost of a party as more and more of the Davidsons' friends discovered that their own kitchens were not safe to use and arrived at the St Francis Hotel for breakfast. Alexa's remaining anxiety, about the safety of Margaret and Robert, was relieved when Brad brought them to join the group. Then the mood changed for a second time, with equal unexpectedness, as the first news arrived that fires were sweeping the city and threatened soon to be out of control: the hotel was declared to be in danger.

Mr Davidson had spent little time at the hotel, but had hurried off first to look to the security of his own business and afterwards to put himself at the disposal of the emergency citizens' committee; and Margaret and Brad soon followed to see what they could usefully do, while Robert later went off to collect her jewels. Alexa knew her own limitations. She could sing, but this was no time for singing: she had none of the practical skills or the brute strength which the present occasion demanded. Bewildered by the sudden turn of events, she was thankful at least that Frank was at hand to look after her and his aunt, and accepted his assurance that he had told Robert

238

where to look for them if the hotel was closed. When they were forced to leave, and had made their way to the Presidio, she sat patiently on the grass with Miss Halloran while places in a tent were found for them.

Daylight began to fade, and there was still no sign of Robert. Alexa began to walk around, looking for him and asking whether anyone had seen a freckled boy with bright ginger hair: but without success. As she turned back, afraid that she herself might become lost when darkness fell, she was conscious of the wind beginning to freshen, catching her long hair and tossing it over her shoulders. The breeze was strong enough partly to disperse the pall of smoke which had hidden until then the devastation of the city. The atmosphere on the Presidio hills, which for the past few hours had been one of an impromptu picnic, was chilled as gradually the chatter of conversation died away. One after another the citizens of San Francisco rose to their feet to watch their city burning. The crimson glow of flames in the east was far brighter than the rich sunset in the west. It was dramatic – in a way, even beautiful – but at the same time it was terrifying. The first shock of disbelief amongst the waiting crowds changed to a feeling of desolation. Even the youngest children, who had spent the afternoon happily playing, were infected by their parents' fear and fell silent with the rest.

Alexa had not yet had time to develop any sentimental attachment to San Francisco, but she searched the disaster area with her eyes as intently as anyone else.

'Where is Van Ness Avenue?' she asked the woman standing nearest to her at that moment. Once it had been pointed out, recognizable by its unusual width, she sighed with relief. The fire was nowhere near it. There was no discernible obstacle to prevent Robert from making his way safely to the hills. If they had so far failed to find each other, it must be only because of the thousands of people around. In the morning light, everything would be easier. As for Margaret, Alexa had felt no real anxiety about her once it was known that she and Robert had not been hurt in the earthquake. As long as anyone needed a doctor, Margaret would continue to work. Returning to the tent, Alexa was able to subdue her fears and hope that all would be well in the morning.

She was accustomed to warm blankets and comfortable beds, and to a sleeping pattern which started very late at night and continued until late morning, not from sunset to sunrise. Stiff and uncomfortable, she awoke in a tetchy mood, made less bearable by the knowledge that she must be careful not to reveal it. Everyone around her had lost his home, his possessions, probably even his livelihood, while she was still only a stranger in San Francisco. True, she had hoped to make it her home, but there had not yet been time to acquire any real stake in the city. The tool of her trade was her voice, and she carried it with her. When she was so much less unfortunate than so many others, she could not expect sympathy. The realization of that fact did nothing to improve her temper.

Like everyone else, she stepped out first of all to look down on the city. The fire had spread during the night. It was moving now so steadily that it could be seen to devour one block after another along a wide front. Alexa heard gasps of horror and hysterical tears as some of her neighbours saw for the first time that their homes had ceased to exist.

Frank, who had slept outside the tent, came to stand beside her.

'You and Aunt Halloran must get out of the city,' he said. 'Cassie will be taking it for granted that we shall all make our way to her as soon as we can.'

'Is it possible to leave?' asked Alexa.

'The ferry is running across the bay to Oakland. There were so many thousand people in the queue already yesterday that I thought it hopeless to join in. But it is the only way out of San Francisco, and San Francisco is ceasing to exist. Even if the wait takes a week, to join the queue now may be the best plan.'

'But the fire, surely, is between us and the ferry.'

'The earliest buildings to burn are now safe from any further fire. The streets are hot to the feet, my father tells me, but there is a way through – it's the way that relief food supplies are coming up here.'

'I cannot leave without Margaret and Robert,' said Alexa. 'Even if Margaret doesn't want to come, I must at least tell her where I am going.'

Frank nodded his understanding. 'Look for them now, then, while I collect some food.'

Once again Alexa began to search, but this time she changed her mind after only a few moments. There were too many people, and most of them were on the move, searching for food or water. While she went in one direction, Robert might pass within a few feet of her, hurrying the other way. She had had a better idea. She climbed on to a rocky outcrop and began to sing.

Although Alexa loved to have an audience, it was not exhibitionism which made her display herself at such a time. She preferred people to stare at her when she was looking her best, not when her clothes were crumpled and her face dirty, and her long hair strained into peasant plaits. But if she sang something high and piercing, her voice would carry over a long distance. And if she chose an aria from *Carmen* which Robert had recently heard her practising in the apartment, he would recognize the sound at once.

Alexa never allowed herself to sing less than perfectly:

241

to be casual or slipshod was to risk spoiling her voice. She ignored the reactions of the people around her – some amazed, some admiring, and some almost angry that anyone could appear carefree when they themselves were despairing. Her interest at this moment was in one possible member of her audience only.

Robert came running, rubbing the sleep from his eyes, before she had finished the song. Alexa recognized at once that he had been distressed. She knew that he found it embarrassing to be hugged or kissed, especially in public, but she also guessed instinctively that he needed the opportunity now to express his relief. Still singing, although less loudly, she stepped down from her makeshift platform and whirled him round in the gypsy dance which the aria accompanied. She felt the tightness of his grip, and returned it in reassurance.

The relief of the reunion lasted for only a short time. She had been worried about him, and conscious that if he had suffered any kind of accident it would have been her fault for sending him out on her errand. Guilt made her first of all press for a quick assurance that at least he had been successful, and then snap at him in annoyance when she discovered that he had not.

Frank returned with the breakfast rations to find them still bickering.

Robert's face was sulky. 'I couldn't help it,' he said. 'They were going to shoot looters. I heard them say so.'

'That's ridiculous! You weren't a looter.' But Alexa sighed, reminding herself that she had no right to be angry. 'My own fault, I suppose. I should have gone myself instead of leaving it to a child.'

'I'm not a child!'

'Obviously you are when it comes to getting past a guard. I wouldn't have let him stop *me* like that. All one has to do is to explain. But I suppose they weren't prepared to take a boy seriously. Well, thank you for trying, Robert. Frank, I must go back to the apartment.'

'You'll do no such thing,' Frank told her. 'What do a few clothes matter?'

'It's more than clothes. I left some jewels there.'

'More fool you, my darling. Why didn't you have them in a bank?'

'Because I'd intended to wear them at the ball. I only changed my mind when Margaret got upset about them for some reason, at the last moment. It didn't seem that one night could do much harm. Anyway, the jewels that I *did* put in the bank are probably lost under a pile of rubble by now.'

'Let them go,' said Frank. He kissed her affectionately. 'I can give you all the jewels you want.'

'I know you can, dearest. But these are something special.'

'Valuable, you mean?'

'They *are* valuable certainly. Worth a small fortune, in fact. Nothing to compare with the Davidson fortune, but enough to make me feel that I shouldn't be marrying you as a pauper.'

'If you hadn't a cent in the world, your face would still be your fortune,' said Frank. 'And your voice is a second fortune. The Davidsons have nothing to offer in comparison.'

'That's not the only reason why I want them.' It came almost as a surprise to Alexa to discover how strong her feelings were for the rubies. Most of her jewels – and she had owned a good many, whatever might by now have become of them – were important to her mainly as a visible token that she need never be poor again as she had been poor in her childhood. 'They're a family heirloom. A legacy from my father. I really do want to fetch them, Frank. Van Ness isn't far out of the way. If

243

you take Miss Halloran directly to join the ferry queue, I could catch up with you almost as soon as you had a place in it. You said yourself that there might be several days to wait, so an hour won't make much difference.'

'I don't want you wandering about the streets alone,' said Frank. 'If you want your jewels, you shall have them. But I'll get them. You concentrate on finding Dr Scott, and when you've met up with her, don't let her get away again. I'll be back as soon as I can, and then we'll set about making our way to Cassie.'

'I'd rather go myself,' said Alexa. It seemed to her that a woman might have less trouble than a man in persuading a guard that she was not a looter; and from what Robert had said it seemed that no other obstacles were likely to present themselves in that part of the city.

'I already told you, *I'm* going,' said Frank. His eyes smiled at her as merrily as ever, but the set of his lips was firm.

Alexa was not accustomed to take orders from the men who loved her. Through many years of adulation she had become spoiled, expecting every whim to be indulged. Only Matthew had been strong enough to impose his own wishes, not once but twice. This was the first argument that she and Frank had had during their courtship, and Alexa was sensitive enough to see how important it was to Frank that he should win it. He was telling her that she would have to surrender some of her independence when they were married. Alexa accepted his decision with a smile and thanked him with a kiss.

The errand was bound to take him a long time. He had not yet returned when Alexa was able to report to Robert that she had found his mother working at a first-aid station. She had been less successful in persuading Margaret to cross the bay with Frank, but this came as little surprise. It was enough that she had been able to pass on

244

Cassie's address, so that they could all be sure of coming together eventually.

After a late breakfast of pressed beef, Alexa set herself to comfort Miss Halloran, expecting that a woman of her age and dignity would by now be upset by the primitive conditions which she was being forced to endure. But to her surprise the old lady was in fine form. All her stiffness of manner had dropped away, almost as though she were enjoying the adventure. She kept both Alexa and Robert enthralled by stories of the way in which she had travelled from Ireland forty years earlier, first in the steerage of an emigrant ship, then in the almost equal discomfort of an immigrant train, and lastly in a wagon across the desert and through Indian country.

Even the exciting experiences she recalled could not distract her hearers from looking frequently down towards the burning city. Alexa watched in horrified silence as the frontiers of the fire relentlessly extended themselves, leaping from roof to roof over the open spaces of streets and gardens. But in the early afternoon a sea mist blew in from the ocean, covering all the lower parts of the peninsula with a familiar white cloud which was immediately darkened by smoke into a black fog. The streets became invisible, and night appeared to fall far earlier than usual over the hills.

A series of violent explosions came from the direction of the built-up area, more startling because nothing of what was happening was visible. Rumours spread through the listening crowds. The arsenal had blown up, the firemen were dynamiting fire breaks, a gas main had been ignited, a warehouse full of spirits had exploded. Miss Halloran's chatter died away, and Alexa's worry and fear returned. She sent Robert off to stand in line for the evening rations of bread and water and Brad, ordered by his father to rest after two exhausting days, returned to join them, bringing with him eggs and milk. They cooked the eggs on a neighbour's fire, and ate in silence.

So the long hours of the evening passed, with the city invisible under its thick blanket of smoky fog: and still Frank did not return.

7

In a new and mobile society, wealth and respect grow at the same rate. By 1906 Greg Davidson enjoyed more of both than could be boasted by most of his fellow citizens in San Francisco, but he had not acquired them without effort.

At the end of a voyage round the Horn, he had arrived at the Golden Gate in 1879 without a penny to his name. William Lorimer, who had provided him with a free passage, saw no reason to contribute any additional funds. Even before the voyage began, David Gregson had died, buried in a new identity: it was as Greg Davidson that he began to earn his living by using the skills of his boyhood apprenticeship. He wound clocks and mended clocks and made new parts for clocks, finding himself increasingly useful in the houses of newly-rich men who were not used to the care of possessions. One of them asked him to repair the lock of a safe; another, to construct a new safe disguised as a bookcase. Greg met the challenges and moved on to make more safes, this time for himself. He acquired a building which, though semi-derelict above ground, boasted a brick cellar, and was soon able to offer secure strong-room facilities for gentlemen who wished to leave their valuables in the city and be sure of finding them again when they returned.

At that time there was still gold coming out of Comstock Hill; and when the new strike was made in the Yukon, the miners who hurried to make their fortunes there left from San Francisco and brought their gains back to the city. Greg's own fortune was founded on the single fact that he was known to be honest. As time went by, his customers became friends. He acquired interests of his own by advancing funds for exploration in return for a percentage of any eventual discovery; and he expanded his safe deposit business until he was making loans and investments on a considerable scale. For the second time in his life he had made the transition from locksmith to accountant, and found that he had become a banker again. He still owned a company which made safes and locks – and he had observed with pride that both his sons had inherited his own manual dexterity – but the capital on which his real wealth was founded was his reputation for integrity.

Often – especially in the early days – he remembered John Junius Lorimer, whom he had once admired for his authority and wiliness. Like everyone else, he had been fooled by the chairman of Lorimer's, and his admiration had changed to hatred long before he left England.

His feeling for Margaret Lorimer had been very different. True, they had parted in a quarrel. But as distance calmed his own anger, he was able to recognize that he had expected too much. A young girl who had always been devoted to her father could not be expected to accept in a moment that John Junius's behaviour was not only criminal but spiteful as well in its intended effect on herself and her fiancé. Faced with a divided loyalty she had chosen wrongly, but Greg could understand her reasons. In the leisure which the long voyage provided, he accepted the fact that he still loved her – and at the same time felt able to hope that she would love him again when she had had time to understand the tangled story.

So he had written to her from a shabby lodging house in San Francisco soon after his arrival. With nothing to offer except his own devotion, he was forced to rely on her adventurous spirit to bring her to his side – but when he remembered the determination which he had so often seen flashing in her eyes, it seemed to him that this would be enough.

He used one of the Lorimer Line captains as his messenger, and calculated as closely as he could how long it would take for his letter to reach Bristol and for Margaret in turn to travel out. In the meantime he worked hard so that she should find him, when she came, well established and with his own home: and when the necessary time had elapsed he met every ship out of Bristol over a period of many months. Only when, with a sick heart, he had accepted the fact that she intended neither to come herself nor even to answer his letter, did he accept the opportunity which for some time had been dangling before him. He married Moira Halloran, the daughter of one of his Comstock customers, and set himself to forget Margaret Lorimer. In this he had largely succeeded.

Certainly, no one could have been further from his thoughts as the earthquake struck the city. He had kept his head even in the first confused hours of the emergency. Realizing almost at once the threat posed by fire, he had hurried away from the St Francis Hotel as soon as his family was safely settled there. Before noon on the first day his staff had carried everything that could be salvaged from his offices and strongrooms to a specially chartered ship which was now moored out in the bay, waiting until it should be safe to return to land. With that anxiety relieved, he added his authority to a committee of the leading citizens of San Francisco who were dividing emergency tasks between them. Some, while the firemen and troops fought to control the fire, crossed over to Oakland. There they were organizing hospitality for the homeless; and newspapers whose rivalry in normal times was notorious were printing a joint edition which listed the names of all those for whom beds were already waiting across the bay. The ferry which took refugees away from the disaster area returned on each round trip laden with food and water. It was Greg's responsibility to see that supplies were fairly distributed.

He would have been glad of Frank's help, and had suggested as much to Brad when he sent the exhausted boy off to rest at last. But it did not trouble him that there was no response to the message. There were a good many ways in which an able-bodied young man might be making himself useful at this time. He might even have been compulsorily drafted into one of the fire-fighting squads which were now attempting to contain the fire by creating fire breaks so wide that the flames could not leap across them.

By ten o'clock on the evening of the second day he was very tired. The opera ball had ended only at four o'clock on the night of the earthquake, so it had been from his first deep sleep that the shock had awakened him, and he had had no rest since then. He made his way towards the position which Brad had described to him as the family base. The smoke which had shrouded the buildings of San Francisco earlier in the evening had been dispersed by the night breeze, and so bright now was the light which came from the city burning below that he had no difficulty in picking his way between the people who lay sleeping on the ground.

The sound of a gasp and a scream, followed by a kind of sobbing, made him pause. Weary though he was, he could not pass by any new emergency, and he knew that in every community there were a few who would try to profit from the misfortunes of others. There might be assaults and robberies: if so, there must be firm action.

He made his way towards the sound and then came to a halt, smiling. A city might be dying, but babies were still being born. This one had already arrived – and in good health, to judge by the furious strength of its cries. A woman, kneeling on the ground in front of the mother, was dealing efficiently with the birth, while other women from nearby groups stood ready with blankets to wrap the child and even a little precious water to wash it.

When it seemed that she was satisfied that everything was in order, the woman who had delivered the baby wiped her hands on the grass to clean them and rose to her feet. She staggered a little with stiffness and exhaustion as she turned. Greg put out a hand to steady her. By the crimson light of the flames he saw her face, and recognized her at once.

He could tell that she had identified him with equal speed – and with none of the surprise, it seemed, that he was bound to feel. For what felt like a very long time, he was too stunned to speak.

'Margaret!' he exclaimed at last. 'Margaret!' He shook his head in incredulity and then laughed, as though some anticlimax was needed to reduce the electric tension between them. 'Last time I saw you,' he said, 'you were soaked through with rain. Your hair was plastered against your face and your black cape drooped with dampness. And now I see you again after so many years, and your hair is still tousled, but this time it's blood and not water which streaks your face.'

'There have been moments of tidiness in between,' said Margaret. In spite of her weariness, her eyes were twinkling with laughter, and the memory of the way she had so often teased him when they were young and in love overwhelmed him with delight. He held out both hands towards her.

'I am very happy to see you again, Margaret.'

'And I you, David.' She accepted his grip, and smiled at him with a pleasure which seemed equal to his own.

'Could you bring yourself to call me Greg?' he asked. 'I am known here only as Greg Davidson. And I imagine that you have long ceased to be Margaret Lorimer.'

'Yes,' she agreed. 'I married Charles Scott, the son of our old family doctor. But he died a good many years ago. I support myself now. I am a doctor as well.'

'I remember that was always your ambition. I'm very glad to hear that you weren't disappointed.'

There were people all around. No more public place could be imagined for such a reunion. Yet the intensity of their reaction to each other seemed to create a fence of privacy around them, and all the nearby bustle of conversation was concerned with the new baby. Greg was conscious of a wish to keep on talking, but every subject – whether of reminiscence or enquiry – seemed too trivial. In the end, he could not resist asking the one question which had worried him for many years.

'I wrote to you, Margaret, after I had arrived here. We spoke unkindly to each other at our last meeting, and it was my dearest wish that we could agree to forget our suspicions, on both sides. I hoped that you might be willing to join me here. But you didn't answer my letter.'

Even in the lurid light of the fire he thought he saw her grow pale.

'I never received it,' she said quietly.

'The captain who carried it for me put it directly into the hands of your brother William.'

Margaret's fists clenched with anger and fell to her sides.

'Oh!' she cried. 'Yes, I well believe that. It seems to have been William's delight to interfere in the lives of every member of his family. Oh David, if only I had known! I had no way of finding out where you had gone. I wanted so much to tell you that I had discovered my mistake, to apologize to you. But I could only wait until I heard from you, and I heard nothing.' She gave a sigh which acknowledged that it was too late for regrets. 'You received a good deal of unkindness from the Lorimer family in England, David – Greg. I'm glad at least to discover that you've found success and happiness here.'

Her comment was accurate enough. His choice of a wife had not proved satisfactory in every respect, but he had adored each of his three children from the moment they were born, and they had responded by developing a relationship of easy friendship with him, very different from the conflicts of autocracy and rebellion which afflicted the households of many of his friends. And he certainly had no complaints about his material prosperity. But at such a moment none of that seemed important. He struggled for the right words to express the pleasure he felt at his encounter. Before he could find them, however, they were both startled by a sudden series of explosions down in the city.

'Not before time,' Greg said, turning to look in the direction of the sound. 'That must be the last of the fire breaks. They're demolishing houses to make wide open strips around the area which there is no hope of saving. The Western Addition was cut off earlier in the evening. Sounds as though they're trying to contain the fire in the south now.' He dismissed the matter from his mind. 'Tell me, Margaret, how it was that you looked so little surprised to see me, if you didn't know my home was here?'

'I caught sight of you forty-eight hours ago, at the opera.'

'Then why did you not come at once – ?'

'I was afraid that if I startled you by a sudden public encounter, you would remember only how angry you had been with me at our last meeting. I wrote you a letter instead, hoping that you would be able to forgive me. But in our hurry to get out into the open after the earthquake, I quite forgot about it. It must still be lying on the table of our apartment on Van Ness Avenue.'

'Then we must assume that it is now a scattering of tiny fragments, since the Van Ness apartment blocks have already succumbed to the dynamite which created the fire breaks.' He looked with sympathy at the alarm on her face. 'And I suppose all your possessions were still inside?'

'Yes. Well, I suppose all of us here are in much the same situation.' It seemed that she needed a moment to restore her courage; but then she made an effort to smile, and returned to the subject of their earlier conversation. 'As soon as I saw you, I knew that we should be certain to meet. The name Davidson had meant nothing to me until that moment, of course. But I learned yesterday – what no doubt you know already – that your son is going to marry Alexa.'

Now she had certainly startled him. 'You are Alexa Reni's guardian, then? Of course – Dr Scott! Women change their names more legally than men, but just as confusingly. My sister-in-law told me – '

On second thoughts, he decided not to repeat the report which Miss Halloran had made to him on his return to San Francisco. She had warned him of Frank's involvement with the new star of the opera house. 'She is a little old for Frank,' had been her comment. 'Twenty-four, I understand. But she is most correctly escorted by her guardian, a Dr Scott. A very respectable woman, although perhaps a shade modern in her views. They both seem well accustomed to good society. I have allowed it to be known that I am receiving them.'

It was possible, thought Greg, that Margaret might not appreciate this last mark of approbation. He smiled at her again without speaking, and offered his arm so that they could walk on together.

'I trust you approve of Alexa,' Margaret said. 'Your son will find her the most affectionate wife possible, but I know that she hopes to continue her career for a few years, while her voice is still at its peak. I imagine that they have discussed this together, and found it no obstacle. I hope that you – '

'I leave Frank to make his own decisions,' said Greg. 'He is twenty-one, he has some money of his own from his mother, and I rely on his good sense. As for Alexa, I have hardly had time to know her.' He had seen her for the first time on the stage, forty-eight hours earlier, in fact, and the effect was disconcerting. She was so convincing an actress that he had half expected to be introduced eventually to a vivacious, sensual gypsy. It came as a shock – although a delightful one – to find himself later, at the ball, meeting a tall, slender young woman, dressed with an elegance which put the ladies of San Francisco in the shade, and with her fair, delicate skin and beautiful face set off by a crown of reddish-blonde hair. It would be no exaggeration to say that her loveliness had for a moment taken his breath away.

'It would hardly be honest of me to pretend that I have thought of you every day since we last met,' he said abruptly as they walked. 'But after the opera, as I watched Frank and Alexa dancing together – so happy, and so much in love – I *did* think of you. I remembered the ball which you and I attended in Bristol.' He knew that Margaret would not have forgotten the occasion he meant. 'I remembered how happy *we* were that night, and how lovely you looked. And for a moment I found myself overcome with hatred of your father, who wrecked it all for us. A useless emotion: I imagine he must have died many years ago.'

'Yes. Soon after you left Bristol,' said Margaret quietly. 'The letter you left behind made his conviction certain. He killed himself rather than go to prison. Did you not hear of it?'

The words brought Greg to a halt. He turned to stare into Margaret's eyes and shook his head. 'So it is I, and not you, who need to ask for forgiveness.'

Still holding his arm, Margaret walked on, so that he was forced to continue beside her. 'What you wrote was the truth,' she told him. 'He was my father: I loved him and I shall always love his memory. But I understand that your feelings must be very different.'

'I have lived on my hatred of him for many years,' admitted Greg. 'My strength very largely came from it. I worked to build myself a fortune that would be larger than his, and more worthy of pride because I started from nothing. My house is grander than Brinsley House, and the treasures it contains are greater.' He checked himself, laughing ruefully. 'At least, that was the case two days ago. There are more ways than one of being deprived of possessions. But even if the house has gone, I can afford to replace it. I was always ambitious, but hatred of John Junius Lorimer has been the fuel of my ambition ever since I arrived here. That is another reason why now, when I am successful, my children may marry whom they choose. Without conditions, without manipulations.'

The outburst was hardly a tactful one, but he needed to express his feelings once in order that Margaret should understand them. They had both suffered greatly in their youth from lies and deceptions imposed on them by others. Now, in control of their own lives, they could afford to indulge in sincerity. His pleasure at seeing Margaret again was so intense that he could feel happiness bubbling to the surface of his emotions even in such a time of disaster. They would be friends again – indeed, they were friends already, for he felt confident that Margaret's reaction to their meeting matched his. Time, and the relationship between Frank and Alexa, would draw them even closer together. She was a widow, she had said, and he was a widower. There was no need to make plans, to put anything into words. It was enough that they should share these impressions of instant sympathy.

In the meantime, he was anxious to learn everything he could about Margaret's life in the years they had spent apart. His mind teemed with questions. He began with the one which came nearest to home.

'Tell me,' he said. 'How did you come to be Alexa's guardian?'

8

Contentment is quickly punctured by interrogation. A moment before, Margaret had been so happy that she had completely forgotten how weary she was, and how terrible were the circumstances in which she had met her one-time fiancé again. The speed with which they fell into sympathy with each other after so many years apart warmed her heart with a peacefulness which could not be disturbed by their unusual surroundings. And then all this was shattered by a simple, inevitable question.

'How did you come to be Alexa's guardian?'

Margaret found it incredible that she had given no previous thought to the problem. From the moment when she caught sight of the man whom she must now remember to think of as Greg, she had been conscious only of the need to talk out her own relationship with him, so that the events of the past should not be allowed to come between them again. She had made no attempt to relate Alexa's situation to her own – indeed, she had hardly acknowledged that any relationship existed.

The unnerving events of the past two days no doubt excused her lack of thought, but did not help her to answer the question. Too many points needed to be considered. Because Alexa used her mother's name, nothing until now could have prompted Greg to connect her with the Lorimers of Bristol. It would not endear her to her future father-in-law when he discovered that she was the daughter of John Junius Lorimer. Doubtless he would be fair-minded enough not to hold it against her, but it was not a fact to be announced without thought. And then there was the minor difficulty of Alexa's lie about her age. A young woman who was only twenty-four years old could not be the daughter of a man who had died twenty-seven years ago. Margaret – although reluctantly – had promised not to disturb what seemed at the time to be a small social lie: but a truthful answer to an apparently unrelated question would quickly reveal that Margaret's information could not be reconciled with Alexa's version of the facts.

Without realizing it, Margaret groaned aloud. The question was simple, the answer should have been straightforward: it was ridiculous to find herself prevented from answering it by a careless promise. It might have seemed equally simple to answer in a different way; telling Greg only that Alexa was the daughter of an old friend, her music teacher, and had been orphaned while she was still a child. But one thing was clear to Margaret. Enough trouble had been caused in her marriage to Charles by her concealment of the details of Alexa's parentage. She did not intend to let the same situation arise again in this unexpectedly renewed friendship. In no circumstances would she lie to Greg. But before she actually told the truth, Alexa had the right to know what the danger was, so that she could prepare herself to meet it. Greg's question could be answered tomorrow; but not today.

Margaret's groan – which she was hardly conscious of having made – was caused by her dilemma. But Greg, who could not have known the complicated thoughts aroused by his straightforward query, must have assumed that her sudden appearance of collapse was caused by exhaustion, or by a natural reaction as an intensive period of work came to an end.

'When did you last sleep?' he demanded.

'I don't remember.'

'You've been working ever since the earthquake?'

'There were so many broken bones to be set,' she murmured. 'And then burns to dress. I was just on my way to rest when I was called to deliver the baby.' Until he asked her, she had not realized how tired she was. Now, suddenly, her weariness overcame her. She stood still, unable even to put one foot in front of the other. She felt Greg's arm move to encircle her waist, steadying her for a moment lest she should fall. Then, without warning, he picked her up and began to carry her towards the lines of tents.

Once upon a time, Margaret remembered through a haze of weariness, she had longed for the day to come when this man would pick her up in just such a way and carry her on her wedding day over the threshold of the home in Bristol which they were to share. It was odd, it was very odd indeed, that it should take an appalling series of calamities before she could at last allow her head to sink on to his shoulder, and sleep.

She was awakened next morning by Alexa, who came to tell her that breakfast was being prepared outside the tent. Margaret looked with distaste at her own dirty and crumpled clothes, but there was nothing to be done about them. As she tried to comb her tangled hair into some kind of tidiness, she asked Alexa about her state of health, and Robert's.

Alexa shrugged off the enquiry. 'Why did you not come to the opera ball?' she asked instead. 'I needed you there.'

'I'm sorry.' Margaret hesitated. A good many explanations were needed, but these surroundings, so lacking in privacy, did not provide the right place to start.

Alexa accepted that she was not to have an answer at once. Her second comment suggested that she had been giving a good deal of thought to Margaret's behaviour and was trying to connect the various puzzles suggested by it. 'Mr Davidson brought you here last night,' she said.

'Yes, I know. I was most grateful to him. I was very tired – too tired to walk.'

'But how did you and he know that you were both looking for the same place, that you both knew me? I had had no opportunity to introduce you.'

'We had met before. A long time ago, in England. It's a coincidence – a happy one, though. I'll tell you the whole story when we have time.'

'I still don't understand –'

'Later,' said Margaret firmly. She was stiff and aching and her head swam with tiredness, but it was time to take a grip on the new day. When today's history was being

259

made all round her, it was no time to begin explaining what had happened almost thirty years ago. 'Is Mr Davidson here now?'

Alexa shook her head. 'No. He had to go early to supervise the rations again. But he's just sent Brad back with a message. A friend of his, who lives on the other side of the bay, has sailed his private yacht over. It's waiting to take us all across. So we shan't need to queue for the Oakland ferry.'

'I can't leave here, Alexa. You and Robert must go, of course, but I must stay.'

'I told Mr Davidson that you'd argue. He laughed and said he betted you would. He said it in an odd way. That was what made me think that you knew him already. Anyway, he said to tell you that the same yacht is already loaded with five women who are expecting babies in the next few days, and the owner proposes to make as many further trips as are necessary to pick up any more pregnant women. So you can make yourself useful organizing a maternity ward as soon as we get to the other side.'

'Will that be anywhere near where Cassie lives?'

'Not very; but nearer than here, of course. We can take a train from Oakland to Napa. Once we're across the bay, we'll be able to telephone ahead, and Cassie will send horses down to the railroad station.'

As Greg had correctly guessed, the pregnant women were enough to sway Margaret's decision. Every factor – of hygiene, food, warmth and peace of mind – combined to make it wise for anyone in need of medical care to escape from a refuge area which was becoming steadily more crowded and insanitary as the city continued to burn. She had already decided to go as she renewed her acquaintance with Miss Halloran and greeted Robert and

Brad, enjoying the meal of bread and beans which they had prepared.

'Where's Frank?' she asked Alexa.

'I don't know. He went down into the city yesterday, and he hasn't come back.' Alexa's voice was tense.

'He'll be all right,' said Miss Halloran. The broadness of her Irish accent seemed to have increased as all other social conventions ceased to be observed. 'They're saying that every fit man in the streets has been rounded up to bury the dead. Frank's grandfather made his start in life digging canals. The boy will come to no harm using a spade for a day or two. And he'll know that we'll be making for Cassie's place.'

Margaret was watching Alexa's face, and noticed the anxiety it showed. But perhaps, she thought, it was not entirely on Frank's behalf. Everyone by now was feeling the strain of the past few days; and Alexa, in particular, who always took such pains with her appearance, could not be expected to look as calmly beautiful as usual when nothing but a great deal of dirt and a very small amount of water had been applied to her complexion.

At the slow pace made necessary by Miss Halloran's presence, the little party made its way down to the pier. The air at the lower level was so hot that even with scarves across their faces they felt their throats burning with each breath, and the very earth underfoot was smouldering. Camping on the Presidio, there had been a sense of devastation but not of actual danger. Amongst the ruined streets, by contrast, fire darted unpredictably, as though from the mouth of a roaming dragon – exploding through the roof of a house apparently unaffected, or roaring through a narrow gap as if the flames were arrows shot by a bow at random. Margaret was relieved when they reached the yacht. To her surprise, she found that as well as the five pregnant women, Greg was already on board. The military authorities had taken over his food station, he told them, leaving him free to escort his elderly sister-in-law and the rest of the family out of danger. Cassie's house was not easy to reach, and conditions on the eastern shore of the bay might well be chaotic. He would feel easier in his mind now that he could accompany them.

Margaret made it her first task, as the yacht slipped away from the pier, to examine the five women and estimate the likelihood of any immediate action being necessary. Robert and Alexa were used to seeing her at work, but she was conscious that the three Americans were looking at her curiously. Miss Halloran seemed hardly to approve, although realizing that the circumstances were unusual. Brad was fascinated. As for Greg, she several times caught sight of him smiling, but could not quite determine whether it was with pleasure or amusement.

When she had finished, there was time to look around. In front of them, a range of heavily wooded hills rose steeply from the sparkling blue water of the bay. But behind, the view was very different. The whole sky was black with a pillar of smoke which, while it dispersed at the top, was continually renewed from below. Even at this distance it was possible to hear the relentless roar with which the flames devoured one block of buildings after another. The breeze off the water was cool, but it was something more than that which caused her to shiver.

Greg came to stand beside her, looking in the same direction.

'A terrible sight,' he said.

'It must be far worse for you than for me,' Margaret recognized. 'Everything that burns down is part of your home. I'm only a foreigner.'

'A foreigner who chose an unlucky time to visit. You

came just to be with Alexa, I guess – for only a few weeks? Or were you reckoning to stay? Now that Alexa's planning to marry, I can see that you may be rethinking whatever arrangements you've made, but what was in your mind when you came?'

'We did come here expecting to settle,' said Margaret. 'It was all to depend on how Alexa was received. If for some reason she'd found that she didn't appeal to American audiences, she knew that she would be welcome back in Europe. But she wanted to make a career for herself in the New World if she could. And as soon as that was decided, I proposed to look for employment here as well.'

'You're saying all that in the past tense.'

'Does San Francisco still have an opera house?' asked Margaret. 'And hospitals?'

'It still has sick people,' Greg pointed out. 'And you may be surprised how quickly we pull ourselves together to deal with them. This must be the worst fire in the history of San Francisco, but it's surely not the first. Rebuilding, rebuilding fast, is something we take for granted.'

'In the same place?' queried Margaret.

'In exactly the same place.'

'Is that wise? Frank said something about a fault in the earth – something that had caused earthquakes here before, and might easily do it again.'

'No, it's not wise,' said Greg. 'It's sentimental. But there's something to be said for being sentimental. I hope you'll decide to make your home here after all, Margaret, in spite of the roughness of your welcome.'

Margaret looked into his eyes, trying to decide on what level of feeling he was speaking. As they talked together on the previous evening, he had displayed a need to interrogate her, to understand what had happened in the past: their meeting must, of course, have come as a considerable shock to him. It seemed as though now he had arrived at some kind of conclusion, which made questions less necessary. As though he understood her deduction, and accepted it, he met her look steadily.

'The memory of love is a very potent force, isn't it?' he asked. 'Different from love itself. More dangerous, I guess. But strong. It doesn't develop over the years, and change, as love does. It takes one straight back to the time of being young and trustful and hopeful. Yes, very dangerous. As insecure a foundation to build on as the San Andreas Fault. But at a time like this, one needs to hold on to anything which promises a little hope.' Unexpectedly he laughed. 'My timing's not too good,' he said. 'I'm fifty-six years old, I haven't shaved for three days and I smell of smoke and sweat. I can hardly imagine a less romantic figure. All I'd better say is, please don't be in too much of a hurry to get away from San Francisco.'

His hands reached forward, and there was a second in which Margaret thought that he was about to kiss her. But whether it was the thought of his own stubbly chin that dissuaded him, or the awareness of Miss Halloran's observant eyes, he did no more than squeeze her waist gently for a moment, smiling, before turning away to join the two boys.

Margaret leaned over the rail of the yacht and stared down into the water. It made no sense that whatever power it was that had first drawn Greg and herself together so many years ago should still be as strong as ever. She knew nothing of his life in these past years, just as he knew nothing about hers. They had, surely, become strangers. And yet, all lovers must start as strangers.

Margaret reminded herself that she ought to be cautious. To have loved a man once was no sufficient reason for loving him again. It could mean merely that she was lonely, resentful of the fact that her married life had lasted for such a very short time, reluctant to admit that she was too old ever again to attract a man's love. But it was difficult, all the same, to control her exhilaration. In an effort to remind herself that only a few miles away there were people weeping for their dead or horrified by the loss of their homes and all their possessions, she raised her eyes again to the sinister tower of smoke. But it was no good. Already, all the moments of fear and strain which the past three days had brought seemed to be pushing themselves into the back of her mind, refusing to be remembered. If anyone were to ask me what happened in San Francisco in the April of nineteen hundred and six, she told herself, ashamed and excited at the same time, what should I want to answer? Not that I watched the destruction of a city. Only that there I met my first love again.

9

When a whole community suffers a disaster, the sympathy it attracts is far greater than would have been earned by the sum of individual losses. When Margaret and the other passengers on the yacht arrived at Oakland, it seemed as though the whole population of the United States was jostling for space along the eastern shore of the bay. There were refugees hoping to return as soon as possible, relatives anxious for news, and relief workers either waiting to help those who fled from the city or struggling to get their supplies through to those who had no choice but to stay. Emergency hospitals were already fully manned, and Margaret found that there was nothing she could usefully do except move out of the area as quickly as possible.

Greg called at a bank and drew out money which he distributed amongst the adults in the party, so that they should all be able to supply themselves with necessities, but they found that no one in Oakland would accept payment. It was not only the relief organizations which were handing out clothes and bolts of cloth: shopkeepers took one look at the blood and dirt which stained Margaret's skirts and pressed replacements on her. Even the train which carried the little party north to Napa was free.

Greg sat next to Margaret in the train. Alexa and Miss Halloran, facing them, must have seen how close the two were sitting, but they made no comment: conventions had crumbled in the emergency, Margaret herself pretended that she had not noticed. She stared out of the window as the train wound its way through pastures and vineyards and woods, as though it were only the pleasant view which kept a smile on her face. Even without looking, she was sure that Greg was smiling too.

Cassie's bright new home welcomed them to peace and rest at last. Cassie herself, sweet-faced and unaffected, hurried from one to another in relief and welcome. She had not expected strangers to arrive with her family, but accepted Margaret and Alexa as her guests without question, sending Brad and Robert to find beds with a neighbour.

'And Frank?' she asked.

'We are the rats who have deserted the sinking ship,' her father told her. 'Frank is one of the captains who has remained behind to keep it afloat.'

'Let's hope he doesn't think it his duty to go down with it.' The subject was not pursued. There was hot water waiting for baths, and feather mattresses for sleep. The nightmare was over.

For twenty-four hours Margaret was content to relax in the fresh country air and the quiet of the valley. Brad and Robert went off at dawn to join the gang of men who were clearing a stretch of scrubland which would soon become part of a new vineyard, after Cassie had anxiously warned her English guest how to recognize and avoid poison oak. Alexa, to whom a constantly changing supply of clean clothes was a necessity of life, set to work at once to make herself new underwear from a length of white cotton which had been given to her at Oakland. She wore one of her gift dresses as well, a country print very different in style from the fashionable dresses which were her normal attire. Although the effect was incongruous, she refused to take off the opals which she had worn to the opera ball. It was as though, having lost everything else, she needed to feel that these last treasures could not slip away from her.

'The rubies!' exclaimed Margaret, reminded of them by the sight of the opals. 'I left them behind in the apartment!'

'You were right to be superstitious about them.' Alexa's attempt to laugh was not altogether successful. 'I have only to try them on for five minutes, and a whole city is destroyed. Powerful magic indeed!' She bent her head in concentration over her cutting-out.

Margaret was surprised that the subject should be dismissed with so little curiosity or regret. But she was relieved that Alexa did not criticize her for the haste and lack of thought with which she had left the apartment.

Greg too had altered his appearance from that of the previous day. His complexion, close-shaven, seemed positively polished with cleanliness and his newly washed hair bounced off his forehead in springy curls. The aura

267

of success clung to him, as well as that of soap. But whereas Margaret's father, in the days when he was a powerful businessman, had never been able to put off his air of authority, but tyrannized his family as completely as his staff, Greg had a different aptitude. No one taking note of his confidence and decisiveness could doubt that he was a man of importance in his community. But he had the ability, it seemed, to forget his responsibilities. In London, Margaret had been attracted to Lord Glanville partly because she was flattered when an aristocrat unbent to confide in her. Now, far more strongly, she recognized that part of Greg's attraction lay in the fact that he was an energetic and successful man who could nevertheless pay her the compliment of completely relaxing in her presence. He took for granted both her contentment and his own in their new relationship.

The country idyll could not, however, remain undisturbed for long. After their second breakfast at Cassie's house, Greg came to stand beside Margaret on the verandah and announced that he must return to Oakland.

'The fire in the city is under control at last,' he said. 'I must be ready to go back as soon as anyone is allowed into the business area. There will be a great deal to decide – about my own affairs, those of my customers, the rebuilding of premises, the state of our home. I may not be able to return for some time. But I shall send Frank up as soon as I can find him. He will need a rest. Margaret, allow me to deal with your affairs at the same time as far as I can. Did you have insurance to cover your possessions?'

'How can insurance companies cover losses on such a scale?' asked Margaret. 'Surely they will all go bankrupt?'

'They'll have to choose between ruining themselves by meeting their obligations at once or ruining themselves by refusing to pay and finding themselves without customers in the future. Give me the facts, and I will see what can be done. What were your banking arrangements? Did you actually transfer your money to San Francisco?'

'Fortunately not,' said Margaret. 'We intended to do that when our plans were settled. But for the time being we had arranged to draw on our London accounts through a local bank. The greatest risk must have been to Alexa's jewellery. Almost all of it is in one of your own company's safe deposit boxes.'

'Then it should have survived,' said Greg, and took down the details. 'I was able to salvage most of the property we held in safe keeping before the fire took hold. I'll bring back what information I can. Margaret, you'll still be here, won't you, when I return?'

'Of course.' Almost intoxicated by happiness and the high, heady air, Margaret turned to smile at him. Whether or not he recognized that she was deliberately inviting him to kiss her, he did so, and left her to marvel at the ease with which their old affection had re-established itself.

As soon as he had left, Margaret went to the sewing room. She would need new petticoats herself, but that was not her chief reason for seeking Alexa's company.

'When Frank arrives, you must tell him how old you are,' she said without preamble.

Alexa looked at her in astonishment. 'But why?'

'It should be enough for me to say that there should be no lies between you.'

'You have said that once already, but then you agreed that I should choose my own time.'

'That was before I met Frank's father.'

'What difference does that make?'

'He wants to know something about your own parentage. It is a reasonable request. I intend to answer his questions, and truthfully. I have avoided them for the moment, so that you can put the facts straight yourself, without being caught out in an untruth.'

'You can answer his questions, surely, without being precise on the subject of age.'

'I told you in the tent,' said Margaret, 'that I had met Mr Davidson before.'

'Even if you had not, I could hardly have failed to notice your intimacy.' There was a note of spitefulness in Alexa's voice, no doubt caused by her annoyance at the instruction which she did not yet understand.

Was it necessary, Margaret wondered, to reveal how close she and Alexa's future father-in-law had once been? She decided that it would merely confuse the discussion.

'Mr Davidson was also well acquainted with your father – *our* father,' she said. 'He knows that John Junius Lorimer was already dead several years before the date you now claim as your birthday. As a matter of fact, he also on one or two occasions met your mother. It is possible that he may have seen you in your cradle. Even if he did not, he certainly was aware that your mother had had a baby. He returned to San Francisco only a few hours before the earthquake, so we need not be surprised that he has not yet thought to connect Alexa Reni with anyone whom he knew in Bristol when he was a young man, a long time ago. But as soon as he has time to reflect calmly and to cast his mind back, he will undoubtedly remember. What I am telling you, Alexa, is for your own sake. If you persist in your lie, it will be discovered even without help from me, and you will suffer for it. I'm not prepared to be involved in a deception of which in any case I disapprove.' She smiled and reached for the scissors. 'We won't quarrel about it, I hope. You are so beautiful, Alexa. Frank will think nothing of birthdays when he comes back.'

270

'If he comes back.'

'What do you mean by that?'

'I mean that I am worried.' Alexa's head was bent over her sewing. 'He should be here by now.'

'He wouldn't have known about the yacht: and I should think that the queue for the ferry will not be cleared for a week.'

'He didn't return to the tent, though.' Alexa sighed, but said nothing more about it. Margaret noticed how eagerly she jumped to her feet every time she heard the sound of a horse approaching, and how great was her dejection as each hope was dashed.

It was Greg, in fact, who was the first to return, a week after his departure, in a carriage hired from the station. Margaret watched from the window as he paid the driver and called Cassie's odd-job man to unload a variety of roped boxes and portmanteaux. All the energy with which he had set off seemed to have drained away from him. His face was grey and tired, his clothes crumpled and dirty again, charred around the ankles to show that he had been stepping through the ashes of the fire. When Cassie came running to greet him, he kissed her but did not speak. As she went to the kitchen to give her orders for a meal, he came into the drawing room without pausing on the way to wash or tidy himself.

'Where are the boys?' His voice seemed cold, and he did not greet either Margaret or Alexa personally.

'Working in the forest. And Miss Halloran is resting.'

'Good.' He had carried inside with him one steel box which he set down before Alexa. 'I think you will find most of your valuable property in here.'

Margaret expected to see her sister's eyes brighten. At the very least, Alexa would surely want to open the deposit box and see whether any damage had been done. Instead, she stared at Greg as though she knew, as he clearly did, that there was something more to be said. Margaret, not understanding the tension between them, knew only that there was something wrong.

'It wasn't all quite so safely stowed, was it, Miss Reni?' he said. 'You owned one more set of jewellery.' He opened a leather pouch which was belted round his waist and took out the rubies which had been abandoned in the Van Ness apartment. One by one he laid the pieces out on the table: the necklace, the ear-rings, the tiara. The tiara had been bent out of shape. He tried to straighten it with his fingers, as though he needed time to steady his voice before he looked up again.

'Of course,' he continued, 'you could not have expected that I would recognize these stones. I have seen them before. I know a good deal about their history – enough to know that you have no right to own them.'

Alexa stood up. Naturally pale at any time, her face now seemed completely drained of blood. But not, as Margaret might have expected, with anger. She was afraid.

'Mr Davidson,' she said. 'What has happened to Frank?'

Greg made no attempt to answer the question. Instead he looked at Margaret. 'You gave her the rubies, I suppose,' he said.

'No.' Margaret was ready to explain, but by now Alexa was so tense that she would not allow any interruption.

'They were a gift to me from my father. I have every right to own them.'

'Then who, may I ask, was your father?'

Whether or not Alexa remembered the warning that Margaret had given her, she could not retreat now. She held her shoulders straight as she answered.

'My father was John Junius Lorimer, of Bristol.'

Greg looked from one woman to the other, as though

272

he could not believe what he had heard. He sat down behind the table on which the rubies lay, and buried his head in his hands.

'After so many years!' he exclaimed. 'Even from the grave this devil stretches out his fingers to snap the strings of my life.'

Alexa stepped forward, pressing the question to which she must already have guessed the answer.

'You have to tell me, Mr Davidson. What has happened to Frank?'

'Certainly I will tell you, although all I know is what is contained in a military report. Frank approached the guard at the entrance to your apartment block and asked for permission to go inside. He was refused permission and told that the building was unsafe. The reason for this was that dynamite had been placed in every building between Van Ness Avenue and Polk Street in order that a fire break could be created. A little while later the guard was withdrawn. The soldiers reported that they had cleared the area and, as soon as they themselves were at a safe distance, the fuses were lit. Frank's body was found three days later, buried in the rubble of your apartment block. These rubies were in his pockets. When his body was dug out, it was labelled as that of a looter.' Greg's fists clenched, in anger as well as grief. 'You sent him to his death, Miss Reni. Just for these.'

'I didn't send him.' Tears were running down Alexa's face, but she stood her ground. 'I was going to go myself – he insisted – what does it matter? You loved Frank, Mr Davidson, and so did I. We should be able to share our grief, not to be angry.'

It was a vain hope. Greg's eyes showed the intensity of his feelings as he looked straight at the young woman who might have been his daughter-in-law, and the sight of her tears did not move him.

'You killed my son,' he said. 'Thoughtlessly or selfishly, it makes no difference now, but don't talk to me of loving him. I ask you just to get out of my life before you do any more damage.'

Margaret, recognizing that no good could come of an argument between two people who were so distraught, moved towards Alexa and tried to lead her out of the room. But Alexa shook her arm free.

'Your anger is with my father, Mr Davidson. He died when I was a baby. I never knew him. If you had some quarrel with him, I know nothing about it. You have no right to be angry with me merely because you hate my father.'

Greg took a deep breath, controlling himself so that his answer came in a voice that was calm and cold.

'Once upon a time – a very long time ago – I loved a woman who was also your father's daughter. I loved her for herself, and I did my best never to hold her parentage against her. If Frank had lived, I would have welcomed you into my family whoever your father was. But thanks to you, my son is dead, and every time I see you I shall remember why. There is no longer any link between us. There is no longer any reason why you should stay in California.'

At last Alexa seemed to realize the uselessness of talking to him. But as she turned towards the door, making no further attempt to control her sobs, he called out to her. 'You are forgetting these.'

She looked back, but was not in time to catch the necklace that he sent spinning through the air towards her. It hit her in the face, just above the eye: the edge of the pendant cut her eyebrow open. Darker than the rubies themselves, drops of blood began to scar the white rug on which she stood.

'Take them away,' Greg ordered. 'Your father had no

274

right to give them to you. They were bought with money stolen from those who had once believed him to be an honest man. But he is dead, and so no doubt are most of the people he ruined. You have made it clear enough how much you value your baubles. Take them away.'

Alexa did not seem to be listening. She had put a hand up to the cut on her face and now looked incredulously at the blood which covered it. With her other hand she stooped to pick up the necklace. Then, in an action which was almost that of a madwoman, she rushed towards Greg, snatching the rest of the jewellery which lay on the table in front of him and holding it up as though she intended to dash it down on his head. Margaret recognized that she had moved from grief and shock into hysteria, and was in time to grasp her hands and pull her away.

'Come dearest,' she said. Alexa began to scream as she was led firmly towards the door, gasping out a series of short, piercing sounds. She broke away and ran out on to the verandah, allowing Margaret to turn back for a moment.

With his head pressed down on the table, Greg was weeping. Margaret was in tears herself as she looked at him. In her first glimpse of him here, at the opera, it was his prosperous, well-dressed good looks which had instantly revived all her old feelings for him, making her long to show her pleasure in his success. Seeing him now, crumpled and distraught, she was overwhelmed by an even greater longing to love and comfort him.

'David,' she said quietly, forgetting in the stress of the moment to abide by his change of name. 'Please, David.'

She touched his hand, and as though he had felt the cold skin of a snake he pulled it abruptly away and used it to cover his face. Margaret looked down at him, as unhappy on her own account as on his. Her heart ached with the realization that he would never again be able to look at her with anything but hatred in his eyes. It had been possible to explain away all their old misunderstandings, but nothing could alter what had happened within the past week. Just for a moment she put a finger on the shoulder of his jacket, so lightly that perhaps he would not feel it. Then she went outside to look after Alexa, whose screams were gradually subsiding into gasps.

It was necessary to be brisk. Margaret sent a messenger to find Brad and Robert. By the time they came, she had already packed together the few possessions with which they could leave. Robert looked in astonishment at the two tear-swollen faces which greeted him, and his bewilderment turned to bad temper when he learned that he must say goodbye to his friend at once.

'If ever you come to London, Brad, I hope you'll come and visit us,' Margaret said. It was the polite formality of the departing guest, but its effect was to trigger off a new outburst from Alexa.

'I can't return to London. I came here to work. I must stay here.'

'There's no work for you to do here,' said Margaret firmly. 'The opera house is burned. The whole world will know what has happened to San Francisco. There will be no disgrace in abandoning our plans and returning home. In London we have friends who will help us to start again. We have no friends here. Get inside, and let us be off.'

She had already asked for the use of the carriage to take them to the station, and had guessed from Cassie's surprised look that the news of her brother's death had not yet been broken to her. Now their young hostess looked even more puzzled as she came running to catch them before they left.

'My father asked me to give you this.' She held out a

276

purse which was heavy with silver. 'When you say you're from San Francisco, you'll get free travel on the railroad right across the continent to New York. But you'll need food on the journey, and then the cost of your passage home.'

Margaret hesitated for a moment; but it was true that they could not manage without some immediate supply of money.

'Thank your father from me, and tell him that of course I'll repay it when I get back to England,' she said.

Cassie's embarrassment increased. 'He told me you'd likely say that,' she agreed. 'And if you did, I was to tell you – '

Margaret recognized that Greg's daughter was too kind-hearted to speak the words she had been given.

'You were to tell me that he never wanted to hear from us again,' she suggested bitterly, and recognized the truth of her guess in Cassie's silence. 'I think your father needs you now, Cassie. Goodbye.'

There was a moment more of delay. Alexa, still hysterically bright-eyed and flushed, was fitting into the box brought up from the safe deposit the rubies which Margaret never wanted to set eyes on again. With her own emotions as near to breaking point as were her sister's, Margaret looked through the window of Cassie's sitting room. It was easy to see that Greg had broken the news now, for he and his daughter were gripping each other in a long, unhappy embrace.

There were explanations which could have been made. Margaret knew that she could have justified her own behaviour, even if not Alexa's. But as she stared, an outsider, at the father and daughter who were attempting to comfort each other, she recognized that she could never again expect Greg to be reasonable as far as the Lorimers were concerned. She had reminded herself when she first arrived in San Francisco that the man she had once loved would have a life of his own which could leave no room for her, and it would have been better for both of them if that assurance had never been put to the test. The interlude in which they had seemed to have carried their old affection over such a long gap of years had been very brief; and it was over. They were strangers again, and this time it would be for ever. The whip cracked and the wheels of the carriage began to roll.

Greg did not lift his head to watch them go.

10

The most useful members of society are those who have the fewest ties of love and family to distract them. So at least Margaret tried to persuade herself as the train chugged interminably across the whole width of the continent. But it was no easy matter to come to terms with the griefs she was leaving behind and the bleakness of spirit which she carried with her. Separately and silently, Alexa was no doubt occupied in much the same way.

Margaret's misery was tinged with bitterness. How much kinder it would have been, she thought, if fate had not allowed her the brief hope of happiness before snatching it away again. But she recognized that what had happened was irrevocable. There was nothing to be gained by looking back; and if the future appeared desolate compared with the life which she had briefly imagined for herself – well, she had been lonely before, and survived it. She must try once again to find her satisfaction in the service of others.

She hoped that her sister would be equally successful

in putting the disaster behind her. Alexa had more to mourn than herself – death instead of disappointment – but that might make it easier for her to recognize the finality of what had happened. The months in San Francisco must be considered as a time out of their lives. Even though they would never be able to forget the events which had taken place, they must go on as though nothing had happened.

Even before they reached London, Margaret was reminded that this was too facile an approach – that no part of life could be completely without consequences. Margaret herself was not a good sailor. She had none of that love of the sea which had driven her Lorimer forebears to seek their fortunes in ocean-going ships: the slightest swell could upset her. Alexa, though, on the outward voyage – excited by the thought of new worlds waiting to be conquered – had seemed able to enjoy even the roughest day. When now she took to her cabin to ride out a mid-Atlantic gale, it seemed possible that her illness was caused as much by her state of depression as by the motion of the water. But the steamship entered the calmer coastal waters of England, and still Alexa was sick. Margaret recovered sufficiently from her own misery to worry about her sister's inability to take any food, and was able almost at once to guess the cause. She stared at Alexa in dismay.

'It is not yet certain,' said Alexa, when Margaret at last put her question into words. 'Everything that has happened in the past month – the shock of the earthquake, the expose to the weather, Frank's death, jolting about on the railroad, the storm – all these things, surely, must upset one's system.'

'Yes,' agreed Margaret. 'But they wouldn't cause you to be sick in this continuing way. I agree that you will need to wait for another month before you can be quite sure. But it is not too soon to begin thinking about what you should do. The baby is Frank's, I suppose.'

'Well, of course.' Unwell and worried, Alexa showed her apprehension by snapping.

'So there is no possibility of marriage. Unless, of course, you could find someone in England, quickly, who would be willing – '

'No!' Alexa sat up in her berth. Pale and bedraggled, she looked very different from the glamorous creature who charmed audiences and dominated balls and parties, but her eyes flashed with all the energy which had carried her so quickly to the top of her profession. 'I'm not prepared to bend my life ever again to fit in with that of a man. I am able to earn my own living and to manage my own affairs. Men may come to me if they wish, but I will not take a step out of my way to go to them. I have had too many disappointments.'

'You speak as though Frank deliberately let you down,' exclaimed Margaret. 'It was not his fault that he died.'

'Of course not. It was not Matthew's fault that I was born his aunt: not Caversham's fault that he needed to marry an heiress. I am not concerned with fault or blame. I am saying only that I do not propose ever again to be the victim of circumstances – of other people's circumstances. I intend to keep my life in my own hands from now on. To marry is always to surrender to a man's selfishness. He sets out a style of living, and his wife is supposed to conform to it in every way.'

'It is what most women wish for,' Margaret said gently, attempting to soothe down her sister's uncontrolled emotions.

'Then most women are welcome to it. What I am saying is that I am not most women. I depend on no one for my income. I can do whatever I like.'

'It sounds as though you are merely claiming the right to be as selfish as the men you criticize.'

'Yes!' cried Alexa. 'That is exactly right. What is selfishness in them is selfishness in me. But if it is praiseworthy for a man to maintain himself, to preserve his independence, to be successful in his career, then it must be equally praiseworthy for me to do the same. You must understand that, Margaret. For twenty years I have admired you because you have managed your life with as much strength and efficiency as any man could do, and have been more use to the world than most of them.'

Margaret made no answer to that. In her heart she knew that she was no different from the majority of women whom Alexa professed to despise. She could have been happy as a wife and mother, and it was not from her own choice that she had enjoyed only the briefest taste of domestic life. It was true that she had used ambition and a wish to be of value to the world as a means of conquering her disappointments, just as she would now need to do again: Alexa's declaration, although it emerged from a deeper bitterness, was not so very different. Nevertheless, there was still one circumstance which she seemed to be overlooking.

'You are not taking the baby into account,' she pointed out. 'Oh, Alexa, how could you be so foolish?'

'Do you think it was intended!' Alexa's temper flared up again. She made an attempt to laugh. 'At least there will be no difficulty in choosing a name. The child of Frank, conceived in San Francisco at the moment when the earth moved. It will have to be Francis, won't it? If it is ever born.'

'Alexa – '

'There are ways,' said Alexa stubbornly. 'You are a doctor, Margaret. You must know how to end a pregnancy.'

'I chose to be a doctor so that I could learn how to preserve life,' said Margaret. 'You can't ask me to kill your baby.'

She met her sister's defiant look with a steadiness of her own, and probably Alexa had known even before she asked that it was too much to expect, for now she shrugged her shoulders.

'There are other doctors.'

'It is illegal,' said Margaret. 'No reputable doctor will do it. And it is extremely dangerous. You must not interfere with nature.'

'You interfere with nature every time you cure someone who has been afflicted by nature with an illness,' Alexa pointed out, but the anger seemed to have gone out of her voice. 'Very well, then, suppose it is to be born. I have two choices, I imagine. I can disappear from London at once and move around Europe from one opera house to another with such speed that no one will notice the time when I am not to be found in any of them. Or I can make no attempt at concealment and receive sympathy for my misfortune in being widowed in the San Francisco disaster.'

'How can you say such a thing when you were not married?'

'And who will ever be able to discover that?' countered Alexa. 'Do you think there is a single official document left unburned in the city? Even the names of all the dead are never likely to be known. The bodies of a good many people who were killed in the first shock must have been consumed in the flames afterwards. I never intend to return to the city. As long as I make no claim on anyone, there can be no harm done.'

'Alexa, you cannot lie about something as important as this.'

'What solution do you propose that doesn't involve

some deception? A moment ago you were suggesting that I should look hastily for a husband. Even though you presumably expected me to tell the truth to the man concerned, you would not have made such a suggestion unless you were intending that the child should be passed off as his in the eyes of the world. A big lie or a little lie, what is the difference? What I suggest would protect the reputation of the child throughout its life, at no cost to anybody. I will keep my own name and refuse ever to mention my husband's, on the grounds that it would distress me too much.'

'And the child himself?' asked Margaret. 'What will you tell him when he is old enough to ask about his father?'

'I shall not be there to be asked. I shall find someone to adopt him.'

During the past hour Alexa had managed to shock her sister with almost every sentence she uttered, but this last announcement was so much more horrifying than the rest that for a moment Margaret could only gasp incoherently in her attempt to protest.

'Alexa – you cannot possibly – your own child!'

'Do you seriously see any alternative?' Alexa's voice was weak and flat with depression. 'If Frank had lived to marry me I would have taken pleasure in giving him an heir. But as things are, I don't want the baby. I have no maternal feelings at all. The birth will be a nuisance. The existence of a baby would be an impediment to my career, and I cannot believe that to be dragged from one opera house to another all over Europe is the best upbringing for any child. I cannot face it, Margaret, now that I am completely alone.' She lay back again in the berth and began to weep, turning her face to the pillow as Margaret stared down at her with a worried look.

'You know you are not alone, Alexa, I'm here to help you.'

'You have refused to help me.' Alexa's voice, like her sobbing, held an undertone of hysteria. 'You criticize every suggestion I make, but you have nothing to offer in its place. And if you had come with me to the Opera Ball, none of this would have happened.'

With an effort Margaret restrained her indignation at the attack. It was true that she did feel some guilt in this respect. But Alexa, although it had suited her to pretend to a younger age, was twenty-nine years old, perfectly well able to know right from wrong and to look after herself. The chaperonage for which she had asked had never been more than a social device.

Margaret was used to dealing with pregnant women. She knew how easily they became upset even when the babies they expected were wanted and would be born into a happy home, and how very much more terrifying their condition became when there was no husband to support them. She considered the situation for quite a long time while Alexa continued to sniff into the pillow.

It was not difficult to guess what Alexa wanted her to say. But a simple offer and promise, quickly spoken, could involve twenty years' responsibility. Margaret reminded herself that she was nearly fifty: too old to play the part of a natural mother to a young child – too old to be certain even that she would live to see the child become an adult. And she, just as much as Alexa, had a living to earn.

Neither of these facts proved, in the end, to be strong enough to influence her decision. Margaret had never felt quite the same sense of family responsibility which had prompted her elder brother to offer his support whenever she was in need, and which had apparently also made him feel justified in interfering in the most personal affairs of his brother and sister just because he was the head of the family. Margaret remembered, in fact, how she had stood twenty years earlier in a filthy farmyard in France, looking at a yellow-haired boy who was Ralph's son, her own nephew, and recognizing that she must not acknowledge the relationship.

But that had been for the boy's own sake. When Alexa talked of having her baby adopted, she was speaking out of adult selfishness. Margaret's appalled reaction to the idea revealed to her the strength of family feeling that she still retained. This baby would be her own niece or nephew, the grandchild of her father, John Junius Lorimer. The child could not be abandoned to strangers. There was no choice.

'You want me to look after your baby?' It was more of a statement than a question, because she knew the answer in advance.

Alexa lifted her head from the pillow and looked at Margaret. 'Would you?' she asked. 'Would you really?' She dabbed her eyes dry and sat up in the berth. 'I know you think I'm being cowardly and selfish,' she said. 'But what kind of a life can I offer a child? I have no home. I don't know how to look after babies. I don't know how to love them. I don't want to be a mother.'

'Be quiet, Alexa. You're just going to work yourself up into tears again.' The sharpness in Margaret's voice was not accidental. Briefly she wondered how much of what the younger woman had said was sincere. Alexa was an actress, and a very talented one. She could cry as convincingly when it suited her to do so as when her heart was broken. But on this occasion it seemed likely that her feeling of panic, increased by her physical weakness, was genuine enough. When she acknowledged that she was being selfish, that was true as well, but to punish her for it by insisting that she must bear the whole responsibility for the upbringing of an unwanted child would also be to punish the child. Margaret's love for Alexa was very deep: but deeper still was her passionate belief that every baby must be welcomed into the world with love. If Alexa was incapable of providing such a welcome, then somebody else must do it instead.

'Yes, I will do what I can,' Margaret said. 'But only on conditions. I know now that when I adopted you I was wrong not to tell you the whole truth about your parentage – and you have suffered from it, in your relationship with Matthew. I'm not going to make the same mistake again. I'm prepared to bring the child up. I'm even prepared to adopt him legally, if only in order that he can have a surname which requires no lies either to him or to the outside world. But I should tell him right from the beginning that you are his mother. I should expect you to behave as his mother – to love him and to spend as much time as you can with him whenever you are in London, and to make him feel that it is your care for his security which prevents you from taking him with you on your travels.'

'And his father?' asked Alexa.

'His father is Frank Davidson. He will need to know that as well, as soon as he is old enough to ask. And you must remember that Robert has to be considered. He will begin to ask *his* questions as soon as the baby is born.'

Alexa considered these proposals in silence. Then she looked steadily into Margaret's eyes.

'If you are to tell him all this,' she said, 'will you also tell him how his father and I ran hand in hand from the ball at which we became engaged, and were married in front of a judge only an hour before the earthquake struck San Francisco?'

Margaret swallowed the lump in her throat, accepting

with distaste the difficulty which Alexa had pointed out earlier, of finding a solution which protected the unborn child without involving any kind of deception.

'You may tell him that yourself,' she said. 'How can I know what happened after the ball, when I was at home in bed?' Staggering with dizziness, Alexa left her berth and held Margaret in a long and tight embrace.

'Thank you, dearest Margaret,' she murmured. 'No one ever had a better friend.' Then, as she drew away, her eyes sparkled with their former liveliness. 'But the baby won't be a boy!' she exclaimed. 'A beautiful girl, with golden hair and Frank's Irish eyes. We shall call her Francisca.'

PART V

Kate in England

1

The daughter of a missionary is expected to be of use to society rather than to decorate it. As Kate Lorimer walked across to Bristow Great House on a steamy Jamaican afternoon in 1909, the wide-brimmed hat which should have protected her complexion against the fierce sun swung from her wrist. After eighteen years of carelessness, one afternoon more or less would make no difference to the freckles which covered her face and arms. Her thick hair, tawny like a lion's mane and almost as tangled, flowed unrestrained over her shoulders, and the hem of her skirt was frayed and muddy.

None of her family had ever tried to nag her into looking either smart or beautiful. Such an attitude would be vanity. Although the young ladies who lived in the city or the rich plantation houses might shield their skins from the sun with parasols and canopies, Kate had always been allowed to expose herself to the weather. It made no difference whether she was burning in the sun or drenched by the island's torrential rain; she regarded the elements as her friends – and never more than now, when she was so soon to leave the extremes of a Caribbean climate to embark on a medical training.

Her parents took few of the home furloughs to which they were entitled, so it was many years since Kate had last visited England. But she remembered how cold the rain was there, and how weak the sun. The skies had always seemed to be grey, and the people in the streets huddled together inside drab clothing as though to escape from the atmosphere. Sometimes she was afraid that she might soon become as colourless as they, but such doubts were chased away by the surging energy which was carrying her at this moment across the banana plantation at a pace which none of the workers on the estate would have tried to copy.

Hurrying towards the house with a springy step which was almost a run, she stretched her senses to catch and imprison all the memories which would have to last her through the drab years to come: the heat battering at her skin, the brightness of the light which dazzled her eyes, the humidity of the air which filled her lungs, the trickle and splash of running water and the lush greenness of the vegetation which grew from it, the scents of blossom and of orange trees, the sudden harsh cries of birds and the hysterical laughter of a distant donkey.

Kate had been very young when, clutching her brother Brinsley by the hand to keep up her courage, she had first pushed a way through a curtain of creepers to find herself in the garden of Bristow Great House. Dusty and rotten though the building was, it had become at once the private retreat of the two children, an enchanted palace in which they could act out the stories they read and invent others of which they themselves were the original heroes.

Later, in the stone ruins of the old slave hospital not far from the plantation house, Kate's earliest determination to adopt her mother's profession had revealed itself in the treatment of a succession of imaginary patients, or in persuading Brinsley to entrust himself to her bandaging. They had never brought their younger brothers and sister to share in the discovery, and neither of them spoke of it at home, lest the magic should be invaded and destroyed. To this day Kate did not know whether her parents had ever realized where their two eldest children spent so much of each day.

Perhaps there had once been a time, in the rich and slave-supported years when the house was first built and furnished, when it had achieved some illusion of grandeur. But Massa Matty had died, and not long afterwards the slaves had received their freedom. The new owner, whoever he was, had never found it worth while to take possession of his West Indian inheritance, and the house had been allowed to decay as the revenues of the plantation declined. Kate had never known it as anything but a ruin.

Nevertheless, it was her own private ruin, more of a home to her in some ways than the plain stone house which stood in the middle of Hope Valley. All the villagers brought their problems to the pastor and their infirmities to the doctor, and were never turned away: there was no privacy in that place. The house in Hope Valley had been Kate's family home throughout her childhood. She belonged there – but Bristow Great House had belonged to her.

And to Brinsley, of course, until he was sent away to school; and also to Duke, who lived with his grandfather, Red Mattison, in what had once been the separate kitchen quarters of the Great House. His mother was Chelsea Mattison, the valley schoolteacher; but she was unmarried and had never made any public acknowledgement of the relationship.

Kate knew that her hopes of seeing Duke now to say goodbye were faint. He was older than she was, and soon after Brinsley's departure for England he had found new employment on one of the neighbouring plantations.

Some instinct told Kate that this would be her last look at Bristow Great House. Although during these past three years she had still brought her books to read on its overgrown terrace, or her notebooks to the little room which they had christened the study, the world of fantasy and dreams had already faded. As she grew up, she had come to use the dilapidated building more as a peaceful refuge in which to prepare for the career she had already chosen. Although she told herself now, as she stood in the mahogany-panelled drawing room, that she had come to say goodbye to her childhood, the truth was that she had already left it behind.

Nevertheless, she went through the rituals which she and Brinsley had invented twelve years earlier, tapping each wall in turn with a long stick to weave a magic fence through which no intruder would dare to burst. More realistically, she supposed that the old house would continue to rot away. Birds would fly between the sagging jalousies to build their nests inside rooms which were now to be abandoned again, fouling the floors with their droppings. Red's goats would wander on to the verandahs, the rain would beat against the walls, and hurricanes would tear at the roof. Jamaica was an island in which new life sprang up exuberantly almost overnight – but decay advanced at very much the same speed.

She called Duke's name for one last time, but there was no answer: she had not expected one. It was time to return to Hope Valley. Her mother would soon begin to worry lest there should be insufficient time for all that had to be done before the journey. Dragging her feet at first, Kate pushed a way back through the undergrowth for the last time, and then began to run. Today she seemed to be more than usually at the mercy of her moods: apprehensive about what lay ahead, but excited too. And England could not be too completely a foreign country when Brinsley would be waiting in Bristol to welcome her and Aunt Margaret had offered her a home in London.

An hour later her old clothes lay crumpled on the floor. Cleaned and mended, they would find a deserving home as soon as she had gone. Kate herself, shy beneath the stares of a continuing flow of well-wishers, stood very straight in her new travelling outfit. Her thick hair, brushed into an unusual orderliness and promptly strained into plaits, was pinned into a coil on the top of her head. She felt as though a single abrupt movement would bring the whole edifice tumbling down.

In a corner of the room, Grant was whining his indignation at being temporarily neglected. Although four years old by now, he tried to cling to his mother's skirts as possessively as if he were still a baby and was fiercely resentful of anyone who claimed more of her attention than himself. This was not, as a matter of fact, something which very often happened. Lydia, who had encouraged independence in her elder children from an early age so that she might herself be free to attend to whichever members of the congregation needed her help, seemed to have changed character since his birth. As though to compensate him for his disability she continued to carry him long after he should have walked, consoled him when he should have been told to be brave, and spoiled him in every possible way.

Kate had an instinctive sympathy for the unfortunate. From her first sight of Grant's deformed body she had been prepared to lavish her love on him, and this reaction had been strengthened when she realized that their father could hardly bear the sight of his youngest child. But as Grant had left the cradle and developed a personality of his own, it grew more and more difficult to remain sympathetic. Kate reminded herself that all young children are selfish, but Grant was remarkable for the force of will which he applied to getting his own way, using tears or tantrums, strength or weakness, as he judged which would best serve his purpose. It had become increasingly clear to Kate that it was her mother, and not Grant, who had become the underdog, and she made no attempt to conceal her disapproval.

'It's very common for an elder child to be jealous of a new baby,' her mother had told her once. 'But you must fight against the feeling, dear. It's unworthy of you.'

'I was never jealous of Brinsley, never,' protested Kate. 'Nor of Mary or Alexander. When the little ones died, I was as sad as you were – you know that. It's Grant who is jealous of me. And you're allowing him to make you too tired, Mother. It would be better for him in any case if he were to play with other small children in a natural way.'

'His misfortune – ' began Lydia; but Kate had interrupted her.

'Yes, he is lame, and of course I am sorry for it. But although he appears awkward, I don't believe he feels any pain when he walks. He needs to have more exercise than a normal child, not less. And he ought not to grow up thinking himself too unusual. His misfortune doesn't make him more important than everyone else.'

At the time of that conversation, Kate had been sensitive enough to her mother's distress not to press the matter too far. But since then, Lydia's tiredness had deepened to the point of exhaustion and Ralph, seeing this as clearly as Kate, had become rougher in his attempts to discipline his young son. This in return had led to quarrelling between the two adults, destroying the calm happiness which had ruled the household before Grant's birth. Finding it hard to be tolerant of her little brother's demanding nature, Kate felt now an unworthy satisfaction in the knowledge that for once she was the centre of attraction, and that Grant realized it.

'I feel ashamed to send you to England with so few new clothes,' her mother fussed. 'But if we'd made more here, I'm afraid they might have appeared dowdy when you reached London, and not warm enough for a colder climate. Sophie will take you shopping in Bristol as soon as you have had a day or two to settle down.'

'It seems wrong to expect too much from the generosity of my relations,' Kate said: although she was well enough aware of her need for a new wardrobe. 'Especially since they already do so much for Brinsley.'

'They won't be out of pocket.' Her father had joined them now that she was dressed. 'I'd intended to explain the financial arrangements to you while we were on the train to Kingston, but I can as easily tell you now. I have my own bank account in England, and I have authorized both William and Margaret to draw on it for your needs, as they already have for Brinsley's. You surely didn't think that your uncle was shouldering the burden of Brinsley's school fees? I don't want to disparage his generosity – the home he provides for Brinsley in the school holidays is something money could never buy. But when it comes to the disbursement of cash, it will be my money that you spend.'

'For my fees as well?'

'Of course. And I've done my best to make it clear to Margaret that she must accept enough from us to pay for the food that you eat in her house, even though the room in which you lodge may cost her nothing to offer. Whatever sums you need for spending-money she will also draw from my account. You will discuss the amount together when you have some idea of your commitments. Naturally I expect you to live as economically as possible, but whatever money you need for your essential expenses will be available to you.'

'I'm very glad to hear it. Thank you, Father,' said Kate.

The news came as a relief as well as a surprise. It had

seemed natural enough that her mother, a doctor herself, should have supported Kate's ambitions when they were first expressed; and she had been grateful, too, that her father raised no objection of principle to her wish to study medicine. Kate knew that in this respect she was more fortunate than many other girls of her own age holding the same ambition.

But although she was glad of her parents' moral support, the question of money had worried her. The Hope Valley community was self-supporting in food, while clothes were as likely as not to be obtained on a barter system and were rarely renewed except on special occasions such as this one. Kate herself never handled cash. She knew that her father did business on behalf of the whole community, and from its profits paid a schoolteacher and bought books for the children and supplies for the hospital. But to finance the long training of a medical student would need resources which a missionary pastor could not be expected to have at his disposal. If Kate had not asked questions before, it was because she feared that to know the truth might be a humiliation. She was aware that her Bristol relations were wealthy – and rather than abandon her vocation she was prepared to accept help from anyone – but she would not have enjoyed being a dependant.

Perhaps, she thought, her father enjoyed the benefit of some family trust in England. Although he himself had chosen to embrace a life of poverty in Jamaica, he might well feel no objection to using for his children's benefit whatever provision had been left to him by his own father. Kate knew very little about her grandfather, who had died more than ten years before she was born, but she did know that he had been a rich man.

'You have another visitor,' called Lydia.

Kate stepped out on to the verandah and her eyes lit

up with pleasure as she saw that Duke was standing there. For his part, he stared at her as though he had never seen her before.

'That's one smart young lady,' he said at last, his white teeth flashing in a grin. Although his skin was so light in colour, his smile was wholly of the island. 'I came to say goodbye and wish you good times. Maybe we don't meet again after this.'

'But I shall come back,' protested Kate. 'I know it's a long training, but this is my home. Of course we shall see each other again. I shall still need someone to practise my bandaging on when I come.'

'I'll wait for that,' said Duke. 'Just so long as you never call me "boy".' He must have seen the flush that showed he had hurt her feelings, for he was quick to withdraw. 'You always did fall for every tease I could think up. You remember that time there was a caterpillar on your foot and I told you the hairs had poisoned your skin and the only cure was for you to hang upside down till all the blood was drained out of your leg.'

'Your teases never were very funny,' said Kate, but she was smiling again. Her father, who had been listening from the back of the verandah, stepped forward to interrupt.

'No time for a session of reminiscence now,' he said, and Duke nodded obediently.

'I wrote a letter for Brinsley.' He held it out to Kate. There was a moment of awkwardness between them, neither knowing how they should say goodbye. Duke solved the problem by holding up his hand in a kind of salute. 'Well, good times, then,' he called out. Grinning once more, he left at a run.

'Look after the house!' shouted Kate after him. He turned and waved again. She was sorry at once for what she had said. Duke, working on another plantation, would not have time to care for a derelict piece of property, which would be no fun without company; and she had given her father the chance to ask awkward questions.

He took it at once. 'Which house? he asked, although – knowing where Duke had spent his childhood – he must have guessed the answer before he spoke.

'Bristow Great House,' Kate answered. 'Duke and Brinsley used to play there. Duke helps his grandfather look after the garden. He's very attached to the place.'

'He writes a neat hand,' commented her father, glancing at the envelope which had been addressed to Brinsley. 'Or did his mother do it for him?'

Although the question was a natural one, Kate was indignant on her friend's behalf. The children of Hope Valley were taught to read and write in the schoolroom, but the lessons did not come easily to them, and in most cases were forgotten as soon as they began to work on the land. Duke, though, as the son of a schoolteacher, had been taught earlier and more thoroughly than the others, and not allowed to forget his skills.

'He's very clever,' she said. 'He's much better at sums than Brinsley ever was. When they played cricket together they used to have great competitions and work out batting averages and that sort of thing, and Duke always got the right answer first. If ever you need an assistant, Father, to help you with all those accounts you have to do, you ought to ask Duke. I promise, you'd only have to show him once what needs to be done.'

'I'll bear your testimonial in mind,' her father promised with a smile. 'And now, are you ready at last?' The luggage had already been taken to the railway station on a donkey cart and it was time to move in the same direction. Her mother, who for the past hour had been pressing messages to Brinsley on her, as well as warnings

297

on her own account, fell silent; and Kate, not normally emotional or demonstrative, found to her surprise that she was on the verge of tears.

'What if I should never see her again!' she thought, suddenly aware of her own youth and good health and exuberant spirits as she embraced someone who looked old beyond her age. The years of Grant's dependence, added to the rigours of the climate and Lydia's self-imposed programme of community health work, had left a woman who had never been plump or pretty looking strained and haggard, her sallow skin stretched tightly across the bones of her face. 'You will come to England soon, won't you?' Kate begged aloud. 'You ought to have a holiday, and Brinsley and I will need to see you.'

As though Lydia shared her fear, the embrace was returned with an almost painful tightness. Grant, excluded, began to shout for his mother's attention and was sharply rebuked by his father. Kate held out her arms to the little boy, anxious to leave in friendship, but he turned away petulantly.

She looked from one parent to another. It was difficult to believe that once upon a time they too had been students, healthy and high-spirited, as sure of their own vocations as she was now of hers, embarking with eagerness on the separate trainings which were to bring them in the end to this obscure corner of the world. Had they been happy, she wondered: was this how they had expected their lives to turn out? There was a moment in which all her excitement and her memories of a loving family life seemed to be obscured by shabbiness and sadness and Grant's flash of spite, causing her courage to falter. Then she straightened her shoulders and smiled for a last time at her mother before she took her father's arm. It was time to begin her own adventure.

2

To a small child every house is large, and a grand house a palace. Memory increases the illusion, bringing disappointment to a return visit if in the intervening years the visitor has grown to fit the scale of the building.

Brinsley House, however, was substantial enough to survive the test of remembered grandeur. Even to an adult's eyes its marble entrance hall was vast, its entertaining rooms numerous and palatial, its terraced gardens spacious. For a moment, as she stood in the doorway, Kate was overcome by shyness. She had hoped that Brinsley might have been at the dock at Portishead to meet her, but instead it was her cousin Beatrice who had come. Beatrice had been polite enough, expressing all the proper hopes for the comfort of the voyage and the enjoyment of her visit to Bristol, but there was a sharpness about her manner which made her seem cold even when her words were friendly.

The difference of fourteen years in age was another barrier. Beatrice, in her early thirties, belonged neither to Kate's own generation nor to her mother's. The two had nothing in common but their relations, and that was a subject quickly exhausted.

Now it was her aunt's turn to greet her. Tall, and tightly laced into a stiff stateliness, Sophie's approach was so formal that for a moment Kate found herself struggling wildly to remember all the petty rules of etiquette which her mother had tried to recall for her benefit. Should she unbutton a glove, or remove it – and one, or both? But of course, even though she might be almost a stranger, an aunt was to be kissed.

Sophie offered first one pale cheek and then the other. Again there were murmured hopes that the voyage had not provided too much discomfort, that her parents were well. She would no doubt like to be shown to her room at once, in order that she could refresh herself: luncheon would be served in half an hour. Brinsley, she was told, had been staying with a schoolfriend for the past week, but was expected back at any moment. The boat which had brought Kate from Jamaica had arrived earlier than had been expected when his plans were made.

Kate had been allocated one of the bedrooms which afforded a view of the Gorge. She stared out of the window at the plunging cliffs and the graceful bridge suspended above them and the calm woods on the further side. The climate was not after all as grey as she had anticipated, but even the sight of sunshine and white puffy clouds scudding across the blue sky could do nothing to disperse her feelings of desolation.

She was not wanted here: it was as simple as that. Before she left home Kate had been unhappy in her belief that she would be an expense to her relations. Her father's assurance on this score had lightened her mind completely – it had never occurred to her that they might feel her mere presence a nuisance. Anyone, even a total stranger, who came to Hope Valley and asked the pastor for hospitality would be given not only food and shelter but also a genuine welcome from the heart. Sophie Lorimer had more rooms at her disposal than she could possibly use herself, and servants to ensure that little of the work of entertaining a visitor would fall on her own shoulders; yet in spite of all this she could put no warmth into her welcome. To provide accommodation for a niece and nephew when requested to do so was merely an irksome duty.

Without warning Kate found herself overwhelmed by

homesickness. She felt completely cut off from Jamaica: from childhood, friends, loving parents, all the sights and sounds to which she was accustomed. How many years would pass before she saw them again! It was even possible that she might never return.

For a little while, pressing her forehead against the cold glass of the window, Kate indulged her misery. Then she straightened her shoulders and tossed her head in the gesture with which she had always before been able to shrug away disappointment or depression. Her thick hair, instead of swirling across her shoulders, remained firmly pinned in place. It was a necessary reminder that she was a young lady now, no longer a child.

And Brinsley would soon be here to greet her. And her stay in Bristol was in any case only an interlude. Everything would be different when she arrived at Aunt Margaret's house in London. It was only four years since her father's sister had visited Jamaica: she was warm-hearted, and not a stranger like these cold Bristol Lorimers. Even four years ago Margaret had been sympathetic to her niece's ambitions: she could be relied upon now for support which would go deeper than the mere provision of a home. Then there would be work to be tackled – hard work, leaving no time for this kind of sentimental self-indulgence, Kate told herself firmly. She had been accepted temporarily into William Lorimer's household merely because she was a Lorimer. In London, she would be able to make a life for herself.

Even that prospect was a subject on which it was necessary to be discreet. Her father had warned her, without going into details, that William and Margaret were not on good terms. The quarrel was no concern of Kate's, he said: there was no reason for her to conceal from either of them the fact that she had visited or was planning to visit the other – but she might find the atmosphere pleasanter if she refrained from talking about her aunt while at Brinsley House, or her uncle when in London. And then Lydia had added another warning, to the effect that any reference to Matthew Lorimer in his parents' presence might bring a chill to the conversation. Kate had never, so far as she remembered, met her eldest cousin, so to refrain from enquiring after him was not a great problem; but it was an odd family, she thought, which found it so difficult to like each other.

Then Brinsley came rushing into the room, and the last of her doubts vanished as she was given a genuine welcome to England at last. There were so many questions to be asked and answered that the sound of the luncheon gong came as an unwelcome interruption. For an hour it was necessary to be formal and polite again, although now that Kate had regained her good spirits she was able to accept that Aunt Sophie's voice did not indicate any active resentment of her young guests' presence, but merely a lack of interest in anything but herself.

As for Beatrice, a positive note of friendly enthusiasm came into her voice as she invited her cousin to accompany her that evening to a suffrage meeting. Kate hardly liked to admit that the word suffrage was unfamiliar to her, but fortunately the invitation was expanded to the point of comprehension by a strongly worded attack on Mr Asquith – who had apparently made promises, or half promises, in respect of the claim by women that they should have the vote. The prime minister, it seemed, had broken his word in a treacherous manner. It was necessary for strongly worded resolutions to be passed and forwarded to Downing Street. Such an abrupt plunge into the politics of a country to which she was still a stranger was bewildering to Kate. For once she was glad of Sophie's calm intervention.

'Stop pestering the child, Beatrice. If she plans to be

one of these working women like your aunt, no doubt she'll form her views on the subject soon enough.'

'But staying with Aunt Margaret will expose her to unsound influences.'

'What *do* you mean, Beatrice? Your aunt's opinions may not accord with mine, but I understood that you and she were in agreement. You both attend that committee of Lord Glanville's, after all.'

'Oh yes,' agreed Beatrice. 'Aunt Margaret's views are reasonable enough. But the same cannot be said of Alexa, and she stays with Aunt Margaret whenever she's in England, so that Cousin Kate will hardly be able to avoid meeting her. And Alexa becomes rasher and more militant with every year that passes.' Beatrice turned to Kate to explain. 'Alexa is much in demand because she is famous and her voice is so strong and her appearance so striking. Whenever the militants plan a procession, they ask Alexa to march at the front, and to sing as she marches. The news that she is going to be present increases the number of people who come to watch. I suppose they think they're being given a free opera performance. Her photograph is always appearing in the popular papers. Would you believe it, the press has nicknamed her "The Singing Suffragette". In my opinion, she does it only for the publicity it brings her – I suspect her of having no coherent views on the subject at all.'

Since it was impossible for Kate to guess the cause of Beatrice's dislike of Alexa, she felt her way cautiously into the conversation.

'Why is it called militant to sing and to march in processions?' she asked.

'Oh, that's only the respectable part of it. The militants throw stones. Not Alexa, as far as I know – I don't imagine she fancies the thought of a few weeks in prison – but a lot of the others. And they've made it almost

303

impossible for any public figure of whom they disapprove to hold a political meeting without disturbance. The result is, of course, that those of us who believe in pleading our cause with rational argument now find that we can't get anyone to listen. Alexa and her fine friends are doing a great deal of harm, in my opinion. She'll almost certainly try to get you under her thumb too. Which is all the more reason why you should come to our meeting tonight and hear a properly argued case.'

'It's out of the question, Beatrice,' said Sophie with surprising firmness. 'Your cousin is bound to be tired after so much travelling. And your father will expect to find her here when he comes home this evening.'

It was a sharp reminder to Kate that Brinsley House had a master and that she still had to face her uncle and his younger son, Arthur. They both worked in the Lorimer Line's offices down at the docks, but had not bothered to step outside to greet her when the banana boat arrived.

An explanation of the apparent discourtesy emerged as soon as Arthur came home that night – although he was past his thirtieth birthday, he was not yet married and still lived with his parents at Brinsley House. He warned his mother at once that there had been trouble at business that day, and that his father was likely to arrive late and in a bad temper. Then he welcomed his cousin more warmly than either Sophie or Beatrice had done, explaining at once that her arrival at the port had coincided with a meeting of such importance that none of the Lorimer staff had dared to interrupt their chairman with the news of her presence. Now he made amends for their neglect. His eyes were admiring as he looked at his cousin, and his voice was friendly when he suggested that they should stroll together in the garden.

The enquiries he made about the voyage were more

detailed than Beatrice's vague politenesses. It did not take Kate long to realize that he was using her to give him a report on the day-to-day running of his banana boat, which had brought her to England. But although the conversation was clearly for his own benefit rather than hers, it did at least leave her with the feeling that he was listening to the answers. She was conscious of him tucking notes away in his mind, to be acted upon, perhaps, the next day: and because she was herself accustomed to observe and note, this amused rather than offended her. It was not long, in fact, before she felt sufficiently at ease to accuse him of employing her as a spy, and the smile with which he accepted the challenge sparked off a friendly feeling between them.

His father's arrival, an hour later, introduced a different mood into the household. William did not come out into the garden to greet his niece. Instead the sound which reached her was the slamming of his study door.

'I'm afraid you're not going to see my father at his best today,' Arthur apologized. 'As well as being Chairman of the Lorimer Line, he's a director of the company which owns the docks. We've had agitators in Bristol recently. They've had some success in forming trade unions in London, and now they are attempting to disrupt the economy of the whole country with their demands. A deputation waited on my father this morning. It was a stormy meeting, to say the least.'

'What did they want?'

'A restriction of the hours to be worked each day. In some industries this sort of thing may be possible, for all I know. But no shipping line can tolerate it. Your own vessel, for example – she arrived in the normal working hours of the morning, as it happened, but only because sailing conditions were exceptionally favourable. If she had docked in the late afternoon, as was originally scheduled, it would still have been necessary for her cargo to have been unloaded at once. What these men don't seem to realize is that if all their demands were to be met, even the most prosperous company could be bankrupted – and then who would pay their wages?'

'So Uncle William was not prepared to agree?'

'He didn't consider that matter even worthy of discussion. I was summoned to attend the meeting to see how he dealt with them – that was why neither of us was able to greet you. There were tempers lost on both sides. One of the men reminded my father that the Lorimer Line could be one of the first to suffer if a cargo of bananas were to be held up in some way instead of being unloaded at once. It was an outright threat. Of course, it won't happen. The trouble-makers will soon be wishing that they had any job at all, however long the hours. But I was afraid for a moment that Father was about to have a fit. He went so purple that I thought he was actually going to burst with rage. You'll have to forgive him if he isn't as attentive to you this evening as he ought to be. It may be better for you not to see him at all tonight than to face him when he's in such a bad mood.'

The conversation was not one which did much to put Kate at ease, so when, later that evening, a message was brought to the drawing room asking her and Brinsley to come to the study, it was with some uneasiness that she obeyed. But it appeared that their uncle's good temper had been restored by a dinner brought to him on a tray, and by a generous pouring of brandy after it. He was affable enough as Kate, for the fourth time that day, reported on her family's health and spirits and handed over a letter which her father had sent by her hand to his brother.

'Young Brinsley here has been telling you, I've no

doubt, how he's been wasting his time this summer,' he said. Although the words were critical, the tone of his voice was more indulgent than might have been expected for a man whom Kate knew to have few interests of his own outside his office. 'The youngest boy ever to play for his school at cricket. And the worst Greek scholar within living memory. His father's son. Not much doubt about that. Well, time you were in bed, young man.'

'Yes, sir. Goodnight sir.' Brinsley stood up to leave, but Kate deduced that she was expected to stay.

'Excuse me, uncle, if I just tell my brother that there is a letter for him in my room.'

'You gave me the one from Mother and Father,' Brinsley reminded her.

'This one is from Duke. I saw him just before I left. Uncle William's mention of cricket reminded me of it. Duke's promised to look after Bristow Great House while we're away.'

Brinsley went off in search of the letter, closing the door carefully behind him. Kate turned back to her uncle and found that he was staring at her curiously.

'Bristow Great House?' he said. 'What is that?'

'Just a place where Brinsley and I used to play as children,' said Kate. 'In the days when the land was worked by slaves, it was the home of the plantation owner. Now it's almost a ruin. Nobody has lived in it for years.'

'You talk of "the plantation". Which plantation?'

'The estate which is worked by my father's congregation,' said Kate. 'He's told you about it, surely.' She was puzzled by the intensity of her uncle's interrogation. Since he provided the shipping which brought much of the produce of the estate to England, he must know how his brother's interests had expanded from religion to agriculture.

'I'm aware that your father owns a plantation,' said William. 'But I've always understood it to be called the Hope Valley Estate. That's the name branded on the crates which he consigns to my ships.'

'That's what it's called now,' agreed Kate. 'But in the old days it was the Bristow plantation, and the house still keeps that name. Not that anyone ever speaks of it except Brinsley and myself.'

'How did your father get his hands on it?' William had sprung to his feet while she was talking. Suddenly he was pounding the desk with such force that the decanter of brandy jerked dangerously towards the edge. The fierceness of his anger terrified Kate, so that she too rose to her feet as though she might need to defend herself. For a moment it seemed that he was trying to control his feelings, but the restraint was even more alarming than the open fury.

'I made enquiries,' he said through clenched teeth. 'Not at once, because it was necessary to wait until all danger passed of the Jamaican property being sucked into my father's estate after his death and disposed of to the benefit of his creditors. I was patient for a good many years. And when at last I put in my claim, I was told that my rights had lapsed. That the land which I should have inherited had been disposed of. And now you tell me that your father owns the property. But I tell you that he has no right to it. Who is the eldest son? Tell me that. Who is the eldest son?'

Kate, bewildered, could think of no reply, but none was expected.

'If there was anything left after the collapse of my father's business, if there was any legacy which could have been honoured as he would have wanted, it should have come to me. It should have come to me, I say. Your father is no better than a thief. I shall – I shall – '

He raised his hand to pound the desk for a second time. Ridiculously, it was for the safety of the decanter that Kate was now alarmed. She put out a hand to save it, but the impending blow did not materialize. William was attempting to struggle from the grip of some kind of paralysis. His upraised hand trembled, but would not obey him. He stood as though posing for a statue, frozen into an ungainly attitude of anger, one shoulder hunched towards his neck, a fist poised to descend. His complexion had flushed to the purple which Arthur had described earlier in the day. Kate, at her mother's side, had witnessed a great many emergencies in Hope Valley, but never anything like this.

'Aunt Sophie!' she called; but guessed at once that the thick walls and mahogany doors insulated the rooms of Brinsley House too well for any call to be heard. She tugged at the bell pull and hurried round to the other side of the desk to support her uncle. Try as she might, she was not strong enough to force him safely into his chair, for all his muscles were rigid. Only his teeth chattered a little as he attempted, but failed, to speak.

The butler came in answer to the bell, only to stand frozen to the spot with shock. Kate called again, this time through the open door, and Sophie arrived with an outraged expression. At the first sight of her husband her expression changed and she fainted dead away. It was Arthur at last who took control of the situation, sending messages to a doctor and summoning more servants to carry his father up to bed.

No one, in the general turmoil, took any notice of Kate, and she was glad of it. More than two hours passed before Arthur returned to the study and found her still sitting there, huddled in a leather armchair.

'How is he?' she asked. Arthur sat down in his father's

chair on the far side of the desk, for there were no other seats in the study.

'Still alive,' he said. 'But the doctors are not hopeful about his condition. He has had an apoplectic stroke, it seems. I'm not quite clear yet what that implies. He has lost the power of speech, and the whole of his left side is paralysed. The right hand, too, is beyond his control at the moment. If there is to be any improvement, it is to be looked for there, they say. However that may be, he will never work again. Never be himself again. I can hardly credit what has happened – that it should be so sudden. One moment an active, astute man with all his faculties; and then within seconds a helpless object, to be carried and nursed. If he had died tonight, Kate, I would have had those men before a court tomorrow morning on a charge of manslaughter.'

'The men?' she queried, not understanding him.

'The trouble-makers. There's not the slightest doubt in my mind that they're responsible for this. I suspect that he came very near to his present condition while they were in his office this morning. No doubt he was going over the conversation again in his mind, so that his anger returned. Or perhaps he was recounting it to you – you were in here with him, were you not?'

'Yes, I was.' said Kate. Even to her own ears, her voice sounded faint, and she was conscious of Arthur looking at her with concern. But he would think it natural that she should be shocked by what had happened. He could not guess, and she dared not confess, what had really been the subject of her conversation with his father.

Nothing had ever been mentioned in her presence at home about the way in which the Bristow plantation had come into her father's possession. She did not even know whether it was his personal property or whether he was a kind of trustee, administering it on behalf of the Hope

Valley community. Although feeling herself accused alongside her father, she had no guilty knowledge which would have allowed her to understand exactly what it was which had so greatly upset her uncle. Nevertheless, it was impossible to conceal from herself one fact of guilt: the fact that his loss of control had been caused by something which she herself had said, though in all innocence, and not by the memory of his earlier arguments with the dock workers.

No doubt his anger on the first occasion had made him more vulnerable to the stress of the second upset, but Kate's conscience was not completely clear, all the same. She would have felt happier if she could have confessed her doubts to her cousin, recounting the conversation in the hope that he could assure her that it was of no consequence. But her ignorance of the background and of the true facts sapped her confidence. If there were truly something wrong, to bring it into the open might cause trouble for her father. There had been talk of a legacy, and the implication that it had been misapplied. What were her uncle's words? 'No better than a thief!'

Everything in Kate's upbringing told her that she ought to be frank and honest. But her uncle's tirade had frightened her – on her father's behalf as well as her own. If her uncle recovered his speech, of course, or the power to write, he would be able to explain to the world whatever it was that had made him so furiously angry. To the confusion of Kate's emotions was added, for one involuntary second, the hope that perhaps he might not recover. Kate was so shocked by the wickedness of her own thoughts that without warning she burst into tears.

Almost at once she conquered her feelings with anger at her own behaviour. 'I never cry!' she exclaimed, gulping herself under control again. But the moment of breakdown had lasted long enough to bring Arthur to her side. He sat on the arm of the leather chair and she was conscious of his hand gripping her shoulder.

'It would be remarkable if you didn't feel upset,' he said. 'None of us has properly imagined what this day has meant to you. You've left everyone you love and sailed halfway across the world to begin a new life. You find yourself in a family of people who – relatives though we may be – are strangers. We expect you to be at ease in a strange house; and give you, no doubt, strange food to eat. And just as you're beginning to relax into the normal routine of this new life, it's all upset by an emergency. No wonder you are disturbed. I can't apologize enough for giving you such a bleak welcome to England.'

'You've all been very kind,' protested Kate. Already she had forgotten her own earlier resentment of her aunt's coldness. Arthur's arm encircling her shoulders was comforting, and his voice was sympathetic: she did indeed at this moment feel herself to be one of the family.

'I'm wondering,' he said, 'whether you would prefer to go straight to London? You mustn't misunderstand me. We had expected you to stay with us for several weeks, and I know that my mother was looking forward to equipping you for your life in England. Beatrice, too, saw you as a new recruit to her campaign and will not be at all pleased if I whisk you away. As for myself, I had looked forward to your company even before you arrived, and now that I have met you I'm even more loath to deprive myself of it. But I'm trying to consider the situation from your point of view. There can be no doubt that the next few days are bound to impose a great strain on my mother. Whether my father's condition improves or deteriorates, she will want to be at his side. In the same way, it will be necessary for me to take control of his business affairs. I'm perfectly well able to do so, but in the past he has been reluctant to allow me too much responsibility, so that at least to begin with it may be necessary for me to work longer hours than usual. If you stay here, I fear you will be neglected. And however much you may protest that you understand the reason, you're bound to be lonely, since you've had no time at all yet to make friends of your own. And so I'm wondering whether you'd like me to telephone Aunt Margaret and ask whether you could begin your stay in London earlier than had been arranged.'

'Do you think it will be convenient?' asked Kate. She was anxious not to cause trouble to anyone, but it was hard to judge where she would be least in the way.

'You probably know that she spends much of her time at the hospital. Whether you go now or later, she may not be able to give you much of her own company. But presumably she has given some thought to the question of entertaining you and introducing you to young women of your own age. And in any case – '

Kate interrupted what promised to be a never-ending list of reasons why she should leave. Her moment of weakness had been caused by guilt rather than either shock or shyness, and she saw the need to form a definite opinion about her own future. It was her aunt Margaret who was her true hostess in England, who had written spontaneously to Jamaica hoping that Kate would live with her while she studied, and had pressed the invitation with warmth and generosity until the offer was accepted. The stay at Brinsley House had been arranged only because it would have seemed rude of Kate to land at Bristol from a Lorimer ship and make no attempt to see her Bristol relatives. But from the first moment she had felt herself to be a nuisance, and circumstances now allowed this to be acknowledged by both sides.

'If Aunt Margaret is prepared to have me, I agree that it would be best for me to move on to London at once,' she said, and Arthur's smile confirmed that she had made the right decision.

3

The home of a warm-hearted woman quickly becomes crowded. Even a small army of servants had not been able to prevent Brinsley House from appearing empty, almost desolate; but as soon as Kate stepped inside her aunt Margaret's much smaller house in Queen Anne's Gate she was struck by the atmosphere of bustle and warmth created by a number of people all living full lives in an affectionate atmosphere.

Margaret herself appeared at the door to welcome her niece and nephew – for when told what had happened she had insisted that Brinsley should travel with his sister and stay until the school term began. The housekeeper, Betty, did not slip silently away as any of Sophie's servants would have done. She waited, beaming, at the back of the hall, and was introduced. Margaret's son, Robert, was there, too, well scrubbed and looking very respectable in his Sunday suit. His eyes were bright with pleasure and mischief, though, and as soon as he had shaken Kate solemnly by the hand he hurried Brinsley off to the room which the two boys were to share.

'You'll find it rather a crush here compared with Brinsley House,' Margaret apologized, but the cheerfulness of her voice suggested that this did not greatly worry her. To prove her words, a small girl – pursued by her nursemaid – came scrambling down the stairs at that moment to see what was going on. Her blonde hair, bright blue eyes and rosy cheeks gave her the appearance of a china doll, but this impression was at once belied

314

by the energy with which she bounced up and down, demanding attention, until she was picked up for a quick snuggle.

'This is Frisca.' Margaret introduced her, gave her one more brisk kiss, and handed her back to the nursemaid. Then she led Kate into the drawing room.

Kate assumed her to say Frisker. 'That's an unusual name!' she exclaimed. She could see that it was appropriate, but was bound to find it unfeminine.

'She was christened Francisca. But from the moment she could walk she's hardly been still for a single second – she seems determined to hop, skip and dance non-stop through life. Her mother began to call her Frisky and the nickname was certainly apt enough. But I felt it to be more suitable to a puppy than a little girl. Frisca is my attempt at a compromise. She lives with me here, because her mother spends so much time travelling. Alexa is an opera singer, you know.'

'And Frisca's father?' asked Kate.

'Her father died before she was born. He was killed in the earthquake at San Francisco. Alexa is in London now, so you will see her this evening – that is to say, if she doesn't have to spend the night in prison.'

'Is that likely?' Kate was startled, but remembered what Beatrice had said.

'There's to be a demonstration in Hyde Park this afternoon. A procession of suffragists. One can never be quite sure what will happen. But now you must give me all the news of your dear parents before I allow you to go and unpack.'

How different it was from Sophie's polite enquiries. Kate knew that as well as being her father's sister, Margaret had been a friend of her mother's since they were both girls. They had shared lodgings as medical students, and even after they had qualified as doctors.

They had shared, too, all the secrets of their hearts in those long-ago days. Margaret, moreover, had been in Jamaica when Grant was born. Kate knew how much her presence then had meant to the whole family.

Only when the subject of Jamaica had been exhausted did Margaret ask after her elder brother. She had already been informed of his stroke over the telephone, and now pressed for details as soon as she realized that Kate had actually been in the room when it happened. All Kate's feelings of guilt revived for a moment, until she realized that Margaret was considering the situation as a doctor rather than as a sister. Even then, she was glad when her aunt nodded thoughtfully and suggested that she might now like to unpack.

After luncheon, Kate felt a sudden return of her normal energy, which had been restricted first by the cramped conditions on the banana boat and then, almost as much, by the stifling etiquette of Brinsley House.

'May I go for a walk in Hyde Park?' she asked. 'I would very much like to see Alexa's demonstration.' She was not quite clear whether Alexa was a cousin or an aunt or connected with the family only by adoption, but she had noticed that her Bristol cousins used the Christian name alone, so presumed that it was in order for her to do so as well. A slight frown on Margaret's face made her wonder whether she had decided wrongly, but it soon appeared that there was a different cause for disapproval.

'These occasions are very crowded. And there is always the danger that a disturbance may develop; even a riot. It depends very much on the police. Sometimes there are huge crowds – thousands of people – and yet no trouble at all, because the atmosphere is sympathetic. But on other days, if the Home Secretary has lost patience, there may be arrests, and attempts to resist arrest, and sometimes very unpleasant injuries are inflicted.' She considered a moment longer and then smiled. 'Well, if you are to live in London, you must be prepared to face its hazards, I suppose, though I had hoped to protect you for a little longer. You've probably realized already that I'm uncertain how I ought to look after you. I've no doubt you think of yourself as grown-up, but I may be conscious of dangers of which you can have no experience. I must behave as though I were your mother.'

'Who has allowed me to run wild all my life,' said Kate, laughing mischieviously, and Margaret's smile showed that she was well aware of this.

'At least you must take Robert and Brinsley to protect you,' she said. 'And I shall ask you for a promise that you will keep well back from the procession. It's the people in the front of the crowd who are at risk from the mounted policemen. Will you agree to that?'

Kate was willing to accept any conditions, and said so, but she was a little surprised by her aunt's apparent lack of enthusiasm for the demonstration. Sophie's comments on her sister-in-law had given the impression that Margaret was a supporter of the suffrage movement.

'Are you not in sympathy with the suffragists, Aunt Margaret?' she asked.

'I believe that women should have the same right to the vote as men. To that extent I am in sympathy with them – and indeed, I expect more than some of them do. But I think it unfortunate that so much attention is concentrated on this one reform, which by its very nature won't have much practical effect for some time, even after it's adopted, when there are so many other ways in which women need to be protected. You'll find, Kate, that in England there are a great many women whose time and energy are under-employed. They have fewer children than their mothers did, but they still have servants to run their houses. If they were to take any kind of paid employment, it would be a reflection on their husbands, who are expected to support them; and in most cases they're not qualified for any useful work. So the greatest element in their lives is that of boredom. I've never been in that situation myself, and you will never be either; but even in a short visit you were probably able to observe the symptoms in your aunt Sophie.'

Kate smiled her agreement, although it came as a new idea that she ought to feel sympathetic rather than contemptuous.

'None of what I've been saying applies to the rich, nor to the poor,' said Margaret. 'But the class in between is larger than you might suppose. And it's from this class, very largely, that the agitation for the vote has sprung. But what seems sometimes to be forgotten is the huge section of society whose women have no time to trouble about the vote, because all their energies are devoted to keeping alive and to keeping their children alive. In the course of your career, Kate, once you're qualified, you'll be able to contribute more to the happiness of women than all Alexa's friends put together. There are thousands of women who are unhappy not because they are disfranchised, but because they are poor; and by far the most usual cause of poverty is ill-health – the ill-health either of the breadwinner in the family, or of his wife.'

Margaret checked herself and laughed, as though embarrassed to find herself making a speech. But Kate was stimulated by the conversation, for the words reinforced all her own ideals and ambitions.

'In Hope Valley everyone is poor,' she said. 'And yet nobody is unhappy.'

'It may be easier to be poor in a hot climate than in one which is often cold and damp,' suggested Margaret. 'The people of your father's congregation wear only whatever clothes are needed for modesty. In England,

318

warm clothes and strong boots are a necessity for health, and those who can't afford to buy them suffer for it. In Jamaica, a house hardly needs to be more than a roof to keep off the rain. Here, walls and windows are needed as well, to protect a family against cold winds, and they can't be obtained without payment of rent. There should be a fire for heat as well as for cooking; but coals must be paid for. Few people in the towns have the opportunity to grow their own fruit and vegetables as your villagers do, or to milk their own goats. They eat only what they can afford to buy, and very often it isn't enough. When the father of a family in England is in work, his wife can usually manage to keep the household warm and fed, although it may be a struggle. But once he loses his job, the cycle of deprivation and sickness begins; and very often indeed the loss is caused by the ill-health of the father. It's a problem which can be tackled from many different directions – by improving working conditions, or housing conditions, or educational opportunities, or health facilities. This year for the first time, as an example, old people with few resources of their own have been allowed a pension of five shillings a week, and this will prevent many cases of malnutrition and despair.'

'I suppose that if women are allowed to vote, they may use their power to press for more measures of this kind,' suggested Kate tentatively.

'They may indeed. But their campaign is taking a long time and is monopolizing the attention of the most intelligent and forceful women in the country, so that reforms which might arouse less opposition are neglected for lack of pressure. We must all work in our own fields, and certainly I'm not criticizing Alexa. It would be very easy for a woman who is well paid and beautiful and famous to ignore the hopes of those less fortunate than herself. But if *I* had time to march in processions, my battle cry would be Happiness Through Health.'

'When I'm qualified I shall work only amongst poor people,' declared Kate.

'Rich men sometimes need medical attention too,' said her aunt, although her smile was sympathetic.

'And have very little trouble in obtaining it,' said Kate.

'I see you are your mother's daughter.'

'My mother is like you, Aunt, in many ways,' said Kate thoughtfully. 'She tries to keep people healthy and helps them to be happy in the way of life in which they find themselves. But sometimes I feel a kind of anger which goes beyond that. Brinsley and I have a friend.' She paused. 'I believe you met him once.'

'The brown boy who played cricket with Brinsley?'

'That's right. Duke. He's very clever. I was telling my father before I left how clever he is. A lot of the people on the island don't try to work very hard, but Duke does. If you had to compare him and Brinsley in almost any way, Duke would win the comparison. I mean, I'm very fond of Brinsley, but he does lark about most of the time.'

'He's younger than Duke, of course.'

'Yes.' Kate hardly thought the point important, but accepted it as a fact. 'What I'm saying is that Brinsley will be comfortable all his life. He's being well taught at school and he'll go to university if he chooses and take up whatever career he likes and do as well in it as he can. All because his father is able to provide for him whatever is wanted. Father isn't even a rich man, but still he can do that. Well, Duke doesn't even know who his father is. His ability and application are greater than Brinsley's, but he'll never get the chance to show them. He'll be an estate worker all his life, at the mercy of anyone who cares to put him out of a job. It doesn't seem right that all this should have been decided, the whole pattern of two lives laid down, at the two moments when the boys were born.'

Margaret laughed aloud. 'It sounds to me as though you're a revolutionary, Kate. Don't dig too hard at the foundations of society. If the whole system collapses on our hands, we may all be worse off in the end. And no two babies can be born with an absolutely equal chance of happiness. One may have a richer father than the other, but he may also have a more neglectful mother. Or some mental or physical defect. Poor little Grant, for example, might have expected to start life with all the same advantages as Brinsley.'

'Yes.' For a moment Kate was subdued by the memory of her younger brother. Then she embraced her aunt in a surge of impulsive affection. 'It's going to be so wonderful living with you and talking to you.'

'You'll find no shortage of people to talk to in London. Though your studies may not leave you much time to reorganize the world. And now, if you want to see Alexa on the march, it's time you left.'

Margaret had been right to warn her niece of the crowds. Kate was accustomed to living in a small community, every member of which she had known from birth. Never in her life had she seen so many people gathered together in one place – and she could tell that even fifteen-year-old Robert, in spite of his attempt to act the part of a blasé Londoner in front of his colonial cousins, was equally astounded.

Hyde Park in itself might have come as enough of a surprise to the two Lorimers, for in Jamaica every inch of ground was either cultivated or else responded to neglect by turning itself into a jungle of dense vegetation. A lawn was a luxury reserved for the rich, and Kate had never imagined anything like this vast expanse of grass. Even in

321

the countryside it would have been remarkable; in the heart of a capital city it was almost unbelievable. But the grass could hardly, in fact, be seen, for it had grown into a garden of flower-trimmed hats and sprigged white gowns. Even the gentlemen in the crowd wore bright ribbons round their straw boaters to add to the general impression of summer gaiety.

All these were spectators, but only a few moments after Kate and the two boys arrived on the scene they heard the sound of music as the procession approached. It was led by a fife and drum band which marched with military precision. All its members – even the drum major – were women, dressed in a uniform of purple, green and white, with shorter skirts than Kate had ever seen on an adult. Behind the band, divided into twenty groups, marched the active supporters of the suffrage movement. They carried banners to proclaim the part of the country from which they came – except for the first group of all, which appeared to be organized on a different basis. It announced itself as the Actresses' Franchise League; and although its members wore the same 'Votes for Women' sashes as the other demonstrators, they contrasted strikingly with those who followed them by reason of the elegance of their figures and gowns. All of them were good-looking; but one, tall and slim, with a pale, translucent complexion and hair of reddish gold, was the most beautiful woman Kate had ever seen.

Robert nudged Kate in the ribs. 'That's Alexa,' he said.

Even as he spoke, Alexa began to sing. It was a marching song, to which the band ahead provided a rhythmic accompaniment, and the effect on the procession was visible and immediate. Shoulders were straightened, heads held higher, hundreds of feet marched with a firmer stride. And the thousands of spectators, who until this moment had been talking and laughing in a picnic atmosphere, fell silent to listen. Alexa's voice was as beautiful as her face, and powerful as well, but there was something more than that which drew all eyes towards her. Something intense in her personality concentrated the attention of her hearers, but at once an outgoing impression of gaiety and love of life rewarded them with a feeling of warmth. Kate found herself smiling – not for any particular reason, but because she was overcome by happiness. She hardly listened to the speeches which were delivered from a series of platforms distributed over the large area of grass, but instead hugged her excitement to herself. How lucky she was to be living at the centre of the world, in a capital city teeming with new ideas – and how doubly lucky to have the prospect of intimacy with such outstanding women as her aunt and Alexa.

'What relation is Alexa?' she asked Robert as at last the crowds began to disperse.

'She's my aunt. Well, your aunt as well. My mother's sister.'

'Same mother, same father?' asked Kate. It was a question which came automatically in Jamaica when relationships needed to be established; because all too often there the answer was 'No, same mother, different father.'

This time there was a variation. 'No,' said Robert. 'Just same father. A half-aunt, I suppose.'

'She doesn't seem old enough to be anyone's aunt. She can't be any older than Cousin Beatrice.' Kate considered the comparison while Robert agreed that the generations did seem to have become rather mixed up. There was something about Beatrice which flattened and depressed the spirits, whereas Alexa had the power to stimulate even those who did not know her. Kate looked forward to their first meeting; but it came on a less joyful occasion than she had expected.

Kate and the two boys returned to Queen Anne's Gate to find that Alexa had reached the house before them, driven in a motor car by an admirer. She was sitting in the drawing room with Margaret, and it was clear at once that something untoward had occurred. As soon as Kate had been introduced, Margaret revealed what it was.

'I'm sorry to say that my brother William has died. The news came while you were out.'

Kate adopted a properly sombre expression, although her uncle was so little known to her: the few minutes of angry conversation which had preceded his stroke had hardly persuaded her to feel any affection for him. Alexa, it seemed, was less prepared to be hypocritical. She stood up and walked with a quick, gliding step to the window.

'I'm not going to pretend to a sorrow I don't feel,' she said. 'He never liked me. When I was a child he resented my presence in his house. And when I grew up he behaved abominably to me. Abominably. I shan't write, and I shan't go to the funeral. Will you go, Margaret?'

There was a long silence. Kate remembered that her father had mentioned an estrangement between his brother and sister.

'I have even more cause to be angry with him than you have, Alexa,' Margaret said. 'Quite apart from the grief he caused me on your account, he changed the whole course of my life many years ago. I may have been a more useful member of society as a result of his deceit, but I should have been a good deal happier if he hadn't interfered. If he had lived, I should certainly never have spoken to him again. And yet – yes, I shall go to the funeral.'

'Why?' demanded Alexa passionately. 'Why must you go?'

'Because it seems the right thing to do. Because I have no quarrel with the rest of his family, and they are the ones who would take my absence as an unfriendly gesture. And perhaps also because a small part of my own life dies with William – the years when I shared a nursery and a schoolroom with him in the house that is now his. Or rather, I suppose, now Arthur's. Arthur Lorimer is likely to find himself an extremely rich young man. William was never interested in anything but making money, and in that he appears to have been remarkably successful.'

'Will his other children not inherit any of his wealth?' asked Kate.

'The contents of wills very often come as a surprise to those who think they know what to expect,' said Margaret. 'I can only guess. I imagine he will have left Sophie some kind of life interest in the house and in a part of his income. I should think also that he must have recognized how unlikely it is that Beatrice will ever marry. It would be only kind to provide her with a competence, rather than forcing her to apply to her brother for money. But after that, William would not be a man to dissipate his resources. He must long ago have recognized that Arthur has inherited his own genius for increasing the Lorimer fortune. He would have realized that leaving the bulk of his property to Arthur would be the best investment for the family.'

'Isn't there an elder son as well?'

Margaret glanced at Alexa, who was still staring out of the window with her back to the others. Kate found her aunt's expression difficult to understand, but the answer came calmly enough.

'Matthew. Yes. But Matthew angered his father a great many years ago by refusing to take his place in the family business. Since then, his way of life has not been one of which his parents could approve. And William had a talent for giving his own relations cause to quarrel with him. He wasn't always honest with Matthew. Even if he had wished for a reconciliation with his elder son before he died, I doubt whether he would have been successful. I would be surprised if his will includes any legacy to Matthew.'

The mention of a legacy brought uneasily back to Kate's mind the subject of the tirade which had seemed to cause her uncle's stroke. Even in such friendly surroundings she did not like to say anything which would cause awkward questions to be asked of her father, in case he might not be able to answer them, but that did not dampen her curiosity.

'When your own father died, Aunt Margaret, what legacies did he leave?'

'My father's situation was unusual, not to say unfortunate,' Margaret replied. 'He was an immensely rich man almost for the whole of his life, right up until its last few months. But he died a bankrupt, owing more to the creditors of the bank he controlled than he could possibly pay out of his own estate. So the strict answer to your question is that he left nothing at all to any of his children. In fact, however, he made one or two substantial gifts before he died – before it became illegal to diminish his estate. William, for example, was given the family shipping company, the Lorimer Line, on his twenty-first birthday – and there could be no criticism of that gift, for it was several years before the collapse. My own twenty-first birthday present was a house. It was intended for my own occupation after my marriage, but when those plans fell through it helped to pay for my medical training. It was more doubtful, perhaps, whether he ought to have given me that, but the gift was never challenged. Your father was the unluckiest of us. He was only a schoolboy at the time of our father's death. In different circumstances I'm sure he would have been given his fair share. As it is, you can feel very proud that he has achieved so much by his own efforts.'

'I was not even a schoolchild when John Junius Lorimer died,' said Alexa quietly, without turning round. 'I was three years old, yet he left me a fortune in rubies to hang round my neck. It's as well that your father is a man of God, Kate, or he would have had cause to be angry at the unfairness of life and the haphazard way in which fortune distributes her prizes.'

'Kate and I have had this conversation once today already,' said Margaret. Her tone immediately lightened the atmosphere, and Alexa was quick to respond. She sat down beside Kate and clasped her hands, demanding to be told all her plans for the future. All the excitement of the afternoon returned, augmented by an extra gaiety when Frisca was brought in for her hour of playtime. By the time Kate went to bed that night she had lost the last traces of the homesickness which had attacked her in Bristol. She was living amongst friends who were determined to love her, and she would soon be beginning the training on which her heart had been set for years. In the contentment of a half-sleep she saw the promise of happiness in both the present and the future, and gave no further thought to her uncle's angry strictures about a misdirected legacy. 'No better than a thief!' he had cried, but it was an accusation which could never be repeated, because the accuser was dead.

PART VI

Alexa at Blaize

1

The death of a king brings fashionable society to a standstill. While the lower classes of England shed a tear for 'poor old Teddy' and then returned to their normal pursuits, the aristocracy was forced to wear black and stay at home.

So Alexa, returning to England for the summer season of 1910 after a winter spent singing in St Petersburg, found London dull. The restrictions on social life, however, applied mainly to the capital. When Lord Glanville invited her to spend a weekend at Blaize, her spirits rose.

'Shall I take Frisca with me?' she asked Margaret. 'Piers says that she would be welcome.'

'You may find her unwilling,' Margaret said. 'Robert is to play in a cricket match on Saturday and I've promised to take her to watch.'

'She'd certainly never forgive me if I interfered with such a treat.' Alexa was well aware that Frisca adored her cousin. 'She makes it quite clear that she intends to marry Robert when she grows up. I don't know how we're going to break the news that a young man twelve years older than herself may not be prepared to wait.'

'Oh, she'll find another hero long before that,' Margaret said cheerfully. 'Well, give my kind regards to Piers. When will you go?'

'He asks me for Thursday, and since the Royal Opera House has cancelled its performances for the whole week, there's nothing to make this impossible. I wonder whether the other guests will be invited for the same time. I've found myself once before arriving at Blaize a day ahead of the main party. It's one of the advantages of widowhood, I suppose, that my reputation is reckoned to be a less fragile flower than a young girl's.' She mocked herself as she spoke, and was amused to see Margaret's fleeting frown of disapproval.

'You've never told Piers the truth?'

'Why should I? The truth is a legal formula which in the circumstances makes no difference to our relationship. And it's a mistake to scatter too many versions of the same story around amongst people who know each other. I'll write to accept, then.'

Alexa felt no qualms about leaving Frisca with Margaret. As the two women had agreed between themselves before the birth, the little girl had always been told truthfully who her mother was. She knew that Margaret was only her aunt – but it was Margaret, all the same, who represented the constant love in her life. It was to Margaret that her nursemaid took her for an hour of play every evening, and Margaret who came each night to see her in bed and hear her prayers. Alexa's own visits, sudden and brief and full of treats and spoilings, provided excitement and the opportunity to chatter to her beautiful mother, but they were no more than holiday occasions. Margaret was Frisca's family.

So Alexa was alone as she was driven up the winding woodland drive of Lord Glanville's estate on the bank of the Thames. The sun was bright and the trees fresh and vigorous, their leaves almost visibly unfolding in the warmth of the afternoon. She breathed deeply in the spring air as she stepped down from the motor car which had been sent to meet her at the railway station.

Her host appeared to greet her with a promptitude which suggested that he had been listening for the sound of the engine. It was interesting, Alexa thought, that he was more handsome today, in his early fifties, than he had been ten years before. His hair, which had already begun to turn grey when she first met him, was now so brightly white that it had the curious effect of making his face appear younger. During his wife's lifetime, too, his eyes had always seemed troubled, and his forehead lined with strain; his shoulders had been perpetually stooped, as though to minimize his height. Now his back was straight and his step springy. He moved like a young man and allowed nothing to disturb the smile of pleasure with which he came forward to take her hand.

'I'm cramped after the journey,' Alexa said as soon as they had exchanged greetings. 'May we walk in the garden for a moment before I go to tidy myself?'

'Of course,' he said, and she could see how much the suggestion pleased him. 'It's too early for the roses. But the azalea walk is at its best.'

He offered her his arm and led her towards the river. The terraces and gardens immediately adjoining the house were arranged in a geometrically formal manner, to suit both the original Tudor building and the wings which had been added to it in the reign of William and Mary. On the further side of the house, the terraces were divided by a ha-ha from the fertile and well-ordered land of the home farm: this was the view which Alexa knew that she would have from the window of the guest room which was always allotted to her. But between Blaize and the Thames the ground sloped down too steeply for cultivation.

Most of it was wooded, but with blossoming or specimen trees which made it clear that this was still part of the pleasure garden. On a meandering bed, artificially lined with smooth grey stones in an apparently random fashion, a small stream trickled down to join the river.

On either side of the stream low-growing azaleas pressed together so closely that it seemed almost to be the same shrub in which pink and red and purple flowers blended, or yellow and white more coolly dipped their heads to reflect in the rippling water. Alexa clapped her hands with pleasure at the rich ribbon of colour in such an unexpected setting.

'Only in England does one find such informal beauty so carefully planned,' she exclaimed. 'I remember that last time I came here in spring you took me to a field of daffodils and primroses. Have you a corner of your grounds for every week of the year?'

'It's one of the happy results of being a landowner,' Lord Glanville agreed. 'One can be prodigal of space. A man who can see his whole garden from his drawing-room window must sometimes feast his eyes only on bare branches or withered blossoms. But I can turn my back on the dying daffodils and come here instead. And within a week the laburnum avenue will be at its best, to lead us on to the first flush of the roses.'

Although Alexa had asked the question, her attention had already been distracted from the answer. They had almost reached river level by now, and she felt sure that she must have been to this part of the grounds before, on one or other of her visits; but she could not remember that she had ever noticed the building which now attracted her attention.

It was large and very long, stretching along the bank of the river. The roof was in bad repair, but the walls were built of the same dark bricks as the Tudor section of Blaize, their upper sections patterned with bleached beams of oak.

'This can hardly have been built since I was last here,' she said, puzzled. 'And yet I'm sure I don't remember seeing it before.'

'Until a few weeks ago it was screened by trees which had grown up far too close to it,' Lord Glanville explained. 'And covered with brambles and creepers. It would have been impossible for you to guess the shape of the building beneath the tangle, even if you'd been able to approach it. Recently I had an idea which would have brought it into use again, so I had the area cleared in order that its structural state could be examined.'

'What is it?' asked Alexa. 'Or rather, what was it?'

'A tithe barn. Pre-Reformation – older than the house. It was built in a period when the family always kept the living in its own hands. The tenant farmers of the time must have had difficulty in distinguishing between what they owed to the church and a simple addition to their rent. It was positioned here because we had land across the river, and the harvest tithe was brought over by boat.'

'I don't imagine your tenants would take kindly nowadays to the idea of giving you a tenth of all their crops, so I take it you aren't proposing to revive that system. What's your new idea for the barn? Shall I guess?'

'You're not likely to be successful,' Lord Glanville laughed. 'There's a game of tennis which is played in an indoor court. The old, royal game – nothing like lawn tennis. One or two of my friends still possess courts which were built in the Tudor period, when it was particularly popular, and others have erected new ones for themselves in the past twenty years. They've introduced me to the game, and I find it fascinating. It has a special advantage that even a player of advancing years like myself can sometimes beat a younger and fitter man by the use of craft. With a court of my own in which to practise, I should improve more rapidly, of course, and it occurred to me to wonder whether the barn could be adapted for this purpose.'

For the second time within an hour Alexa contrasted

the energy which her host displayed nowadays with the languid tiredness of those earlier years when he had borne the anxiety and responsibility for an invalid wife.

'And could it really be used in that way?' Alexa asked. She lifted her skirts so that they should not catch on any of the cut brambles which lay on the ground, and stepped inside the barn; if ever there had been a door to close the entrance, it had rotted away a century or two before. There was a smell of musty dampness, of air which had not been disturbed for many years, but enough light filtered through the gaps in the roof to reveal a structure that seemed closer to a cathedral than a farm building. Alexa studied it curiously while Lord Glanville answered her question.

'It would be simpler – and less extravagant into the bargain – to erect a completely new building,' he said. 'A real tennis court has special requirements. The floor must be smooth, naturally, and of stone – but that could be arranged easily enough. The game is played off the walls, so these also must be smooth and true, with windows running the whole length of the court at a high level, above the playing area. And there are various architectural oddities which are incorporated into the rules of the game – apertures and galleries which enable winning points to be scored; and a sloping penthouse roof above the galleries, to be used in the service.'

'A roof inside the building?' Alexa found it difficult to visualize the appearance of the court from his description.

'It's thought that the game may have been developed by monks playing in the cloisters of their monasteries, and using every feature of the courtyard,' Lord Glanville explained. 'Anyway, my conclusion, alas, is that the conversion would be too complicated.'

'So the barn will be abandoned again, to decay still further? What a pity. The old brick is so attractive. And the size is unusual.' For a moment or two longer Alexa wandered about inside, picking her way with care over the rough ground. Then she turned to smile impishly at Lord Glanville. 'You should convert it into a little opera house,' she said. 'It would be perfect. The length of the barn would allow plenty of room for an audience, an orchestra, a stage, and space behind the stage for the cast. There could be a gallery at the end there, where there seems to have been a loft once. It might be necessary to incline the floor and to raise the other end of the roof to accommodate the scenery, but really the alterations would be very simple. And there could be a landing stage on the river, allowing the audience to arrive by boat. Just think how romantic that would be on a summer evening.'

'Romance on a small scale,' laughed Lord Glanville. 'Before you could make room for a Soldiers' Chorus, you would have to evict the audience.'

Alexa shrugged away the objection. 'Mozart wrote operas to be performed at court, in theatres no larger than this would be. And in Russia, you know, many of the noble families who have town palaces in Moscow and Petersburg also own theatre palaces a few miles outside. I was invited to sing in one by Prince Aminov – a private performance for his family and friends. It was a most agreeable experience.'

'One may reasonably assume that the theatre would have been built by the family's serfs, in the days before their emancipation,' suggested Lord Glanville. 'And it's my impression that the servants of the Russian aristocracy haven't changed their expectations too markedly since those days. In England, the economics of staging opera privately might prove more daunting.'

'Certainly it would be necessary to charge admission,' agreed Alexa. 'To charge a very high price, in fact, so that to attend a performance became something to boast about. But the casts could be small and the sets modest. Even the orchestra, in such a small building, need not be too enormous. New composers could be found, who would write for a particular place. There's a need for patronage in music.' She realized that she was allowing herself to speak too seriously and made a gesture of insouciance. 'I'm sorry,' she said, 'I mustn't bore you with my hobby horse. I travel round the world keeping an eye open for my ideal opera house. But I'm in no real hurry to find it, because it would tie me down to one place.'

'If it would tie you to Blaize, I would willingly give you the barn and the money to adapt it,' Lord Glanville said. Just as Alexa a moment earlier had twirled her parasol in an attempt to pretend that she was only indulging a fantasy, so now he laughed to suggest that he was joking; but Alexa suspected that that was an equal pretence.

The conversation was an unsettling one. Alexa spent so much of each year singing in opera houses abroad that her meetings with Lord Glanville were necessarily infrequent. But at each reunion she was amazed by the ease with which they resumed their friendship as though there had been no gap. It had become a friendship of equals. The time when Alexa had been dependent on the help and protection of the Glanvilles was long past. Every new year and every new success brought her more confidence and, as she grew more mature, so the twenty-year difference in age between herself and Lord Glanville seemed less important.

If only he would be a little less restrained, she would be able to judge whether the pleasure she felt each time she saw him could be transformed into something deeper. But she could hardly expect him suddenly to become passionate when her rejection of his proposal of marriage four years earlier had been so brusque and unkind. He had chosen the worst possible moment then to ask her to marry him, coming to join her on the ballroom terrace of Blaize while her heart was still breaking with love for Matthew, who had left her for a reason she could not accept and whom she would never see again. She had told Margaret at the end of that evening that she could not possibly love Lord Glanville. Now she was not so sure.

This, however, was not the moment to find out. Without making any comment on her host's suggestion, Alexa turned to lead the way out of the barn and up the steep woodland slope at a pace which left her breathless. Her carefree smile as Lord Glanville caught her up masked an anxiety which she was determined to conceal. He could not be expected to know about the difficulty which she had recently brought upon herself by her own impulsive behaviour. Nor could he guess how frightened she was. The temptation to confide in him was very great, but pride held her back. She had chosen a way of life which placed no reliance on male support, and it would be cowardly to appeal for help when the first small problem arose. The friendship which gave them both such pleasure was built on the foundation of two independently satisfying lives, and nothing must be allowed to spoil it.

As they emerged together from the woodlands, Alexa straightened her shoulders and held her head high. With one hand resting lightly on her host's arm she allowed herself to be taken into the house as a lady of fashion, calm and elegant, without a care in the world. A guest at Blaize – and nothing more.

2

Political opinions can be altered by argument, but a man's conception of what constitutes good manners is less susceptible to change. In the course of Lord Glanville's campaign to remove the constitutional inequalities between men and women, he had grown to respect the intelligence of his allies in the battle. Even when his disagreements with the Pankhursts were at their most acute on questions of timing and tactics, he acknowledged the brilliance of Christabel's intellect. The fact that – although her sex disqualified her from practising as a lawyer – her name had headed the honours list in the Bar Examination, confirmed his belief that if educational opportunities were to be made equal from childhood, the intellectual differences between men and women would also disappear.

But in his social life he found it less easy to treat women in the same manner as men. He was courteous by nature, and had been brought up to behave chivalrously to what he still regarded as the weaker sex, even when he saw its representatives beating policemen over the head with their banners. The most ill-favoured of his female colleagues in the suffragist movement could expect to receive his most polished compliments.

Alexa was further from being ill-favoured than any other woman he had ever known, but to her Lord Glanville paid no compliments. Although he had adored her for many years, he no longer made the mistake of telling her so. Instead, he worked hard to develop a friendship between them which owed nothing to the fact that he was a man and she a woman. It was not always easy – in fact, if he were to be honest with himself, it was never easy – and the strain which it imposed was hardly diminished by the knowledge that society gossip assumed the relationship to be what he would have liked. He was forced to snatch his rewards where he could: when she kissed him with the same spontaneous affection which she would have offered to a female friend; or when he advised her on her financial affairs and could enjoy her intelligent concentration as he explained the intricacies of investment policy to her as though she were the orphaned son of a friend, acknowledging ignorance but determined to understand. Her visits to Blaize were always a pleasure to him, but there was pain at the heart of them.

For this reason he found it difficult at first to think of a safe subject with which to open the conversation when Alexa appeared later that evening, dressed for dinner. She had been correct in guessing that his other guests for the weekend house party had been invited to arrive a day later than herself. He wanted her to himself, and now that she was here he wanted to tell her how lovely she looked. But he knew that he would be unable to phrase the compliment lightly enough to be acceptable.

'How is Kate the firebrand?' he asked instead.

Alexa looked startled, either by the abruptness of the question or at his description of her niece. 'I didn't realize that you'd met her,' she said.

'She was at home when I called on Margaret one day just before Christmas. Within half an hour of being introduced, she was expounding her theory that all privilege must be paid for, that the aristocracy has no right to continue in the possession of wealth and property if they evade their responsibilities to their dependants.'

Alexa tutted angrily. 'The girl has no tact.'

'Her heart is in the right place, even if her tongue is undisciplined. And as a matter of fact, she was trying to

338

pay me a compliment. Margaret had taken her to see the model housing estate I've had built on some land I own in Whitechapel. Kate approved in particular of the sanitary arrangements there, but what really drew her praise was the discovery that because the rents are low, my income has been reduced by building the new houses. For that sacrifice, I gather, I may be allowed to enjoy the possession of Blaize and Glanville House for a little longer without a guilty conscience.'

'We must hope, then, that Kate never goes to Russia,' said Alexa. 'I've never seen so many jewels as those on display every night at the Mariinsky in Petersburg. The men, with all their Orders, gleam just as brightly as their wives and daughters do in tiaras and necklaces. It may be that the hundreds of grand-dukes and princes and counts and all the rest of them are benevolent enough to the people who work their estates and provide their huge incomes, but it would take a good many model housing estates, I should think, to justify a single one of those diamond necklaces in Kate's eyes.'

'She must naturally have been influenced by the conditions in which she was brought up. I understand it was a community organized to be self-supporting on a basis of mutual help, with her father as a kind of benevolent despot.'

'Yes, you're right. She has no quarrel with a paternalist order of society, in which some command and others obey, as long as any benefits are distributed throughout that society. But I suppose that before she came to England she had never seen poverty of the kind which London reveals. It's to her credit that she's shocked by it. Margaret has had to be quite stern with her, though, telling her that for the time being she must concentrate all her energies on studying and passing her examinations.'

'That must have been why she didn't come to the

suffrage meeting at my house, although she had expressed interest in it. And talking of suffrage, I take it that your friends have told you of the developments which took place while you were abroad, and our hopes of the Conciliation Bill.'

'I would prefer *not* to talk of suffrage,' said Alexa.

Lord Glanville was disturbed both by the tone of her voice and by the manner in which she turned away so that he could not see her face. 'Has something happened?' he asked.

'Yes, something has happened.' Alexa made an attempt to laugh. 'I've made a promise, and now I regret it. You've often told me how much you disapprove of the more extreme actions of the Franchise League, and how unwise you think me to be involved with them. You are quite right, of course – you have always been quite right. I've allowed myself to become too deeply involved, and now there seems no way to withdraw without humiliation.'

'But even the League is surely not foolish enough to plan anything this year! Every section of the suffrage movement has agreed to a truce – an end to all forms of militant activity until the Conciliation Bill has been considered in Parliament.'

'There are different definitions, I suppose, of militancy. Processions and demonstrations are still to continue, are they not? What the League has in mind will not cause any physical harm to anyone. But all the same – ' Her voice trailed away. She was frightened, he realized; and the knowledge increased the protective love which he felt for her.

'Tell me.'

'It's a secret,' she said. 'I promised . . .'

'You surely don't think I'd betray you.'

For a moment longer she hesitated. Then she turned

340

back to face him, clearly relieved by the opportunity to discuss her anxieties.

'There's to be an unusual kind of demonstration,' she said. 'Not a mass meeting. No speeches. Just one person singing a very special song.'

'The one person is yourself, I take it. Well, that certainly doesn't sound too militant. Where are you proposing to sing this song?'

'In Westminster Abbey,' said Alexa. 'In the middle of the Coronation service.' Lord Glanville's incredulity must have shown clearly on his face, for she hurried to defend herself. 'There will be nothing subversive about the song, nothing at all. It's a kind of hymn, in fact, and sung to a hymn tune. But the words are intended to remind King George, as he takes the oath, that half his subjects are women and that he has responsibilities towards them as well as to the men.'

'My dear Alexa, you cannot possibly – ' Lord Glanville was horrified, and saw no reason to pretend otherwise. 'For a start, you would never be allowed inside the abbey on Coronation Day. And even if you were to gain admittance, you would be arrested as soon as you began to sing.'

'There's a peeress who is sympathetic to the cause,' said Alexa. 'I mustn't tell you her name. But it was her idea in the first place. She wished to make the gesture herself, in fact, but she has no voice; she wouldn't be heard. So instead, she is prepared to make her invitation and her robes available to me. And I shall be in the middle of a block of peeresses. It will be a little while before anyone realizes what is happening, and a little longer before anyone will be able to force a way through to me. Outside the abbey, other women will be distributing leaflets bearing the full text. It will be printed in the newspapers the next day. Even if King George doesn't receive the whole message at once, it will reach him eventually.'

'Have you considered what the penalties are likely to be, Alexa?' Lord Glanville was aghast.

'There's no law that I know of which makes it a crime to sing a hymn in a place of worship.'

'I doubt whether that will prevent the Home Secretary from drawing up charges. Women are being sent to prison merely for trying to push their way into the House of Commons. But this – I'm no lawyer, but I'm sure that if the authorities can find no simple offence, they will invent a complicated one. Sacrilege, for example, or blasphemy if the words of the hymn in any way justify it. For all I know, it may even rank as treason or sedition to create a disturbance in His Majesty's presence. You will certainly be sent to prison.'

'Yes, I know,' said Alexa. 'I realized that when I agreed to do it. Obviously I couldn't expect a prison sentence to be a pleasant experience, but when so many of my friends have accepted the risk, I didn't think I ought to shirk it. I still don't think so.'

'But a few moments ago you mentioned that you had come to regret what you promised. Why is that, if nothing has changed?'

'Something *has* changed.' Alexa began to walk up and down the room in an agitated manner. 'It changed some time ago, but because I've been abroad I was slow to discover it. When I promised to sing, I was prepared to endure a spell as an ordinary prisoner. What I didn't know was that it has now become a point of honour for all imprisoned suffragists to go on hunger strike. If I were to refuse to do so, I should earn the contempt of all my friends in the movement. Well, I wouldn't even mind starving if it could be of any help. But then I learned something else – that every hunger-striker is forcibly fed.

342

And do you know how that is done, Piers? I've had it described to me, and I can tell you. They put a steel gag into your mouth and open it until your jaws are wide apart. Then they force a large rubber tube down your throat. It chokes you until you retch and vomit: they hold your head and wait and then push the tube down even further before at last the food is poured down. You struggle, I'm told, you can't help but struggle because the choking robs you of breath; and the result is to leave your chest aching and your throat raw.' She had worked herself up into tears, and now buried her head in her hands, trembling with the effects of her own imagination. 'I can't do it, Piers. My voice is the only asset I have in the world. If I lose it, I have nothing. I'm thirty-three years old. I can't expect to be beautiful for very much longer, but there's no reason why my career shouldn't continue for a long time yet. I can't take the risk of having that tube forced down my throat, but I shall be mocked for a coward if I withdraw altogether from what I've promised.'

'Is that so important to you?' he asked.

'Yes. What respect would you, or any other man, have for a soldier who deserted in the middle of a battle? I shall be ashamed for the rest of my life. But I can see no way out.'

'Calm yourself, Alexa.' He stepped forward and put his hands on her shoulders, drawing her towards him so that her head was pressed against his chest. He could feel her panting, almost sobbing, and for a moment his grip tightened. But caution warned him not to frighten her still further by embracing her with the passion which he longed to show. He stood for a long time without moving, until her breath gradually steadied itself and she was able to raise her head.

It was not the first time, he remembered, that they had

held each other for comfort in just such a manner. On the very first day of their acquaintance Alexa had clung to him for protection against his own brother. And later, in Heidelberg, he in turn had sought consolation in his grief for his dying wife. On neither of those two occasions had he expected Alexa to appreciate his emotions. But now she was older, an experience and sophisticated woman. As soon as she had emerged from the tangle of her own feelings, she would become conscious of his.

She knew them already, in fact. More than four years had passed since the moment on the ballroom terrace at Blaize when he had asked her to marry him. On that occasion he had misjudged her mood completely. From the proud stiffness with which she held her head, the sparkle in her eyes, the vivacious gaiety with which she held the attention of everyone in the room, he had recognized her excitement as that of a woman demanding to be loved. Perhaps he had been right in that, but quite wrong when he hoped that his was the love she wanted to attract. Now, if he was very careful, he might be able to make a second chance for himself.

This time his hopes were more rational. He could not pretend that Alexa loved him. It would be enough, he told himself, if she would agree to marry him. But to approach without frightening her required a delicacy difficult to achieve when his emotions were in such a state of turmoil. He held his breath, approaching in silence what seemed to be the most important moment of his life.

Behind him, the door opened. The butler had come to announce the serving of dinner. Lord Glanville took one hand away from Alexa's shoulders and flicked his fingers in a gesture of dismissal. The butler hesitated, interpreted the instructions rightly and withdrew without speaking. As the door closed behind him, Alexa lifted her head and forced herself to smile. Glad after all of the interruption which had lowered the emotional temperature, Lord Glanville smiled back.

'Let me tell you,' he said, 'the story of Lady Constance Lytton and Miss Jane Warton. For I have a suggestion to make.'

3

Throughout the centuries the story-teller has had the power to calm and control an audience. Lord Glanville could see that Alexa was startled by what must have seemed to be a complete change of subject; no doubt it was curiosity that helped her to accept it.

'I've never heard of Jane Warton,' she said. 'Lady Constance's name is familiar, of course. I know that she sympathizes with the militant movement. But I've always understood that her health was too uncertain for her to take any active part in it.'

'Sit down and let me tell you what happened while you were in Russia,' said Lord Glanville. 'Jane Warton was arrested in Liverpool for throwing stones. As a matter of strict fact, she was so anxious not to hurt anyone that she wrapped the stones in paper and merely dropped them over the hedge belonging to the prison governor, but that was enough to earn her a prison sentence. Like the rest of the women arrested, she went on hunger strike, and was forcibly fed on eight occasions in exactly the horrific manner you have just described. She has a weak heart, and it's feared by her brother that permanent damage may have been done to it. That's half the story.'

'Where does Lady Constance Lytton come into it?' asked Alexa.

345

'Some weeks before Jane Warton's imprisonment, Lady Constance was arrested in the same way, in Newcastle. Like Miss Warton later, she went on hunger strike. The authorities were highly embarrassed to discover that they had in their charge the sister of an earl. No attempt was made to feed her forcibly. Instead, she was released from prison. The point of the story is that Lady Constance Lytton and Miss Jane Warton are the same person.'

It was easy to see that Alexa was still puzzled. 'I see the point, but not the relevance,' she said. 'Has this anything to do with me?'

'I told you that I had a suggestion to make, and it's this. You're proposing to go to Westminster Abbey disguised as a peeress, dressed in robes you are not entitled to wear and using an invitation not addressed to you. But there's another way. You could go genuinely as a peeress, wearing your own robes and entitled to your own seat. There would be no charge of impersonation or unauthorized entry. You would still undoubtedly be arrested for causing a disturbance; you might well be imprisoned. But no prison officer would dare to assault you in the way which forcible feeding entails. Not only because of the publicity the case would arouse, but because the Home Secretary would be well aware what the effect on his own political career might be. I may not be a member of the government, but my voice is not without influence in the House of Lords. He would think twice before he offended me in such an unsympathetic cause.'

Slowly Alexa rose to her feet again. 'What are you saying, Piers?' she asked incredulously; although she must have known the answer.

'Once before I offered you everything I had to give – my name, my fortune, myself. They were of no interest to you then. Now I'm making the offer again, because you could find that my name at least might serve a useful purpose.'

Was it his imagination, or did he see a flash of pleasure in her eyes? He held his breath as he waited for an answer. The silence continued for a long time, encouraging his hopes to rise. Last time he had asked her to marry him, she had hardly seemed to listen, flinging a brusque refusal from the depth of some private unhappiness which her vivacious manner earlier in the evening had given him no chance to anticipate. But today there was a warmth and softness in her expression which must surely be to his advantage. It came as all the more of a shock when at last she shook her head.

'Do you expect me to take your name only to degrade it? Piers, you are kind and generous – yes, and ingenious too – but you haven't allowed yourself time to think what you're saying. Your name might protect me, but in return for your kindness you would hear it read out in court, attached to a criminal charge.'

Disappointment silenced him briefly, but he could not prevent his hopes from feeding on what was surely a trace of regret in her voice. Perhaps all she wanted was to be convinced that she would not do him too much harm by accepting his proposal. Lord Glanville applied himself to reasonable argument.

'I don't agree, as you know, with the methods of the militant campaign.' He spoke calmly, as though it were the most natural thing in the world to discuss the political situation when his heart was pounding with anxiety. 'I wish that I could persuade you to join me and support the constitutionalist approach. This is another point you might consider. If you were to marry me, even your most fervent friends might accept the necessity for you to conform, publicly at least, to your husband's known views. There would be no shame in using marriage as an excuse for withdrawing from your undertaking.'

'My own views are as well known as yours!' Alexa exclaimed. 'I see no reason why a woman should alter her opinions to conform with those of her husband.'

'You interrupted me too soon.' Lord Glanville recognized that he had made a mistake and hurried to correct it. 'I said that I didn't approve of the militant methods. But obviously I agree with the eventual aims. What I was trying to indicate was that it would cause me no embarrassment to hear my wife's name linked with those aims, even in court. Marry me, Alexa.'

For a second time she shook her head. 'I'm sorry, Piers, but it's out of proportion. Marriage is too important to be traded for such a small thing as a temporary humiliation. I know already that I shan't be able to face the forcible feeding. But no doubt I shall be able to invent some diplomatic illness at the last minute. I shall be ashamed for the rest of my life, but it will be no more than I deserve for being so impetuous. I'm truly sorry, but I can't accept your offer.'

It was a moment of complete humiliation. To hear Alexa reject his love would have been bad enough. But when he could offer her an arrangement entirely to her advantage and found that she still regarded marriage to him as too high a price to pay, he was bound to feel a bitter sense of rejection.

Except for that mistaken moment during the ball at Blaize, Lord Glanville had never deceived himself into believing that Alexa loved him. Her attitude now only confirmed what he had always accepted, but it was enough to make him desperate. This might be his last chance to hold her to his side, for it seemed all too likely that his proposal had already bruised the fragile friendship with which he had been forced to content himself during the past few years. If the damage had been done, there could be no harm in testing whether a higher offer would be more successful.

'If you need a more positive inducement, I can offer that,' he said.

'What do you mean?'

'An opera house of your own. I know you've always wanted one, however small. We were talking of it earlier today. If you marry me, I'll give you that for a wedding present – the tithe barn, converted to your own specifications. And however much money you need to run it.'

'Really, Piers! What do you take me for?' Alexa exclaimed, and the fierceness of her anger startled and dismayed him. Obviously he had misjudged her mood, but he could not understand how. Half an hour earlier she had been frightened and depressed, drained of all her usual vitality as though, for the first time since she became an adult, life had grown too much for her to manage alone. Five minutes earlier she had seemed warm and affectionate, tempting him to take the initiative in what had immediately been revealed as a bad mistake. Now the colour flooded back into her cheeks and her eyes flashed with their familiar fire as she attacked him.

'I was anxious when I came here, yes, and tired; glad of your friendship and company,' she said, with what seemed a disproportionate indignation. 'But comfort was all I asked for. You're treating me as though all I want is to grab whatever anyone will give me. Do you see me only as someone who can be bought if the bribe is big enough? Am I so selfish that you believe I'd marry you just because you have so much to offer? I won't allow you to think of me like that. How could I possibly accept such an arrangement?'

'If you think I regard you as selfish, it's because you're looking at what I suggest from a purely selfish point of

349

view.' With nothing any longer to lose, he allowed his unhappiness full rein. Only once before, in Heidelberg, had he lost his temper with her as he did now. On that occasion she had responded with understanding and sympathy. Now she looked at first startled and then resentful. It was difficult, no doubt, for her to recognize that part of his anger was with himself for his inability to find the right approach to her heart.

'How can you say such a thing,' she protested, 'when I decline an offer which would have so many advantages for myself just because it would bring no good to you?'

'I can call you selfish because you're rejecting my proposal without even considering what you might have to offer me. You're thinking only of what I suggest you might take, and not of what you might give.'

'That's not fair, Piers.' Her flush had deepened at the criticism, but she made no attempt to retreat from the argument. '*You* are the one who is emphasizing what I would gain from being your wife. And what *could* I give you? You have so much already. Wealth, property, a title, the respect of everyone who knows you. What could I add to all that?'

'When I die, the respect of which you speak may earn me a kind obituary notice. And all the rest – the title, the money, the land – will be inherited by my brother Duncan, a man whom I dislike and despise; and so, I think, do you. I have more sense than to say that you could give me your love if you tried, because I know that love can't be forced. But you could give me an heir, Alexa. No one else can.'

'Why not?'

'You know the answer to that. Because I can't look at any other woman while you're dazzling my eyes. I love you, Alexa. I want you, and I want a son. Your son and mine.'

350

He had surprised himself enough by losing his temper a moment earlier, but that was nothing to the shock of realizing that he was no longer able to maintain the polite restraint of a gentleman. As he pulled Alexa into his arms for the second time that evening, he was aware that the tight grip of his fingers must be bruising her arms, that the rough pressure of his kiss was forcing her head back until she could hardly breathe. Because he was hurting her, she fought against him, but her struggles only spurred him to imprison her more tightly than before. When at last he released her, he expected her to slap his face or leave the room in anger, but she made no attempt to move away. Instead, as she faced him, she seemed to be panting with the same effort and excitement that he felt himself.

'I ought to apologize,' he said when he had brought his feelings under control. 'But I won't. Even if you're going to tell me now that you never want to see me again, it was right for you to know how I feel. You seemed to think that all I was offering was some kind of cold contract.'

'And so you were,' she said. 'You've always been so calm, so cool, so protective. You've never told me before that you loved me.'

'But you must have known.'

'Perhaps,' she admitted. 'All the same, I needed to be told. It's easier to accept a gift of love than an opera house. You've done so much for me, Piers. My whole career has been built on your generosity. From the first moment I met you I've been carrying a burden of obligation that I've never had any chance of repaying. Well, it hasn't seemed like a burden until now. But when you tried to pile more and more on top – if I'd married you on those terms, how could I have ever made you believe that I felt anything more for you than gratitude?'

351

'I'm sorry,' he said. He felt emptied now, exhausted by the draining of his emotions. 'If I seemed to be bribing you – and I have to admit that I was – it was because I couldn't think of any other way to approach you.' He sighed at the hopelessness of his position. 'But I had no right to be angry. Nor to ask so much of you. You couldn't be expected to give up a brilliant career, even if it was only for a few years, just to have a baby.'

'Couldn't I?' said Alexa. 'Why don't you ask me? You were quite right, as a matter of fact, in thinking that I could be bribed. You chose the wrong bribe, that's all.'

'Then what's the right one?'

'You've found it already. I needed something to give you. Now you've told me what you want. And I'm ashamed that I didn't think of it for myself long ago.'

'I don't understand,' he said. That was not quite true. He understood enough to feel an excitement which came near to joy, but it was necessary to restrain it. He had misjudged Alexa's moods too often and too recently to be sure now that his hopes would prove to be justified.

'When I was young,' she said, ' – younger even than when you first met me – there was a time when I believed that the most important thing in life was to love and be loved. I wasn't always hard and flighty. I would have given my love and loyalty for a lifetime if I could have found anyone to accept it. But first of all – ' She hesitated, apparently changing her mind about what she was on the point of saying. 'Caversham couldn't afford it. He had to marry an heiress who would shoulder the burden of his estate. And in San Francisco – I would have stayed, you know, even after Frisca's father was killed, if his family had wanted me. But they didn't. One grows to expect disappointment. When I sing on the stage I can give the whole of myself to the audience and feel them accepting me, loving me. That's why I find my work so exciting. In private life it's never seemed so easy. The best defence against rejection is never to offer anything important.'

'There was never any possibility that I would have rejected anything you had to offer me. We could have discussed this a long time ago, at the ball.'

'No,' said Alexa. 'You chose the wrong moment then.'

'And ten minutes ago?'

'You were asking the wrong question. Offering far too much and demanding far too little. So that was the wrong moment as well.'

'Then how shall I find the right one?' He almost laughed aloud for happiness. 'Am I expected to plunge a skewer into your heart, like one of my cooks testing the centre of a cake to test whether it's ready to be taken from the oven?'

'After the Coronation, when I've dealt with my own difficulties, that would be the right moment,' she said.

More gently than before, he took her into his arms and kissed her again. 'I can't wait so long,' he said. 'And I think you realize already how unnecessary it is to ask me to. There's no virtue in being proud when you could be generous. Tell me that you'll marry me. Say it now.'

Her soft acceptance of his kiss was encouraging, but when he allowed her to speak again he was not given the direct answer for which he hoped.

'There's something I need to tell you first,' Alexa said instead. Her hands moved through his hair and pressed his head against her cheek as she hesitated before continuing. 'About Frisca.'

Lord Glanville stared at her with a bewildered expression.

'Frisca?' he queried. 'She would come here with you, of course. There's no problem about Frisca.'

'I was never married to her father,' Alexa said. 'I've passed myself off as a widow, but that isn't true. It *is* true

353

that her father died in the earthquake, and I would have married him if he'd lived, but – well – ' She shrugged her shoulders. 'That's all.'

'Why do you tell me this now?'

'Because I believe that there should be no lies or concealments within a marriage. That proves, I suppose, how different I am from the women who are born into Society. You'll have to accept a good many shocks if you marry me, Piers. I'm prepared to study the conventions, but not always to accept them.'

She had made her answer clear enough, but he still needed to be reassured.

'I was afraid I'd frightened you,' he said.

'You've been frightening me for years.' The lightness of her laugh contradicted the words. 'How could I ever have promised a son to someone who always seemed so detached? At first you treated me almost as a daughter, and afterwards I felt you'd put me on a kind of pedestal. It's not in my nature to play the part of a goddess. Off the stage, that is. But if you're prepared to behave like an ordinary man and treat me as an ordinary woman, you shall have your heir. With pleasure.'

'And yourself?'

'And myself.' She had – he realized with delight – none of the prudery of the unmarried daughters of fashionable society. Part of his mistake had lain in not discovering more quickly that she could only be reached through the sincerity of her own affections and her wish to give pleasure. The smile in her eyes showed that he had reached her now. 'And like you,' she said, 'I don't think I can wait until after the Coronation.'

He was kissing her again, as fervently as before, when the butler made a cautious reappearance and a second silent withdrawal. Alexa noticed the closing door and freed herself laughingly.

'I suspect,' she said, 'that dinner is served. And if one thing is absolutely clear, it's that I mustn't start my reign as mistress of Blaize by alienating the cook.'

Taking his hand, she turned to lead the way towards the dining room, but Lord Glanville held her back. He took time to consider what he wanted to say. As Alexa herself had pointed out a moment earlier, she had not been born into Society. But she had had opportunity enough to observe its members and perhaps to adopt some of their insincerities. The daughters of the British aristocracy were expected to behave impeccably. Their mothers guarded them with fierce attention, their fathers were quick to punish any breach of the conventions, and even the most notorious rakes accepted the fact that while a married woman was fair game, a young debutante must be left to enjoy her innocence until she married. But these same virtuous young women, once they had snared their title and provided an heir to it, behaved with a freedom which came close to promiscuity. Lord Glanville could hardly tell Alexa in so many words that he loved her far too deeply ever to be a complaisant husband. But the thought, however indirectly, must be expressed.

'Frisca's father is dead, you tell me,' he said. 'And Caversham is married. But what about the other one? The young man with the thick fair hair. Matthew Lorimer, I believe his name was.'

Alexa was silent for a moment. Then she looked him straight in the eyes, and the honesty he saw there made her words unnecessary.

'I loved him once,' she said. 'But that was a long time ago. I haven't seen him since the night of the ball here at Blaize. I shall never see him again. I shall never even think of him again. It's finished. You don't need to worry about Matthew.'

4

A family which traces its descent from the Norman Conquest hardly needs to acquire other ancestors by marriage. Nevertheless, when Margaret arrived at Blaize for a visit on New Year's Day of 1913, she took with her the portrait of John Junius Lorimer. One of Lord Glanville's footmen carried it into the house and leaned it against a wall to await his mistress's orders.

Margaret sent Robert off at once to look for his little cousin. Frisca had become part of the household at Blaize as soon as her mother married Lord Glanville, but she looked forward impatiently to every visit from the young man who had been a big brother to her during her babyhood. Margaret herself followed the portrait into the drawing room. She found Alexa lying decoratively on a day-bed, and guessed the reason at once. The little girl born to the Glanvilles nine months after their marriage had died only three days later, and a second pregnancy had ended in miscarriage. It was clear that in this third attempt Alexa was determined to take no chances.

'How beautiful you look?' Margaret exclaimed as she kissed her hostess. 'And how well!'

'You disappoint me,' laughed Alexa. 'I'm doing my best to act the part of an invalid. But of course I'm perfectly healthy – with nothing to do all day except look languid and think beautiful thoughts. Piers is being very stern with me. He won't even let me walk as far as the river to see how my little theatre is getting on. I'm sure that by the time this baby appears I shall have lost the use of my legs altogether. I try to persuade Piers that some exercise must surely be necessary, but he's quite adamant that I'm to be pampered. So here I lie, seething with suppressed restlessness.'

'I can see it means a great deal to him.' From the day of their first meeting Margaret had known how passionately Lord Glanville longed for a son.

'And no less to me, I assure you,' said Alexa. 'How can I feel that I've earned all this luxury until there's an Honourable little boy in the nursery? I distinctly promised Piers an heir – and besides, I have an unladylike desire to spite Duncan, who must be gnawing his fingernails at the prospect of the estate he'd reckoned on suddenly slipping away from him. When little Lucy died, and I was so distraught, I quite seriously found myself wondering whether Duncan had been sticking pins into a wax image of her.'

'You dismissed the thought, I hope.'

'Oh yes. A girl would have been no great obstacle to his hopes. Piers could have provided for her well enough out of his private fortune, but the land is entailed in the male line and will go with the title. All the same – ' Alexa looked at Margaret almost shyly, as if wondering whether it would be foolish to confess whatever thought was troubling her. 'All the same, I did find myself overcome on that occasion by another superstition. I know it was foolish; but the death upset me, of course, and I suppose I was looking for something to blame.'

'What superstition was that?' Margaret asked.

'You remember the Lorimer rubies?'

'Am I likely ever to forget them?' Margaret frowned at the memory, and Alexa was quick to take her up.

'Yes, you were superstitious about them once yourself,' she said. 'I remember that you asked me not to wear them to the Opera Ball in San Francisco. They had brought bad luck on every appearance you told me. I mocked you a little, because you've always been so sensible and practical: it seemed out of character that you should be nervous about an object which couldn't possibly affect the course of events. And I made a joke of it again when the earthquake came, as though merely to take a few jewels out of their case for a moment could destroy a city. But then they really did become evil, didn't they? They killed Frank. And although you've always been too considerate to say so, I know that they ruined your own friendship with his father.'

'What had all this to do with Lucy?' asked Margaret.

'As you know, I'm not at all superstitious by nature,' said Alexa. 'I believe that everything that happens can be explained in a rational manner by a real cause. And yet the history of the rubies – so much ill-fortune in such a short time – did make me uneasy: and then I became ashamed of myself for it. So on the day after Lucy was born I asked Piers to bring the jewel case to my bed. What harm could it possibly bring to an innocent new-born baby? I showed the jewels to Piers. I knew that he had a strong-box full of Glanville jewellery, waiting to adorn his daughter or his son's wife. But I wanted Lucy to have just one heirloom from her mother's family as well. The Lorimer legacy. I put the jewels at the foot of her cradle for a moment, and then Piers took them away. Within forty-eight hours she was dead.'

'She was dying already!' exclaimed Margaret, appalled at the implications of what Alexa was saying. 'Nobody dared to tell you while you were still so weak from the birth. But from the moment she was born, the imperfection in her body made it inevitable that she couldn't survive. She wasn't able to feed herself, or be fed. The rubies could have had nothing at all to do with that. Nothing whatever.'

'I know that, of course,' agreed Alexa. 'That is to say, I accept it with my reason. But at the time, when I was distressed and angry, it was tempting to look for an explanation and find it in some kind of malevolent fortune. The curse of the Lorimers, I exclaimed to myself, remembering how you told me once that your father – *our* father – could be said to have stolen the jewels from his creditors. So, although I still won't admit to being superstitious, let me put it a different way. The rubies have been associated with too many disasters for me ever again to take pleasure in wearing them. The accumulation of coincidences is too high. So before this pregnancy started I sent them away to be kept in the strongroom of a bank – and not even my own bank, since it seemed all too likely that the unfortunate repository would be blown up or burgled or bankrupted.' She smiled, as though to show Margaret that she was joking, but her eyes were serious. 'They are to stay there for the rest of my life. Unless the time should ever come when I feel that I've lived long enough. Then I shall send for them, and adorn myself with them, and sit back to see what happens.'

'You're very foolish and very wise, my dear.' Margaret bent to kiss her again. 'Wise, not because of any damage the rubies could cause, but because it's important that you should be completely calm and untroubled until this new baby is born.'

'Now that we've talked away the family curse, you see in me the very model of calmness. The rubies aren't of the least importance, and my child will inherit a quite different kind of legacy from the Lorimers.'

'What's that?'

'You,' said Alexa. She put out a hand, drawing Margaret closer so that she could be kissed again. 'Often and often I've tried to imagine what my life would have been like if it hadn't been for you, and the picture terrifies me every time. I know what a burden it must have been for you to accept responsibility for me, and how much of your independence you had to sacrifice for it. And the only claim I had on you was that my father was John Junius Lorimer.'

'I saw you as a legacy to me,' said Margaret, deeply touched by Alexa's affection.

'And a very unwelcome one I must have been. An undisciplined guttersnipe. But I've had time to realize that I've never been the only one you've loved. Matthew told me long ago how you mothered him when he was small and longing to be cuddled. You were willing to take responsibility for Frisca even before she was born, and if Piers hadn't given her a home here, I'm sure you'd have looked after her until she was ready to leave. You've welcomed Kate and Brinsley into your life as though they were your own children. So you can see why I feel so confident that my son will have a fine inheritance – the best kind of inheritance, because it doesn't depend on anybody's death. From the moment he's born, he'll have his Aunt Margaret to love him.'

'He will indeed,' Margaret agreed. 'But you mustn't take it for granted that you'll have a son rather than a daughter.'

'Oh, but I do. This pregnancy is quite different from the others. I'm as convinced as I've ever been of anything that this time it will be a healthy boy.'

'How can you possibly tell!' Margaret was teasing, but pleased by the confidence behind Alexa's peaceful radiance.

'On every other occasion I suffered from nausea from the very beginning. Do you remember how ill I was on the voyage home from America? I realize that a good many women are affected like that for a time, but with me it seemed to be worse and it lasted longer. That was why I couldn't go to the Coronation when I was pregnant. I was so convinced that I shouldn't be able to sit through the whole service without disgracing myself. Just think of being sick over all that red velvet and ermine! I should have been ostracized by Society for the rest of my life!'

'I thought perhaps it was nervousness which caused your nausea at that time,' commented Margaret. She had known of the plan to disrupt the Coronation service and had disapproved. It had seemed tactful not to ask too many questions when Alexa suddenly announced that she was not well enough to attend the service.

'I'm never nervous about singing,' Alexa said. 'And with Piers to support me I wasn't even frightened of being arrested. No, it was only the pregnancy which made me feel so ill. But this baby seems pleased to be part of my body. We're flourishing together in a quite different way.'

'It could still be a girl.'

'No girl could possibly kick as violently. Even Frisca, who's hardly been still for a second since she was born, wasn't able to make her presence felt before that with quite such gusto. No, I shall have a son. As tall and as kind as his father. With as much love of music as his mother. And, on his own account, with perhaps a touch of wildness. His kicking suggests that, at least. I think I shall call him Alaric. The barbarian, invading the civilized life of his parents. I wonder what he'll *really* be like. There was another thought I had, Margaret, when I sent the rubies away. Do you remember – oh, years and years ago – I asked you whether your father had left any legacy, and you said that the only true inheritance was one of character?'

'I don't remember the occasion,' Margaret said. 'But I'm prepared to believe that I expressed some opinion of the kind.'

'You were talking about your father's children: William and Ralph and yourself. At the time, I didn't even know

361

that I ought to be counted in with them. Well, I was thinking the other day about the next generation, to which my son will belong: the grandchildren of John Junius Lorimer. They must all have inherited something from him. Some part of themselves, I mean – I'm not talking about objects. But what? It's not easy to pick these things out, especially since the grandchildren are all so very different from each other.'

'Perhaps his different attributes have been scattered between them,' suggested Margaret, willing to enjoy a moment of speculation. 'Matthew and Arthur, for example. Arthur has certainly inherited his grandfather's talent for making money. But Matthew has his eye for beauty.'

'I remember Matthew himself saying that to me once.' A silence hung in the air, as though there were something else that Alexa would have liked to say. Margaret equally had to restrain herself. She saw Matthew from time to time in London and, although she could make no sense of his curiously angular paintings, they still shared the affection for each other which had been established in Matthew's babyhood. She never talked about the meetings to Alexa, however, and did not propose to do so now unless she was asked.

'Yes, they seem to have divided their grandfather's character neatly between them.' Alexa, accepting Margaret's verdict, then moved decisively away from that illustration of the subject. 'But of all the other grandchildren, it might have been expected that at least one would be the John Junius Lorimer of his generation. I don't see which one, though. There are plenty of contrasts among the cousins, but none of them has quite the right weight to be the head of a family.' She laughed to herself. 'Who could think that Beatrice and Frisca have anything in common, even as small a thing as a grandfather – Beatrice so prim and sharp and cold, and little Frisca bouncing

362

about, determined to make the whole world smile by her antics.'

'There's not much of John Junius Lorimer in either of them,' agreed Margaret. 'And even less in Ralph's children. Kate wants to set the world to rights, although she doesn't yet see how to do it. I sometimes think that she only has eyes for the miseries of society. She's still too young, I suppose, to realize that even the poor are able to be happy for part of the time. I have a great admiration for Kate. She'll have a good deal to offer the world when she's finished her training. But I'm afraid that the price she's paying for it is the sacrifice of her youth.'

'While Brinsley is a golden boy who sees all the delights of life spread in front of him for the picking.'

Margaret agreed with the description. Where Kate's earnestness aroused admiration, Brinsley Lorimer brought gaiety everywhere he went, infecting everyone with his light-heartedness. It was difficult to imagine him settling down as a hard-working member of society. For a good many years it had been tempting to postpone any suggestion that he ought to begin taking the future seriously, so great was his delight in the pleasures of boyhood. Margaret herself had often excused his escapades on the grounds of his youth. But he was not a child any more – the year that was just beginning would see his twentieth birthday. Ralph, who had devoted his own university years to hard work, seemed to take a vicarious pleasure in learning that his son would captain the Oxford cricket team this summer. At least Brinsley was serious about something; but to play cricket was hardly a career.

'I've never seen Grant, of course,' said Alexa.

Margaret's knowledge of him, too, was nearly all secondhand. Because she had been present at his birth, she had seen for herself his crippled condition and knew it to be incurable. Both Lydia's letters and Kate's angry comments on them had made it clear that even so young he was tyrannizing his parents. There seemed no useful comment to be made on this particular grandson of John Junius Lorimer.

Sometimes Margaret wondered whether there might not be yet one more Lorimer, unacknowledged. There had been a moment of unhappiness in the life of her brother Ralph – before he married Lydia – when he had confided some of his secrets to his sister and had seemed on the point of revealing others. But that was only speculation. If Lorimer blood was flowing in the veins of some dark-skinned boy or girl in Jamaica, she was not likely now ever to be told of it.

That left only Robert, and Robert – except in the bright redness of his hair – bore no greater resemblance than any of his cousins to the man whom Margaret remembered from her youth as so rich and autocratic, so solid and old. She stared for a moment at the portrait propped against the wall. Then she walked across the room to the mullioned window.

The terraces and lawns of Blaize, and the fields of the home park beyond, were covered with a crisp sheet of snow. It had fallen on Christmas Eve and remained until today undisturbed by anything but the arrow-headed tracks of birds. But now the side of the shallow hill beyond the ha-ha was patterned with other tracks. Robert, rosy-cheeked with cold and effort, was dragging Frisca's sledge up the slope and sending it down again with a gliding push. Frisca's cries of delight at each speeding journey broke through the frozen air of New Year's Day while Robert, at the top of the hill, rested for a moment, sharing her pleasure, before running down with his scarf flying from his neck to pull his little cousin up again. His bright hair, tousled and shining, gleamed against the white background of the snow.

John Junius Lorimer had had red hair in his youth. He too must have been a lively boy once, waving his hat, perhaps, to cheer the news of the victory at Waterloo. But it was impossible for Margaret to take the leap of imagination which would enable her to envisage her father as young, and exactly the same limitation of vision made her unable to see Robert as old. It was enough, she told herself, that he was healthy and clever and loving; eighteen years old, with his life as an adult just about to begin.

'What are you thinking?' Alexa asked from the day-bed behind her.

'I was looking at Robert and thinking how good it must be to be eighteen years old,' she said.

It was a lie. She was thinking that there must have been a moment in 1800 when Alexander Lorimer and his wife had looked down at their red-headed baby, John Junius, hoping that he would have a happy and successful life. Alexander could reasonably have nursed these hopes until the day of his death, for he lived long enough to see his son, born into a time of wars and revolutions, survive into an age of prosperous stability. And yet, in the end . . .

Margaret closed her mind to what had happened in the end, but a forgotten sentence from a schoolroom translation flashed unbidden into her memory. 'Who but a god goes woundless all the way?' On the day of Robert's birth she had been frightened lest she should prove unable to protect him on her own. She had done her best, and her best had been good enough to provide security during his childhood, but there was no kind of security which could be guaranteed for ever against accident and disaster.

The unwelcome thought made her shiver with an apprehension which had no reasonable foundation. To cheer herself again she looked back at the happy scene outside. Frisca had jumped off the sledge now and was throwing snowballs at her cousin. Without warning Margaret remembered another snowy afternoon when she herself was only a year or two older than Robert was today. She had looked out of a drawing room window in Bristol then at a snowscene just as beautiful as the one which stretched in front of her eyes now. She still remembered the unbroken smoothness of the lawns, the dramatic highlights of a line of elms in the background, the cold blue cleanness of the silent air. She had stood beside the man she loved and the future stretched itself in front of her eyes like a carpet of happiness.

None of the happiness she envisaged at that moment had ever come her way. Instead, it had melted like the snow itself, one casualty amongst many others in her father's ruin. To look into the future and hope was to ask for trouble. But that thought, which so inopportunely and unreasonably chilled her heart, was not one which ought to be expressed to a woman expecting a child. The future must be all-important to Alexa now; her own future, and the child's. And the new baby would have the best possible start in life: loving parents, a secure and comfortable place in society, the right first of all to enjoy and later to own a peaceful corner of the beautiful English countryside.

'How fortunate your son will be,' Margaret said. 'Born with a silver spoon in his mouth, with all the advantages that you and Piers can give him – he'll have no need of any legacy from the Lorimers.' She looked down at Alexa and touched her shining strawberry-blonde hair with an affectionate finger. 'Although I do suspect,' she said, 'that he may inherit his grandfather's red hair.'

Anne Melville, daughter of the author and lecturer Bernard Newman, was born and brought up in Harrow, Middlesex. She read Modern History at Oxford as a scholar of St Hugh's College, and after graduating she taught and travelled in the Middle East. On returning to England, she edited a children's magazine for a few years, but now devotes all her working time to writing. She and her husband live in Oxford.